PRAISE FOR THE NOVELS
OF ANNE O'BRIEN

Queen Defiant

"*Queen Defiant* lives up to its title as Anne O'Brien, with sensual lyricism, gifts readers with the lesser-known story of Eleanor of Aquitaine before Henry Plantagenet swept her away to immortality. Married to the monk-king of France, Louis VII, Eleanor fights Louis, the church, and the French nobility to go on crusade to Jerusalem, where she finds unexpected sexual fulfillment before a much younger Henry pursues and wins her to an even greater love. We are more familiar with her tumultuous story as England's great queen, but O'Brien brings us the equally fascinating tale of Eleanor's little-known earlier years—the years that gave her an enduring defiance and strength that she would need for the rest of her life."
        —Jeane Westin, author of *The Virgin's Daughters* and *His Last Letter*

The Virgin Widow

"Packed with royal intrigue and stunning reversals of fortune, *The Virgin Widow* is a thrilling romance drawn from history, beautifully told. Anne O'Brien's spirited and courageous heroine, Lady Anne Neville, a traitor's daughter and future Queen of England, vividly narrates her incredible journey through treachery and heartbreak into the arms of the man she loves—the last Plantagenet King of England, Richard III."
        —Sandra Worth, award-winning author of *The King's Daughter*

"O'Brien pulls us by our heartstrings through the power struggles between the House of York and Lancaster, telling the story through the seemingly hopeless love of Anne Neville for the man who would become Richard III . . . a little-known story that you will never forget."
        —Jeane Westin

"*The Virgin Widow* is a novel so engrossing that I couldn't put it down. Anne Neville comes to full and glorious life on these pages—a courageous woman of her own time, timeless in her appeal to readers."
        —Kate Emerson, author of *Secrets of the Tudor Court: Between Two Queens*

continued . . .

"Anne O'Brien's *The Virgin Widow* takes the reader on a compelling journey through medieval history and the heart of Anne Neville, a pawn and power in Plantagenet England. The vibrant characters, especially the narrator heroine, leap off the page. O'Brien weaves love, lust, tragedy, and triumph into a rich historical tapestry to treasure."

—Karen Harper, national bestselling author of
Mistress Shakespeare and *The Irish Princess*

"Better than Philippa Gregory." —*The Bookseller* (UK)

"All of the right ingredients: romance, intrigue, betrayal, glamour, history, murder . . . brilliant!" —The Anne Boleyn Files

"With this winning book, Anne O'Brien has joined the exclusive club of excellent historical novelists." —*Sunday Express* (UK)

Other Novels by Anne O'Brien

The Virgin Widow

QUEEN
DEFIANT

A NOVEL OF ELEANOR OF AQUITAINE

Anne O'Brien

 NEW AMERICAN LIBRARY

NEW AMERICAN LIBRARY
Published by New American Library, a division of
Penguin Group (USA) Inc., 375 Hudson Street,
New York, New York 10014, USA
Penguin Group (Canada), 90 Eglinton Avenue East, Suite 700, Toronto,
Ontario M4P 2Y3, Canada (a division of Pearson Penguin Canada Inc.)
Penguin Books Ltd., 80 Strand, London WC2R 0RL, England
Penguin Ireland, 25 St. Stephen's Green, Dublin 2,
Ireland (a division of Penguin Books Ltd.)
Penguin Group (Australia), 250 Camberwell Road, Camberwell, Victoria 3124,
Australia (a division of Pearson Australia Group Pty. Ltd.)
Penguin Books India Pvt. Ltd., 11 Community Centre, Panchsheel Park,
New Delhi - 110 017, India
Penguin Group (NZ), 67 Apollo Drive, Rosedale, Auckland 0632,
New Zealand (a division of Pearson New Zealand Ltd.)
Penguin Books (South Africa) (Pty.) Ltd., 24 Sturdee Avenue,
Rosebank, Johannesburg 2196, South Africa

Penguin Books Ltd., Registered Offices:
80 Strand, London WC2R 0RL, England

First published by New American Library,
a division of Penguin Group (USA) Inc.

First Printing, June 2011
10 9 8 7 6 5 4 3 2 1

REGISTERED TRADEMARK—MARCA REGISTRADA

Library of Congress Cataloging-in-Publication Data
O'Brien, Anne, 1949–
Queen defiant: a novel of Eleanor of Aquitaine/Anne O'Brien.
    p. cm.
ISBN 978-0-451-23411-7
1. Eleanor, of Aquitaine, Queen, consort of Henry II, King of England, 1122?–1204—
Fiction.   2. Queens—Great Britain—Fiction.   3. Great Britain—History—Henry II, 1154–1189—
   Fiction.   4. France—History—Louis VII, 1137–1180—Fiction.   I. Title.
    PR6115.B7355Q44 2011
    823'.92—dc22   2011003173

Set in Simoncini Garamond
Designed by Alissa Amell

Printed in the United States of America

For George, who has succeeded in living harmoniously with both me and Eleanor for many months.

And for my father, who gave me my first love of history.

Acknowledgments

All my thanks to Jane Judd, who continues to be enthusiastic about my versions of medieval history. To Jennifer Unter, whose participation on my behalf in New York is beyond price. To Ellen Edwards and her team at New American Library, who make it all possible. And finally to Helen Bowden and all her experts at Orphans Press, for making my hand-drawn maps and genealogy look splendidly professional.

The Dukes of Aquitaine

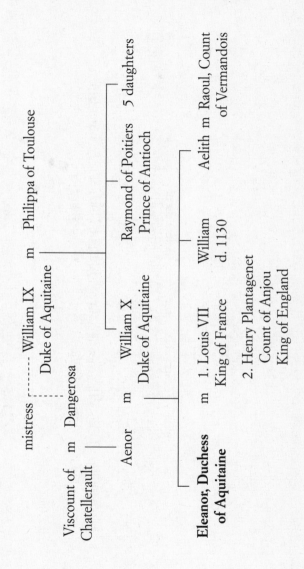

The Kings of France

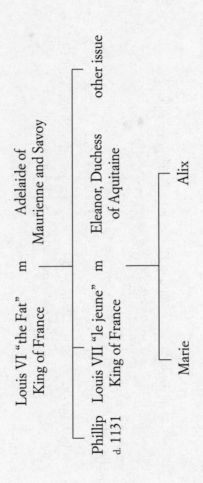

Louis VI "the Fat"   m   Adelaide of
King of France   Maurienne and Savoy

Phillip   Louis VII "le jeune"   m   Eleanor, Duchess   other issue
d. 1131   King of France   of Aquitaine

Marie   Alix

England and Anjou

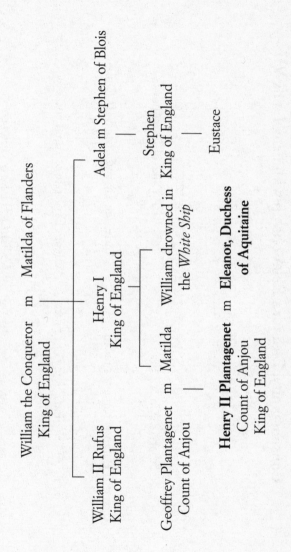

William the Conqueror m Matilda of Flanders
King of England

William II Rufus
King of England

Henry I
King of England

Adela m Stephen of Blois

William drowned in
the *White Ship*

Geoffrey Plantagenet m Matilda
Count of Anjou

Stephen
King of England

Eustace

Henry II Plantagenet m Eleanor, Duchess
Count of Anjou **of Aquitaine**
King of England

Consanguinity: Eleanor's Relationship with King Louis VII

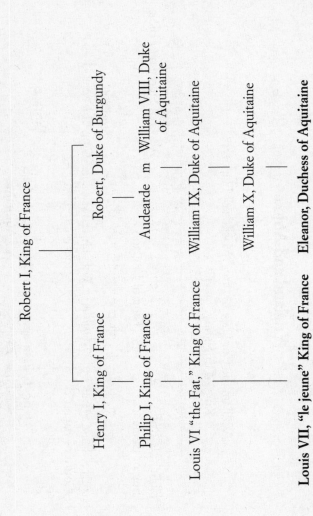

Consanguinity: Eleanor's Relationship with Henry Plantagenet

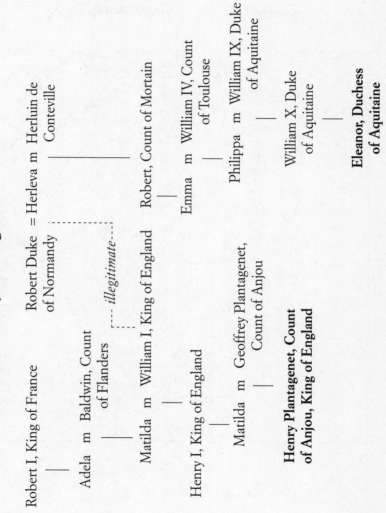

Robert I, King of France
|

Adela m Baldwin, Count
            of Flanders
|

Matilda m William I, King of England
|

Henry I, King of England
|

Matilda m Geoffrey Plantagenet,
              Count of Anjou
|

**Henry Plantagenet, Count
of Anjou, King of England**

Robert Duke = Herleva m Herluin de
of Normandy   Conteville
          - - - illegitimate - - -

Robert, Count of Mortain
|

Emma m William IV, Count
              of Toulouse
|

Philippa m William IX, Duke
                of Aquitaine
|

William X, Duke
of Aquitaine
|

**Eleanor, Duchess
of Aquitaine**

Dominions of Aquitaine, Anjou, and France in the Twelfth Century

London •
England
English Channel
Rouen
Normandy
Vexin
Paris
Champagne
Maine
•Angers
Anjou
Blois
Touraine
Poitou •Poitiers
Bay of
Biscay
Aquitaine
Bordeaux•
Gascony
Toulouse
Mediterranean
Sea

 Dominions of Eleanor of Aquitaine

 Dominions of Henry of Anjou

 Dominions of Louis VII of France

If all the world were mine
From the seashore to the Rhine,
That price were not too high
To have England's Queen lie
Close in my arms.

          —Anonymous German Troubadour

An incomparable woman . . . whose ability was the admiration of her age. Many know what *I* wish none of us had known. This same Queen in the time of her first husband went to Jerusalem. Let no one say any more about it. . . . Be silent!   —Richard of Devizes

Chapter One

July 1137

The Ombriere Palace, Bordeaux

"**W**ell, he's come. Or at least his entourage has—I can't see the royal banners. Aren't you excited? What do you hope for?"

Aelith, my sister, younger than I by two years and still possessing the enthusiasms of a child beneath her newly developing curves, battered at me with comments and questions.

"What I hope for is irrelevant." I studied the busy scene. I was betrothed to Louis Capet whether I liked it or not.

I had thought about nothing else since my father's deathbed decision to place me under the protection of Fat Louis—the King of France, no less—had settled my future beyond dispute. I wasn't sure *what* I thought about it. Anxiety at the choice vied with a strange excitement. Queen of France? It had a weighty feel to it. I was not averse to it, although Aquitaine was far more influential than that upstart northern kingdom. I would be Duchess of Aquitaine *and* Queen of France. I need not inform my newly espoused husband which of the two I considered the more important. Although why not? Perhaps I would. I would not be disregarded in this marriage.

I was Eleanor, daughter and heir to William, the tenth Duke of Aquitaine, the eldest of my father's children, although not born to rule. Not that I, a woman, was barred by law from the honor, unlike in the barbaric kingdom of the Franks to the north, but once I had had a younger brother who was destined to wear the ducal coronet. He, William—every firstborn son was called William—was carried off by a nameless fever when still an infant, the same as relieved my mother, Aenor, of her timorous hold on life, leaving me and my younger sister, Aelith, to the far from affectionate ministrations of my maternal grandmother. In the seven years since then I had grown used to the idea that I would be duchess. It was my right to rule.

But I was nervous. I did not think I had ever been nervous before: I had had no need, as my father's heir. My lands were vast, wealthy, well governed. I had been brought up to know luxury, sophistication, the delights of music and art. I was powerful and—so they said—beautiful. As if reading my mind, my troubadour Bernart began to sing a popular verse.

He who sees her lead the dance, sees her body twist and twirl,
Can see that, in all the world, for beauty there's no equal
Of the Queen of Joy.

I smiled. The Queen of Joy indeed. My looking glass confirmed what could be mere flattery, the greasy, self-seeking compliments of a penniless minstrel toward his patroness. But I was not ingenuous. Alone, unprotected, *unwed*—there would be a limit to my powers. I needed a husband with a strong sword arm, and powerful loins to get an heir on me—for him and for myself. A puissant lord who would stand with me and secure the future for Aquitaine, a man who could lead men and demand the obedience of the power-hungry lords who would snatch what was mine. A man who would be a fit mate for such as I.

Ah, but would Prince Louis fit this mold?

"Well?" Aelith nudged me.

"What do I hope for? A prince, of course," I replied.

"That's no answer."

"A man after my own heart."

"Self-important?" Leaning against the carved window ledge, Aelith ticked her observations off on her fingers. "Opinionated? Arrogant?"

But I sidestepped my sister's chuckling malice and answered seriously enough. "Why not? He will rule my lands. He must do it well. He'll not do it if he has neither the backbone nor the spirit for it. Better a man with arrogance than one who'd sell himself short to make friends. My vassals need a firm hand."

We were standing in my bedchamber, Aelith, my women, and I, high in the old keep, a spacious, graceful room with large windows to catch the light and any breath of air on this day of impossible heat. A room that I loved, full of my own possessions, and from where I could look out across the Garonne to observe the whole scene unfold hour by hour. It was July, hot as the gates of Hell, and I was restless with impatience as Aelith and I observed the settlement grow. Tents, pavilions, sprouting like mushrooms, covered the open meadows, transforming them into a town in its own right. A vivid, richly colored Capetian town on Aquitaine soil. A foreign presence, and above it all the fleur-de-lys of France. A portent for the future, I acknowledged, a French symbol of ownership over the mighty Duchy of Aquitaine. Before me, horses and armed men swarmed. Farriers and wheelwrights set up their booths. A market was soon under way. Small boats plied back and forth with Frankish noblemen or mounds of cabbages. My vassals, I was well aware, would question the relative importance of the two. It would not be a popular marriage, but we would all have to live with it.

"He must be handsome, of course," Aelith announced. She was already precociously aware of the male sex.

"Of course." I had no thought of a husband who was less than pleasing to the eye.

"Like Raymond." Aelith sighed a little.

Raymond of Poitiers, my father's young brother, now ruled as Prince of Antioch in distant Outremer.

"Yes. Like Raymond," I agreed. My only meeting with Raymond had been of the briefest, four years ago now and for a mere few weeks, but my memory of his golden beauty had not faded with time.

Raymond was to my mind the epitome of the perfect knight. "If the French Prince is in any measure like Raymond, I shall be everlastingly grateful." My attention was caught by a flurry of movement across the river. "Look! That's the royal standard!" I pointed. "So Prince Louis *is* here at last."

Aelith leaned over to see the blue pennants with the gold lilies of France. "As long as he's prettier than Fat Louis," she remarked. The laughter in her face did not quite hide a real apprehension. Tales of the grotesque bulk of the King of France abounded.

"I'll give you my gold circlet if he's not. Fat Louis is naught but a mountain of lard ridden with dysentery."

But I knew better than to underestimate King Louis. His body might be corrupt but his mind was still keen. He might be too corpulent to rise from his bed, too obese to mount either a horse or a woman, so rumor said, but he had seen me as a gift dropped from Heaven into his enormous lap.

We watched as another pavilion was erected, larger than all the rest. The Capetian banner was planted beside it to hang limply in the windless air. A group of horsemen drew up and dismounted. Impossible to make out one figure from the next at this distance.

"They won't like it, you know." I spoke softly. "My vassals will detest it."

"But they have no choice." Aelith pursed her lips. "And if the Prince keeps the brigands from our doors, they've no right to complain."

True in essence, but far too simplistic.

Was this, this Frankish marriage, what the Duke, my father, had intended when he had placed me into King Louis's keeping? *Arrange a marriage for my daughter*; he had left instructions for Louis as his life drained from him on the pilgrim's road to Santiago de Compostela in Spain. *And do it fast, before rebellion can take hold. Until that time, I give her and Aquitaine into France's safe hands.*

What was my father, Duke William the Tenth of Aquitaine, thinking? Surely he'd understood that King Louis would never allow me to escape from his fat fingers. It would be like expecting a fox to show goodwill by keeping out of the hen coop even though the door was left invitingly open, and the King of France was no kindly fox. Arrange a fast marriage for me? By God, he had. Between the vomit and the bloody flux that tied him to his bed, Fat Louis had moved heaven and earth to secure me for his son before anyone could voice a protest.

And there had been plenty. My father's vassals might have sworn an oath of homage to me in his lifetime, but with his death our lands were torn by unrest. The Count of Angoulême, a vassal lord of Aquitaine, was vicious in his condemnation of my betrothal, and was not alone. The vassals would have accepted someone like Raymond, one of their own. They would have just about tolerated a noble lord of the south who might win my hand. But not this Capetian interloper, this foreign northerner from some insignificant Frankish tribe. I knew what they would be thinking as they too watched this impressive arrival. They would see Louis Capet as a foreign power who would drain us to further his own ambitions. My father might have insisted with his final breath that Aquitaine remain independent from France, ruled separately, to be inherited in some distant future by the heir of my own body; he might have insisted that Aquitaine must not be absorbed into French territory. But how many of my vassals would remember that, when faced with this invasion of unveiled power?

"It might have been more politic," I spoke my thoughts, "if my father had not thrown us into the hands of a Frank."

And I marveled at my father's unwarranted stupidity in drinking water fouled by a horde of pilgrims, all of whom had doubtless washed and spit and pissed in its shallows. Did he not see, scooping up the bad fish, gulping the rank water, his mind taken up with the successful culmination of his pilgrimage? All he got was a night of fever, of vomiting and flux, rapidly followed by a pain-racked death before Saint James's altar.

An excess of piety can make us all stupid.

"Perhaps the vomiting addled our father's brain," remarked Aelith dryly.

And perhaps the outcome would be civil war. It might be like setting a brand to dry timber, insurrection sweeping through Aquitaine and Poitou before we had finished dancing at my marriage feast.

A quick wash of fear replaced the nerves and the anticipation.

Behind me the troubadour, obviously listening in, struck a strident note on a lute so that I turned to look, seeing the lifting of his brow in my direction. When I smiled in appreciation of his intent, Bernart began to sing a popular if scurrilous verse in a soft growl.

Your Frank shows mercy, just to those who can pay him;
There's no other argument ever can sway him. . . .

He hesitated, breath held, fingers lifted from the strings, to assess my reaction, and even though I knew what would come next, I waved him on. Bernart struck another heavy chord.

He lives in abundance, his table's a feast,
But you mark my words: He's a treacherous beast.

My women joined in with relish on the last line. The Franks were not well loved. They were a coarse, aggressive, unpolished people compared with our Roman sophistication in Aquitaine.

"Enough!" I moved into their midst. "We'll not be discourteous."

"No, lady." Bernart bowed over his beloved lute. "We'll make our own judgment when the Prince becomes Duke of Aquitaine."

I frowned at the smooth cynicism but could find no fault with so obvious a statement.

"It's an honor that Prince Louis should come to you," Aelith said, still leaning her arms along the sill, unwilling to abandon the entertainment outside. "Traveling all this way from Paris in this heat. They say he traveled at night."

It was true. Everything had been settled with such speed, as if the King of France had the Hounds of Hell baying at his heels, although what Prince Louis thought of it I had no idea. Perhaps he would have preferred a Frankish bride. I lifted my chin. I too could be cynical.

"The Prince came to me only because his father, the King, instructed him to. Fat Louis and my guardian the Archbishop feared that if I set foot outside this palace I would be abducted by some scruffy knight with an eye to a rich wife. I'm far too valuable to be allowed to travel the breadth of the country." Impatience tightened its grip now that the Prince was in my sights. "How long do I have to wait before I can see him?"

Aelith laughed and gave a pert toss of her head. "At least he's old enough to play the man and not so old as to be near his grave."

"He's two years older than I."

"Old enough to keep you in line?"

"No." I didn't like this line of humor. "I'll not be a vessel merely to bequeath my royal Aquitaine blood to my children. I am no brood-mare, without opinion or wit, to slave and carry at the behest of a husband. I'll rule my own lands. The Prince must accept that."

"But can you protect them, lady?" Bernart asked with grave familiarity.

Before I could reply, the Archbishop of Bordeaux, Geoffrey of Lauroux, my kindly guardian since my father's death, was announced and entered. Resplendent in clerical robes despite the heat, he bowed, puffing from the effort of climbing the stairs.

"Lady. The Prince is come."

And I knew immediately what I wanted. "I would go out and meet with him."

"No."

I thought I had misheard. "I wish to see the Prince. Will you arrange it, sir?"

"Regretfully no, lady. You will wait here."

"But I wish it." I would not be thwarted in this.

But the Archbishop remained adamant. "To arrive before your future husband, windblown and hot, in the middle of a camp of soldiers and the usual rabble of camp followers? Less than perfect, my dear Eleanor. I think not. You will wait here. You will allow Prince Louis to come to you. As he should, of course." The Archbishop's eyes twinkled with crafty appeal to my pride. "The Kingdom of France cannot compare with the Duchy of Aquitaine. You will stand on your dignity. You will control your impatience."

Dignity. Control. Maturity was rushing up to meet me so fast that it took my breath. And I knew it must be so. The days of my willful girlhood were gone forever.

"How long must I wait?"

"Not long. Tomorrow I will bring him to you."

Another whole day. But to ride into the Capetian camp, as any common sightseer to peer and pry . . . No. I would not do that.

"Tomorrow then. We will hold an audience in the Great Chamber."

"I will arrange it." The Archbishop bowed again and departed, well satisfied, as was I.

I went back to the window, straining to see whether I could make out the distant figure of my future husband. I could not, of course. My gaze strayed to the nearer, familiar vista of Bordeaux. My days here were now numbered. I would have to leave all this, my well-loved home, the dry, sunbaked south. I had known Bordeaux all my life, the warm, golden walls enclosing vineyards and gardens as well as our own ducal palace. Churches with their spires arrowing to Heaven. The market and port with ships landing goods from all the known world. Paris? What did I know of it? Very little, I admitted. Landlocked. Cold and damp and northern. Whatever it was, it was about to become the center of my new life.

"And have you decided which language you'll use to address your most puissant Prince?" Aelith murmured, coming up to tuck her hand through my arm. She was definitely in the mood to annoy.

"I shall speak my own language, of course."

"You'll not make it easy for him?"

"Why should I? He'll gain far more from this marriage than I. Our new combined kingdom—"

"Never mind the politics, sister. You're too solemn. Far more important—what will you wear to meet him for the first time?"

"Aelith . . . ! Life's not all about dresses and mantles. . . ."

"Sometimes it is. Which reminds me—will you lend me your pleated undergown, the blue silk patterned with silver . . . ?"

"No." It was new and precious.

"Well, if you're of a mind to be bad tempered . . ."

It was in my mind to snap at her but I could not; marriage might demand a parting between us, a thought that brought me no happiness. Moreover she had a point. It mattered that I make an impression on Louis Capet. I would force him to notice me. I was Duchess of Aquitaine, not some poor petitioner to fall on her knees and beg the Capetian hand of charity to raise her from the dust.

The Devil whispered in my ear.

Are you sure you want to be bound to a man, to be dependent on his yea or nay? Is this how you see your life—at the beck and call of this unknown prince, for you to be his vassal, his possession, obedient to his commands?

No, I didn't want it but I had no choice. I was fifteen years old, Duchess of Aquitaine and Gascony, Countess of Poitou in my own right. Unable to defend my lands from the jackals and vultures, I must bow to the inevitable. I had made up my mind to it.

I would mate with the Devil himself if it would keep Aquitaine safe.

Aelith borrowed my undergown anyway, but by then events had overtaken me: Blue silk undergowns became entirely inconsequential.

"You are magnificent," Aelith observed.

I raised my chin. I knew it. True to his word, early the next morning, before the heat of the day built to a furnace, Archbishop Geoffrey had himself ferried across the river to escort the Prince to meet me, his affianced wife. I sat in my audience chamber, a vision of Aquitaine splendor, and waited for him.

Aelith's advice in mind, I had chosen a gown of deep blue. To be the possessor of hair the rich red-brown of a vixen's pelt put many colors out of bounds, but the blue of the Virgin's robe was becoming. Beneath it I wore undertunics of silk and fine linen, while over it a long flowing surcoat so that the full skirts lapped around me, trailing as I walked in gilded leather shoes. A jeweled belt clipped my waist, with another loop around my hips. A long transparent veil secured by a gold and jeweled filet did not hide my hair but drew attention to it, braided along its length with blue and gold ribbons to hang almost to my knees. All in all a statement of imperious power—if not entirely comfortable in the sultry heat. Attention was drawn to my eyes, lips, and cheeks by the judicious use of artificial color. Rings flattered my hands; earrings dripped from lobe to shoulder.

And I waited.

"Shall I play, my lady? Or sing? To while away the time?" Bernart, lute to hand and expression blandly innocent, stood to my right with my women.

"No. No music," I replied curtly. I was too tense to appreciate music.

An hour passed.

He kept me waiting.

I was not used to being kept waiting in a life where servants leaped to do my bidding. But I would show neither anxiety nor anger. I would not go to the wall-walk to look out. I sat on my high-backed chair on the dais and stilled my fingers that wanted to tap their impatience. I watched the door at the far end of the vast chamber. The sun lifted toward noon and sweat trickled down my spine.

Still I sat. Temper began to hum beneath my skin. He dared to keep me waiting! Me, in whose veins ran the blood of a long line of victorious warrior knights. He would slight me, Eleanor. . . .

Where was this Prince of France? By God—I'd wait no longer . . . !

And then the tramp of an armed guard. The soft murmur of voices. The Frankish soldiers marched into my audience chamber—much like an invading force—to position themselves into a protective phalanx at the door. But I focused on the man who came to a halt under the arched doorway, looking around with wide eyes, stepping forward only at a murmur from my archbishop on his right.

Louis Capet walked slowly toward me. Louis *le jeune.* Now that the moment was here my palms were slick with sweat. I resisted the urge to wipe them down the silk of my skirts.

The Prince halted, as if looking for encouragement.

I studied him while he was still distant from me, gaining a fistful of impressions. My heart sank. Whom would I compare him with? The only men I had known, of course. My grandfather. My father. My father's younger brother, Raymond, now Prince of Antioch. With these men as my only measuring stick, I had expected a warrior, a bold knight to march forward to claim the prize, a lord with presence, as much at home in a chamber of government as in the lists or on the battlefield. As a Prince of France he should have a supreme confidence. When the men of my family had entered a room, it was instantly full of their authority and forceful personalities.

The lingering shades of the rulers of Aquitaine faded as Prince Louis walked slowly forward, the Archbishop once again at his side with an encouraging smile. This, then, was the man I would wed. He stopped before me, bowed with a nice degree of poise, and smiled. As good manners dictated, I stood and, lifting the trailing hems of my skirts, stepped from the dais and held out my hand in greeting.

Louis was tall, as tall as I, for which I was grateful. His hair was long and fair, waving to his shoulders. His blue eyes, the blue of a summer sky, were direct and almost childlike in their openness. He had fine features: a straight nose and austere cheeks. His mouth was well molded, curved into a sweet, disarming smile. He had taken a razor to his cheeks and chin, his skin soft and smooth. Without doubt, as any woman would see, he was an attractive man.

Will he be attractive in bed?

The thought that leaped into my mind as silkily as my rosary beads might slip through my fingers at Mass did not surprise me. After all, what was the purpose of this union if not to safeguard the future of my domains through the begetting of a child? Would he be pleasing? I thought he would. His shoulders were broad, his figure elegant. His hands were beautiful and slender. I would not object to intimacy with this man.

"My lady." His voice was soft, pleasant to the ear as he bowed again with exquisite grace.

"My lord, you are right welcome," I replied in similar Latin, the formal diplomatic language of the court.

As he bent his head to press his lips to my fingers, I assessed his clothing with some surprise. His garments were of fine wool, the best I had seen, and in the most magnificent red that I did not wear but coveted—a red-haired woman would not choose to wear such a hue unless she were totally witless—but the garment was in what I would have called an outdated fashion. The overgown reached Louis's ankles, rather than his knees, over a plain linen undertunic that showed at neck and hem. No bands of braiding or embroidery to enhance around the collar or sleeves, only a minimal stitching around the neck, and that without style. He wore no jewels. His belt was of good quality but plain leather, as were his boots. He had dressed well but completely without show to draw attention to his rank.

He wore no sword at his belt. The Dukes of Aquitaine always wore a sword, except in their bedchamber—and even then until persuaded to remove it by the lady who shared their sheets.

How could the heir of France not wear a sword, the ultimate symbol of power?

I pursed my lips faintly through my smile, trying not to be overcritical. So he did not like display and ostentation. That did not make him less of a man. Perhaps as a Prince of France he saw no need to emphasize his status with sword and poignard on the day he met his intended bride. But his hands and face were pale, unweathered. The fingers that held mine bore no calluses from sword or shield or even horse harness. He was no warrior, no fighter for sure. He bore no trace of hard campaigning through rain and sun.

Nor was he finding it easy to choose what to say next to me. An awkward silence fell between us. Which I broke.

"I have looked forward to this moment when we would meet, my lord," I said.

Louis flushed, his fair skin pink as an early rose. I saw his throat convulse as he swallowed.

"Lady. I have heard much of your beauty. The rumors were not false. Your eyes are as fine and rare as . . . as emeralds."

His flush deepened. I saw myself reflected in his eyes and knew that he was much taken with me. But that was not the reason for the ripple of surprised pleasure that stirred the fine hairs at my nape. Oh . . .

His flattering words were not in Latin!

At first I had not noticed. He had gone to the considerable trouble to learn at least some words in my own language, the *langue d'oc* of the south, the official language of Aquitaine, rather than the *langue d'oeil* that Louis would speak in his Frankish kingdom.

"You honor me," I murmured, failing to hide my astonishment.

"I have tried. I learned the phrases on my journey here," he admitted with a soft laugh. "But my conversation would be limited. Perhaps we should revert to Latin. God give you good health, my lady."

And so we slid smoothly into Latin again because we must, but the gesture to me was a fine one.

Louis kissed my fingers, then my cheeks, enveloping me in a cloud of sweet perfume. His lips were gentle on my skin. So he had bathed and anointed himself before coming to me. My pleasure deepened.

"Forgive me that I did not greet you sooner," Louis explained. "I ordered a Mass to be said. I had to give thanks to God for my safe arrival."

"You are certainly well protected," I observed with an eye to his guards.

"My father and Abbot Suger—my father's chief counselor who has accompanied me at my father's orders—both insisted. They must guarantee my protection in dangerous territory."

It was said completely without guile, despite the covert slur on the state of law in my lands; nor was it the reply I had expected—naturally, his father would be concerned. "Of course." I raised my hand to indicate a table with two low chairs set for us in a window embrasure. "Here is wine, my lord. Please sit and be at ease."

We sat. At a signal my servants approached to pour the wine and uncover gold dishes of candied fruits and sugared plums. Louis accepted the cup from my hand.

"Let us drink to our union." I raised mine to my lips. "May it be long and fruitful, to the advantage of both France and Aquitaine. As sweet as the sugarplums." I gestured to the bowl.

"It will be my greatest delight."

Louis took a small sip before pushing the cup aside. He declined the sweetmeats. His gaze was fixed on my face. Again an uneasy silence fell between us.

"What is it?" I asked. I did not care to be stared at quite so fixedly.

He shook his head, formally grave. "I can't believe my good fortune. If my brother had lived, he would have wed you. His misfortune is my gain. You are the most beautiful woman I have ever seen. How can I not love you?"

My breath caught on a little laugh of surprise at his lack of worldliness. "I am deeply grateful." It was impossible to respond in any other fashion to so ingenuous an admission after ten minutes of acquaintance.

Louis was unaware. "I have brought gifts for you, lady, to express my esteem." He motioned forward one of his servants, indicating that he lift the lid of a little gold-bound coffer. "My father considered these to be a suitable gift for a young bride."

His father considered . . .

If I was disappointed I did not speak it. Nor did I show my initial reaction to the choice of adornment for a new bride. In the coffer was coiled a heavy chain of gold. A brooch to pin a mantle. Heavy matching bracelets. Valuable without doubt, set with magnificent cabochon gems, large as pigeon's eggs, but heavy, as suitable for a man as for a woman. And somehow *northern*, without finesse or the delicacy of form that I knew. Chains of gold, I thought, to tie me to the marriage. I promptly buried the thought and expressed my thanks.

"Rubies are the most prized of jewels," Louis informed me. "They preserve the wearer from the effects of poison."

Poison? Did he expect me to be poisoned in my own domain? Or in Paris? It was in my mind to ask him. And rubies, for a red-haired woman. How unfortunate. And then not least—why had the Prince not chosen them himself for the woman he would marry?

How could a gift have been so unacceptable on so many levels?

"I will value them," I replied graciously. My upbringing had been superb. "I have a gift for you too, my lord."

I had thought long and hard about it. What to give a man on the occasion of our marriage? Not a sword—far too warlike. A stallion? Perhaps. I had rejected jewels. Then I had decided on something lasting, of beauty, an object of great value that would remind Louis of this moment every time his glance fell on it.

It stood on the table beside the wine flagon, wrapped about in silk. With a twist of my wrist I loosed the shroud to reveal a truly spectacular piece of workmanship from our own treasury in Aquitaine. It was old and very rare, a vase of rock crystal decorated with gold filigree work, inset with pearls. The crystal shone with inner fire in the sunlight.

Louis touched it with one finger, his face solemn. "It is beautiful, but no more beautiful than you, lady."

And that was it. He neither touched it nor looked at it again. Was it not to his taste? How could a thing of such exquisite workmanship not please him? It cried out to be handled, the crystal facets stroked and warmed between palms and fingers. I felt a frown gathering and struggled to smooth it out.

He does not look at it because he cannot take his eyes from your own face! You should be gratified indeed.

True enough.

Louis clasped my hand again, holding it strongly between his as if he needed to urge me. "We'll wed immediately. I must return home to Paris—as soon as we can settle our affairs."

Oh! So soon! My days in Aquitaine were fewer than I had supposed. "I had hoped to show you the hospitality of Aquitaine, my lord," I suggested. "We can take our time. Do you not wish to know your new land, your new subjects? What need to hurry so?"

Louis leaned forward so that his face was close to mine, lowering his voice. For one brief moment I thought he was actually going to kiss me, and stiffened at his boldness. No such thing.

"Are your lords so peaceful and welcoming then, to a Frankish Prince?" he asked, his breath warm on my cheek. "I do not think so. Abbot Suger is wary of staying longer than necessary."

"My lords are not hostile," I remarked carefully, unsettled by his openness, reluctant to admit to the lukewarm acceptance he would receive. "It is just that they don't know you."

Louis smiled immediately. "Then I'll speak with them and win them over. I'll be a fair ruler. I know they'll accept that."

Was he quite so innocent? So guileless?

"They'll come and swear fealty to you," I assured him. "They have been summoned."

And pray God they buried their sour temper and bent the knee or we'd have trouble on our hands. How would this gentle, unassuming man deal with open defiance?

"Then we'll await their coming. Two weeks, my lady, but no longer. My father is ill. I am instructed to return by Abbot Suger."

I chose my reply carefully, preferring soft acquiescence until I knew him better. "Then we will leave in two weeks, my lord, as you wish."

Louis rose to his feet, drawing me with him, his hand on my arm. "There's no need for concern, lady."

"Concern?"

"I can understand your trepidation at being taken so far from your home. Nor have you your mother to give you advice."

"I don't fear it, sir." My voice had more of an edge than I had intended.

"We'll make you welcome in Paris. My own lady mother is keen to meet you. I trust you'll not be lonely there. I wouldn't want you to be unhappy to any degree."

My reaction at what I had considered to be a slight to my maturity softened. Here was a care for my well-being, where I had not expected it. It wrapped around my heart, a warm hand, that the Prince should even give thought to my isolation in a foreign land, in an unfamiliar court.

"I would bring my women with me, sir. My sister."

"Of course. It's my wish that you be comfortable."

Whatever else this Prince was, he was kind, generous. I curtsied deeply. "Tonight we hold a feast in your name, my lord."

He placed his hand on his heart and bowed. "It will be my pleasure."

And then as Louis departed, surrounded by his bodyguards, I was left to sort through those first impressions. A mixed bag, for sure.

He had great charm, a winning smile. He was good to look at. But Prince Louis was not his own man, his actions, even his choice of gift, under the thumb of his father. How . . . disappointing! I had expected a more forceful personality from a Frank, with their reputation for drawing swords first and asking questions later. Louis had not even worn a sword.

I ate one of the neglected sugarplums, licking the sugar from my fingers, considering the weight of jewelry in the casket.

Could this Louis Capet protect my lands for me? Hard to imagine at first sight. Louis was no war stallion, forsooth! More a gentle palfrey. I suspected that, if it came to a fight, the rebel Count of Angoulême would trample him into the dust of Aquitaine before the Prince had buckled on his weapons.

I sighed.

But perhaps all was not lost. Perhaps there were advantages to be gained here. If the Prince came readily to his father's hand on the bridle, then why should he not come equally readily to mine? Could I not replace Fat Louis's influence with my own? Surely it was not an impossibility. Since the Prince admired my person and my face so greatly, could he not be persuaded to listen to me and take my advice? I would tutor him in how to deal with my vassals. I would educate him in ruling Aquitaine. I would make myself indispensable to Louis Capet.

I smiled as I ate another plum.

Prince Louis might not be the worst husband in the world.

I stood and brushed the crystals from my sleeves. As I prepared to leave the chamber, waving my women to go before me so that I could fall into step with Aelith, my eye was caught by the soft gleam of glass and gold and pearls. Louis had left the vase. There it stood, the sun still creating tiny rainbows within its crystal. Conscious of a little knot of disappointment, I instructed a servant to wrap and pack it carefully for the long journey to Paris. Then I closed the lid on the French casket. I supposed I would have to wear the gift for my wedding, but I would not choose to wear it again. Still, I had hoped that Louis would have admired the vase. . . .

"Well?" Aelith.

"He's good to look at. He's thoughtful and considerate."

"He's as pretty as a girl. So your husband will protect your lands for you, will he?" As ever, my sister was not slow to voice her opinions. "Will this *boy* do it, do you think?"

"Why should he not?"

"He's milk and water compared to our father!"

A flash of my eye silenced her. The fact that she had mirrored my own misgivings did not comfort me. I wanted a hawk. An eagle. I feared I was being matched with a dove.

"He's young." My reply was diplomatic. "We'll grow together. And I will be at his side to strengthen him."

"I think your pretty Prince is a virgin, lady," Bernart advised, tapping an impudent rhythm against the belly of his lute.

I was feeling beleaguered here. Were Louis's shortcomings as obvious to everyone as they were to me? I hoped not. To be the object of pity was more than I could tolerate.

"Perhaps he is a virgin still. He is a perfect knight." I tried for magnificent sangfroid.

"But will he be able to couch his lance?" Aelith smirked, squeezing my hand.

A jest as old as time. I think I laughed with her.

I did not laugh later.

Chapter Two

"How long will this . . . this *affair* last?" The Prince's lips tightened into a thin line of disapproval.

As was customary at so momentous an occasion as a ducal marriage, after God's blessing in the great cathedral of Saint Andre, we gathered in the antechamber of the Ombriere Palace to lead the procession through the Great Hall and up to the High Table. Louis looked weary, as if he would gladly cancel the whole affair and make a run for it. It could not be. Today, the day of our marriage, we were on show, and I was alert for even one disparaging expression, one whispered aside.

"As long as it takes to impress your new vassals!" I smiled at him with clenched teeth, my new husband of less than an hour, and closed my hand over his arm to shackle him to the spot. Words hot enough to scorch sprang into my mouth. Did this Frankish Prince not understand what he was getting from this marriage, how much land was now his? Surely it was worth an hour or two of feasting, of building bridges. I almost lost my struggle not to lecture him on the value of diplomacy over a cup of wine and a platter of succulent meats—until Aelith attached herself to my side. She pulled me a little away.

"We've no time for gossip," I remarked, seeing Louis almost physically retreat from the crush without my restraining grip.

Had I said that all was done in a hurry? Two weeks was all it took to get us to the altar. Two weeks that gave my vassals ample time to respond to the summons to attend the wedding and pay homage to their new overlord. Most did, with ill grace, but at least they put in a stiff-necked, close-lipped appearance. Some were conspicuous by their absence—the Count of Angoulême being the one to cause tongues to wag—but enough were present to raise their voices in acclaim of Louis, who in joining his hand with mine was now Duke of Aquitaine and Gascony, Count of Poitou. As we had walked through the streets afterward to cheering crowds, music, and green leaves cast before our feet, Louis's guards had pressed close about us, but still it was an auspicious beginning. The cries were not hostile, although, in truth, the roasting carcasses of beef and the hogsheads of ale craftily provided by the Archbishop for the populace would have sweetened the voices.

Now the deed was done.

In those two weeks I never set eyes on the Prince unless he came as a reluctant guest to a celebratory event, and never alone, always hedged about by soldiers and under the watchful gaze of the man I learned directed his every step: Abbot Suger, right-hand man of Fat Louis. I knew no more about the Prince now than on that first day. Rumor said he had spent the hours in his pavilion on his knees thanking God for the success of this venture, and praying equally for a safe return to Paris. For certain he had no stomach for outstaying his welcome in Bordeaux, just as he had no stomach for the feasting so beloved by the Aquitainians.

Now back in the Ombriere Palace for our marriage feast, I fixed Louis with a stern regard, willing him not to move, ignoring Aelith's whisperings as I renewed my own silent vow. Louis *le jeune* might now be my sovereign lord, my husband, and able to command my obedience. I might have moved seamlessly from the dominance of a father to the authority of a husband, but I would not be an impotent wife, destined to sit in a solar and stitch altar cloths.

"Eleanor . . . ! Who is that?" Aelith persisted.

"Who?"

"The lord in the blue silk and gray fur—the man who's looking at me."

Her eye gleamed and I followed its direction.

It was worth the looking. Tall and impressively built, the Frankish lord was well on in years, but his dark hair was untouched with gray and his face was striking, with a hawklike nose and heavy brows. At this moment his mouth was taut in consideration of something that had taken his attention—perhaps my sister. His dark eyes were fixed firmly and with appreciation on her. And why not? I thought. Aelith's burgeoning shape was revealed by the clinging deep green silk and silver embroidery of her gown. Obviously the lord was one of Louis's entourage, but I did not know him. Perhaps he was newly arrived.

"Find out for me," Aelith demanded, not so sotto voce.

"Aelith! In the middle of my wedding feast?" But I humored her. "Who is the lord with the fiery eye?" I murmured to Louis.

He looked across, face open in welcome. "My cousin, Raoul. Count Raoul of Vermandois. Why?"

"No reason. He looks very proud."

Louis raised his hand to draw the lord's attention. "And rightly. He's Seneschal of France. His wife is sister to Count Theobald of Champagne. Powerful connections."

The Count approached, bowed, and was introduced.

"Lady. A happy occasion."

His voice was as smooth as the silk I wore. When he had retired back into the crowd, to the side of an austere lady with a calculating slant to her eye—his extremely well-connected, powerful wife from Champagne, I presumed—I relayed the information to Aelith as the procession formed behind us.

"He's married. He's also old enough to be your father."

She looked at me solemnly. "He's handsome. A man of authority. A man—not a boy."

"And of no interest to you!"

As ever, Aelith was an open book and I saw her intent: a frivolous flirtation at the feast to pass the time between one extravagant course and the next. I paid it no heed other than to consider that sometimes my sister, for all her high breeding and lack of years, had the heart and inclination of a camp whore.

"Don't demean yourself," I warned.

"I would not!"

So now we processed down the length of the hall, took our seats, and looked out over the no-expense-spared glory of our celebration. Louis and I acknowledged the good wishes and sipped from the marriage cup. I could not help but regret the clash of my braided hair as it lay on my breast with my red damask gown and Fat Louis's rubies flashing in the sunlight. But the Prince would not be gainsaid. Red was a royal color, he had said. I should be clad as the future Queen of France. I humored him in the color and jewelry—by the Virgin, the gold was heavy!—but not in the style of my gown. Its cut was opulent and pure Aquitaine. Louis's pale brows had risen at my trailing skirts and oversleeves that had to be tied in elegant knots to prevent them from dragging in the dust. I was right—he did not approve of ostentation.

At least for once Louis looked the part of a prince, fair and comely beneath the Aquitaine gold of the ducal coronet, despite his compressed lips. His servants had come to grips with him and turned him out as if he had more than two silver pennies to rub together. In fact, he dazzled the eye. Perhaps his father and the omnipresent Abbot Suger had insisted on the red-and-gold tunic, heavy with embroidery, which gave bulk to his figure and an unquestionable air of majesty to his mien.

The feast began; the troubadours sang. The great lords of Gascony and Aquitaine were spread like a mosaic before us. Lusignan and Auvergne, Périgord and Armagnac. Châteauroux. Parthenay. My father had kept them tightly controlled by a clever show of force coupled with an open hand of generosity, but I knew that as soon as I was in Paris they'd be gnawing at the edges of my land like rats on a decaying carcass. The image made me shiver. I sent platters of food and flagons of ale in their direction and bent a beaming smile on them. There was nothing like a feast to soften hostilities. Along the table to my right I tried not to watch as Aelith cast inappropriate glances toward the forbidden Count Raoul, who was not slow in returning them, despite his wife's obvious displeasure, her hand fastening like a claw on his wrist to keep his attention. On my left Louis was toying with a meager plate of roast suckling pig while everyone around tucked in with hearty appetite.

"Does it not please you, sir?" I asked.

Before us on the white cloth was spread a beribboned swan, proud and upright, its neck skewered with iron to keep it erect, the whole resting on a lake of green leaves. Accompanying this masterpiece was a peppered peacock, a spit-roasted piglet, and a haunch of venison, while servants carried in an endless procession of ducks and geese and sauced cranes.

Louis frowned at the display. "I am not used to such opulence."

"But this is a celebration."

"And it would be wrong of me not to enjoy it." He speared a piece of the meat on his knife and ate it. But only one piece, unlike my vassals, who stuffed piece after piece into their mouths until they were sated. Perhaps, I made the excuse, his restraint was a reaction against his father's gluttony. I could not fault him in that.

Bernart, my favorite of all my troubadours, sank to his knee before me.

"I ask permission to sing of your beauty, lady." And not waiting for assent, because no Aquitainian ever refused a song, he broke into the familiar verses.

> *For beauty there's no equal*
> *Of the Queen of Joy.*

I threw a pouch of gold to land at his feet in acknowledgment of his compliment, as he slid into a verse I did not know.

> *From afar the King has come, come to interrupt the dance,*
> *For he fears another man may boldly seize the chance to wed the*
> *April Queen.*

So the gifted Bernart had written this verse for the occasion—and my heart fluttered a little at the compliment. My troubadour knew my value to the King of France and would broadcast it to the winds. April Queen. I liked it almost as much as Queen of Joy—and I certainly approved the idea that I was much sought after. What woman would not? And so I turned to Louis, laughing in surprised delight.

"Well, sir? Do you like the sentiment?"

"No. I do not."

"Why not?" The flat denial astonished me. "Any woman would be delighted with the idea of rivals for her hand. It is the essence of Love."

The muscles in Louis's jaw tightened. "I don't like the sentiment of having to snatch you up before another man forestalls me." I saw his nostrils narrow as he inhaled. The corners of his mouth were tightly tucked in, as if the scents of the spiced meats were suddenly distasteful. "And I have feasted enough." Casting down his knife, he signaled for a finger bowl.

"Do you not find the dishes pleasing?" I asked, suddenly uneasy, uncertain of his intentions. He seemed to me petulant beyond words. Did he want the feast to end? Did he intend to leave? It would be the height of bad manners. Did Louis not see that?

"I do not find the dishes inordinately pleasing. Not as much as you do, it seems." His soft voice had acquired an edge as he turned to stare directly into my eyes. "Do you know what they say of you? The lords at my father's court?"

"Of me? No. What do they say of me?"

"Not of *you*," he amended, "but of your people. They say that men from Aquitaine and Poitou value gluttony rather than military skill."

How patently untrue! Was he being deliberately gauche? Surely he would not be so coarse in his criticism on this day of all days. "Is that all they can find to say?"

"They say you're talkative, boastful, lustful, greedy, incapable of . . ."

The words dried on his tongue, and his cheeks flew red flags as he suddenly realized to whom he spoke. "Forgive me." He looked down at his dish with its uneaten mess of meat and sauce. "I did not think. . . ."

Resentment stiffened my spine. How dared he slander me and my people on so short an acquaintance. I might see their shortcomings, but it was not this Frankish Prince's place to denigrate them. By what right did he measure them and find them wanting? "Do you not feast and sing in Paris, then? Do the Franks not find time away from government for pleasure and entertainment?"

"*I* did not sing and feast. Not at Saint-Denis."

"What is that? A palace?"

"A monastery."

"Did you visit there?"

"I was brought up there."

The words sank in, but with them not much understanding. "You were brought up in a monastery?"

"Did you not know?"

"No. As a priest?"

"More or less."

"Did you enjoy it?" I could not imagine it. My quick anger was replaced by interest.

"Yes." A smile softened the tension in his jaw, and the feverish light in his eye faded. "Yes, I did. The order of the day, each one like the last. The serenity in the House of God. Can you understand?" His voice took on an enthusiasm I had not heard before; his pale eyes shone. "The perpetual prayers for God's forgiveness, the voices of the monks rising up with the incense. I liked nothing better than to keep vigil through the night—"

"But did you not learn the art of government?" I interrupted. "Did you not sit with your father and hear good advice and counsel?" Surely that would have been of far greater use than the rule of Saint Benedict.

"I was never intended to rule, you see," Louis explained. "My elder brother—Philip—he was killed by a scavenging sow at loose on the quay. Philip fell from his horse when it reared." Louis's voice was suddenly rough with suppressed grief. "There was no hope for him. His neck broke in the filth of the gutter."

"Oh!"

"He was an accomplished warrior. He would have been a great king. . . ."

"My son." A soft voice from Louis's other side broke in. The ever-present Abbot Suger, sent by Fat Louis to keep his eye on the son and heir. He leaned forward, a slight, elderly man with a deceptively mild demeanor, to look at me as much as at Louis. "My son, the lady does not wish to hear of your life at Saint-Denis. Or of Philip. You are heir to the throne now."

"But the Lady Eleanor asked if I had enjoyed my life there."

"You must look to your future together now."

The Abbot had the thin, lined face of an aesthete. His hair was as glossily white as an ermine, his small dark eyes just as inquisitive. They summed me up in that instant and I suspected they found me wanting.

"Of course. Forgive me." Louis nodded obediently. "That life is all in the past."

"But I think you miss it." I was reluctant to allow the Abbot to dictate the direction of our conversation.

"Sometimes." The volume of noise rose around us again as Louis smiled self-deprecatingly. "I was intended for the Church, you see. I was taught to value abstinence and prayer. To give my mind to higher pursuits than . . . than this." The sweep of his hand to the now rois-tering crowd was, whether he intended it or not, entirely derogatory. Unfortunately Bernart, roaming the room with lute to hand, chose the moment to swing into a well-loved song, with a raucous chorus for all to join in. Since the wine was flowing, the merrymakers were in good heart.

> *Don't marry this cheat, sweet Jeanne, for he is stupid and*
> *unlettered.*
> *Don't take him to your bed, sweet Jeanne; your lover would be*
> *far better.*

Louis smacked his hand down on the cloth, making the silver dishes dance. "Listen! How can you approve of that? Your minstrels sing of a lust and intimacy not sanctioned by the Church nor by any moral code. They have no respect for women and encourage them to behave without restraint."

The hearty phrase *these flaming whores* was bellowed from a hundred throats, both men and women.

"It is immoral. Degrading. Such verses should be forbidden. Such foulmouthed braggarts as this . . . this scurrilous minstrel should be whipped through the streets for their impertinence. . . ." Louis's voice rose alarmingly.

"But he is not a scurrilous minstrel," I objected. "He is Bernart Sicart of Maruejols."

I received a blank look, and a derisory one at that.

"He is famous throughout Aquitaine. My father thought very highly of him."

"His words are insulting and offensive! I don't want him at my court."

A trickle of fear, as hard and cold as ice, invaded my chest. It hadn't taken my new lord long, had it, to wield his new authority over me. He did not know me very well.

"I'll not dismiss him."

"Even if I demand it?"

"Why should you? He is mine and I'll remain his patron. You'll not change my mind in this—" I closed my lips against *my lord*. I was beyond terms of respect.

As Louis sought for a reply, a quietness fell, as sometimes happens in a crowd.

"Colhon!"

I heard the comment drift across from my left. No attempt was made to mute it and I froze, my fingers clenched around my spoon, in humiliation for Louis—for myself. I felt my skin flush as bright as his. Abandoning the spoon, I curled my fingers around Louis's wrist. I could feel my temper rising.

"Do you think that of me? As ruler of Aquitaine? That I am immoral, my thoughts fit only for the sewer?" My cheeks might flame, my temper might burn, but my voice was tight with control.

"No. I think you are beautiful beyond measure," Louis replied with disarming candor, his voice returning to its low timbre. "I think your mind is as fine as your face. I can find no fault in you. I can't believe you are my wife."

My mind struggled to grasp the quick lunge and feint of this conversation. Was Louis so naive that he would think to win my favor by this lurch from condemnation to flattery? How dared he pick and prod at my own people, at my way of life, within an hour of our marriage? So he could find no fault in me. I admitted to no fault in me! Nor with the uninhibited behavior and language of my guests. Temper remained hot in my blood as I retrieved my spoon in a pretense of sampling a dish of succulent figs.

Clearly disturbed at the flash in my eye, Louis lifted his cup, intending to take a hearty swallow of wine, but Abbot Suger was instantly there to place a hand on his wrist.

"Perhaps not, my lord."

And Louis immediately pushed away the cup. "No. It would be better if I did not."

"Do you always take his advice?" I demanded.

"Yes. My lord Abbot always has my best interest at heart. He would never advise me wrongly." Louis looked puzzled. "Do you have no one to advise you, lady?"

"No."

"Then how do you know what to do, which decisions to take?"

I had to think about that. It was not a question I had ever been asked, to justify my desires and needs. The answer was simple enough. "When my father was alive, we traveled constantly. I watched and I learned. And now I act as I know he would have done. He was a good man. I miss him," I admitted.

Louis's face was transfigured by a blinding smile. "You need me, Eleanor. *I* will advise you."

Could a child raised as a monk give *me* advice, brought up as I was in my father's court? I did not think so. "I hope we will come to an agreement," I replied, compromising.

"My lord will rule your lands wisely, my lady," Abbot Suger interposed.

I bit back a sharp reply. Of course, it would happen whether I liked it or not. I lowered my voice, leaning toward Louis, suddenly intent on mischief.

"If we are speaking of advice, my lord—try this dish." And I offered him a silver platter stacked high with translucent gray shells. "Oysters are known to raise the humors and make a man think of a night heating the bed linen with a beautiful woman. Oysters give a man magnificent stamina."

He looked at me as if I had struck him. "My lady!"

"I am your wife. Is this not a proper conversation?"

Louis swallowed. "I think it is very forward, madam. . . ."

I hooded my eyes. "It would please me if you would try them. *I* shall. We might both be pleased with the result tonight."

Louis *le jeune* looked like a hunted rabbit. With regret, I thought we were both in for some inexpert fumbling before we came to know each other. I wished my husband might have some experience, even if he lacked finesse. Entirely oblivious to my anger, my barely concealed scorn, Louis accepted the oysters without comment. I prayed silently that the old wives knew the efficacy of the succulent shellfish.

Barely had he lifted one, unenthusiastically, to his mouth than a courier approached down the length of the hall, pushing aside servants and guests alike. I expected him to come to me, but of course he would approach Louis—no, he bowed before the Abbot, which spiked my irritation further. The messenger stooped, whispered in Suger's ear so that I could not hear. The Abbot issued a number of terse replies, brusque enough to fix my attention, then relayed the information to Louis. There passed between Abbot and Prince a welter of instructions and affirmations as the courier left the hall as fast as he had come.

I had been involved in none of it.

"What is it?" I would not be kept in the dark.

Louis turned reluctantly to me. "A problem."

"Well?" I raised my beautifully plucked brows.

"We leave now."

"Leave . . . You mean, the palace? In the middle of the feast?" The news must be as bad as I had feared.

"We leave Bordeaux. It is not safe."

"Not safe? How could it not be safe in my own streets, my own city? No one would dare harm me here. . . ."

Abbot Suger offered the explanation, speaking around Louis, his expression bleak. "An ambush, I am informed, outside the walls, my lady. Planned for tomorrow, under the auspices of the Count of Angoulême. Your vassal. He will take you both prisoner and assume the power in Aquitaine for himself."

"Angoulême? I don't believe it. A show of force would soon drive him off. . . ."

Louis took my hand, actually patted it as if I needed his comfort. "I'll not risk it. I've given orders for my camp to be struck and your immediate possessions packed. We ride at once."

So he would order the disposition of my own possessions. "Are we to run away?" I asked between disbelief and fury.

"No, no. We'll forestall him. A far better course of action."

"It seems cowardly to me. Where do we go?" To leave now before the bridal night? I had a sudden vivid picture of spending it in a ditch, beside a road.

"It's arranged, by my lord Abbot. We stay at the castle of Taille-bourg tonight."

"It's . . . it's more than eighty miles to Taillebourg!"

"It's owned by one of your vassals who did homage to me—so safe for us." Louis stood. Everyone on the dais surged to his feet, startled. Louis ignored them. "Make ready, my wife."

I had, of course, no choice but to comply. It was as if the prospect of action had given Louis a much-needed bolt of confidence, and I could do nothing but walk at his side between the ranks of guests. Pairs of eyes followed us, in shock or amusement. Did they think we would preempt the bridal night? That Louis was too urgent to wait? All I saw on his face was strain, perhaps even fear.

Stopping only to change my marriage splendor for garments more suitable for an all-out flight, I was hurried from the palace—my vassals still unaware and feasting in the Great Hall—and rowed across the

Garonne to where Louis was already preparing to mount and waiting for me, clad in mail as if expecting trouble to descend on our heads at any moment.

"Lady!" He waved his hand impatiently as I stepped from the boat, Aelith and some baggage following me. "What took you so long? Do you really need all of that? We mustn't stay. I've ordered a horse litter for your comfort. . . ." He pointed to the cumbersome transport with its enveloping curtains, slung between four sturdy horses. I had traveled in such a palanquin—but rarely—and remembered the bruises and bone-shuddering jolts. And the tedium.

"I thought we were in a hurry," I remarked.

"We are."

"Then what point in a litter? I'll ride."

"I think not. It's too slow," Louis fretted, pulling me to one side with a hand around my forearm as if he would rather not have me question his decision in public view.

"Slow?"

"Too slow, with a sidesaddle and planchet for your feet and a groom to lead."

Now I understood. I despised the litter, but not as much as I despised the wooden seat with its solid footrest to allow a lady to ride in safety. I shook off Louis's hand. He might be my husband of five hours but this was not good sense. "I'll ride astride. No need of a groom or a leading rein. I've ridden all my life." I pulled on a pair of serviceable leather gloves, keeping my eyes firmly on his.

"What?" He was horrified.

"I can keep up with you, my lord. Fetch me a horse to match your own."

Louis cleared his throat and looked askance. Would he deny me that right, to decide the manner of my travel?

"That is what I wish. And I will do it." I left him in no doubt.

"The lady is right." The Abbot, stripped of his ecclesiastical garb for leather and light mail, strode up to chivy us along. "If she is willing . . ."

"She is!" I flashed a warning look, by now thoroughly exasperated. "And we are wasting time here, if the danger is so great."

So I had my way. Louis, his face flaming with high color, was obviously nettled by my boldness, but I left him no choice. "Good!" I nodded at the well-muscled mount that was brought forward for my approval, and raised my foot for his hand. "Lift me, and then we can be gone." As I mounted astride, I tried not to look for any sense of grievance in his resigned expression. But it was there.

We rode at breakneck speed, changing horses at every river crossing, soon outstripping the escort of Frankish knights who at first pounded around us, a human wall of defense against my recalcitrant vassals. I tried not to let the snarls against treacherous southerners hurt my heart, even as I accepted the rightness of them. So we rode as if the Devil himself pursued us rather than the Count of Angoulême—and we saw no trace of him, hour after hour, without rest except to snatch a mouthful of bread and a gulp of wine to sustain us. Abbot Suger urged us on at every brief halt. And since he had our safety at heart, and my own people were the cause of our flight, I could hardly resist, even though I could have fallen from my saddle with weariness toward the end. Aelith, as rank and filthy as I from sweat and dust, fared no better, but Louis showed surprising stamina. Or perhaps it was a determination not to be bested twice in one day by a woman.

As the hours and the miles passed, I felt his anxious eyes travel over me when my muscles shrieked their weariness and my eyelids threatened to close. Yes, he had a concern for me, I thought. There was no malice in the frequent glances, even though I had insisted and must now pay the price. I doubted there was a malicious bone in his body. But I would give him no cause for complaint. I stiffened my shoulders, set my mind against quivering muscles and chafed skin, and pushed my horse—a clumsy, rawboned creature, but the best to be had in the circumstances—on again into a gallop.

"Did you hear what they called him?" Aelith whispered over a shared cup of wine at the next brief halt. "At the feast?"

"Yes."

"*Colhon!* Stupid as a testicle!"

"No need to repeat it!"

What woman would wish to be wed to a figure of ridicule?

Taillebourg. At last. In the considerable fortress belonging to one of my more loyal vassals, I was shown into the private quarters of Geoffrey de Rancon, where comfort closed around me. Too exhausted to do more than give passing thanks for the hospitality, I took possession. A bathtub was commandeered, hot water ordered. My body might ache unmercifully from the crown of my head to my feet, but I would go clean to my marriage night. I looked at the lord of Rancon's bed, appreciating the solid wooden frame and silk hangings complete with down mattress and fine linen sheets. The whole might not match the splendor of mine, but it would suffice. Better than the threat of the dank and very public ditch.

Anticipation was a pleasant murmur in my blood as the servants arrived with a tub and buckets of water. I was neither unwilling nor anxious. I sensed that Louis, an ignorant child-monk, would have more qualms than I. I laughed softly, perhaps unfairly. Louis would not have the good Abbot to offer advice on this occasion. The water steamed; the herbs filled the room with aromatic fragrance; my limbs cried out for the soothing. Aelith fussed to unlace me. I cast off my gown, my undergown, my full-length shift, leaving me clad in one more layer.

A knock sounded on the door. I raised my hand to the chambermaid to forbid entry, but too late. The door opened and Louis himself, still in tunic, boots, hose, and mail, stepped in. He halted on the threshold, pushing back his coif, thrusting a hand nervously through his matted hair that clung wetly to his neck.

"Forgive me." With a shy smile and what could only be described as a charming little bow, mailed gloves still clutched in his hand as if he had come straight from the stabling—as perhaps he had—he took in our surroundings. "I came to ask after your well-being, my lady. I see that everything has been provided for. . . ."

His words dried. His jaw dropped. His eyes focused on my legs, where they became fixed, until they slid nervously away to my face.

"My lord?"

"Madam!"

I waited.

"That . . . that *garment* . . ."

It had been made for me, of chamois leather. Soft, figure hugging, hard wearing, and above all protective, it enclosed my body, covering each leg as with a soft skin of its own. Wonderfully supple, delightfully liberating, it enabled me to move and stretch with great freedom. And to ride without discomfort. It was as accommodating as a man's chausses, on which it was clearly modeled.

"Excellent, is it not?" It pleased me to tease him. His opinions were as inflexible as stones set in gold. His reaction was much as I had anticipated.

"It is indelicate, madam!"

"Do you expect me to ride well nigh a hundred miles, astride, in a shift? In linen drawers, perhaps?"

"No . . . I . . . that is . . ." Louis stammered.

"I had them made for me. For hunting. We enjoy hunting in Aquitaine."

"It is not seemly. The women at our court in Paris would shrink from wearing such a garment."

"A woman from Paris would not shrink from it if she had to flee for her life on one clumsy animal after another! But do your women not hunt? I think I must instruct them on such a garment's practicality."

"You will do no such thing. My mother would be appalled."

"How so?"

Louis shook his head, refusing to elaborate. He did not see a need to, only to enforce my obedience. "As my wife, you will not wear that again." The expression that settled on his face was not attractive, almost vicious in its intensity.

Would I not? As if I, Duchess of Aquitaine, did not know how to conduct myself, how to present myself. "Really?" I opened my mouth to tell him exactly that, but realized that I was just too tired to cross swords with this man who was almost squirming with embarrassment. If the floor had opened before his feet, I swear he would have willingly leaped in. Glancing around, I saw the sly smile on Aelith's face. I could not humiliate him more. Louis would soon learn and become accustomed to my ways. Taking pity on him, I donned a robe to cover the offending article. But that was as far as I would go.

"I should inform you, my lord—I shall wear this garment again tomorrow when we ride on to Poitiers. You have no right to forbid it."

"But I am your husband." His response was brutally frank.

"As I am your wife."

"You have sworn to obey me."

"You will not dictate what garments I choose to wear. Particularly when they are covered by my skirts and not obvious to any onlooker. Only to a man who entered my chamber without my invitation when I might—after the day I've had—expect some privacy!"

As a standoff it was magnificent.

"As I see it," I continued before Louis could draw breath, "we're set to travel another vast distance tomorrow. I will ride at your side, my lord, but not without protection."

"As you say, madam." He glared his rancor but I knew I had won. Louis's response was as tight as the muscles in his neck and shoulders. "I advise you to take some rest. You must be exhausted. We leave early tomorrow." There was that flare of color again in his face. "I'll not make more demands on you. Your sister will keep you company tonight."

It took a full minute for his words to make sense.

"You will not stay with me?"

"I need to pray, my lady." Again almost a rebuke, as if I were thoughtless and inconsiderate of any needs but my own. "For my father the King's health. For our safe travel. Abbot Suger says that I must—he awaits me in the chapel."

"How old are you, Louis?" I demanded. For suddenly, as his eyes fell before my stony stare, he seemed far younger than I—that he should follow the orders of Abbot Suger rather than any inclination of his own.

"I am seventeen," he replied stiffly.

"Then why not . . ."

But the door was already closing behind him, and I was left with nothing but the sound of Louis's rapidly retreating footsteps.

I wrapped my dignity around me with the chamber robe. He had no intention of spending our wedding night with me. Dismay and disappointment twined to create a bright fury that I could barely contain. "Of course it is necessary to pray," I lashed out at the closed door. "You must not keep God or the Abbot waiting."

What did it matter if he did not hear me? Louis was immune to my barbs.

The water in the tub was cooling as I stepped into it and sank up to my chin, my mind not at ease. Despite the relish of victory over what I might or might not wear, I was mystified by the Prince's rejection of me. My pride was hurt, and I resented the fact, for was I not descended from an impressive company of proud women? I considered myself not the least of their number. How could I not see my own supremacy in them? Their fire was in my own blood. Their knowledge of what was due to them colored my own self-worth. Their ghosts had stalked me; their exploits had been the tales of my childhood.

What would they say if they had seen my weak compliance in Louis's absence? Forsooth, my female forebears would have taken me to task.

Women such as Philippa, my paternal grandmother. High-minded and unbending, she lived by the principles of duty and obedience to God, and the respect due to her as the heiress to the county of Toulouse. She was a formidable woman, although I found it difficult to condone her decision to spend her final days with the nuns at the Abbey of Fontevrault, assaulting the ears of God with her prayers for revenge, when the ninth Duke, her husband and my grandfather, lived openly with his lover under Philippa's very nose, in Philippa's own favorite palace. *I* would not have left the field. I would have waged war against my neglectful husband who dared humiliate me, and against the upstart whore who usurped my bed.

Or perhaps I would not.

Because that whore—Dangerosa—was my maternal grandmother. Originally wife to the Viscount of Chatellerault, she saw my grandfather William in full glory of mail and weaponry, and fell into love, like a gannet diving headfirst into the waves off Bordeaux. So too did William fall, so heavily that he must abduct Dangerosa from her bedchamber—with no obvious protest on Dangerosa's part—and carry her off to his palace at Poitiers, where he established her in the newly constructed Maubergeonne Tower. They were besotted with each other, making no secret of their sinful union. Dangerosa raised her chin at the world's condemnation, while Duke William had the lady's portrait painted on the face of his shield. It was, he boasted, his desire to bear her likeness into battle, as she had borne the weight of his body so willingly and frequently in bed.

A tasteless jest. My grandfather had a strong streak of coarse humor.

Dangerosa never regretted her choice. She was his whore until his death, keeping her unpredictable lover more or less faithful with a will of steel, and with fearful cunning. Since she could not get Duke William legally into her bed, then her daughter would get William's son. Thus Dangerosa's daughter Aenor was wed to my father. Dangerosa keeping it in the family, if you will.

So this was my mother, Aenor—who did not fit the mold of strong-willed Aquitaine women. What a mouselike creature Aenor was, according to Dangerosa. Timid, manipulated, she did what she was told without complaint. I suppose there were extenuating circumstances, neglected as she was by a mother who was branded a harlot, bedded by a husband who viewed his father's mistress's daughter with less than enthusiasm. Aenor even abandoned life before her time. I recalled little of her. I was eight years old when she and my brother died.

And so my upbringing, strong in practical advice if not in maternal affection, fell to Dangerosa.

"Never underestimate the power of a good dose of lust," she advised me, waving aside my nurse, who would guard me from such inappropriate sentiments. "A handsome, virile man in your bed is more fulfilling than any number of hours on your knees before the

Almighty. Your grandmother Philippa was a fool. What happiness did she get out of enclosing herself with a parcel of nuns?"

What indeed? I never knew Philippa. But what would Dangerosa—or Philippa—think of me now?

"Am I so ugly? So undesirable?" I asked Aelith. But I knew I was not. What I did know was that it would be common knowledge that my husband had chosen not to share my bed, that he would find more fulfillment on his knees before a crucifix than with me. "Do you think he dislikes me?"

"I think he finds you too beautiful," Aelith crooned to comfort me as she combed out my hair.

"But not in chamois drawers."

"He is a man. What does he know?"

"I thought he would erupt in a storm of temper when I refused. . . ."

"I doubt he has a temper in him," Aelith disagreed.

"Perhaps you're right." Yet there had been that one moment when I thought I had seen a bright flare of barely controlled rage. . . . "But why does he not want me?"

"He does not know women. He does not know how to please them. Now, his cousin Lord Raoul would not hold back, I swear. . . ."

I slapped her hand away when she tugged on a painful tangle in my hair, but she only laughed.

"I don't even know that he wants to please me." I frowned at my knees emerging from the water.

"You didn't make life easy for him, Eleanor," Aelith pointed out, fairly enough, I suppose. "You challenged him over how you would and would not travel, and what you would and would not wear."

"And that wasn't the first. I'd already been more than forthright over the court position of my troubadour Bernart," I admitted with a twinge of guilt.

"What's wrong with Bernart?"

"Nothing—that's the point. Never mind—we just didn't agree."

"And you haven't been wed a full day. . . ."

"I suppose I've not been a dutiful wife, have I?"

"There you have it. He's a prince. He's not used to a woman taking him to task."

My thoughts circled around to the main issue. "He seeks the company of God before mine." For the first time in my life I was touched with a true uncertainty.

"Then you'll just have to show him the error of his ways, won't you?"

I was not much comforted. Aelith shared my pillows. I rose next morning from my marriage bed as much a virgin as I had entered it.

Chapter Three

What a welcome we received as we rode into the city of Poitiers, making our way toward the Maubergeonne Tower, Grandmother Philippa's tower, the home I loved the most. There was not the slightest hint of the rebellion that troubled the Abbot's mind. The streets echoed to the cries of joy of my people so that even Louis was forced to smile and wave at their overt approval. And the crowds responded, urged on by Abbot Suger's largesse. I saw the coin passed from the bound chests in the baggage wains to the hands of the greedy populace even if Louis did not. Louis accepted the acclamation as his right. And why should he not? When his face was printed with happiness and he was clad in mail astride a high-blooded destrier, as had been arranged for this entry, he was superbly striking, a prince whom they could take to their hearts.

Hope surged within me. This night would see the fulfillment of my marriage.

I was stripped and bathed by my women and taken to the soft canopied bed in my own bedchamber. Nervously, expectantly, I waited. A soft knocking at the door. It was pushed open and there, at last, was Louis, under escort from Abbot Suger but otherwise alone. Well, this would be no riotous bedding ceremony with coarse jokes and bold innuendo, and I was not sorry. But it seemed to me that Louis looked as if he were under guard to prevent a precipitate flight. His expression was mutinous.

"It is time, my lord," the Abbot murmured. "It is your duty to the lady. This marriage must be consummated."

"Yes." Wrapped about in a furred brocade chamber robe, Louis stood, hands fisted at his sides, face sullen like that of a child caught out in some misdemeanor.

"Perhaps if you joined your bride in the bed, my lord . . . ? Now, my lord!"

It might have been a request, but Suger's face was implacable.

Allowing the robe to fall to the floor, Louis stalked across the room. I was impressed. He stripped well, as I had thought, revealing broad shoulders and slender hips. The ascetic life had suited him. Lean, smooth, good to look at, he was well made—but obviously not aroused.

That could surely be rectified. My nurse, left behind in Bordeaux, had been explicit in what was expected of me. I had not been raised to be timid with thoughts of the flesh.

At a further impatient gesture from the Abbot, Louis slid between the sheets and leaned back against the pillows beside me, his arms folded across his chest. Making every effort not to brush against me, leaving a chilly space between us from shoulder to foot, he sighed loudly. Was it resignation? Distaste? I think he sensed the sudden leap of trepidation in my blood, because he turned his head to look at me. With another little sigh, more a controlled exhalation, I saw his body relax. His smile was warm, reassuring. No, I had no need to be anxious after all.

"My lord," the Abbot intoned, wasting no time. "My lady. God bless your union. May you be fruitful. May an heir for France come from your loins this night, my lord."

From his capacious garments he produced a flask of holy water and proceeded to sprinkle us and the bed with a symbol of God's presence. With a brisk nod in Louis's direction, he looked as if he might be prepared to stay to see the deed done. We were not an ordinary couple, to order their lives to their own wishes: our marriage must be consummated before the law.

Such a necessity proved not to be to my husband's taste. Louis scowled. "We'll do well enough without your presence, sir," he said.

"It is a matter of witnesses, my lord. . . ."

"God will be witness to what passes between myself and my wife."

"His Majesty, your father, will—"

"His Majesty is not here to express his desires. It is my wish that you leave us."

Well! Louis's decisiveness impressed me. Abbot Suger bowed himself from the room, leaving us sitting naked, side by side. The room was still, the only sound the soft hush as ash fell from the logs in the fireplace. I sat unmoving. My husband would take the initiative, would he not?

Louis slid from the bed.

"Where are you going?" I demanded when I found my scattered wits.

Without replying, shrugging into his robe again, Louis crossed the room and knelt at my prie-dieu, clasped his hands, and bent his fair head in prayer, murmuring the familiar words with increasing fervor so that they filled the room.

Ave Maria . . . Hail Mary, full of grace, the Lord is with thee.
Blessed art thou among women
And blessed is the fruit of thy womb, Jesus.
Holy Mary, Mother of Grace, pray for us now
And in the hour of our death. Amen.
Hail Mary, full of grace, the Lord is with thee.
Blessed art thou . . .

On and on it went. Should I join him on my knees, to pray with him? But he had not invited me; nor did I think it appropriate when this occasion demanded a physical rather than spiritual response. I clawed my fingers into the linen. I'd wager Dangerosa and my grandfather did not begin their reprehensible relationship on their knees before a cruxifix.

"Hail Mary . . ."

"Louis," I said cautiously. Should I disturb him in his prayers?

"Blessed art thou among women . . ."

"Louis!" I raised my voice to an unmaidenly pitch.

Unhurriedly, Louis completed the Ave, rose, genuflected, and returned to the bed, where he once more removed his robe and slid between the sheets. But he brought with him my little Book of Hours, which he proceeded to open, turning the pages slowly from one illuminated text to the next.

"This is a very beautiful book," he observed.

I was tempted to snatch it from him and hurl it across the room.

Instead, I asked, "Louis—did you not wish to marry me?"

"Of course. My father wished it. It is an important marriage to make our alliance between France and Aquitaine. The Scriptures say it is better for a man to marry than to burn."

I did not think, on evidence, that Louis burned.

"But do *you* not want me?"

"You are beautiful."

So was my Book of Hours! "Then tell me, Louis." Perhaps he was simply shy. Was that it? A boy brought up by monks might be reserved and indecisive in the company of a woman who was naked and expecting some degree of intimacy. I would encourage him. "Tell me why you think I am beautiful. A woman always likes to know."

"If you wish." He did not close the book, keeping one finger in the page, but now he looked at me. "Your hair is . . . the russet of a dog fox. Look how it curls around my fingers." He touched my hair. "And your eyes . . ." He peered into them. "Green." Lord, Louis was no poet. My troubadours would mock his lack of skill. "Your skin . . . pale and smooth. Your hands so elegant and soft but so capable—you controlled your horse as well as any man. Your shoulder . . ." His fingers skimmed lightly along the shoulder that had won his attention, until he snatched them away as if they were scorched by my flesh.

"Look," he said suddenly, urgently. "Here." He lifted the Book of

Hours so that I might see and thumbed through the pages until he came to the illustration he sought, the inks vibrant. "Here's an angel with your exact coloring. Is that not beautiful?"

"Well, yes . . ." It was beautiful, but unreal, with its painted features and gold leaf. Did he see me as a gilded icon? I was a woman of flesh and blood.

"What about my lips?" I asked. Daring, certainly forward, but why not? Once, my troubadour Bernart had compared them to an opening rose, pink and perfectly petaled.

"Sweet . . ."

I despaired. "You could kiss them."

"I would like to." Louis leaned forward and placed his lips softly on mine. Fleetingly.

"Did you like that?" I asked as he drew away.

His smile was totally disarming. "Yes."

I placed my hand on his chest—his heart beat slow and steady—and leaned to kiss him of my own volition. Louis allowed it but did not respond. He was still smiling at the end. As a child might smile when given a piece of sugared marchpane.

"I enjoyed it too," I said, my desperation keen. Did he not know what to do? Surely someone would have seen to his education. He might not have been raised to know the coarse jokes and explicit reminiscences that to my experience men indulged in, but surely . . . !

"I think we shall be happy together," he murmured.

"Would you like to hold me in your arms?"

"Very much. Shall we sleep now? It's late and you must be weary."

"I thought that . . ." What to say? Louis's eyes were wide and charmingly friendly. "Will the Abbot not wish for proof of our union—the sheets . . . ?" I wouldn't mince words. "The linen should be stained to prove my virginity and your ability to claim it."

And saw the return of the initial stubbornness as his brows flattened into a line. His reply had a gentle dignity. A complete assurance. "The Abbot will get his proof. When I wish it."

"But, Louis . . . my women—they will mock me."

"I care not. Nor should you. It is not their concern."

"They will say you have found me wanting. Or"—even worse—"that I was no virgin."

"Then they will be wrong. I have never met a woman who has touched my heart as you have. And I know you are innocent. There, now, don't be upset. Come here. . . ."

Abandoning the book, Louis folded me into his arms—as if he were a brother comforting a distressed sister. His manhood did not stir against my thigh despite his appreciation of me. Should I touch him? I may not have had the practice but I knew the method.

But I couldn't do it. I dared not touch him so intimately. In the presence of God and the Book of Hours and Louis's strange sanctity I just could not do it.

When Louis released me to blow out the candle and we lay side by side like carved effigies on a tomb, I was mortified. My marriage was no marriage at all. I knew that Louis slept, as calmly composed as that same effigy, his hands folded on his breast as if he were still summoning God to take note of his prayers. When I turned my head to look at him, his face was serene and completely unaware of the disillusion that I suffered.

Eventually I slept. When I awoke with daylight, he was gone, the Book of Hours carefully positioned on the empty pillow at my side, the page open to the gilded angel. The linen of my bed was entirely unmarked. There were no bloody sheets to testify to my husband's duty toward me or even his desire.

Well, I could have faked it, couldn't I? A quick stab to my finger with my embroidery needle . . . But I did not. It had not been my choice, and Louis must answer for his own lack. Faced with the Abbot's gentle inquiry on the following morning, I was haughty. I was defiant but icily controlled.

"If you wish to know what passed between us in the privacy of our bed, then you must ask the Prince," I informed him.

I silenced my women with a blank stare and a demand that I would break my fast as soon as they could arrange it. Perhaps *now* rather than in their own good time . . . ! I would not show my humiliation but coated it in a hard shell, as my cook in Bordeaux might enclose the softness of an almond in sugar. As for Aelith's obvious concern . . . I shut her out. Even to her, I could not speak of what had not occurred. If I had, I think I might have wept.

What passed between the Abbot and the Prince I had no idea.

In a bid to impress my subjects, Abbot Suger himself, in the glory of the great cathedral, placed the golden coronets to proclaim us Count and Countess of Poitiers. Louis accepted his new dignity with an unfortunate show of shy diffidence, whereas I spent the ceremony taking note of those who bent the knee and bared their necks in subservience, and making an even more careful accounting of those who did not.

Such as William de Lezay, my own castellan of Talmont, my hunting lodge. So personal a servant to me, he should have been first in line. He was not. Always an audacious knight with an eye to his own promotion, he sent me an insolent verbal message by one of his knights, who trembled as he repeated it. He had a right to tremble. I considered consigning him to a dungeon for a week for his weasel words—except that the sin was not his. One does not punish the messenger, my father had taught me. It only increases the trouble tenfold.

De Lezay was unable to attend my coronation: there were too many demands on his time. Such a ceremony was not to his taste, to acknowledge a Frank as his overlord. Such dislike of all things Frankish even overrode his sincere allegiance to *me*, with my pure and undisputed Aquitaine blood. I almost spit my disgust at the sly insincerity. With careful questioning, I discovered that the man had recently increased the number of troops at Talmont and was preparing for siege conditions.

So he had taken my castle for himself, had he?

He would hold it in the face of my objection, would he?

My temper began to simmer. That he should dare to inform me so blatantly of his defection. But that was not the worst of it. De Lezay's messenger, remarkably straight-faced, handed over a small flat leather packet. And within it as I tore it open? A handful of white wing feathers, beautifully barred and speckled with gray and black, fluttered to the floor.

By God! I knew the original owners of those magnificent feathers.

The simmer of temper bubbled and overflowed. The sheer insolence of the gesture! The birds were mine! My rare white gerfalcons, a gift from my father, kept and bred for my own use. Not fit for the wrist of a commoner such as William de Lezay.

"God rot his soul in Hell!"

The messenger, now fallen to his knees before me, trembled.

"May he burn in everlasting fires!" My voice was close to becoming shrill.

"What is that?" Louis inquired mildly, entering the antechamber as my rage reached its zenith. He gestured to the knight to rise to his feet. "What has this man said to disturb you?"

"News of de Lezay." I could barely force the words out. "My own castellan at Talmont. He has stolen my birds. And my hunting lodge. And—before God!—has the audacity to inform me of it." I still did not know what hurt most, the loss of the lodge or the gerfalcons. "My castellan! My father's chosen man!"

Louis's features relaxed. "Is that all? Most have taken the oath. He's the only one to refuse."

All? Was that how he saw it? My temper did not abate. "One is one too many! And he thinks he can get away with it because I am a woman. . . ." I rounded on Louis. I stared at him.

Louis Capet, Prince of France, looked purposeful and surprisingly efficient in wool and leather hunting clothes, a knife in his belt. I tilted my chin to appraise him. His hair gleamed beneath his felt cap. Today he looked like a knight capable of holding his own. And there it was. . . . *I* might not lead a punitive force against my errant castellan, but . . . Of course! Louis would uphold my rights for me, because they were now his rights too.

Ah . . . but would he? I was not certain of Louis's mettle. When Louis had suspected Angoulême of setting an ambush, he had been quick to hitch his tunic and flee. What price de Lezay keeping his lowborn fingers latched onto my property! But I strode to Louis's side and took his arm, tightening my fingers into the fine cloth. I was determined. Louis must not be allowed to run from this. He must be a warrior lord, not a fool to be ridiculed and despised.

"What will you do about it?" I demanded. "De Lezay defies you as much as he defies me. He usurps my power and yours. Let him get away with this and we'll have an avalanche of insurrection on our hands. I can just imagine him with one of my—of our—priceless white raptors on his fist, laughing at us from the battlements of Talmont."

Louis studied the floor at his feet. Then stared thoughtfully at the messenger for a moment, to the man's discomfort. Finally he looked at me. "What would you have me do, Eleanor?"

"Punish him for his temerity. Take back my property."

"You wish me to launch an attack against him."

"Yes."

Louis blinked as if struck by this novel idea. "Then if it will please you, I will," he replied, as if it were the easiest thing in the world. "I would not have you distressed in any way." Astonished pleasure lit his face. "I will restore your birds to you. And your castle."

"Thank you, my lord." I made my smile gracious to hide the flood of satisfaction, and reached up to kiss his cheek. I was not powerless in this marriage after all.

"It will be my wedding gift to you—the restoration of your property. . . ."

"Ah, Louis. I knew you wouldn't fail me."

Before the end of the day Louis and a band of well-armed Frankish knights set out for Talmont, to teach de Lezay a much-needed lesson. I watched them go, wishing that I had been born a man and so could ride out to protect my own, but accepting that I must be content with my triumph so far. With Louis ready enough to respond to my promptings, perhaps I could yet magic a dominant, forceful man out of the sweet, shy trappings that made up this Prince of the Franks. A warrior out of a bookish man of thoughts and dreams rather than deeds. Perhaps I could, if I could get him into my bed to do more than praise my hair. The sight of him, face stern and beautiful, clad in chain mail with his royal tabard and glossy stallion, fired my hope.

"Have you led an expedition before?" I stood at his side as he prepared to mount.

"No. It wasn't considered a necessary part of my education at

Saint-Denis. But I must start somewhere." His mouth twisted ruefully.
"I dislike the idea of shedding blood." He squinted at the stallion tossing its head in impatience.

"Even if it's warranted?" I gripped his hand to steady his nerve. "I
know you'll do the right thing. God go with you. I'll pray for your safe
return."

"I too have prayed," he replied solemnly.

A little tremor of worry unsettled me, but I thought there was no
need. Louis was well enough armed and escorted. I could see nothing
but victory for him. Surely they could put de Lezay in his place without
bloodshed. As I stepped back from the melee of departing horsemen,
I saw Abbot Suger watching us. He approached, bowed, but his eyes
were on the departing figure of his Prince.

"I hope the outcome will be as you wish, lady."

"Do you not approve, my lord?"

"I do. It's vital to the peace of the realm to put down any breath of
treason at this early stage of your union. But the Prince is not always
wise in his choices."

"He needs guidance," I replied coldly.

The cool eyes now turned on me. "As long as it's wise and measured guidance. I advise you to have a care, lady."

I bridled. "Is that a warning, my lord?" My suspicion grew that the
royal counselor condescended to my intellect, believing me incapable
of understanding the nuances of government. "As my husband's wife,
I will stand at his side. You must accept that. He is no longer the child
under your jurisdiction at Saint-Denis."

"As long as *you* accept that I might not always allow you free rein,
lady. On this occasion it is to our advantage, but it may be that in
future . . ."

It was a challenge, issued and accepted on both sides. I learned in
that one short exchange that Abbot Suger would stand against me,
keep me from influencing Louis if he considered it best for the future
of France. Was he my enemy? No, nothing so extreme. But a clever,
astute man, with government at his fingertips, in his blood, the Abbot
was not a man to underestimate.

Barely had the sky paled into dawn than I heard the noise and commotion of Louis's return in the courtyard below the window of my chamber. Before I could do more than leap from my bed, pull on a chamber robe, and lean to look down, Louis was bounding up the stairs, flinging back the door, flushed with excitement. The energy still lay hot on him, whilst on his gauntleted fist sat a white gerfalcon, hooded but in a serious state of ruffled disturbance. The bells on its jesses rang as it lifted its wings and flapped wildly, uttering harsh cries.

"I did it!" Louis announced in the doorway.

"Perhaps you should place the bird on the bed pole . . . for all our safety."

"Yes. Of course." He strode across the room to transfer the magnificent bird to the carved pole, where it sat in a sullen hunch and rustle of feathers. Clad in leather jerkin and chausses, all heavily stained with sweat, Louis was jubilant, hair wild, eyes blazing. Stripping off his gauntlets he swooped on me, gripping me by the shoulders. And then he transferred his hands to cup my cheeks, hold me still, and he kissed me full on my startled mouth. A hot, demanding, intemperate kiss that broke my lips against my teeth. He lifted his head.

"Eleanor!"

And he kissed me again.

"I've brought your gerfalcons here for you. All of them."

I felt an urge to laugh at the foolish extravagance of the gesture, but I could not spoil Louis's pleasure. Nor did I have the breath to reply at length. The passion in him astonished me.

"That's wonderful," I managed.

I don't think he heard me. His fingers dug into my flesh, hard enough to bruise. "I led the expedition. It was a glorious success. You'll need a new castellan, Eleanor."

"What?"

"A new castellan!"

He swung away to pace the room as if he could not contain the energy that victory had brought, brushing at the bed hangings with one hand, stroking the other down the feathers of the now quiescent hawk.

"Is de Lezay dead then?"

"Yes. By God, he is. And deserved it. I've no regrets." The words spewed out, heated, excited. Uncontrolled. "It was so hot. And we were not careful. We took off our chain mail and sent it on ahead with our weapons on the baggage carts. . . ."

Stupid! Louis must have read it in my astonished stare, for he came to stand in front of me again and tempered his voice.

"It was very quiet—no danger, our scouts reported—but when we followed our baggage into Talmont, the first knights were taken prisoner. So we had to fight it out with the rebels." Suddenly the exhilaration snapped into furious temper. "No one will dare to stand against me in future. We killed them all. Including de Lezay . . ."

As quickly as it had appeared, his anger faded. The satisfaction drained from his face, leaving it set in strained lines as his thoughts turned inward.

"Did you fight well, my lord?" I asked.

"Yes. I did." Louis's eyes flashed back to mine, surprise at his achievement causing his mouth to curve into a tremulous smile. "It was so simple. A sword was thrust in my hand and I fought. . . ."

"And de Lezay?"

Louis blinked at me. "He was guilty. I chopped off his hands. The punishment for theft, you see." He looked down at his own, turning them over, as if he would see blood on them. I tried not to shudder at the thought of those palms so recently framing my face. "I ordered my men to hold him—arms outstretched. I lifted my sword and I struck. . . ." Louis looked as shocked as I. "I've never spilled blood before." He swallowed heavily. "But I did what was expected of me—I punished a disobedient vassal. The rest will fall into line now—not one of them will dare rebel when men recall the name de Lezay. My father will be proud of me." Again he searched my face as if the answer there were all-important. "Are you proud of me, Eleanor? Do you approve? I reclaimed your castle. Your falcons . . ."

I saw my chance, since my praise mattered so much to him.

"More proud than you could ever imagine," I soothed. "How could a wife not be proud of the husband who has won back her lands and her possessions? And her pride. You'll make a magnificent king, Louis—when the time comes, of course."

"I shall!"

Raising a hand, I touched his cheek with my fingertips, followed by my lips. His skin was hot, the scent pungent—of man and horse and outdoor living. A heady mixture. Even the pallor of religious life had been overlaid by the effects of the sun. I transferred my lips to his mouth in experimentation, a soft, virginal kiss.

With a grunt of pleasure, Louis banded his arms around me, pulling me hard against him, without thought for the sweat and dust and the effect of their proximity to my silks. His blood ran as hot as his skin—I could all but feel it as he trembled against me. His kisses rained down on my face—lips, cheeks, temple—undoubtedly extravagant but disappointingly without finesse.

"I want you, Eleanor," he croaked. "I love you."

And he was pushing me back onto my bed, almost tripping over his own feet in his haste, fumbling with the lacings of his chausses as he climbed beside me.

"Wait, Louis . . ." I tried.

But already he was pushing aside my robe and shift, parting my thighs with his knee, spreading himself over me with clumsy haste. At least he was erect, I observed, as if I were not truly involved in this event, but aware of the hardness of him against my belly. I hoped, indeed I prayed, that this time it would happen. . . . A heave, a thrust, and he was inside me. I gasped at the dry pain that seemed to tear apart my body, but Louis, his face buried between the pillows and my neck, oblivious to my own responses or lack of them, thrust in increasing urgency, to end in a final, tense shudder and groan.

And that was it. All over before I had concentrated my mind to it, Louis spread-eagled still, heavy on my body, gasping for breath like a floundering plaice cast up on the fish dock at Bordeaux—an unfortunate thought in the circumstances—the heat of him all but suffocating me. Crushed and uncomfortable, I wriggled beneath him.

"Forgive me. . . ." Immediately Louis propped himself on his elbows and looked down at me, eyes feverish, a little diffident as the extreme energy drained from his face to leave it lax as if his features were blurred. "Dear, beautiful Eleanor. Now you are my wife." His mouth on mine was dry lipped and tender. "Did I hurt you?"

"No," I lied.

"I'll never hurt you, Eleanor." He searched my face. "Are you sure? You're very quiet."

I was very sore. I could not lie again, but, moved by a surprising rush of tenderness, I pushed my fingers through his sweat-slicked hair. It seemed to reassure him.

"You fired my blood; I pray God will forgive me if I took you too forcefully. I must go and order a Mass—for my safe return and the health of my lovely wife. I'll pray for an heir." His face broke into a radiant smile. "Do you think you have conceived?"

"I have no idea."

"My father will be doubly proud if you already carry my child when we return to Paris. Will you kneel beside me and pray for a son of our begetting?"

"Yes. I'll pray with you."

"God's Wounds! I feel like shouting our good fortune from the roof of the palace."

"I hope you won't," I replied dryly. Everyone would wonder why it had taken us so long to get to this point. But Louis was no longer there to listen. With a bound he was gone from the bed, straightening his clothing, making for the door.

Leaving me to lie on the disordered linens, and consider—was this what all the fuss was about? I could not believe it. A discomfort, a sharp pain—nothing to write eloquent verse about. I had felt no pleasure in the deed. All rather messy and undignified, I decided, conscious of the slick stickiness between my thighs. *Your innards will become as liquid. Your belly as the sweetest honey, your skin as hot silk.* My nurse had had a way with words, but not, it seemed, with truth. My muscles had tightened, clenched against what had seemed a hostile invasion rather than a longed-for consummation. Giving pleasure to a man was one thing, but should I not receive pleasure too? Was the fault mine or that of Louis? He seemed pleased enough. It had all been rather . . . *brief*! And I thought his desire for an heir took precedence over his enjoyment with me, despite his sensitivity in asking whether I had survived the experience.

Did I think I had fallen for a child? I buried my face in the pillow. Was he so untutored to think I would know so soon? The door opened and I rolled onto my back. Since it was Aelith who approached the bed with a smug smile, I pushed myself up, pulling down my shift and clasping my knees as I met her avid expression.

"Well! The bloodletting aroused him, I see. Was he a good lover?"

"Too quick to tell," I admitted ungraciously.

"Was it as magnificent as the troubadours say? I'd arrange another expedition if I were you."

"Perhaps." I forced a smile. I'd not tell her of all my misgivings. I was not sure of them myself. Louis had been so thoughtful, and yet . . . "At least I am now his wife in the eyes of God and man."

"And in need of a bath!" She wrinkled her nose. "Horse and sweat!" She laughed. "So he was successful."

"Yes. Order some hot water for me—and then I must pray with Louis for an heir. Do you know . . . he thanked me as if I had bestowed a miracle on him."

"And so you had. Not everyone beds a Princess of Aquitaine! Did you enjoy it?" she asked.

"Not greatly." I saw her disappointment as I began to loosen my hair from its night braid and was sorry for my brusqueness. "It's early days, Aeli. We need to grow to know each other, I expect."

It was true, after all. We had made a start. I could teach him more of the intimate pleasures of the bed, to his and my benefit. Once we had settled into our accommodation in Paris, life would become simpler. Louis would not feel so pressured by constraints of time and those around him. I would live with him, replacing Suger's voice with mine. I would teach him what he needed to know about me and the vast lands he had taken on.

"Do you know what he did?" I found myself asking her. It had preyed on my mind through all that had followed Louis's blurted confession. "He chopped off de Lezay's hands."

Aelith's lips made a soundless, *Oh!*

"Louis said it was a just punishment for a thief."

"Our father spilled enough blood in his time," Aelith considered.

"I did not think our father was so . . . so vindictive."

"It's nothing out of the way, as I see it," Aelith concluded, as if it did not merit further discussion. "De Lezay was an arrogant fool." She carried my ruined shift to cast it on the bed. "I see we have the proof at last. And not before time." She had lifted the bed linens, stained with Louis's sweat and semen and my blood. "What shall I do with them?"

I pushed aside the persistent scrape of concern that Louis could be unpredictable in his response to threats or danger, and smiled with not a little malice.

"Send them to Abbot Suger, of course. I trust he'll be satisfied. You can tell the Abbot to parcel up the sheets and send them to Fat Louis. His prayers have been answered."

Fat Louis was never to receive the happy news of his son's consummation of our marriage. Next morning when we were on our way to Paris before the sun had risen, when we had traveled no longer than one hour, a hard-riding messenger, his fleur-de-lys all but obliterated by dust, intercepted us. He flung himself at Louis's feet.

"Your Majesty!"

Which was enough to tell us all the news. The courier gasped it out. Louis the Sixth, Fat Louis, was dead.

Louis wept into his hands. And when he finally raised his head and turned his face toward Paris, his blue eyes held the panicked fear of an animal caught in a snare. It was in my heart to feel pity for him, but not much. Why would he not want to be King of France? There had been no close affection between father and son, as far as I could tell.

I did not weep for a man I did not know. Instead I appraised my new horizons.

I was Queen of France.

Chapter Four

I had traveled all my life. We in Aquitaine were an itinerant, restless court, winter and summer alike, journeying from one end of our domains to the other. Since my father insisted that I travel with him, I had stayed in every variety of accommodations, from castle to hunting lodge, from palace to northern manor to villa in the south. From campaigning tent to luxurious pavilion, in Limoges and Blaye, Melle and Bayonne. I knew gardens and tiled fountains, light airy rooms in summer, satisfying heat in winter.

Nothing could have prepared me for my new home in Paris to which Louis brought me with such pride. Louis might appreciate his inheritance. I did not. Grim and decaying, the Cité Palace seemed nothing to me but a pile of stones, a frowning bleak tower standing on a drear island in the center of a sluggishly running river. The Île de la Cité, as I learned to call it, connected to the two banks by stone bridges.

A place of great safety, Louis enthused, protecting us from our enemies.

A prison cut off from the world, I thought. Cold, uncivilized, unwelcoming.

Even before I set eyes on the palace, my heart sank, for Paris, the world outside my new home, stank. With unpaved streets, and gutters running with the effluent of two hundred thousand souls clustered along the River Seine, Paris squatted in a thick cloud of noxious stench. Black flies swarmed in the fetid air. The welcome of our entourage did nothing to hide the stink. More likely, I decided sourly, the mass of cheering hordes probably increased it, but I acknowledged the welcome. I knew what was expected of me, their new queen.

But my spirits fell to the level of my inadequate footwear as Louis escorted me through the corridors and endless chambers of my new home. I walked at his side in horrified silence. I shivered. Even in the heat of summer it was so cold, so bone-chillingly damp. And dark. The only light to enter was through the narrowest of arrow slits, so casting every room into a depressing gloom. As for the drafts . . . Where the air came from, I could not fathom, but my veils rippled with the constant movement of chilly air. I wished I had one of my fur mantles with me.

"The windows have no shutters!" Aelith muttered from behind me. "How do we keep warm here?"

"There!" Louis gestured, hearing her complaint. He pointed to two charcoal braziers that stood in the small antechamber we were passing through. "I think they give enough heat."

"And enough fumes to choke us!" I replied as the smoke suddenly billowed and caught in my throat. "How do you warm the larger rooms? The Great Hall?"

"A central fire."

"And the smoke?"

"Through a hole in the roof." He sounded mildly amused, as if I were a fool not to know.

Letting in the wind and the rain too, I had no doubt, as well as the occasional exploratory squirrel or unfortunate bird. In Aquitaine we had long moved past such basic amenities, borrowing what we could learn from the old villas of Ancient Rome, with their open courtyards, hypocausts, and drainage channels. I did not speak my dismay; I could not. Unnervingly I could feel Louis's eyes on me as he smiled and nodded, as if he might stoke my tepid enthusiasm from spark to flame. It was a lost cause, and since I could think of nothing complimentary to say, I said nothing, just stood in shocked, shivering silence.

"And we are to live here?" Aelith marveled as Louis stepped aside to speak with a servant who approached with a message. "Will we die of the ague?"

"It seems that we will." My heart was as coldly heavy as the stone floor beneath my feet.

"I wish we were back at Ombriere!"

So did I.

Perhaps my own accommodations, prepared and decorated with the new bride in mind, as surely they must have been, would be more comfortable. Momentarily I closed my eyes as the shadowy form of a rat sped along the base of the wall, claws tapping against the stone, to disappear behind a poor excuse for a wall hanging that did nothing to enhance the chamber. A woodland scene, I surmised, catching the odd shape of wings and the gleam of stitched eyes, except that the layer of soot was so thick the scene could have been the black depths of Hell. The rat retraced its scurrying steps, and I wished the livestock were confined to the stitchery.

When the rat—or perhaps there were many—reappeared to gallop once more in its original direction, I requested that Louis show me to my private chambers immediately, but he had other ideas. Taking my arm in a gentle hold, he detached me from my women and guided me through a doorway, down a long, dark corridor, and knocked on the door at the end.

"What is this?" I whispered, since he did not explain. I felt a need to whisper as the stone pressed down on us. It was like being in a coffin.

"Dear Eleanor." Encouragingly, Louis enclosed my hand in his. "My mother has asked to meet with you."

It was the only warning I received. I had not known that the Dowager Queen even resided in this palace. The door was opened by an unobtrusive servant into an audience chamber, the walls bare and shining with damp, the furnishings few and unremarkable. Except for one attendant woman, Louis's mother sat alone, waiting. Hands clasped loosely on her lap, she gave no sign of acknowledging our entrance. The emotion in that small room was chilling; my flesh crept with it.

"Madame." Louis left my side to approach her.

The Dowager Queen of France raised her head and looked not at her son, but at me. It was an unambiguous stare, and I swallowed at the animosity I read there, my throat suddenly dry. I had not expected this. I was instantly on guard.

Louis bowed, the respectful son, took his mother's hand, and saluted her fingers. "I regret your loss, Madame."

The Dowager Queen bowed her head in cold acknowledgment. I suspected her loss was not as great as her son might fear. There was an air of fierce composure about her. Her features were small and pinched, but from a lifetime of dissatisfaction rather than from present grief. The lines between nose and mouth had not been engraved in a matter of weeks.

Adelaide de Maurienne. Queen of France. Whose position I had just usurped.

She was a pious woman, judging from the presence of a prie-dieu, numerous crucifixes, and books of religious content, and a rosary to hand on the coffer at her side. Clad in black from her veils to her feet, she all but merged with the shadows. I sensed she had been invisible for most of her life as the neglected wife of Fat Louis.

"My son. At last." She did not immediately rise to her feet, even though her king and queen had entered the room.

"Madame," Louis urged with a not-so-subtle tug on her hand. "I would present my wife. Eleanor, Duchess of Aquitaine. Now Queen of France."

Without haste—an insult in itself, to my mind—Dowager Queen Adelaide stood, her hand clamped on her son's wrist, and managed a curt inclination of her head rather than the curtsy she should have afforded my rank. The welcome from Louis's mother was as grim as the stench of mold from the wetly gleaming walls. Did she think to intimidate me, a daughter of Aquitaine? I knew my worth. And I knew my power as Louis's wife. With a genuflection as conspicuous as her lack of one, I sank into a deep curtsy. My face, I made sure, was full of remorse.

"Madame, I trust your faith gives you consolation. If I can do anything to alleviate your grief during your visit to the Cité Palace, you have only to ask. Do you stay long?" A neat little challenge to her presence, deliberately spoken in my own language.

Adelaide looked to Louis for clarification. When he could not provide it, I repeated my greeting in Latin. Adelaide flushed at the implication that the days of her occupation of these rooms might be numbered. Her spine became rigid.

"You do not have a facility with the *langue d'oeil*?" she asked in that language.

"I do," I replied smoothly. I understood her perfectly well. I had made some progress on my journey to Paris. "But I prefer the *langue d'oc.*"

"Here we speak the *langue d'oeil.*"

Sensing the imminent clash of will, Louis eyed his mother cautiously. "We will, Madame, converse together in Latin."

Adelaide inhaled. "As you wish, my son." And then to me, sliding into rapid Latin, "My advice is to learn our language. As a mark of courtesy to your husband and your new country."

"If I deem it necessary, then I will, Madame," I responded promptly, switching to perfect Latin. "I have great skill with languages."

The Dowager Queen allowed her pale eyes to travel over my figure, taking in every aspect of my clothes and appearance. For a brief moment I wished I were not so travel stained, but I raised my chin. I was not answerable to this woman for what I wore. And I deliberately caught her eye.

There! I had not been mistaken. Loathing. A rampant hatred. The depth of it startled me. I had never experienced such abhorrence—one did not exhibit such flagrant emotion toward the Duchess of Aquitaine—but it was impossible to mistake it. Adelaide's nostrils flared; her lips narrowed into a curl of disdain. The glitter in her eye was an acceptance of my challenge, a return of my gauntlet to signal the onset of warfare between us.

And the prize for the victor?

Louis, of course.

Abbot Suger's warning had arisen from political necessity, as he saw it. He would control Louis's ruling of France and thwart me if I demanded a voice. Here before me was quite a different level of opposition: vindictive jealousy, entirely personal, and perhaps all the more dangerous. Adelaide would control the heart and soul of her son.

And the object of so much desire to control and manage? I glanced at him. Did Louis see this potential battle of wills between the two women in his life? Would he stand for me against Queen Adelaide if it ever became necessary? Was he even aware of the tone of our exchange?

Of course he was not. Louis was irritatingly occupied elsewhere, astonishingly oblivious, leafing through the pages of one of his mother's devotional missals. So be it. I must rely on myself in a conflict that Adelaide must not win. I was not raised to bow before an inferior force.

Adelaide deliberately turned her shoulder to me and addressed Louis. "We shall meet again at supper, my son—a banquet has been prepared to mark your return and your marriage." She fixed him with a commanding stare, as she must have done at any time over the seventeen years of Louis's life. "You will be there, of course. There must be no excuses."

A strange comment, one that caught my attention; then it slid out of my mind as Louis bowed and ushered me rapidly from the room.

"Will you show me my own rooms?" I asked, trying to keep up with him, holding my skirts away from contact with the walls, watching my footsteps in the gloom.

Suddenly Louis was in a hurry. "Yes." He did not slow his pace. There was an urgency about him.

"Where are your own chambers?" I asked.

"Through there." He waved vaguely toward a distant door before ushering me into my suite of rooms. "There!" A light kiss on my cheek, his words delivered in a rush. "If anything is not to your taste, then you must tell me. This is now your home. I want you to be as comfortable here as you were in your own lands in the south."

Looking around the stark rooms, taking in their air of abandonment, I doubted it.

But before I could reply, Louis had gone and closed the door behind him. I sat on the bed, sneezing as the mildew from the hangings released its unpleasant odor. Whatever was pulling at Louis was far more important than his staying with me. But at least now that we were here, in Paris at last, even in the face of the Dowager Queen's disapproval—which I intended to ignore—we could start to make some sort of life together.

By the end of that day I was more exhausted than if I had—in my imagination, since I had no experience of it—been on a military campaign. Moreover it proved to be an education, a squint into what was to be my future. How little of my life I had lived so far—a mere fifteen years; how much still stretched before me with all its promise and excitement. The promise was smothered by my experience of that day, the excitement all but snuffed out. What I had seen so far in the palace, the lack of any refinement or luxury, was merely replicated in the royal apartments. The vast bed with its moth-eaten hangings and damp linens made me shudder. My women for once were smitten into silence.

Except for Aelith. "By the Virgin!" she exclaimed.

"By all means pray to the Blessed Virgin," I remarked, spurred into action at last, "but any immediate improvements will be of our own making." I looked around my chamber in despair, shivered in a cold current of air, and gave orders. "Unpack my linens and hangings. Find a servant to bring one of those atrocious braziers. And do you think it possible to have more lighting in here?" I peered into the shadows. "Find some damned candles . . . !"

We made a start, but after two hours there was little improvement.

And then there came the ceremonial feast to acknowledge the new King and Queen.

Louis presided. Why had his mother found the need to insist? He led me to the dais and presented me to my new subjects. I felt their interested gaze, heard the whispered comments, particularly of the women of the court, who were so far behind the fashions of the day as to appear ridiculously outré. Louis attracted no such attention. He looked no better than a well-to-do merchant, in a plain tunic and hose. His chamberlain was better garbed. How could he demand their respect as King when dressed little better than a servant? I determined to take him in hand. But for tonight I settled myself to be celebrated and entertained.

I did not expect to be astonished, to be so rudely awakened into the reality of the Frankish court. But I was.

Where was the procession of courses at the royal feast? The peppered peacocks, the candied fruits, the rice cooked with milk of almond and powdered cinnamon? The lobsters fried with egg? There was no shortage of food, for sure. Meat upon meat upon meat—venison and wild boar, game birds aplenty—but so coarse and unflavored. Fish appeared—and languished on its platter; it was not popular. No delicacies of tarts or junkets or fritters. No leaves or salads. Vegetables abounded—particularly onions and garlic, a matter for much regret—stewed or pounded without finesse into an unrecognizable mush.

Louis ate sparingly. I did what I could. And made a point of ignoring the fastidious grimaces of my women. But even I could not pretend indifference forever to the presentation of the food.

"What is it?" Louis raised his cup to sip the thin wine.

I found my attention fixed on a congealing pool of strangely green sauce on the scrubbed table surface, where a clumsy page had spilled it and failed to mop it up. Nor was the wooden planking that made up the tabletop particularly clean despite the scrubbing. It looked no better than the butchery block from the kitchens, and the scars might suggest a pig had been dismembered on it. Did no one care?

"Do you have no table linen?" I asked bluntly.

"No." Louis was surprised.

"Not even for the High Table?"

"No."

I focused on the charred-edged flat bread before me, a trencher to serve in the way of a plate, beside it a drinking vessel and a knife to hack off portions of meat.

"Are there no spoons?" I eyed a dish of stewed elvers that would be impossible to deal with if a knife was all I had to hand.

"Do you want one?" Louis asked solicitously. "I'll send for one from the kitchens if you wish. . . ."

I shook my head, repressing a sigh. Glancing along the table, I watched one of Louis's barons scoop up the elvers with the flat of his knife, from dish to lips with a noisy slurp. I would forgo the elvers.

The Dowager Queen, clad entirely in black in a markedly unfestive manner, as before, raised her chin. "I have always found the provisions of our High Table satisfactory."

"Have you?" I gave a long look at a thick, glutinous dish that defied recognition. Louis had already given his attention to his seneschal, Raoul of Vermandois, on his right, so I felt at liberty to allow my dissatisfaction to show.

"You will find life very different here, Eleanor," Adelaide reprimanded with a humorless smile. "My advice is to learn the ways of the Frankish court and accept them. It is what I did as a bride."

"It is certainly different from my experience."

The feast continued, memorable for its crudity. No songs. No entertainments. Our eating was accompanied by nothing more than the slurp and chewing and belching of Louis's barons, and an increasing volume of coarse comment and laughter as the wine flowed. At the end, a finger bowl was presented to me. It was more than I expected. But I flinched from the layer of grease and traces of food floating on the top. I dipped in the very ends of my fingers and looked up at the page. He stared back at me with an uncertain fear in his youthful eyes. Clearly he did not know what I was waiting for.

"Fetch me a napkin," I whispered.

He looked askance, toward Louis and back to me. Did he expect me to wipe my fingers on my skirts? I found my attention straying from the rank water in the tarnished silver dish to the black-edged nails of its holder. Perhaps he had scoured the fire grate before serving me.

"I don't think we have a napkin, Majesty," he admitted in a hoarse whisper that echoed along the board, his face glowing with embarrassment. "I could try. . . ."

The lack was not his fault. But when the flat breads were collected, some given to the servants, some thrown to the scavenging dogs that fell on them with enthusiastic snarls, I had had enough. I signaled to my women to leave, gathering my dignity around me to curtsy to Louis. I found it impossible to smile.

"I will retire, my lord."

"It's been a long day for you, Eleanor." He leaped to his feet, and with gentle respect he handed me from the dais. "I trust you will sleep well."

I gripped his fingers for a moment. "I hope you find the time to visit me, my lord, before you retire."

"Yes." I thought Louis gulped, but perhaps it was a trick of the guttering and inadequate rushlights. His eyes shone with warmth and, I decided, admiration. "I hope you are happy with your new home."

"I am happy." I would make my immediate wishes plain, since it seemed that I must. I leaned close. "If you come to me I will show you how happy I am to be here as your wife."

"I will. . . ."

I ordered candles to be lit. I bathed and combed my hair, robed myself in a lavender-fragrant linen shift heavy with embroidery. The bed had been newly made up with my own linens, obliterating much of the damp, and the brazier was stoked, a handful of herbs from the sun-filled gardens of the south thrown on to scent the air and ward off the chills.

I dismissed my women to find what comfort they could in their own chambers.

Settled against the pillows, I waited.

The brazier dimmed into a dull glow and the candles extinguished in their own wax.

Louis did not come to me. I did not think I could have been more obvious in my invitation, and there was nothing I could do to remedy his decision. I could hardly summon him, like a lord sending for a lackey; nor did I care to advertise my own failure—my continuing failure—in bringing my husband to my bed.

Climbing from the high bed, I opened the door to rouse my women.

For the rest of the night Aelith curled beside me as she had every night when we were children. For once she was sufficiently sensitive to make no comment. For my part I seethed with frustration and fury.

I was not a child. I was a wife. I was a woman and I wanted a man in my bed.

Where was my husband?

Next morning I was up betimes. Really it was very simple. I knew what I must do and how to do it. Before I had broken my fast, leaving Aelith asleep, I was off in search of the absent Louis. I would talk to him, tell him of my own needs, and his, not least the need for an heir. He must see sense. If it was shyness that kept him away, I would try to put him at his ease. I would make him talk to me. If necessary I would *demand* his presence with me at night.

I would not be neglected in this way.

First, to his own private apartments after asking directions. I entered without knocking—why should I not?—and walked through corridors and antechambers, finding no trace of life. Eventually, opening doors indiscriminately, I discovered what must be Louis's bedchamber. The bed was as vast as mine, hung with the blue and gold of the Capetians, the never-ending fleur-de-lys glinting in the shadows.

Empty.

And as far as I could see, unused for many weeks. None of Louis's possessions were strewn about the room. Neither brazier nor means of lighting. The room was cold and unoccupied, with dust on coffer and floor. When I punched the bed curtains with my fist, I sneezed on the resulting cloud. I doubted he had been there since his return to Paris.

So where was he?

In an antechamber I came across a servant—a young boy, probably a page—who looked startled to see me but bowed.

"Where is His Majesty?" I asked in careful *langue d'oeil*.

"At his devotions, lady."

Of course. Why had I not thought of that? "Does His Majesty have a private chapel in the palace?"

"Yes, lady. The chapel of Saint Nicholas."

"Will you take me there?"

"Yes, lady. But it'll do no good. . . ."

"Why not?" Had I misunderstood his reply?

"I would take you, lady—but His Majesty is not in the palace." I thought the page looked pityingly at my ignorance. "His Majesty is at the Cathedral of Notre Dame." The vast edifice that shared the Île de la Cité with the palace.

"He rose early?" I asked.

"He stayed there, lady. Through the night. His Majesty often stays there, rather than here in the palace. The Prince—His Majesty—has rooms set aside for his use there."

"And when will he return here?"

The lad shrugged. "His Majesty spends all day at Notre Dame. He observes the offices and . . ."

I raised a hand to stop him as truth dawned. So Louis had returned to the monks almost as soon as he had set foot back in Paris. Better a hard bed in a monkish cell than mine. The thought resurrected a moment in the previous day. Now I understood the Dowager Queen's insistence that her son put in an appearance at the banquet. Clearly she knew him well, fearing he would run hotfoot to the monks as soon as he left her rooms. She knew him better than I! I would remedy that soon enough. A little heat thrummed through my blood.

"I need you to take me to the cathedral," I ordered briskly.

Notre Dame crouched in the gray dawn, dark and looming like a sleeping dragon painted in one of the old books in my grandfather's library in Poitiers. My young guide—Guillaume, he informed me— for the most part silent, overawed by his royal companion and unsure of why I should wish to go to Notre Dame at this early hour, led me along the vast arched nave toward the chancel, where I could hear the monks' voices uplifted in singing the order of Prime.

Where was Louis? Impatient though I was, I could not interrupt the holy brothers. I looked inquiringly at the page, who shrugged his shoulders and ushered me to a seat in the chancel, bowed, and left me as if he considered his task done.

I looked around. It was difficult to see anything in the cool shadows, the early-morning light barely illuminating the vast building, but for sure I could not see Louis, neither in the choir stalls nor kneeling before the High Altar, where I might have expected the King to pay his respects to the Almighty. So I set myself to wait until the service was over. And because it seemed appropriate I knelt and bent my head in prayer. I prayed for my strange marriage with Louis. For strength to make my new life here.

The blessing was administered; the service ended; the monks filed out toward the refectory for bread and beer before taking up their appointed daily tasks. With an eye to accosting the Abbot I rose to my feet. And looked . . . and looked again at Louis, my husband, his pale hair curling to his shoulders beneath the cowled hood. Now I knew why I had not picked him out. Clad in a rough monkish robe, girded with the knotted rope of the monks, Louis walked silently amongst them as if he were one of their number, under vows of obedience and poverty. His hands were clasped in prayer, his eyes downcast. He had no sense of my being there at all.

But then, why should he? His mind was not centered on me. I played no significant part in his life at all. *And I seem hardly likely to do so,* a caustic voice whispered irreverently in my head, *if this is where he chooses to spend his time.*

I stepped out, almost into his path.

"My lord . . ."

Startled from his inner prayers, Louis glanced up. It seemed for just a moment that there was irritation in his face at being disturbed by an impudent petitioner, until he recognized me and the lines around his mouth softened, although I thought he was still not altogether reconciled to my sudden appearance.

"Eleanor. What are you doing here?"

"I came to find you." I would be patient. Louis looked so young, so unassuming, that the hard words I had practiced during the night hours drained completely away.

Taking my hand, Louis maneuvered me adroitly out of the path of the monks. "Did you wish to speak with me?"

"Yes. Why would I be here if I did not?" The words sounded sharper than I had intended.

"Come, then." And with a genuflection toward the altar, he led me to his room, closing the door to give us some privacy. "What is it?"

At first I could do nothing but look around me. It was a cell. Nothing better than a monk's cell, with bare stone floor and bare walls except for a small crucifix over the bed. And the bed on which I sat, since there was barely room for us to stand, was a narrow cot with a single thin covering. Nothing else.

This for the King of France.

"Well?" Louis asked, sitting beside me.

"Do you stay here?" I asked.

"When I can."

"But why? You are the King of France!"

Louis tilted his head. "I was brought up with this," he reminded me simply. "I think it is what my life was meant to be. I should not have been king."

The admission, the rejection, startled me. He did not wish to be king. He would rather return to his old life of worship and service. I had not appreciated how deep they ran still: his past, the childhood influences on him.

"Do you never stay in your own rooms in the palace?" A dark fear, a fear with claws, began to squeeze my heart.

Louis stared at the crucifix as if he realized that he had been indiscreet. "Of course." He linked his fingers with mine, although his eyes remained on the crucified Christ. "I know that I can't stay here as I would wish. I am king now and have other duties that demand my time."

And I am one of them! "Why did you not come to me last night?" I asked, although before God I knew the answer.

"Because I was here." How simple a statement.

"A husband has a duty toward his wife."

"And I will fulfill it. I have fulfilled it. For the past weeks I have put my father's demands before my own, neglecting my path to God's grace. My father did not understand. But now *I* am king and returned home. And yesterday was a holy Saint's Day, so I kept a night vigil, as we are instructed to do. I could not stay with you, Eleanor." Now he looked at me, leaned over, and pressed the lightest of kisses against my brow. "You are so very beautiful—but it is not permitted that I share your bed on a Saint's Day."

The claws sank deeper; the fear intensified.

"And tonight? Will you come to me tonight?"

"No. You must understand, Eleanor. It is no reflection of my deep affection and respect for you, but today is Friday." He was very serious, as if explaining to a child.

"And you are not permitted to enjoy intimate relations on a Friday?" My tolerance was fraying rapidly at the edges, like an old, much-worn girdle.

"No."

"But . . . you need an heir."

"As I know. You did not conceive from our last coupling?" From our only coupling! And I did not yet know the outcome of Louis's virility. "If you did," Louis continued, not waiting for a reply, "then there's no need for me to demand intimate relations with you more frequently than seems appropriate."

Appropriate. Frustration built within me, stone upon stone. I fixed my eyes on his. This was no time for shyness. "Do you not think, Louis, that sharing my bed could bring pleasure—to both of us?"

A little frown creased his brow, although he lifted my fingers to his lips. "But that is forbidden. It is sinful, Eleanor. The Scriptures teach that the purpose of a man knowing a woman is for the procreation of children, and for no other reason."

"But God made us in His image—to experience physical satisfaction, together."

"Of course—but within the bounds of Holy Scripture."

Louis looked at me quizzically, as if amazed that I should not understand this. He was so gentle, so considerate, his certainty so absolute, that I knew I was right to be afraid, as I saw my future in his calm explanation. How could any woman—even I—compete for his attentions with God and the demands of Holy Mother Church?

"God determines the course of my life, although I will always be concerned for your happiness. I'll not neglect you, Eleanor—but you must understand that I dedicate my life to God."

"Will you at least eat with me? Tonight, in my chamber. Privately. Just the two of us, so that we might . . ." I shrugged helplessly, clutching at a passing straw. If he would at least spend time with me, then I might convince him that intimacy need not be sinful.

"No. I cannot. On Fridays I fast—on bread and water. It is a day of penitence for our sins." He stood, releasing my hands. "And now you must go. I keep vigil every day when royal duties permit, between Prime and Vespers. I must pray for my mortal soul. For my country. And I will pray for you too, dear Eleanor." Hand firmly at my waist, he was almost pushing me from the cell.

"When will I see you again?"

"When my time permits."

His smile held the sweetness of honey, the emptiness of a stone tomb. Without a second look, Louis walked away from me, back toward the body of the church and the brotherhood of monks, not caring whether I followed or not.

"Louis . . ."

He did not turn his head.

"Louis . . . !" This time I did not moderate my voice.

And this time Louis turned his face, which even at a distance appeared a study in reproach. "You must not shout, Eleanor. Not in church. It is not respectful to God."

Which left me with nothing much to say. Louis departed and I stood there, my blood colder than the stone that surrounded me. Isolated. Adrift. Uncertain as the truth hit me. Here I was no longer Duchess of Aquitaine, a ruler with power in her hands; I was merely a woman with no place except as wife to King Louis.

And Louis did not want to be king. Nor did he want me as his wife.

I was thoughtful on my return, seeking a firm footing in the swamp that had suddenly spread around my feet, threatening to suck me down. How easy it would be to wallow in misery. Instead, I summoned my women. Quiet, pretty Mamille. Florine and Torqueri, sharp and sly, lovers of gossip. Flirtatious Faydide. Solemn, thoughtful Sybille, Countess of Flanders. There was no laughter here. They were as unsettled as I. Seeing their doleful faces as they huddled in their furs made me decisive. There were changes to be made.

"Come and walk with me," I invited Aelith. "And you too, Sybille. Tell me what you think of our new home."

"You don't need me to tell you." Aelith grimaced at the encrusted muck from the brazier that our slippers and skirts spread across the floor.

"Pull it all down and start again!" Sybille stated with unusual candor.

I laughed, my spirits lifting in their company. "Our thoughts run together."

At the end of an hour I sent for parchment, pen, and ink. The result was a list, not long but with consequences. I set it aside until Louis could satisfy God and visit his wife.

The changes I foresaw would not be only in my living arrangements.

Chapter Five

*I*t took three days for Louis to feel his soul safe enough, restored to the bosom of the Almighty, to emerge from Notre Dame and come to my apartments. He came after the order of Tierce and greeted me as if no time had passed, and he had no apology to make for his absence. He bowed, kissed my fingers, my lips and cheeks with tenderness, but fleetingly, as if he greeted a friend.

"Have you ordered affairs to suit you? Are you comfortable, dear Eleanor?"

He was so certain that I would say yes!

"No. I am not comfortable. How can I be?" I ignored his startled expression. "I cannot be expected to live like this."

"Are you unwell?" he asked uncertainly.

"Of course I'm not unwell! Do I look unwell?" Louis needed firm handling. Pressing a cup of wine into his hand as I drew him toward the detested brazier in my solar, pushing him into a cushioned chair beside it, I presented him with the list.

"What's this?"

"You said you wished me to be comfortable. Did you mean it?"

"Nothing is closer to my heart."

"Then I need improvements to my rooms. These!"

His gaze slid to the parchment. "Can you write, Eleanor?"

"Of course I can write!"

"Not many women are considered able to acquire the skill."

I ignored this. Did he think I'd been raised an illiterate commoner in a peasant's hut? "And as you see, Louis, I have made a list."

I watched him as his gaze traveled down it. His lips pursed, twisted; he glanced up to me, then back to my demands. If I was to live out my days here in the sweet Virgin's name there had to be some concessions to the life I'd been raised to.

"So you have." Louis continued to read—how long would it take him!—tapping the page with one hand. "Windows? Why do you need windows? You have windows."

"These are not windows. These are defensive slits for shooting arrows."

"I need to be impregnable. This is a fortress."

"Is the King of France not safe in the heart of Paris? My women do not shoot arrows. We need larger openings to let in air and sunlight. How can we see to sew and read? How can Faydide see to play the lute? Surely your stonemasons can create some wider, taller windows without too much difficulty."

"I suppose they could. But would that not allow cold air in . . . ?"

"Shutters! It's like sitting in a gale even now. I want wooden shutters for all the windows in my apartments. And in my own chambers—I want glazing."

"Ah! Glazing." Louis's fair brows climbed as if my extravagance were as gaudy as a peacock's feathers, but he did not refuse. He tilted his head. "It says here—'remove smoke.'"

"So it does." To my good fortune a chance draft wafted a curl of poisonous fumes to envelop him and reduce Louis to coughing. "I'll die of the smoke if I have to live with it much longer. My hair, my garments reek of it."

"But the Great Hall—"

"Yes, yes—I know the Great Hall must keep its central fire, but in here I want stone fireplaces, Louis, with chimneys built into the thickness of the walls to carry the smoke away."

Louis eyed the formidable wall of stones before him as if he personally would have to take a hammer to them. "A major building program then . . . The cost will be great, of course. My treasury—"

"A little thing," I disagreed.

"Well . . ."

"In the palaces of Aquitaine we have chimneys," I added slyly. "Do you not have the wealth to encompass it?"

He thought for a moment. "I do."

"And I want tapestries," I added.

"As I see."

"You have none to my taste. Not one wall in this palace displays a tapestry of any size or quality. Those I've seen are in a state of disintegration or covered with soot. What can you be thinking?" I allowed him no time to retreat. "Think of the display of your wealth and style, Louis. You are not some insignificant lord, still residing in a stone keep, but King of the Franks. Your palace should be a stamp on your authority, not a rough fortress no better than your ancestors could build a hundred years ago. And if that does not appeal to you—think of how much warmer the rooms will be, keeping the damp and drafts at bay."

"I don't feel the cold," Louis observed. "But if that is what you wish—then order them as you will. The tapestries from Bourges are thought to be the best."

I reached to kiss his cheek, delighted with the resulting quick blush, and tugged at his sleeve. Louis was open to suggestion, a blank scroll on which I might write. And I *would* write on it. Not Abbot Suger. Not Dowager Queen Adelaide. I would be the one to map out Louis's future.

"Will you give the orders for the stonework immediately?"

"If it pleases you, then I will. I should be thankful you've not gone ahead and done it already, so that I find us knee-deep in stone dust and chippings." His smile was charmingly rueful despite the ponderous humor. "I've been told that you've already dismissed one of my appointments."

So Adelaide had complained to her son, had she? It had taken her less than twenty-four hours.

"Yes," I acknowledged airily. "The cantor at the palace chapel."

"My mother was distressed that he'd been removed."

"That's hard to believe." I opened my eyes wide. "Perhaps you misunderstood her, Louis. The man had no ear and could scare hold a tune. As for leading a choir . . . When you hear his replacement, one of my own household with a fine voice, you will admit my choice is good." I saw the muscles in his jaw twitch as he prepared to refute this, so I pressed on with an argument he could not deny. "It's only fitting that God be praised to the best of our poor talents." I was getting the measure of my husband.

"That is so, of course. . . ."

"Do you object to my plans, Louis?"

"No. Not at all."

"You would say if I displease you, wouldn't you?"

"You'll never displease me. I admire you."

Victory fluttered in my breast. It seemed I could play the obedient, grateful wife with skill. I had no experience of it, but a quick-witted woman can learn and learn fast. I had achieved exactly what I wanted.

"And you will give your orders to the stonemasons today?" I persisted.

"Yes. Eleanor . . . ?"

"Hmm?" I was already halfway across the room to order my women to pack away the most fragile of my gowns.

"Is there anything you *do* like here? In Paris?"

I halted. Turned back. He still sat, looking almost dejected at my lack of enthusiasm for my new home, my list in one hand, the untasted cup of wine in the other. How woefully deficient in authority and importance he could be. Poor Louis. He really had no presence.

As if he read my thoughts, he stood and walked toward me, while I sought desperately for something to say to make him look less of a cowed child who had been refused a promised treat.

"Perhaps you like the gardens," he suggested. "They're thought to be very fine. Will you walk there with me?"

How could I refuse without appearing churlish? I walked with

Louis along the pathways enclosed for privacy by walls and trellised vines, bordered with acanthus. Willow, fig, cypress, olive, and pear trees gave welcome shade in the heat of the day. They would do very well with some statues and the occasional water display, but these formal plantings were no compensation for the chains on my freedom to travel the length and breadth of my dominions, as I had once done at my father's side. They were no compensation for the stultifying life I had been dropped into. My new existence was almost as rigidly curtailed as if I had taken the veil. The ordered beauty of sight and scent was no compensation at all for Louis's continued absence from my bed.

"Louis." I touched his hand as we halted beside a bed of fragrant lilies. "I am not carrying your heir."

My courses had come on time. Louis's energies after the matter of the white gerfalcons had failed. Our one step into the intimacy of matrimony had not had the desired effect.

Louis's face fell. "I must lay the matter before God."

That was all he said, or at least to me. I presumed God was the recipient of his disappointment.

"It is a waste of money. A sheer waste of money," Adelaide raged when the stonemasons moved into my apartments and the air was filled with dust along with the cheerful cursing and tuneless singing of the workmen. "And to what purpose?" She raised her voice above the racket. "A soft lifestyle. It is not necessary." She glared her dislike of me and the upheaval combined. "You should learn to live our Frankish lifestyle. You are too soft, with your flighty southern ways. . . ."

"Do you not approve, Madame?" Soft, dulcet. My talent for acting improved daily, and I had learned fast that to humor the Dowager Queen was more satisfying than to oppose her directly. To annoy, Adelaide had deliberately addressed me in the *langue d'oeil*. I replied equally deliberately in Latin.

"No, I do not. What have you persuaded my son to do?"

"Simply to make my life tolerable."

"It is not right. . . . I have told Louis so. . . ."

"You do not have to tolerate the changes, Madame. I will instruct the masons to leave your chambers alone. If it is your desire to live in squalor and cold and choking fumes, then that is entirely your own choice."

She had waylaid me in the corridor to the royal chapel, after Mass, where my cantor had just surpassed himself in singing the canticles. I made to walk past her, then halted, faced her. It was not in my nature to remain silent after all, when my authority was under question. I fell easily into the harsh syllables of the *langue d'oeil*, since it seemed appropriate to express my feelings thus. "If you wish to complain about my actions, Madame, come to me, not to your son. It does not please me to have Louis troubled by your petty dislikes."

"I will complain as I wish," she snapped back. "I will complain where I think it will have the most effect."

"So you think you can persuade Louis?"

"I am his mother. He listens to me." But her furious stare slid from mine.

"Excellent!" I smiled thinly. "Perhaps you would instruct him that he is no longer a monk but the King of France."

"He does not need to be told."

"I think he does. We both know that he is at this moment celebrating High Mass and that he will remain at Notre Dame for the rest of the day, despite the official deputation from Normandy that Louis himself summoned. They are kicking their heels in the audience chamber, as they were for much of yesterday." I paused for the length of a heartbeat. "Your son does not listen to you, Madame, does he?"

"You are discourteous!" Adelaide hissed. "Without respect!"

"I am Queen of France and Louis's wife, and as such beyond reproach." I performed a polite curtsy. "Louis is grown to be a man, away from the woman who gave him birth. Good day, Madame."

"You will not have it all your own way." The final words floated after me.

Would I not? I smiled a little. I did not fear Adelaide. I doubted that she had ever commanded Louis's full attention. And now Louis would listen to me and to no one else. Who would hinder me?

*   *   *

"You are a Daughter of Satan, madam! You should be ashamed!"

Ashamed? I froze, my mind alive to this new threat.

We were in the city of Sens, Louis having moved his whole court to the royal palace there so that we might make an appearance at the formidable Council of Bishops. It had been an occasion of heavy debate, ending in the disgrace of Peter Abelard, the Paris lecturer whose infamous affair with the beautiful Heloise had had such terrible consequences. Here at Sens, Abelard's elegant assertions that logic should be used to question and strengthen faith, so popular in Paris with the educated elite, came under vicious attack from the Church heirarchy. And the man who had emerged from monkish seclusion to achieve this victory, the man who now addressed me in such vulgar terms, was Abbot Bernard of Clairvaux.

"Look at you, woman! All airs and graces and mincing steps, laden with ornament."

Seated beside Louis for a formal audience, I smoothed my hands down my silk-damask skirts, aware of the shimmer of rich, tawny cloth. Had I not taken utmost care with my appearance to honor my husband before this important clerical delegation? Would this visitor to our court address me, the Queen of France, in such a manner?

He would if he were Bernard, Abbot of the Cistercian order of monks at Clairvaux. There he stood in the very center of the Great Hall, dominating the vast space, spittle flying with his words of condemnation, his flowing white hair giving him an air of prophetic sanctity, as if he were a figure come alive from the Old Testament.

"Your hair—revealed for all men to see . . . ! Have you no understanding of what God demands from the fallen daughters of Eve, in recompense for her seduction of Adam into sin?"

Nor was he finished.

"Daughter of Belial! Your appearance is an affront to God! If your husband will not take you to task, then it is my duty to do so, in God's name!"

I held the pale gaze, marveling at the passion and presence of this man, skeletally thin as he was from fasting and the rigors of his holy life. So frail, he looked as if a buffet of storm wind would lay him low, but still he claimed the authority to rebuke me.

"I recall your execrable grandfather, madam." He was quivering with holy fire. "I recall his flouting of God's teachings."

True enough. The ninth Duke had preserved an ambiguous relationship with both the Almighty and His Church, upholding the motto: *I will do as I please.* The Duke would honor God, as long as God's will did not conflict with the Duke's. My grandfather had spent much of his life excommunicate for one reason or another, chiefly his unholy liaison with Dangerosa.

"My grandfather respected God well enough," I remarked frostily, looking to Louis for help and getting none. My husband appeared predictably tongue-tied. I decided it would not be politic to recall Dangerosa to Abbot Bernard's vicious judgment. It would not help this situation.

"You must learn to curb your tongue, daughter," Abbot Bernard challenged, his hostility unabated. "How can it be seemly in a woman to voice her opinions? It is not your place."

"It is my place, my lord Abbot." I would not be silent before this crude attack. "I was raised to have opinions and not fear to express them: I shall continue to do so. My lord the King does not object. Why should you?"

Which predictably failed to silence my vicious-tongued adversary. "I will preach to this misbegotten court what is acceptable in the eyes of God!"

And he did, every point sharpened like the tip of a poignard to rip my outrageous appearance to shreds.

The skirts of my gown—". . . a virtuous man might think such a woman to be a *viperous snake* by the tail she drags after her in the dirt . . ." The embroidered and furred decoration on my hem and cuff—". . . skins of squirrels and the labor of silkworms—all to clothe a woman who should be content with plain cloth . . ." Cosmetics to enhance, as any woman worth her salt would wish to do—". . . a thrice-damned superficial beauty, put on in the morning and laid aside at night . . ."

Such was holy Bernard's condemnation, his voice trembling with ire, his fist hammering against the lectern, whilst I sat, backbone straight, unmoved by the vitriol. How dared he condemn a daughter of Aquitaine. I would never bow my head before the Abbot of Clairvaux, but I was aware that beside me Louis sat transfixed. His face glowed as if Bernard's delivery came straight from the mouth of God.

This was dangerous. In that moment I knew I had an implacable enemy. Abbot Suger would undermine me in a subtle, subterranean manner. Adelaide was as vicious as a vixen, snapping at my heels with sharp teeth, but without real influence. Now, Bernard of Clairvaux— he was the wolf at my door. I could not afford to underestimate Bernard of Clairvaux. With Louis's ear, he might cause me harm.

But then Bernard's virulence was forgotten, swallowed up in the excitement of my presentation to my new people. I was crowned Queen of France on Christmas Day at Bourges. In the great cathedral, in a sumptuous ceremony under the astute hand of Abbot Suger, Louis and I were acknowledged as King and Queen of France. Although Louis had already been crowned in his father's lifetime, the Abbot considered it no bad thing to remind the cynical and battle-hardened vassals of the Frankish King that Louis was their new monarch. I watched as the crown was placed on his head.

Louis twitched with apprehension, as if he expected the crown to fall at his feet.

I sighed.

Why could he not have been better matched to the position he held? Why could he not have resembled the men of my own family: proud, confident in his demeanor, power at his fingertips? Even with the weight of gold and jewels on his fair hair he looked more boy than man. Why did he have to fidget so? Why could he not stare down these lords who had an eye to every weakness? Louis had the crown and God's blessing. Why did his hand have to clench nervously on the hilt of the sword of state?

God's Bones! I could play the role with more conviction than Louis ever could.

I was crowned too. I felt the thrill of it run through my blood. I was still young and inexperienced enough to believe that the mystical symbols of crown and oil and holy water would mean something. How could they not bring me happiness and contentment? In those days my heart was full of hope, and Louis did his best to make my experience in Bourges memorable.

By the Virgin! It was!

Louis ordered the creation of a masterpiece to impress me and his vassals. At the climax of the coronation feast, four men staggered from the kitchens under the weight of a giant platter bearing a subtlety worthy of one of my own master cooks.

"I had it made for you." Louis beamed, beckoning the men forward.

It was manhandled onto the table before me, a vast pastry crust on a pottery base, the whole fashioned and gilded into a castle with towers and crenellations, just like the Maubergeonne Tower. With its moat of green leaves, ribboned banners imprinted with fleurs-de-lys floating from its towers, it was a tour de force indeed. With an ingenuous smile of delight, Louis indicated for the lid to be raised.

"What's inside?" Sweetmeats? Flowers? Some impressive creation of precious sugar? Or perhaps even a jeweled coronal to match the official one of my crowning?

"Wait and see. . . ."

A knife was run around the circumference. I leaned forward. A hush fell as all waited. The lid was raised in a piece. . . .

A gasp.

A murmur of agitation from the women as, with a frantic flutter of wings, a flurry of small songbirds escaped from their prison up into the rafters and roof spaces, or flew with swooping panic over the tables. The women shrieked, hands to their veils; the men shouted with ale-fueled appreciation. In mounting terror the birds flew more madly, with loud cheepings, their droppings splattering down indiscriminately on tables, food, and clothing.

I think I gawped. I certainly hiccupped on an entirely inappropriate laugh. I might have ducked below the level of the table to escape a darting flock of finches.

"Shit!" Raoul of Vermandois guffawed crudely.

"Your Majesty!" Abbot Suger deplored, retaining his ecclesiastical dignity against all the odds.

Poor Louis! If he had hoped for melodic tweetings, he was disappointed. Shrill and tuneless, the creatures merely added to the pandemonium. Nor was that all. With shouts of laughter from the barons, crossbows appeared in eager hands, arrows aimed—dangerously—at the unexpected targets. Their aims were remarkably good, all things considered. As the barons roared their approval at every hit, my own vassals amongst them, the songbirds began to fall, to be snapped up by the hounds that swarmed and waited below.

I watched with growing dismay.

Aelith giggled in horror.

"Well, Louis . . ." I sought for words through my distaste at so much thoughtless bloodshed, through the pity for the small corpses. "That was truly spectacular!"

Louis, on his feet, paled to the blue-white of a corpse. "I did not mean for this."

Of course he did not. But did he not think? Two score or more birds encased in a pie, released from their captivity, would assuredly cause havoc.

"Clear them out . . ." he ordered as one wounded, cheeping creature fell onto the table under his nose.

"How is it possible?" I asked, angry now. "If you wait long enough your barons will dispatch most of them."

It was indeed pitiful. Blood and death and poor little bodies. I tried not to mind the smirks and ridicule from the lords who were sober enough to mock Louis's failure. The whole was brought to a halt only when a casually loosed arrow buried itself in the shoulder of one ill-fortuned squire.

Poor Louis.

Even his best efforts were crowned with disaster.

When Louis solemnly gave the formal kiss of peace on the mouth of each of his barons, I shivered with uneasy premonition. He was no leader of men and never would be.

It was impressed on me in those early days of my marriage after my crowning that I had misjudged my self-appointed task to make Louis attend to me. Louis continued to apportion his time spent with me and in matters of government to the barest of necessity. Almighty God ruled Louis's world. God demanded his devotion, his meticulous observance of the offices, the measuring of his days. Oh, he was always pleased when his path crossed mine. I could never fault the depth of affection and kindness in him. He would kiss my cheek, give me gifts. Sometimes he would kiss my lips and stroke his hand down my hair, looking at me in delighted, innocent amazement, as if he could not quite understand how he had come to have a wife at all.

Sometimes I did not see him for days on end.

Before God, I was patient with him. I would not shout. I would not scold or upbraid him for his neglect of me. Sweet Virgin, I would not! I had to keep a tight hold of my temper as my life was smothered by the flat, tedious, all-encompassing monotony of it all.

Boredom had a heavy hand.

How did I pass my time?

With my women I set stitches in belts and altar cloths. We played chess; we sang and read and gossiped when the weather was unkind. We strolled in the gardens. On bright mornings we rode out to hunt and hawk.

It was stultifying! Suffocating!

Sometimes Louis came to my bed, but not before praying through the order of Compline, as if his soul could not survive the night with me without the click of the rosary beads through his fingers. He slept beside me. He did not touch me.

My courses came regularly, again and again as the months passed. How should they not? Although Louis's face fell at my failure to conceive, he had not felt moved to repeat the experience beyond that first brief occasion.

"How do I bear a child if you will not play the man?" I demanded, furious with him, unable to contain my frustration when he inquired yet again after my health.

Louis turned his face away.

But not before I experienced that first flutter of fear. What if I failed to carry an heir for France? What would be my future then? Even more important to me—what if I conceived no heir for Aquitaine? I stamped down the thought before it could bear fruit.

I was thrown back on my own devices. What did I do with my time, my energies? What did I do to warm this cold northern existence, to exercise my mind and my imagination? Songs and stories had a finite quality. The constructions Louis had promised me continued apace. Soon I had my glazed windows and fireplaces, my beautiful tapestries that filled the rooms with vibrant color and tales of daring and courage, but my heart remained lodged far away in Aquitaine. In Poitiers. I yearned for the warmth, the beauty, the songs and dancing that stirred the blood to passion. I wanted feasting and laughter and . . .

So there it was. It was no great leap to set up my own court, a close mirror image of what I knew and loved. I would be Duchess of Aquitaine first, Queen of France second. I would drag this backward court into an Aquitainian world of rich hues and sensual pleasures. I would create a little Aquitaine in the heart of Paris. And surely, somewhere in the novelty and excitement of it all, I could bring Louis to my bed as man and lover instead of an affectionate brother.

"You've been busy again, Eleanor." His hands plucked uncomfortably at the embroidered band around his cuff as he surveyed what I had done to the High Table. A linen cloth stretched fair and stainless along its length, white as snow, with a napkin, a glass, and a knife and a spoon at every place. Plates of polished pewter and silver. No more bread trenchers for those who sat at my table. The pages' hands were scoured to red-fingered purity, the finger bowls perfumed with citrus and rosemary, frequently replenished. A troubadour warmed the strings of his lute. "Does it make you happy?"

"Yes, indeed." I smiled encouragingly. I had his full attention.

"One thing would please me far more," I whispered in Louis's ear. "One thing would make me *very* happy."

"Then I will grant it. You only have to ask."

"Come to me tonight. We will pray together"—a lure he could not refuse—"and then I will tell you. Will you come?"

"Yes." There was no hesitation. Louis smiled at me.

"Promise me."

"I promise."

Excellent. I had a plan. My experience told me that there was perhaps one pathway to Louis's reluctant loins.

"Do you recall the success of your expedition against de Lezay at Talmont, Louis? When you rescued my gerfalcons?"

We had prayed. At some length. Now at ease Louis lay beside me in the bed. The room was warm, the bed hangings sumptuous, the linens soft against our naked flesh. Louis's skin gleamed in the light from the single candle. I had hidden the Book of Hours in the bottom of one of my coffers.

"Yes." He produced a smile, swiftly followed by a little frown. "I recall de Lezay. . . ."

"It was a victory," I broke in to obliterate his memory of de Lezay's severed hands.

"Yes. A victory." Still he was troubled.

"To impose your authority on an impudent vassal who had stolen what was mine."

"I recall. I had God's protection." Smiling again, Louis rolled to prop his head on his hand and look at me. "What of it?" His eyes shone with benign contentment, and I leaped in before he could think of another prayer to offer.

"It's Toulouse. I want you to get back Toulouse for me."

"Toulouse?" A large kingdom abutting Aquitaine to the southeast, stretching almost to the Mediterranean. Louis looked quizzical. "Do you have a claim on it?"

"Certainly I do. My grandmother Philippa was Countess of Toulouse in her own right. It was snatched from her when my grandfather was too old and ill to fight to retain it for her. The present ruler, Count

Alfonso, has no right of blood, only the right of power," I explained simply. "It should not be. It should be *mine*." Which was not untrue, even though Toulouse had been lost to us for the past twenty years. But here was a circumstance that might just play into my hands. "Now that I have a powerful husband of my own . . ."

I left the words hanging, for Louis to snatch up. Was this not what I had always wanted, a strong right hand to hold my lands? So why not get back what had been stolen from me? And if success in battle should strengthen Louis's manhood . . . So many possibilities here. I let the idea settle in the still room as I reached and handed Louis a cup of spiced wine from the nightstand.

"Think about it," I urged as he sipped, as a faint color tinged his cheeks, a glow that had nothing to do with the heady spices. "It would extend your lands, as well as enhancing your prestige if you launched an assault and crushed the man who dared to steal what is rightfully mine." I cupped his cheek with my palm so that he focused on my eyes so close to his. My unbound hair curled with sensuous effect onto his chest, his shoulder. "I would be so proud of you, Louis, if you could renew my claim to Toulouse and restore it to me—to us. . . ."

I had planted the seed. I could see it grow in his face, in his eyes. Or more like I had lit a little flame that bloomed and consumed. Louis drank deep as the vision of fame and glory struck home.

"What a reputation you will build for yourself," I added. "No lord will dare to threaten you."

"True . . ."

"And you will have all my admiration. . . ."

"Do you mean it?"

"Yes."

Louis took another gulp, wiped his lips with the back of his hand. "Then I will. Toulouse will be yours again."

Taking the cup from him, setting it aside, I kissed him on the mouth. "My powerful husband. My victorious lord . . . I can see it now, the point of your sword at Count Alfonso's throat so that he has no choice but to hand Toulouse back. . . ."

His lips warmed beneath mine. His hands clasped my shoulders with surprising strength. His erection surged and stiffened against my thigh.

"Louis!" I sighed against his mouth.

God was pleased to allow him to complete the deed. Briefly, in truth, but not before Louis had spent the royal seed in me. I felt nothing. How could I, when Louis's interest was fast and tepid at best? My body remained unresponsive beyond the success at getting him to this point. Through it all I prayed that my womb would quicken.

"Thank you, Eleanor."

Louis fell asleep.

I lay awake in some sort of stunned horror. All I could think of was my grandmother Dangerosa, who had spent her whole life embracing the physical allure that could bind a woman to a man. Her passion for my grandfather had led her to abandon husband and family, to live as a kept woman, to ruin her reputation. What fervor must have existed between them. How hot the desire. My experience was the palest of shadows compared with hers, and in a moment of pure despair I doubted I would ever know what Dangerosa had known. Had Louis seduced my emotions? Had he beguiled or captivated me? He had not. He was not interested.

My blood chilled.

Chapter Six

L ouis acted. The extent of his enthusiasm astonished me as much as it horrified his mother and drove his royal counselor into a fury. I had not thought he would take my advice so much to heart, nor quite so precipitately. I had thought it would take more than one night in my bed to stir him to open hostility against Toulouse, but Louis leaped on the excuse for invasion as a hungry cat leaps on a bird that threatens to escape. The voices raised against such a project were loud and vociferous, but Louis was deaf to them all.

"Why in the blessed name of God make an enemy of the Count of Toulouse?" Abbot Suger, excruciatingly civil but furious that Louis had made his decision without once consulting him, questioned both the cost and the ultimate value to France.

"Because he has no claim to it," Louis stated. "Toulouse is Eleanor's."

"You have been ill advised." Suger's flat stare encompassed me before returning to Louis. "Are you not aware that your vassals will not support you, Sire? They'll refuse to supply you with knights. Not one of them wants an angry neighbor on his doorstep. We have no argument with Toulouse."

"I will defeat Count Alfonso, my lord Abbot. He will no longer be a neighbor and his anger will be a thing of no importance."

Suger lifted his hands helplessly. "I pray God thinks you worthy of victory, Sire."

"I will ask Him. He'll not refuse me."

And Adelaide? Her civility was negligible. "You will not go, my son."

A mistake. I saw Louis's nostrils narrow.

"I will, Madame."

"Louis! You will listen to me, even if you refuse to heed Abbot Suger."

Ha! Adelaide still had not learned. Louis listened to me, and we set out for Poitiers together, where I prepared to stay as Louis gathered his troops. I wished with all my heart to travel farther south with him, into the center of my own lands, and the temptation to do so stirred my blood from its northern languor—but a miracle had happened. That one night when I had painted for Louis the glory of his victory over Toulouse, his ownership of me, however brief and perfunctory, had been effective. My courses had stopped and nausea struck in the morning hours.

Praise the Virgin! I would carry an heir for France and for Aquitaine.

My delight superseded my wretched mornings when my belly heaved and the thought of food made me retch. Louis proved to be mildly sympathetic to my sufferings but was more taken up with the magnificence of his own achievement, glowing with masculine pride. If he stated once, eyeing my flat belly with a proprietary gleam, that this fruit of his loins would be the longed-for son, the heir to the kingdom, he said it a dozen times. I swear my nausea increased. And as I wallowed in misery I tried not to fall prey to cynicism. The heir would enhance my importance and win over those of Louis's court who still saw me as an undesirable southern influence in France. No one would dare to slight me when I bore the King a son.

Even Abbot Bernard would be forced to temper his denunciations.

But for now Louis was intent on conquest in my name. Emerging from my chamber, a linen cloth pressed to my lips, I listened to his enthusiastic explanation that they would take Toulouse by surprise and starve the city into submission. Even through my misery

I noted that for a siege Louis employed few siege engines. Nor was Louis's army particularly impressive in size. Was the whole operation too small, too ill prepared? Yet Louis was so confident that I too saw no impediment to his success. If Count Alfonso did not expect the descent of an armed force, he would be unprepared and the campaign brought to a swift end. Louis would return to me, full of courage and male pride. Perhaps his rejoicing would take him from the long hours on his knees.

"I will return and lay Toulouse at your feet," he promised. "I'll drag Alfonso before you to ask your forgiveness."

I kissed Louis farewell and retired to vomit into a basin.

How many days before Louis returned. Two weeks? Three? We saw the cloud of dust from Poitiers and knew there had been no effective siege. We knew the outcome anyway, long before I saw Louis's crestfallen face. Rumor traveled faster than the Capetian troops. Count Alfonso had been warned and was waiting for Louis. Formidable defenses, banks and ditches and wooden palisades sufficient to repel Louis's meager army, had been hastily thrown up.

And my noble, all-powerful, ambitious King of France, drunk on pride and certain victory? Louis did not even stay to make a token attack but turned on his heels and retraced every inch back to Poitiers without one blow being struck, whilst in Toulouse, Alfonso thumbed his nose from the castle walls, catcalls screeching the derision of the Toulousians, the soldiers' gestures obscene and graphic.

Alfonso could not believe his luck.

I despaired.

Louis begged God's forgiveness for the unspecified sin that kept him from victory.

A humiliating disaster all around.

I did not use such words to Louis, although it was in my mind to blame him. Where else to lay the faults of lack of preparation, even of abject cowardice in making no show of force?

"I failed to take Toulouse," was all he said. The misery of failure sat on his shoulders as surly as a thundercloud. The chapel at Poitiers saw more of him than I did.

After a gloomy progress through my domains, we returned to Paris, where the reaction of Abbot Suger and the Dowager Queen would await us. With one look at Louis's doleful expression, Suger desisted, doing nothing more than frown sternly at both of us, as if we were errant children, then unbending enough to take Louis's arm in a fatherly manner with a sigh. No point, I suppose, in ringing a peal over his head so long after the event.

Adelaide would have something to say about it; she would not hold back. Nothing would keep her silent when she had been proved right. I steeled myself. But her apartments were empty and a message had arrived for Louis during our absence. Adelaide had gone to her dower lands in Compiègne, where her eye had fallen—with astonishing speed—on an obscure lord of the de Montmorency family who was unwed. Adelaide expressed the intention of marrying the lord and not returning to court. Poor man. Louis appeared to have little interest in his mother's remarriage. It astonished me that the Dowager Queen could accept a return to comparative insignificance, but perhaps it was in her nature to keep house in a distant keep, where she could concentrate on God and her stitching. Obscurity would suit her very well.

It would not suit me.

So we were returned to Paris, Louis's reputation smeared, the weight of Abbot Suger's disapproval heavy, and perversely I missed Adelaide, her acerbic wit and the sharp cut and thrust that had become the essence of all our dealings. Conversation with Louis was as dull as a boiled mutton pudding. Abbot Suger, rigidly diplomatic, had no conversation at all. Adelaide spoke her mind with no hiding of her disapproval of me, and I had relished our verbal combat.

At least the child grew and thrived in my belly. It was my only consolation.

Adelaide's departure had its consequence. Returned to my rooms, I set my women to unpacking my traveling chests, since Aelith, who would normally have supervised such a mundane matter, had expressed a desire to remain behind in Poitou. There was the faintest scratch at the doorpost. I turned to find the dark-clad figure of a woman—a servant, judging from her garments—watching me.

"Yes?"

"You do not recognize me, lady."

"Should I?" I was out of sorts and missed Aelith's easy company. My nausea had settled, but I had found the long journey in the lurch and sway of the litter more than exhausting. Louis had been no company.

"I am Agnes," she replied with a quiet assurance surprising in one of her status. "I was tire-woman to Queen Adelaide."

I recalled her, Adelaide's shadow, silent and unobtrusive as she fetched and carried for her royal mistress. She was short and slight, fine boned, her hair covered by a wimple, her figure concealed in dark wool, a woman, I decided, who would pass unseen through life. I could not understand why she had come to me.

"Why did you not accompany Queen Adelaide to Compiègne and her new life?"

"I do not wish to retire, lady. I have no desire to disappear into the depths of the country."

"Did she allow you to stay?" My interest was piqued.

"I did not give her the choice, lady. It was not my wish to go and so I refused."

I looked at her sharply, reconsidering. Behind the unassuming exterior of this woman of indeterminate age was a remarkable composure.

"And so?" I let my cloak slip from my shoulders. Agnes stepped neatly forward to retrieve it before it reached the floor. Impressive! "What is your wish?"

"I wish to offer my services to *you*, lady."

"I have enough women to wait on me." I indicated the women from noble families who made up my household, their sole existence to meet my desires.

"To wait on you, yes. But you need me, lady." She placed the fur on the bed, brushing down the soft pelt with her hand.

"I don't think I do." I yawned. Oh, I was tired.

"You need me to help you survive at this court."

What a strange thing to say. I did not think I had any such need. What could a servant offer me? I raised my brows in inquiry.

"How many friends do you have, lady?" the tire-woman asked.

"Friends?"

"I think you have none. Which of these women would tell you the truth?"

I considered. She had a point. They would tell me what I wished to know.

"My sister would. . . ."

"Your sister is in Poitou, lady. I would be your friend," Agnes stated. "I would be your eyes and ears. And I would tell you the truth. To know the truth is to have strength."

"Why would you do this?"

She gave no reply. Her eyes were dark and direct as she allowed me to make my own judgment. Truth? Truth was a valuable commodity, not to be sneezed at. I walked across the room, singling out Florine, whose ear for gossip was keen.

"Florine . . ."

"Yes, lady?" She looked up from her task of shaking out my robes from the chest.

"What is the court saying about Toulouse?"

The change in Florine's demeanor was imperceptible, but I saw it. A tightening of a muscle here, a flicker of an eyelid there. Her hands stilled on the silk sleeves she had just lifted from a coffer.

"That it was unfortunate that Count Alfonso was warned of His Majesty's campaign."

"Is that all?"

Florine could not quite look at my face. "Yes, lady."

"Thank you." I beckoned to Agnes. When we were out of earshot in the deserted anteroom, I said, "Tell me, then. What *do* they say about Toulouse?"

"They put the blame at your door, lady. They say . . . the advice that His Majesty acted on was not good." She looked me full in the eye.

"And the lack of forces, the insufficiency of siege engines for such a campaign? The ignominious retreat without a blow being exchanged? Where is the blame for them apportioned?"

Agnes shook her head.

"How can that be put at my feet?" I demanded.

"It can if the initial plan was not considered to be sound. And that plan was yours, lady."

So I was at fault. My claim to Toulouse might be right and just, but blame for France's defeat would not be leveled at Louis. The Aquitaine Queen must be the cause of France's failure. I felt the bitterness of it, the unfairness of it. Perhaps it did not altogether surprise me—but I learned the lesson well. I must guard my vulnerability.

Agnes came into my employ. A friend? How would a tire-woman be a friend to the Duchess of Aquitaine? But I kept her because she was right—truth was strength.

There were repercussions from Toulouse. Abbot Suger had his revenge for my interfering where I had no right to interfere, with the result that I found myself shut out of Louis's meetings with his Council. It was not right! The wife of the King of France had always been given access to decision making, had always been consulted. Even Adelaide had scrawled her signature on any number of Fat Louis's charters. I had made it my business to know this.

But after Toulouse there was a wily conspiracy, a change to the custom, quietly done. I was not to be allowed to sit in Louis's consultations with his advisers. My role as Queen was to be ceremonial. I was to be a cipher, a lovely face and elegant body to stand silently at Louis's side in royal robes and bear the royal children. All I had feared. Neither my consent nor advice would be sought or acted upon. I was barred. My presence at royal discussions was de trop.

Abbot Suger's little victory.

I allowed it. Would I embarrass myself by being turned from the door of the Council chamber? But in my heart I refused to accept defeat. I would say what I wished in the privacy of my bedchamber, where the worthy Abbot had no power. But first Louis must make amends for cringing so weakly before his minister. I was carrying the heir to France, was I not? I had every right to punish him.

I withdrew from Louis. I distanced myself from him, made no

attempt to seek him out, absenting myself from the formal meals with the excuse that I was unwell. When he came to my apartments, I had a dozen excuses to deny him entry. Indeed, one word of my possible ill health put him to flight like a rat into a sewer in the streets of Paris. I would bring my husband to his knees for his slighting of me. And I did, of course. It was a cunning woman's ploy, to pretend disinterest. After no more than a se'enight of the fictitious headache, the trouble-some cough, the inexplicable rash, I brought him to me where I had closeted myself in my solar. Abjectly apologetic, Louis had a little cof-fer clasped to his chest like an offering.

"My lord." My voice held the bitter cold of January, while I contin-ued to give my attention to the troubadour who knelt at my feet pour-ing out an impassioned love song. I would not be ignored, and Louis would be left in no doubt of it.

—she is my heart's one joy, crown of all ladies I have ever seen,
Fair, fairer still, fair above all the fairest is she, my lady, as I must
avow—

My troubadour sang with pain and adoration, all plaintive emotion in his voice.

"My lady . . . !" Louis approached.

I waved him to silence as the singer fixed his eyes on my face and completed the sentiment.

—now it is time, lady, that you grant your lover his reward—
or else it would be folly for him to praise you—

"Lover? Reward?" Louis's words were bitten off.

"Certainly." I graced him with barely a glance. "My troubadour demands my love in return for his." How convenient that he should be singing those sentiments at such a moment—if one believed in such coincidences. "This is *Cortez Amors*, Louis. Courtly love." I yawned behind my fingers. "The love of a troubadour for his lady. His worship of the unattainable woman of his heart."

Louis strode forward to tower over me. "I'll not have that man here, expressing such sentiments to my wife."

Better and better . . . "Why ever not?"

"You refused to obey me on the day of our marriage. That was in Bordeaux, your own city. This is Paris. I'll not have that man in your chamber."

My troubadour still knelt, head bent, fingers stilled on the strings. Marcabru, another favorite of my father, was a songsmith full of wit, of scurrilous verses or the sweetest love songs to turn a woman's knees to water, renowned throughout Aquitaine and Poitou. I had brought him to Paris with me from our recent visit to Poitiers. He was a handsome man with great charm and a heart-melting smile. A smile that was now wickedly in evidence at the exchange of words.

Louis waved him away. Marcabru looked at me for confirmation. I hesitated, just for a second, then nodded, smiling at him and watching as he bowed and retreated across the room. My women withdrew too, leaving the pair of us in a little space of hostility.

I turned to Louis. "Did you wish to speak with me, Louis?" I asked sweetly. "Did you want my advice at last? Or will you continue to shut me out of your deliberations?" He slammed the little coffer down, to the detriment of its hinges. "Did Abbot Suger allow you to come to me?" I pursued.

Louis snarled, not diverted. "You were flirting with him, Eleanor."

I made my face grave, hurt. "I do not flirt with my servants."

"I'll not have it."

I lifted my chin a little. "By what right do you take me to task, my lord?"

His reply was becoming tedious with repetition. "I am your husband."

"My husband? I think I've not seen you in my bed anytime this week—this month, in fact. Even longer than that . . ."

"Such comments don't become you, madam. As for your paid

songster . . . How typical of the louche south," he accused viciously, "to encourage such wantonness. . . ."

We had been here before, of course. "Do you dare accuse me of lascivious behavior, Louis? The woman who carries your child?"

"How should I not? Look at your hair, your dress. . . ."

"I am at leisure here in my own rooms to dress as I please. . . ." Deliberately I drew my hand down the length of my hair, wrapped about in silk ribbons, the ends clasped in gold finials. Louis's eyes followed the gesture. "I recall a time when you wound my hair around your wrist, my lord. . . ."

"I'll not discuss that . . . !" His face was suffused with color. "I'll not have you looking like . . ." He sought for a word.

I supplied it. And not quietly. "A harlot?" I suggested.

It silenced Louis. It drew all eyes in the chamber to us. With a furious look, Louis leaned close to whisper, the syllables harsh in the quiet room, "You will dismiss your troubadour, Eleanor."

"I will not. I am his patron."

Louis stalked out. The jewels—his peace offering but left behind with bad grace—were atrocious, solid enough to decorate a horse's harness. I remained obdurate. I knew what I was about. Hardly had the week expired than Louis marched in with another box, small and carved of wood. Without apology or explanation he thrust it into my hands.

"A gift, Eleanor. To remind you of your home. I know you love the perfumes of the south, so I've had this made for you."

I opened the little box to release a sweet scent of orange blossom with a deeper note that tickled my nose. It was pleasant enough and I was touched that he should think of me with so personal a gift. Feeling magnanimous, I put aside my embroidery. Now was the time to welcome him back into my affections. I kissed his cheek.

"I had the ingredients from a merchant here in the city," Louis explained, as he took the box from me, strode across the room to the open fire, and . . .

"Take care, Louis—only a little—the merest pinch . . . That's too much . . . !"

Louis cast a hearty handful of the contents onto the fire. His enthusiasm was a fine thing.

Smoke rose. There was the sweetness of the orange blossom, perhaps a little jasmine scenting the air, and beneath that . . . I sniffed. Sandalwood I expected, or even frankincense as the base notes. That was what I would have ordered. We in the south had much experience of the skills of Ancient Rome, now practiced and polished by our alchemists. But that was not it. . . . I sniffed again. One of my women sneezed. Louis coughed discreetly. Then not so discreetly as the smoke billowed and the pungency caught at the back of the throat.

There was no escape. The perfume burned, the smoke filled the room, and we coughed, sneezed, eyes watering as we were all overwhelmed with the cloying, animal heaviness of it.

"Open the windows," I ordered when I could breathe. "Douse the flames."

To no avail. The perfume continued to give off its secrets, and the mingled scents hung like a miasma in the air. By this time any sweetness was entirely obliterated, the drafts from the open windows merely stirring the fire into fresh life.

We fled to the antechamber, where we continued to wheeze.

"It was very expensive," gasped Louis, beating at his tunic, dragging his hands down over his face.

"I can imagine." And I began to laugh.

Musk, of course. The most valuable, the most sought-after of base elements. To be used circumspectly, and totally overwhelming when applied with too liberal a hand. Laughter took hold and I could not stop. Everything was permeated with the scent of musk. The tapestries, the very stones of the walls. And ourselves.

"It was too much, Louis," I managed. But Louis was already beating a retreat, still spluttering, as I mopped my eyes. "They say its perfume remains detectable for a hundred years. . . ." I gasped.

"One week on the skin would be too much," Agnes muttered. "Your hair, lady! It reeks of the stuff. Who concocted it for His Majesty? They ought to be suffocated in their own product."

"Probably the master of horse, used to making liniment! They say it's an aphrodisiac. . . ." I burst into laughter again.

"And will you inform His Majesty of that?"

We laughed until we could laugh no more, before Agnes ordered up hot water to scrub and scour our skin and hair. The remains of Louis's gift we consigned to the garderobe.

Poor Louis! Even his kindest efforts went awry, but at least we were reconciled.

I was still not readmitted to Louis's councils.

I lost our child. For no reason that I could understand. Although my belly was hardly rounded, the birth far distant, I gave up hunting. I danced only moderately. I ate and drank circumspectly. Nothing must harm this precious child. But then a sharp pain struck in the night, a pain that became agony where there should have been no pain. The child was stillborn, almost too ill formed to recognize as a child, certainly too small to take a breath on its own and too incomplete for me to know its sex. Only a mess of blood and disappointment. Of the pain in the bearing of that child as it tore its way from my body I gave no thought; only the loss that lodged its despair in my heart concerned me. I had failed. I had failed France and Aquitaine. My grief surprised me.

Did Louis blame me?

No, he never did. He thought our loss was brought about by some nameless, undisclosed sin of his own that he had not confessed, thus driving him to endless hours on his knees to seek God's forgiveness.

Perhaps it was. Or was the sin mine?

It was Agnes who held my hand when I wept, when the pain was almost too great to bear, not Louis, who was banned, as were all men, from the birth chamber.

"What do they say, Agnes?" I asked when the grief ebbed, to be replaced by empty reality.

She pursed her lips.

"Whom do they blame?" I pressed her.

She gave an eloquent shrug. "The child was born before its time. It is always the fault of the woman. It is the burden we have to bear."

A caustic reply but not without sympathy. I knew she was right.

As for Louis, his despair might have driven him to his knees, but he still found time to banish Marcabru from my court. I did not know my troubadour had gone until I emerged from my chamber to be told that Louis had sent him back to Poitiers on the understanding that he would never return to Paris. I missed him, that bright flavor of the south in his words and music that might have helped me to heal. I was heartsore, but kept it close within me. I never talked of it to Louis, this callous dismissal of my troubadour when my spirits were at their lowest ebb. This was deliberate retribution on Louis's part. I had not thought him capable of it.

I think in those days my heart began to harden against the King of France.

Chapter Seven

I did not see it, but my feet tottered at the edge of a slippery slope that would take me tumbling down into a black void. It was my own fault. Had I not been so taken up with the loss of my child, with Louis's disregard, I would never have neglected Aelith. What possible harm could come to her in Poitiers, where she was known and well loved? I should have remembered that she could be too passionate for her own good. But in fairness I could never have imagined the consequences of the freedom she enjoyed there.

She returned to Paris, her face alight, as full of joy as I had ever seen her.

"Aelith!" I hugged her. "I missed you. . . ."

"I'm so sorry, Eleanor. I should have been here."

"What could you do?" I studied her, suddenly suspicious. "You look pleased with yourself!"

"Oh, Eleanor! I'm in love."

I laughed, relaxed a little. "Which troubadour this time?"

"No, no." Gravity and an unusual maturity settled on her features. "I love Raoul of Vermandois. I want him. I want to marry him, and, before God, he wants me. Will you help us?"

Raoul of Vermandois. The man Aelith had cast her eye over at my marriage feast. Count Raoul, the Seneschal of France with the well-connected wife. Of an age to be wed, Aelith had distracted me when I suggested it was time and beyond to find her a husband. And why was that? Because she had Raoul of Vermandois in her sights. And why had she remained behind in Poitiers? To be with him, since Count Raoul had been ordered by Louis to remain there and take soundings of any incipient uprisings.

Aelith's voice was urgent, her fingers digging into my arm. "I am in love with Raoul of Vermandois."

Simple words, but heralding such disaster if I had but known it, so that it was to be Aelith who unwittingly brought me great distress. I meant well. All I wanted was happiness for her, happiness and fulfillment such as I did not have, with the man she loved and who loved her. I did not see the outcome for her, for Louis, for me. How could I? It was beyond what anyone could have foreseen.

"Tell me," I said.

And she did. Aelith moved restlessly around the room, her eyes sparkling, her words extravagant with infatuation. In Poitou, as I had guessed. Late summer, the weather had been fine, offering good hunting and long, lazy days. It gave so much more. Aelith and Count Raoul, free from too many interested glances, had stopped attempting to deny the strange fascination they had for each other.

I produced all the arguments. She would not go blind into this relationship.

"He's married, Aelith."

"I know."

"He has a wife with powerful connections. And children."

"I know that too."

"He's old enough to be your grandfather."

"He loves me. He's more of a man than Louis!"

Which was true. I sighed. "What makes you so certain he's not in love with your dower, more than your mind and body?" Aelith was a wealthy woman, a desirable bride for any man, with estates in Normandy and Burgundy. Vermandois would be a fool not to see Aelith's value.

"He likes my mind and body very well." She blushed.

So that was it. I tried not to appear shocked at what my little sister had been doing in Poitou. "Have you slept with him?"

"More often than you have with Louis, I warrant!" she retorted with uncomfortable percipience. "At least when Raoul looks at me, it's with a man's desire for a woman, not veneration at the feet of the Madonna!"

"Aelith!"

"Well, it's true!"

True it might be, but I was not prepared to admit it.

"Please, Eleanor," Aelith continued, wrapped up in her own problems. "Talk to Louis. Get his support."

"The Count is married, Aelith." It was the final nail in the coffin of Aelith's love, as far as I could see.

"So Raoul divorces his wife!" She gave a distinct flounce, unworthy of her claims to adult emotion. "If Louis will support him, why should he not demand his freedom? The Church will agree."

"Are you sure about this, Aeli?"

"I am. Raoul's come to Paris with me. I love him." She looked so radiantly happy. "Would you deny me love because there's precious little in your life?"

It was not something I had ever talked of, not even to my sister. How could a proud woman confess that the man she had married could barely tolerate her body? But how true her accusation. Jealousy! It struck home, a fist to my belly, and I was ashamed. How could I not give her my blessing? I promised to test Louis's feelings, and soon discovered that I did not need to. Count Raoul had already broached the subject with Louis over a cup of ale. Taking time off from his daily appointment with the Almighty, Louis sought me out to complain of my sister's flighty ways and questionable morals.

"Needless to say, I don't approve," Louis remarked, fist clenching on his knee as he sat and frowned at me.

"Why not?" I was completing my dressing, choosing jewels from a casket. "They love each other."

"So Vermandois tells me. He threatens to leave his wife and children and carry Aelith off and live with her, whether I say yea or nay."

"So what are you going to do about it, Louis?"

It had become very important that I win this chance of happiness for Aelith. If guilt was to be apportioned for the events that unfolded, then I could not claim my innocence. For I had watched Aelith and Raoul together, in public, marveling at the latent passion that arced between them. Raoul might be an aging wolf but he was still a wolf, tough and vital. The desire when they looked at each other made me shiver. Though he was never less than courteous and respectful, Raoul's touch on Aelith's hand, the deep caress of his voice, the slide of his eyes over her face, all announced his feelings for her to the whole court. Oh, yes, they loved each other.

What did I have?

Nothing. How long since Louis had last touched me? I burned with longing. My heart and my bed were a wasteland, empty and barren, and I could do nothing to remedy it. It almost reduced me to weeping until I reminded myself that Duchesses of Aquitaine did not weep. They took action to remedy the problem—and I could at least remedy Aelith's lack. She would have her much-desired marriage; she would have her lover. All I had to do was open Louis's eyes to the advantage for him, for France.

Louis's brow creased in a familiar worry of uncertainty. "Raoul says his first marriage is unlawful. He and the lady are third cousins and no dispensation was sought—so he could demand an annulment."

"I know." The Church and the laws of consanguinity were a positive quagmire into which the unwary fell. No man and woman related within the scope of four generations could wed. Without a dispensation and the passing of much gold from the disappointed couple to the Pope, such a marriage was unlawful. "I think you should support Vermandois."

"I've no wish to become embroiled with the Pope." I saw Louis almost physically retreat, but I knew how to play him, a fish on a line.

"But, Louis—surely you have realized . . ."

"Realized what?"

I pushed onto my finger a pretty amethyst ring and leaned from where I sat to grasp his sleeve. "Have you considered the connections of Raoul's wife, Louis? Is she not sister to Count Theobald of Champagne?"

Champagne!

It was as if I had struck Louis. If Louis hated any man it was Count Theobald of Champagne, the very man who had refused point-blank to support Louis in the debacle of Toulouse, denying his feudal obligation to send troops to aid his overlord. If Louis was of a mind to blame any man for his ignominy before Toulouse, it was his disobedient vassal Theobald of Champagne.

How fortunate!

Louis blinked. He had snapped up my bait and the possibilities swam in his eyes: revenge of a very personal nature cloaked in political support of Vermandois's new marriage.

"Champagne's sister . . . of course she is," he muttered. "I'd forgotten. . . ."

"So . . . Now, will you support Vermandois and Aelith?" I purred. I had stirred the pot—a woman who had never stirred a pot in her life—and now I must leave it to simmer. No need! It took all of ten seconds to come to a turbulent bubble.

"I'll do it!" Louis declaimed. "I'll do it. I'll have a parcel of French bishops annul the Vermandois marriage immediately."

"The Count of Champagne won't be pleased." I held out my wrist and a bracelet of amethyst stones for Louis to clasp there. Which he did with brisk efficiency, as if fastening a bridle to a horse, his mind already distant and planning.

"No, he won't, will he?" He smiled, quite wolfishly for him.

So it was done. Louis found three compliant bishops to grant an annulment on the grounds of consanguinity within the third degree. The same bishops, almost in the same breath, joined Aelith and Vermandois in matrimony.

All highly satisfactory.

We rejoiced at the celebrations. Aelith shone with happiness. The Count preened. Abbot Suger's scowl was swept aside. Louis celebrated his moment of victory at the expense of Count Theobald with more cups of wine than was habitual. Was that the influence, the stimulus? The wine or the splendor of the well-executed revenge? He came to my bed that night and took me as a man should take a woman. My heart lifted. Might he not become the husband I desired?

Ah, but the repercussions! Perhaps I should not have been so blinded by my sister's happiness and Louis's magnificent erection. Why had I not seen it, even when it must have been obvious to all but the most dull-witted?

The political aftermath was instant and cataclysmic.

Vermandois's rejected wife took herself and her children back to her brother's household in Champagne, putting herself under Count Theobald's protection with loud complaints against the validity of her annulment. Count Theobald appealed to the Pope—Pope Innocent it was then, as sly a creature as all popes, to my mind. Theobald claimed that Louis and I had pressured the French bishops into their decision, which I suppose Louis had, but to accuse him so openly, so viciously, was not wise. Nor was it within the realms of acceptable diplomacy for the Pope to respond by stamping his holy foot.

I could have told Innocent it would not work. With Louis it was a matter of soft words and gentle suggestion, not issuing directives. He might have been raised a monk but he had as strong a sense of his monarchy as Fat Louis.

The outcome was like a ridiculous scene from a bad mummers' play, except that there was no humor in it. I listened to the succession of couriers who brought us news and papal directives, each one over-lapped by the next. Pope Innocent raged from Rome, deploring Louis's part in the proceedings, and ordered Vermandois to return to his first wife. Vermandois, now happily ensconsed with Aelith, refused. The papal wrath building, Innocent excommunicated the French bishops who had acted under Louis's orders. Louis blamed Count Theobald for the whole mess. Disastrously, the Pope gave his final challenge. The penalty for such disobedience was God's ultimate judgment. Innocent excommunicated Vermandois and Aelith.

And then? Pope Innocent excommunicated Louis as well.

Our whole royal household was placed under an Interdict, thrust outside any relationship with the Almighty. No services, no confession, no penance, no absolution. We were abjured from the bosom of God. Louis was left with nowhere to hide.

"By God! He'll not do this!" Louis gasped in horror, lured into blasphemy. "I don't deserve this damnable judgment! The King of France is not answerable to Rome! God's Bones! I'm no cur to be whipped back to my master's heels!"

The Interdict fed the flames of Louis's wrath to a conflagration. He raged, paced the length of the Great Hall and back again, damning the Pope and Count Theobald indiscriminately, his face strained and drawn with fatigue, barred as he was from the comfort of the Church. I made no attempt to placate him. He was beyond soothing.

"This is all at Theobald of Champagne's door," he snarled when he returned to where I watched him from the dais. "If he'd not gone sniveling to the Pope in the first place . . . He'll pay for this. I'll teach him a lesson he'll not quickly forget. A vassal does not stir the Church against his liege lord with impunity."

He was already marching out of the door, calling for his steward.

Oh, Aelith!

My premonition of disaster was now strong, storm clouds gathering to engulf us. I prayed her marriage was worth it, for all of us.

For the rest of the day the palace was a mass of shouted orders and running feet. Rumors flew, multiplying, growing more extravagant. By the time Louis descended on me in my chamber late in the evening in a state of nervous excitement, I knew what he planned. Bright eyed, exhausted but yet vividly alive, he sat on my bed and laid his campaign before me.

"We leave tomorrow, Eleanor. I've summoned my vassals with their feudal levies. I'll invade Champagne. I'll bring him to his knees. Abbot Suger disapproves, but I'm not listening. I'll have Theobald's head on a platter. . . . It's good policy, isn't it, Eleanor?"

A shiver of caution passed over my skin. I hesitated. "Will you be strong enough?" I remembered Toulouse.

"I've no intention of facing Theobald in pitched battle. If I lay waste to his crops and villages, he'll soon come running to ask forgiveness.

Followed hot on his heels by the Pope, who'll cancel the Interdict fast enough. It wouldn't be wise for Innocent to be at odds with the King of France with a victorious army at his back." He surged to his feet and gripped me by the shoulders. "And before I go, Eleanor—I'll bed you." He planted a kiss full on my mouth. "Remove your gown!"

"It's a Friday," I remarked waspishly. Louis's idea of seduction was not mine.

"I'm aware, but this is urgent." He had already released me and was stripping his tunic over his head. "I've no thought of my defeat, but I pray God it's His will that I leave you with my heir growing in your belly."

I submitted with ill grace, but I doubt Louis noticed. He prayed and maintained an erection with feverish intent. I prayed for his success in Champagne and in the power of his loins. I think I might even have prayed for some vestige of pleasure, but it was a brief, businesslike occasion. Louis seemed pleased enough and kissed me before he left. It crossed my mind that he had come to me because he was forbidden to approach God. I think by now I was resigned to it.

But Louis's plan for revenge disturbed me. I could see no good coming of it, only worse conflict. Nor did I like the lack of courage that made Louis turn aside from battle with Count Theobald to wage war on the villages of Champagne. It was not the policy of a principled warrior.

Louis marched into Champagne with banners and pennons fluttering gold and blue, and I stayed in Paris, trying not to remember his brave descent on Toulouse and his ignominious return. Would he emerge the victor? I sent a stream of prayers to the Holy Virgin to come to his aid. Surely he could not lose, surely . . . As I prayed I closed my eyes tight, trying not to visualize the tales that were trickling back to us, of fire and blood, of indiscriminate killing and looting and abominations committed by the French troops across a swath of Champagne.

What happened at Vitry-sur-Marne I could not ignore. No one could.

It was imprinted on my mind in sickening detail.

"We were victorious, lady. We could have made our own terms with the Count of Champagne."

Victory. My relief was overwhelming. But no terms? The flat report, the uneasy manner of it, did not ring true with victory. The atmosphere in my tapestried audience chamber pulsed with tension. Our armies had returned showing few signs of depredation, flags flying bravely, but where was Louis? He had not ridden in at the head of his troops to receive the acclamation of his capital. It was now drawing toward evening, and one of Louis's captains, a man I did not know, had, strangely, asked to speak with me.

"You didn't make terms," I stated.

"No, lady."

"Why not?"

"It was a hard campaign," he replied. The captain paused and looked away to study his hands as they tightened white-fingered around his gauntlets.

"Where is the King?" I asked, by now unnerved.

"I have to tell you, lady. . . ." The captain raised his head at the sound of approaching footsteps from the antechamber, and I saw sweat slick on his brow, although the room was not warm. "Here is His Majesty. I have presumed to come and warn you. . . ."

His anxiety was now spreading strongly to me. Something was amiss. I felt an invisible hand, as cold as ice, grip my throat. A weight lodged in my belly.

"Is the King wounded?"

"No, lady. Not exactly." Which did not reassure me to any degree.

"Tell me," I snapped.

The captain, a man of experience in the battlefield, chose his words carefully. "His Majesty is . . . unwell. He has not spoken or eaten since . . . since Vitry-sur-Marne. We felt constrained to return to France in the circumstances. I gave the order. . . ." A footfall made him turn his face toward the half-open door. "As you see, lady . . ."

By the Virgin! I needed the warning. Louis was led into the chamber by another Frankish knight whose hand was firm on my husband's shoulder. Louis's feet were hesitant, stumbling, his shoulders bowed.

"Your Majesty. You are home." The knight touched Louis's arm to bring him to a halt.

Louis blinked and looked around, a crease digging between his fair brows. I think he did not recognize his surroundings. Gray and insubstantial, eyes dulled and lacking life, Louis seemed to cower, searching the room for some point of recognition. Then his gaze fell on me.

"Eleanor!" His voice cracked, broke on the one word.

"Your Majesty . . ." Louis's captains bowed themselves out, relief potent in their speed, and left him to me.

For a moment shock held me in place. Little more than a walking shadow, Louis seemed to have aged a score of years in the time since he had left. Was this the man who had embarked on his campaign with such assurance, such energy? He was still clad in his mail, the royal colors on his surcoat proclaimed him the King of France, but there was no majesty here, no military might. Here was a drained husk of a man.

"Louis?"

My voice too broke a little, so great was my appalled astonishment. I could never have anticipated such a change in a young man. He might recognize me, but there was no communication in his empty gaze. He simply stood silent, unmoving, as if waiting for orders. His hair was lank and filthy, his clothes mired. This was far worse than Toulouse. The majesty of kingship had been obliterated—and now I knew why. The vicious rumors had prepared me.

Vitry-sur-Marne. The name that must not be mentioned.

Practicalities took over. I took his hand and led him into my apartments. He followed me like a loyal hound, unquestioning, his hand lax in mine. It was just the strain and stress of war, of travel, I tried to convince myself. I would see to his bodily comforts and then when sense and reason returned, I would talk with him. A good night's sleep and a hot meal and Louis would come to his senses. I drew him into my own bedchamber, where, with Agnes's help—it was not my wish to subject him to my women's gossip—Louis stripped, bathed, put on clean hose and tunic, ate and drank a little, and sat before a fire. All without a word.

This was not right. It worried me more and more as Louis followed my instructions without complaint. Not once did he express his own preference. His eyes were focused beyond me, his lips clamped tight. At last, alone, Agnes dismissed, I pulled up a stool and sat beside him, taking his hand in mine when he paid me no heed.

"Louis . . ." Nothing. "Louis!"

He pulled his mind back from some great distance, and looked at me.

"Are you comfortable now?"

"I am guilty."

Rough and raw, his voice sounded unused. I considered encouraging him to speak of the campaign in general but decided to draw out the blade. Brutally painful it would be, but it would release the poison faster.

"Is it Vitry?" I asked.

A shudder ran through his frame and his hand clenched on mine, the nails digging into my flesh. His mouth framed the word, but he could not speak it. Ashen, body shaking, he turned his face away from me. When I looked, tears were running silently down his cheeks to drip onto his tunic. Nothing I could do would stop them. All I could do was put him to bed.

At first he sank into a deep sleep, but then the nightmares took their hold. Louis thrashed, cried out, then woke to weep into his pillow.

"Tell me what troubles you. Let me help you," I begged.

But he remained silent, sunk into his own private hell.

With dawn came Agnes carrying a tray of ale and bread. When he refused to respond, between us we pulled Louis from the bed and dressed him. When he shook his head at the offered ale, I held the cup to his lips until he drank. And then my patience gave out.

"Get him to talk to you," Agnes advised. I did not need her to tell me. I had no intention of allowing Louis to continue like this. I pushed him into a chair, pulling up a low stool so that he must look at me.

"Louis. Tell me what happened."

"I . . . can't!"

"I won't go away until you do, so set your mind to it."

And he told me, the words tumbling out from his stiff lips like a river in spring, its flow without restraint. I don't think Louis saw me, but merely let the memories loose.

"It was Vitry. We attacked the keep at Vitry. They fired back at us with a hail of bowshot. So I gave orders to retaliate—we fired flaming arrows. The wooden keep was soon ablaze. They deserved it, didn't they? They should have offered a truce. . . ." Tears began to track down his cheeks again, but he was unaware of them. Licking his dry lips, he continued. "My troops—I lost control. Bloodlust swept through them. They stormed through the streets, killing, hacking all who came in their path." He spread his palms and looked at them as if the scene were painted there. "The thatch and wood of the houses caught fire fast in the breeze. I was on the ridge above and saw it all. . . . The whole town ablaze . . . I couldn't stop it. They fled." He stopped, breath catching.

"Go on," I urged, even though I knew the pain of what he must recount.

"The people fled into the cathedral. They thought they would be safe there, you understand, under the protection of God. They should have been. . . . But they weren't. The flames engulfed them. The roof caved in. I saw it—heard it. Every soul trapped and perished." His voice dropped to a whisper. He leaned toward me. "Over a thousand people, they told me."

I gave him a cup of ale again but he could scarce hold it, his hand shaking as if he had the ague. I guided it to his lips once more but he shook his head and raised his eyes to mine. They were haunted. Horror and remorse swam there beneath the tears.

"I heard the screams of the dying, Eleanor. Smelled their burning flesh. I could not stop it. I am responsible. The destruction of God's house. All those innocents, women and children. How can I ever atone for that?"

And he wept into his hands, harsh rasping sobs that I could not soothe. For a time I absorbed the extent of the massacre done in Louis's name and mine. It was an abomination and I could make no excuse for it. I would have wept too for the loss, but I forced my mind back to my weeping husband.

"It was not your fault," I tried. "You did not order the sacking of the town."

I don't think he heard me. "God will blame me. And how can I ask for His forgiveness? I am forbidden God's presence."

For that was the crux of the problem. Excommunicate as he was, Louis counted himself forever damned, without hope of spiritual ease. No confession, no absolution, no comfort of the Blessed Sacrament. The fear of the Last Judgment hung over him and would until the day he died, a death without the hope of salvation. All his life had been spent in the arms of Holy Mother Church, and now when he needed its care and compassion and forgiveness most, it was closed to him. Throughout that day, Louis wailed as a soul in torment. I could not comfort him as he lay in my bed staring up into the canopy, or curled onto his side like a child.

He had my compassion, of course. At first. But as the days passed and I saw no signs of recovery, my tolerance spun out to its allotted length. I could not understand his refusal to take hold of his life again.

"What are they saying?" I asked Agnes, as I frequently did in these troubled days.

"That the King is mad and incapacitated from grief." Her bluntness was a relief.

Even Abbot Suger was helpless, turning to me in open appeal when Louis refused to speak to him. "You have to get him up, lady. If his barons see him in public, wearing the crown, well, the damage is not so great. If not, I fear insurrection. Get him up and dressed, for the love of God. . . ."

Easier said than done.

"You must get up, Louis." I gripped his shoulder, aware of the press of bone against my palm from his fasting. Still I shook him. "You are King of France."

"I am damned."

"Lying here will not change that. Your people need to see you."

"I cannot." His eyes were sunken, his cheeks hollow.

"You can. You must."

"How can I face my people when I'm guilty of the slaughter of so many?"

"How can you not face them? You are the King. You can't stay here forever."

"I need God's forgiveness."

"And I'm sure you'll get it. But for now you have to face your people. You have to be *seen* or discontent and rumor will spread."

"I'm damned, Eleanor. I'll never be forgiven. I don't deserve to be king." Pushing my hand away, Louis turned his head on the pillow. Weak tears collected in the harsh runnels beside his mouth.

How many tears could the man weep?

I had to leave the room or I would have slapped him. I had done what I could for him, but this was too much. Short of dragging him from the bed I could do nothing more. I could neither understand nor cure him, so intent was he in wallowing in misery. In those days it seemed that the crown of France rolled in the gutter, its owner sinking under a glut of misery and self-pity, incapable of rescuing it.

I prayed to the Virgin to stiffen Louis's backbone—and suddenly there was hope when I had all but lost faith in his recovery.

"His Holiness Pope Innocent is dead, Your Majesty."

I hid my joy from the papal emissary who, suitably sonorous, had ridden hard to bring us the news. The Pope had been summoned by his Holy Father; God had come to my rescue. The new Pope, Celestine the Second, I was informed, in a spirit of compromise to get his Papacy off to a good start, was pleased to welcome his errant son the King of France back into the fold and remove the ban of excommunication.

Thank God! My thoughts skittered over what this would mean, and the news was good. All would now be well, with Louis free to renew his relationship with God. He would confess the sins of Vitry and would be absolved. Good, good. I could barely take it in when despair had been so strong in me. Louis's spirits would be restored; he would resume his authority in the eyes of his barons. Surely he would also rediscover his need for me and I would conceive that much-desired son. I dispatched the news immediately to Louis whilst I assured the papal emissary that relations between France and Champagne would be put to rights. As soon as I had seen to the man's hospitality—it all seemed to take an age—I allowed myself to celebrate this miraculous reversal of our fortunes.

First to find Louis. I went to my solar, where I had left him, but he was not there; nor was he in his own apartments. Of course—how foolish—I knew where he would be. He would have rushed to Notre Dame to give thanks and confess his sins before a priest.

I followed him with light steps and a heady sense that all had been made well.

There he was, just as I had expected, before the High Altar, prostrated on the floor, arms spread as Christ had spread his arms for the sins of the world on the Cross. In my newfound optimism, I hung back. I would give him this time alone, to put himself right with God, before I rejoiced with him at Pope Celestine's mercy and celebrated his taking back the mantle and majesty of the King of France.

An hour passed—or was it longer? Louis lay as unmovingly prostrate as a corpse, while I waited, my feet and heart growing colder. Then, at last, Louis stood and bowed to the altar. And turned to face me as I walked forward, hands held out in greeting.

"You've heard the good news, Louis." Of course he had. "You are forgiven. . . ." The smile on my face froze. I halted abruptly. I let my hands fall to my sides.

"Yes. I am forgiven." He kept his distance.

I formed the words carefully, my voice little above a whisper. "In God's name, Louis. What have you done?"

"I have made my penance to God."

"But this?"

"This is what He desired of me."

The anger in me could not be borne. I shook with it. My fingers clenched into fists with it. I could barely temper my words.

"What have you done?" I repeated.

The man who stood before me was not Louis, King of France. This was not a soldier, a lawgiver, an administrator. This was not the handsome young prince who had come to Bordeaux to claim me. If nothing else, he had destroyed all his beauty.

He had cut his hair. Those beautiful fair waves of silk that I had admired when we first met, hacked off now to a rough crop and the crown of his head shaved into a tonsure. No tunic, not even a plain undecorated one, hung on his spare frame, but a monk's habit and rope girdle. He was barefoot, wearing coarse sandals. Even his stance was monkish, his hands clasped and hidden within his sleeves, shoulders curved inward. And his face—how frighteningly austere and harshly carved it was, cheeks gaunt from his recent lack of sustenance, eyes deeply sunken—was the face of a man in extremis.

"Oh, Louis!"

Here was Louis, my husband, truly transformed into the monk he had always wished to be.

"I can't believe you've done this!" I heard my voice rise and echo in the vast space.

"Hush!" He addressed me as if I were a fool, not capable of seeing the truth as he saw it. "I have to make amends for all the blood I've shed."

"But you can," I urged, struggling to push aside the barrier he had erected between us. "The Interdict is removed. You are no longer excommunicate. You can pray again, receive absolution. . . ." Did he not understand?

"It is not enough. I must make penance. Fasts, observances . . . night vigils. We must all do penance for the blood that stains our souls. . . ." His words trailing off, he would have turned away, back to the altar if I'd allowed it. I strode forward and grabbed his sleeve with considerable force, voice harsh enough to destroy the sanctity of the place.

"Did God tell you to do *this*?"

"Yes. God must see my sorrow. How can He know my repentance if it is invisible?"

"God is omnipotent. Can He not see what is in your heart?"

Louis smiled with utter conviction for himself and pity for me. "Of course He can. You must not mock, Eleanor. But it seems to me that I must show Him in the way I live my life. I must grow closer to Him. I can do that only if I give up the trappings of my earthly existence."

"You will give up your crown? Surely you'll not do something so . . ." *Stupid!* I bit down on the word. There was a holy fanaticism in his face that frightened me.

"No, no. Am I not anointed with holy oil? I am king, but even a king must make amends for vicious sins committed in his name." His eyes became stern. "Even a queen must repent."

The quiet words were like a sword between the ribs. My breath caught. "Do you blame me too, Louis?"

But his smile softened into kindness; he touched my cheek with gentle fingers. "No. It was not your doing. It was my orders that took us into Champagne. I was the one guilty of the bloody horror at Vitry." Now he did turn away from me, but not before I had seen that his fingernails were bitten to the quick, their ends bloodied, skin torn. "I will stay here tonight."

The future for me suddenly loomed, terrifying in what was not spoken. It must be spoken! "What do you mean?" I demanded.

"I need to be here," he murmured, his gaze on the altar, its silver crucifix shining with reflection of the candles. "I need God's presence. I need His forgiveness. I must dedicate my life to Him. I must listen to Abbot Suger and Abbot Bernard in future. They will lead me in God's path. . . . I must lead a holy life, pleasing in God's eyes."

How I controlled my fear and anger I did not know. "But you *are* forgiven, Louis. There is no barrier between you and God's forgiveness. Come back with me to the palace. . . ."

He shook his head as if I were still that fool who could not encompass so grave a matter. "Try to understand, Eleanor. I cannot return with you. I must not listen to you. Your advice leads me into dangerous waters. . . ."

I needed to hear it in plain words, although I already understood with terrible clarity. "Will you not come to me tonight?"

"No, Eleanor. I will not." Louis's lips softened in compassion.

I snarled, a show of teeth. If he smiled at me once more in that tolerant manner, I would surely strike him! I deliberately uncurled my fingers and took a breath. I must not give in to the fury that raced through my blood, that darkened my vision, threatening to blot out everything but the stupidity of Louis's rejection.

"You still do not have an heir, Louis," I choked out in an amazingly level voice.

"I know." He sighed. "But I must stay here."

"And what of me?" He almost shrugged. For sure he did not look at me. "Is this what you want for me? To be old before my time, to live as a nun? To turn my back on the world? I won't do it. I'm young, alive. . . . You won't imprison me as you imprison yourself."

"You will do as you wish, Eleanor. It is no longer my concern."

"Yes. I will live as I wish. I'll not be bound by your constraints."

I had hoped to provoke him—and failed. Covering his face, Louis walked once more to the altar, his shoulders shaking, and knelt before it.

What now?

I sank to one of the empty choir stalls, my knees suddenly too weak to bear me as my husband once more prostrated himself and wept in an agony of repentance. No! For a moment I resisted what was impossible to resist. I would not allow this! I would shriek, cry out, destroy the silence, rend the air with my tangled emotions. I would demand that God return my husband to me. But with my nails scoring my palms I bent my head and kept silent. Nothing I could say or do would change Louis's decision. He had finally withdrawn, choosing God over me. The humiliation was biting.

How long I remained there in frozen horror I had no idea, until a sound brought me back to the present; then soft footfalls of monastic sandals caused me to lift my head. Louis had gone. He had left me, to retire to his cell rather than stay and comfort me. He had said all he needed to say, and I would have to live with the choice he had made.

"How could You do this to me?" I raged against God, not caring who heard my outrage. "How could You condemn me to this empty existence?"

Only when the echo of my harsh cry startled me was I driven to plaster my hands over my mouth to cut off the agony, until I felt my anger drain away to leave me astonishingly calm. And at the still, cold center of my heart a new emotion unfurled. I felt it creep in, encroaching slowly, until it filled every space in my body. Contempt. Hard, cold contempt. That was all I could feel, contempt for the excuse of a man who wept and sniveled and made excuses. For the man who could not come close to the warrior prince of my dreams and had now chosen the life of a monk. Respect? Understanding? Affection? There was room for none of those in my icy heart. Louis had effectively murdered any soft emotion when he had faced me and informed me that I could live as I wished because he had no interest in me and my concerns.

As I drew my cloak around me to walk back to the palace, I saw my life for what it was and what it would be. Lonely, isolated, empty. I was only twenty years old, in full vigor and beauty. As I had told Louis, I was young and alive. But my bed was cold, I was as virginal as it was possible for a wife to be, and my body burned with empty longing. I was like to become as dried-up a husk as Louis. Must I live like him for the rest of my life, a shadow in a shadowy court where my friends were few and my enemies keen to grasp any weapon they could use against me? My vulnerability had never been more clear. I would never bear the child that would silence my enemies. Aquitaine would never have a ruler of my blood.

For a moment I stood beneath the cold arches and made my own choice to mirror his.

"Yes, Louis, I will live as I wish." I repeated my earlier affirmation so that my voice echoed in the empty reaches of Notre Dame. "I will live as I wish, and to Hell with you!"

Later I was not so sanguine. I dismissed my women, even sensible Sybille of Flanders, and flung myself on my bed, regretful that I did not have Aelith to comfort me, although I could not have told even her of the misery that engulfed me.

"What shall I do?" I asked in despair when Agnes came to help me dress for supper.

"To what purpose, lady? If it's His Majesty's strange preferences, I don't see there's much you can do." Agnes was always brisk and well-informed.

I turned my face away from her. "I have no husband."

"Take a lover," Agnes whispered.

My head whipped around. A lover? "I cannot."

"Why not? Do you love His Majesty?"

"No."

"So there is no obstacle. Will you burn with desire forever? His Majesty will not be the man to ignite that flame." Her lip curled with the same contempt that had swept through me.

"I have never burned with desire." I sighed.

"I say you lie, lady." Her smile was caustic. "I warrant *he's* as much use as a eunuch between the sheets—but those southern singers of yours could ignite the blood of any woman, with their sighs and soft eyes and sensuous words."

Uncertain, I plucked at the edge of the sheet.

"Will you live out the rest of your life without that experience, that knowledge?"

I was honest. "No."

"So do it," Agnes said, as if the decision were made.

I balked. "How do I know it will be any different with another man, Agnes? Perhaps the problem is mine."

She snorted. "And you a beautiful, passionate woman!"

"I have never felt passion."

"You have never known the right man. Will you go to your grave never knowing the pleasure to be found in a man's arms and loins? Take a puissant lover, my lady; that's my advice."

I turned my face into my pillow, much as Louis had done.

"Go away!"

We were not finished with Vitry. Bernard of Clairvaux descended on us without warning. Despite the ill health that had reduced him in recent months to little more than skin and bone, he demanded an audience with Louis on the instant that he set his holy foot inside the palace. Fragile he might be but he wasted no time, haranguing Louis before the whole court. I think he hoped to shock him out of his sorry existence as a penitent. For once *I* was not the object of his wrath, and Abbot Bernard had my sympathies.

With me at his side, Louis sat, pale and set-faced, clad in an ankle-length tunic in honor of the saint's visit, although I detected the edge of a hair shirt peeking above the neck opening. He listened to the diatribe in bleak-faced silence.

There was nothing new in it, but the Abbot was shockingly forthright. What was Louis thinking, to wage a war—unwarranted at that—against Theobald of Champagne? What sort of behavior was it for a Christian king?—slaying, burning, destroying churches, consorting with bandits and robbers. It was time he put Vitry-sur-Marne aside and turned his mind to ruling his country. A king's place was with his hands on the reins of government, not clasped in prayer every hour of the day. Even Abbot Suger was raked from head to foot for failing to give Louis good advice, before the barbs were turned once more on the King.

"What persuaded you to support this matter of Vermandois's marriage? You allowed yourself to be led down the path of evil by your wife." Disgust dripped from every one of Bernard's accusations. "You let yourself be led by the nose by Raoul of Vermandois. You should be ashamed, Majesty! You should—"

"Stop!"

The whole court shuddered on an intake of breath. So did I. I could not recall hearing Louis raise his voice before in so commanding a tone.

"You would silence me?" Bernard demanded.

"I would! I will! Led by the nose . . . ? You overstep yourself, my lord Abbot!" Louis leaned forward, hands planted on his knees. "You are not my conscience."

"Before God, you have need of one!" Abbot Bernard gave not one inch.

"You'll not speak to me like that." Louis surged to his feet, striding forward as if he would strike the Abbot. "I will act as I see fit. I am king here!"

"Then conduct yourself as one, in the eyes of man and God," Bernard thundered back. "In God's name! Why would you go to such lengths to please the woman who is your wife? Could you not see the danger? What persuaded you to disapprove of the consanguineous relationship between Vermandois and his first wife?"

"Because it's against the law of the Church," Louis snarled. "Of God."

"You fool! You misguided fool!" Bernard's eyes blazed. "To draw attention to consanguinity! When you yourself are related to your own wife within the forbidden degrees. Consanguinity is a dangerous game to play. What's sauce for the damned goose can become sauce for the thrice-damned gander!"

Silence!

The atmosphere was suddenly as thick as a smoke-filled chamber. A strange hiatus held us all. No one moved. Not a breath could be heard. What was this? My whole attention was caught up.

"What?" Louis's voice dropped as his eyes flickered from Bernard to me. "That is false."

"Of course it's not false." Bernard's voice once more blasted all present. "Are you saying you are not aware?"

"No. I deny it. . . . There's no proof. . . ."

"Proof? The Bishop of Laon himself has exposed the consanguineous affinity."

Louis's voice rose into a shout of fury. "No. I'll not believe it. I'll not have it spoken of, d'you hear? Eleanor is my true wife."

The proceedings, such as they were, continued to disintegrate around me. I paid them no heed. The matter of consanguinity remained hanging in the air, like a dust mote in a sunbeam, waiting for me to snatch at it and see its meaning. It was a revelation that I must pick apart. And since I knew who had the knowledge to help me . . .

Louis had denied the accusation, but I would wager Abbot Bernard had the truth of it.

"Your Majesty . . ." The Bishop of Laon scrambled to his feet, then bent his portly form at the middle into a bow. I heard the intake of heavy breathing, exertion and anxiety in equal measure. "Your Majesty . . ."

He could think of nothing else to say. How could he? I had not advertised my coming. Nor, I imagine, was my expression conciliatory after a long, hot journey into Aquitaine on what I hoped would not be a matter of chasing a wild goose.

"My lord Bishop." I walked forward into the sunny room. The Bishop lived in some style, some comfort, and I admired the light-filled chamber with its tapestried walls, its spread of books on every surface, its cushioned seats that invited a visitor to stay and be entertained. If I had my choice I would live again in Aquitaine. If I could regain control over my own life . . . I pinned the Bishop with a stare. "I wish you to show me the results of your recent studies."

The round face flushed; the little eyes, remarkably porcine, widened between the pouch of cheek and forehead. His pursed mouth pursed even further. An unappealing man—but an erudite scholar who owed his primary loyalties to me, not to my husband, although one might be forgiven for disbelieving that, seeing supreme discomfort shift over his features.

"My studies, Majesty . . . ?"

I advanced, forcing him to look up. He was barely over five feet in height. It pleased me to take advantage of my inches.

"I beg you will not play the fool with me, sir. You know why I'm here. Show me."

"Majesty . . . indeed." To do him justice, he did not pretend further ignorance. "But I cannot. . . ."

I allowed a little smile, watched as his rigid shoulders relaxed. "Why would that be?"

The Bishop swallowed. "The document you seek—confiscated, Majesty."

"By whom?"

"His Majesty the King."

I swung around toward the window, gazing out over the lake and wooded hills. So Louis had already taken it, destroyed it, had he? He'd wasted no time over it. How typical of him. But did he really think that to destroy the written evidence would destroy the fact, if that fact existed? His naivete continued to amaze me. Quickly I turned my head, to catch the Bishop eyeing me. Cautious, speculative, a hint of victory perhaps. Just as I thought . . .

I turned a bright smile on the Bishop of Laon. "And you did not make a copy of your valuable investigation before it was seized? Do I believe that?"

Not expecting a reply, I wandered around the room, touching the expertly worked tapestry, picking up a document from the table where he had been working, running a cursory eye over it, rejecting it. Lifting another. The Bishop cringed as if he would like to smack my hands away. He sank his teeth in his fleshy underlip.

Now sure of my ground, I relaunched my attack. "Come, my lord Bishop. We're wasting time. I don't mean to leave without satisfaction."

"Majesty! I dare not."

Well, at least he had changed his denial from *can't* to *daren't*. I leaned on the table, lowered my voice. "Show me. Show me what my husband the King thinks important enough to destroy and forbids you to discuss with his wife."

He gulped like a carp in a fishpond. And capitulated like a pricked pig's bladder.

"Yes, Majesty. But could I beg your discretion?"

"Do you fear His Majesty?"

"I do!"

I smiled with a show of teeth. I think he feared me more.

Allowed to return to his own milieu, a man of letters rather than of high politics, the Bishop busied himself, finding a key and rooting in the depths of a coffer. He scooped out rolls of parchment, dropping them on the floor, then took a flat sheet from the bottom and smoothed it on the wooden surface before me. It was a sheet of parchment with a raw edge, as if it had been torn from another. The words and lines were hastily scribbled, a quick copy. There were some blots, crossings out, but I believed in its authenticity. I made myself comfortable in the Bishop's own cushioned chair and beckoned.

"Show me, my lord Bishop. There's no blame. I merely wish to see for myself."

"Yes, Majesty. I imagine you might." I registered the dry tone as the Bishop prepared to point with stubby fingers.

"Where am I?"

"Here, Majesty." My tutor lost himself in the enthusiasm and detail of his discoveries. "And here is His Majesty King Louis. See, joined in matrimony. Now your own family—here is your own noble father and his father before him." I traced the lines the Bishop had sketched in. My father, William, and before him my famous grandfather William, knight and conqueror, troubadour and lover.

As far back as my own memories stretched.

Before my grandfather was another William, wed to a lady I had no knowledge of. Audearde.

"This lady is the key to this!" The Bishop rubbed his palms as if he had discovered a gold nugget in a mountain stream. "She is the connecting link, Majesty. . . ." His words dried as he realized he had just handed me dangerous material; then with a shrug the Bishop dived in. "*Her* father was Robert, Duke of Burgundy. Do you see? And *his* elder brother was Henry the First, King of France. Both sons of King Robert the First of France."

"Ah . . . King of France." I followed the parallel set of lines, tracing them with my finger from that far-distant King Robert of France, through Henry, then Philip, to Louis the Fat, and then to my own husband.

I frowned. "We are related." If the evidence was correct, it was irrefutable.

"Undeniably, Majesty. Within the fourth degree."

"That is forbidden."

"By the law of the Church, it is." The Bishop nodded furiously. "Within the laws of consanguinity, such a marriage is prohibited."

I set my elbows on the table, on either side of the document, clasped my hands, and rested my chin there, absorbing the implications. My hands trembled; my mouth was dry. The names swam in my vision. The implications were not clear, but I knew they were vastly important to me. Raising my eyes, I found the Bishop regarding me intently.

"But we were wed, were we not?" I queried. "By the Bishop of Bordeaux, under the supervision of Abbot Suger himself."

"Indeed you were. But that does not mean to say that it was legal. There was no dispensation applied for from His Holiness."

"Did Abbot Suger—did my husband's father not know of this?" I swept my hand over the evidence.

The Bishop raised his brows. "I cannot say, Majesty." Or would not! There was a knowing glint in those little eyes. "As I recall, Majesty"— he leaned close—"the marriage was very fast. Considering your extreme youth and vulnerability on the death of your father . . ."

"Ha! You mean Fat Louis saw the chance of a wealthy, unprotected heiress for his son and snapped her up before anyone else could get his hands on her, with or without the stamp of papal approval!"

"It is true, Majesty—or so I believe"—the Bishop's eyes were bright with the spirit of complicity—"that the Bishop of Bordeaux was well rewarded for his compliance. He was granted complete freedom from all feudal and fiscal obligations. The charter was witnessed by His Majesty's father and by Abbot Suger."

"So they knew. They all knew." I considered. "What do I do with this?"

I did not expect a reply but the prelate gave one. "Your marriage is not in danger—if His Majesty refuses to accept this proof."

"His Majesty might not accept it, but I will."

"What do you wish to achieve, Majesty?"

"I don't know." Nor did I. It was still too new.

"If you will take my advice, Majesty—take care how you use your knowledge."

"I don't know how I will. Or even if I will." My mood swung from a sudden ray of blinding hope to bleak frustration. I needed to think. "I shall keep this." I handed over a purse of gold for his troubles.

I traveled back to Paris, my thoughts still scattered. The document in my hand was a fiery brand. I did not doubt for one minute that the connection was accurate. So I was wed outside the law of the Church and the blessing of God. Was this the reason for my failure to quicken? Many might have thought so, God's punishment for disobedience. Quickly I discarded that thought. I did not believe it—the fault was not from the sin of the marriage. How was it possible to conceive if Louis failed to plant the seed? I could count on the fingers of two hands the number of occasions Louis had shared my bed with carnal desires. Our failure had nothing to do with our common ancestor.

A different seed uncurled within my breast, springing into life.

If my marriage was in sin, should it exist?

This is a way out for me . . . an annulment of an illegal marriage.

Annulment. Freedom. In the confines of my litter, the curtains pulled against the world, I felt my heart begin to beat heavily against my ribs.

Aelith has achieved it; why should I not pursue it?

The little bubble of hope expanded, only to burst as soon as it grew, because of course it was not possible, Louis having rejected the illegality out of hand. It was useless even to contemplate it. If by some miracle Louis agreed to give me my freedom, he would have to be willing to give up Aquitaine too. He would never do that. Even if he could be persuaded that I was not a comfortable wife for him, Louis would never give up half his kingdom.

Abbot Suger would never allow it.

The door that had opened was suddenly slammed shut.

I had the document now tucked within my bodice, where it all but burned a hole. I could truly laugh if it were not so tragic. Aelith and the Bishop of Laon had inadvertently shown me a means of escape from Louis, from France, from a life that clipped my wings, but a means I was not free to take. I had found the doors and window to my prison but was not free to open them.

Chapter Eight

The occasion of the consecration of Abbot Suger's new abbey church at Saint-Denis in June of the year 1144 brought Adelaide out of retirement and, reluctantly, into my company. We took our seats, prepared to be impressed, and so we were. The building was without doubt incomparable, if somewhat austere and northern for my taste, pointed arches and towering vaults replacing the more sensuous rounded style of the southern cathedrals I knew. Vast stained-glass windows allowed the light to pattern the floors with jeweled mosaics. Abbot Suger might have renounced the sin of luxury for himself but nothing had been spared on this monument to his place in God's scheme of things. Nothing could take the eye from the High Altar, dominated by a twenty-foot gold cross lavished with diamonds and rubies and pearls. Crammed with treasures and gifts from every feudal lord in France, the church glittered like a festive woman.

My eye was drawn to one spectacular offering that graced the altar.

I was at first disbelieving. And then speechless. But I vowed I would not be when I next had conversation with Louis.

Louis led the procession into the church, of course. As a symbol of his restitution, he was given the honor of shouldering the silver reliquary holding the bones of the martyred Saint Denis, placing it on the altar, where it would rest amidst more gold and precious stones than the saint could have imagined in his lifetime. The procession was lengthy, the singing endless. The heat and smell of ranks of pilgrims overpowered me as every inch of the cathedral was jammed with those who could push themselves within the four walls.

I played my part with appropriate opulence, wearing a pearl-encrusted diadem and a damask robe overlaid with cloth of gold. Even Adelaide drew the eye, gleaming with royal gems that she had removed with her to Compiègne. Louis, on the other hand . . . He had, of necessity, abandoned his ridiculous pilgrim's staff, but he was still clad in the drab gown, with the leather purse and crude sandals of a penitent that he had worn the previous day on our seven-mile journey from Paris. Had he even washed? He could be taken for any obscure pilgrim with filthy feet and shorn hair, one of the hundreds of riffraff that swelled the crowds. I felt unable to look at him.

"Before God, he is no son of mine," Adelaide murmured, her dislike of me buried beneath her despair over Louis. "Of all my six sons, that he should be the one . . . Do you hear what they're saying? It's dangerous."

The whispered conversations around me made no effort to hide the contempt for the King's posturing. At least I was silent in my abhorrence. He was oblivious to the scorn of his subjects, his bare feet caked with dust, his face emaciated with fasting, yet Louis's eyes were aglow with the assurance of God's blessing as he lowered Saint Denis to the altar. They never glowed like that in my presence.

I saw the brilliance of his pleasure fade only once.

As he came to take the seat beside me, he was forced by circumstance to come face-to-face with Theobald of Champagne. Louis's saintly aura dissipated in an instant. His features took on a set and unforgiving cast. If there had been hope of a rapprochement between the two at this holy event, Abbot Suger might find a grub in the heart of his sweet fruit. Forgive your enemies? Louis glared hatred at Count Theobald and the Count glared back. What would Louis's God make of that?

But I had my own bones to pick over with Louis. As he sat and the choristers surged into soaring notes, I leaned toward him, mouth against his ear.

"You gave away my gift to you!"

His eyes flickered. "Which gift?"

"The one I gave you on the occasion of our marriage. The crystal vase that now graces the High Altar in Abbot Suger's abbey! A gift from you to Saint Denis! Or to Abbot Suger? It doesn't matter which! You gave away my marriage gift!"

A look of bewilderment crossed his face. "I thought it a fitting offering. It was very precious to me."

"*I* gave it to *you*. I chose it as a symbol of my . . . my respect and hope for our marriage."

"I know. Do you not approve that I considered it precious enough to offer it—as a gift from us both?"

"I did not choose it as a gift for Abbot Suger, who barely tolerates me!"

"It is for God, not for Abbot Suger."

The gentle chiding, the soft, tolerant closing of his hand over mine, stirred my anger to another level. "God has no need of more gifts. Look at it." I raised my hand toward the glittering array, now partially masked by the gray swirls of incense.

"It is a mark of my repentance, Eleanor."

I flicked my fingers over the coarse cloth of his sleeve. "I think you've shown your repentance quite clearly enough in your less than kingly display. Within the past hour I've heard you described variously as a fool, an idiot, and a poor excuse for a monarch. I'm not sure which hurts me most. It's ignominious, Louis. You should have shown yourself to your people as a man of power, not as a beggar in the gutter."

"God understands." He clasped his hands and bent his head in prayer. He was beyond my tolerating. "Pray with me, Eleanor," he murmured, suddenly gripping my hand.

"*I* will pray for an heir, Louis." My tongue was acid. "I hope *you* will do more than offer petitions to the Almighty."

His smile was serene as he fixed it on the distant reliquary of the saint. "Thank you, Eleanor. I too shall pray that we shall be blessed."

And did he come to my bed that night, in our comfortable accommodation in the abbey lodgings? He did not! The lure of a night vigil with the monks at Saint-Denis before the glittering crucifix was too strong.

I cursed him.

But it forced me to accept that the path I had set myself, here at Saint-Denis, however distasteful to me, was now inevitable.

I had a purpose. A twofold purpose for being here at Saint-Denis. I needed help, and was driven to acknowledge that there was only one man who had the power to help me. Oh, how I resisted. How I shrank from making my requests. Would I willingly prostrate myself, laying myself open to his sneering hatred?

Holy Virgin! My belly curdled. But I would do it. After seven years of arid marriage, two whole years now since Louis had rejected me to play the monk, I had no pride. The two worries that crowded my days and nights were beyond my solving.

The one possible source of my redemption, the one voice Louis might listen to below God, was Bernard of Clairvaux, that most holy and intractable of saints on earth, who had honored Saint-Denis with his presence, the glamour of the occasion luring him from his austere cell. There was no man with such influence in Heaven or on earth. He might damn me as the Daughter of Satan, but I had nowhere else to go.

I requested a private consultation with him.

I went to our meeting as Queen of France, in robes and diadem, ermine and cloth of gold. I spared no effort, and I had my arguments thoroughly marshaled, my campaign well planned. I would flatter, put my case, and hope that the saint could not resist the sin of pride in achieving what the King and Queen of France could not accomplish alone. When I stepped into the little audience chamber where he granted me a few precious moments of his time, I approached him boldly and held his eye, my recent tearful meeting with my sister close in my heart.

Aelith might have achieved her heart's desire, but it had come at a terrible price.

"Help us, Eleanor." She had wept in my arms from grief as she had once wept from happiness in the early days of her love. "I've condemned Raoul and our children to Hell. You've got to help me, Eleanor." Her tear-drenched eyes were raised to mine.

Pope Celestine might have shown compassion to Louis and lifted the Church's ban, but my sister, Aelith, and Vermandois were still excommunicate, their marriage not recognized by the Church. They were living in sin, their children conceived in sin. I could not allow the Pope to plunge them into everlasting fire on a whim. I had to act, since Louis was a man of straw. I would persuade Abbot Bernard to use his influence.

"What do you request, lady?" Abbot Bernard was more emaciated than ever, more skin and bone than saint. "Is it forgiveness for your part in the horrors of Vitry?" he asked bitingly.

"No, my lord Abbot." I would be respectful. I must be respectful! "This is a matter dear to my heart." I choked out the words. "I would ask your help, my lord Abbot." His eyes stared without compassion. "I am in great need."

His voice held no softness. "And so, my daughter?"

I stated my argument, for Aelith and Vermandois, as plainly and forcefully as I could, ending with a plea that surely he could not resist.

"I wish more than anything to bring my sister back into the love and communion of the Church. She weeps for her sins and can find no comfort without the sacraments. Would you condemn her, and her innocent children, to eternal damnation?" I took a breath. "If you would add your voice to those who petition His Holiness to reconsider, my lord Abbot—I am convinced His Holiness would listen to you."

Bernard's fine-grained skin flushed an unhealthy red. "Such subjects are not for discussion by a woman."

"Not even by a woman for the saving of her sister's soul?"

"You should be ashamed to raise such matters."

A bitter taste of defeat rose into my mouth, yet I pressed on. "I would make a pact with you, my lord Abbot." He regarded me in unpromising silence. "If you will speak for me—for my sister—with His Holiness, I will do all in my power to persuade Louis to come to terms with Theobald of Champagne and restore peace between them."

It was the best I could offer.

"One does not haggle with God!" Bernard observed, entirely unmoved. "I'll not mediate. It was *your* advice that your husband acted upon when he invaded Champagne. It was wicked, evil advice, and yet you have no penitence, no contrition. You are responsible for His Majesty's fall from God's grace . . . and your advice came from the Devil. . . ."

I shook my head, fighting against despair. He was not listening to me. "Why should my sister have to suffer when nothing she did was outside the law of man or God? She committed no sin."

The Abbot all but spit the words at me. "You would discuss the fruits of adultery with me? You would excuse the sin committed by Vermandois and your sister?" This was a disaster. "My only advice to you, lady"—he sneered over the respectful address—"go home and stop meddling in affairs of state that are nothing to do with you!"

He turned his back on me and walked from the room, leaving me trembling with righteous anger at his intransigence and my own helplessness.

I was furious with him, but I was equally furious with myself. I had thought I could argue the rights of my case with him, with calm, legal precision. What a miscalculation that had been. Through the night hours I mulled it over.

With dawn came no satisfaction, but a change of plan.

"Go to Queen Adelaide," I instructed Agnes, "and borrow one of her gowns. And a veil." I gave very specific instructions.

Brows raised in curiosity, Adelaide herself came with the selected items. They rose even higher when she saw me clad in them. Meanwhile I requested another interview with the Abbot. And was granted one. Adelaide pursed her lips and wished me well. I thanked her with dry appreciation.

In the same audience chamber, Abbot Bernard waited for me. I saw the tightening of the muscles in his jaw as I walked forward. I saw myself through his eyes: a petitioner in a state of abject penitence.

By God, I discovered a talent for deception that day.

Face cleansed of cosmetics, not one jewel except for a plain silver cross on my bosom, all my habitual sparkle doused under severe black damask, I approached the Abbot. I even wore a despised wimple and full veil, neat as any nun, to hide the red hair Bernard considered to be a mark of the Devil. Adelaide's plain gown was without ornament, no dagged edges, not a hint of fur. No fur slippers, no train, no long sleeves, nothing that I recalled from that notable sermon that could arouse his disfavor. Since Adelaide was shorter than I by a hand span, I had to wear an undershift so that my ankles were hidden from unseemly view.

I found it hard not to laugh at my outrageous appearance. I was the source of the counsel of the Devil, was I? Eve with the apple of deceit? Not so. Here I was as discreet as the Holy Virgin herself. Or more like a widow who wouldn't stand out in a field of autumn rooks.

Even Adelaide had managed a smile.

"Well, my daughter." Dry and rusty, Bernard's aged voice was almost astonished.

I sank to my knees. The seams around the bodice strained. I would make it hard for Abbot Bernard not to listen to me. I would make it impossible. I would play the role of a penitent that even he could not withstand. And so I bent my head and covered my face with my hands, remembering how once in my childish defiance I had vowed never to bow the knee before this man. How immature I had been. What extremities are we driven to by necessity.

There was a little silence. Then: "God bless you, my daughter."

To give him his due, Bernard acted with all Christian charity. I heard the shuffle of his feet as he approached, felt his touch on my opaque veil. How I resented it! But I must humble myself. I bowed my head, my eyes on the hem of his robe.

"I have seen the error of my ways, my lord Abbot. I have prayed through the night."

"Your confession does you credit, my daughter. Have you come to do penance for your outburst of yesterday?"

"I have. I was in the wrong."

"Do you confess your malign influence over Vitry?"

I could not! I could not do it. "My words to my husband were perhaps not wise," I managed.

Bernard allowed it to go unchallenged. "Have you a request of me?"

I had to ask. And not about Aelith, who was suddenly not my priority. However much I shrank from it, I had to beg.

Seven years of marriage and only one dead child.

Even Aelith had borne Vermandois a child in sin, a son.

I cared little for Louis, even less for France. But I did care for Aquitaine. I must give my domains their own heir for the future. I needed a child.

I lifted my face to look at the Abbot and spoke, my voice soft and raw with real grief.

"My lord, I come to ask your aid. There is no one else in France who can make his voice heard in the courts of His Holiness the Pope or beneath the arches of Heaven. In God's name, please help me." Tears flowed down my cheeks, and not all to do with artifice. "I have no one else to turn to."

The tears flowed harder.

"My child! Such emotion does not become you."

"But it does. It is a high matter of state." A catch in my voice, I sniffed delicately. "My life is empty and barren." I added an impassioned tone, as I had practiced, and bowed my head again. "In seven years I have carried only one child, and not to term. Since that tragic loss, almost six years ago now, I have failed to quicken—my woman's courses have continued to flow." I could feel Bernard flinch at so intimate an observation but I held to my plan. "I beg of you, pray for me. The gift of motherhood is all I ask, as our Holy Virgin experienced. Intercede for me, my lord."

My voice broke on the request. I risked a glance. Bernard's face was strained with some severe emotion. Perhaps he would reject me after all, unable to consider relations between man and woman, much less pray for them. I covered my face with my hands and managed a good bout of weeping.

Bernard responded with a hint of panic. "My child. So much distress . . . I cannot deny you." It sounded as if the words were wrenched from him. "I will help you—but there are conditions. There are always conditions. Do you understand?"

"Yes."

"You must promise to seek the things that make for peace. You must not meddle in affairs of the kingdom but guide His Majesty into good relations with the Church. If you will agree to that, I will entreat the merciful Lord to grant you a child."

I sniffed again. "I should tell you, my lord," I whispered, glancing up. "The King will not come to my bed. He does not do his duty by me. I am dutiful to him . . . but he will not. I cannot persuade him."

Bernard's features stiffened; his mouth disappeared into the thinnest of lines.

"That is not a matter for you to discuss with me. . . ."

"How can God grant my prayer, or even yours, my lord, if Louis will not fulfill his role as my husband?"

"This is disrespectful. . . ."

"But true. The Holy Virgin conceived knowing no man, but I cannot! His Majesty needs an heir. I think he will never achieve it. And that is not good for the kingdom. How can I not meddle in this, when it is within my female power to put it right? If only Louis will consent to honor his vows before God . . ." It was the strongest argument I could wield. He *must* listen to me. Bernard was silent for so long I feared I had lost. "I thought I had wed a king," I murmured, "and found I had married a monk."

Bernard sighed. Good or bad?

"Stand up, my daughter."

I did. My eyes remained on the begrimed hem of his robe.

"I will take the burden onto my own shoulders," he stated somberly, "as long as you agree to remain obedient and humble, as is the role of womenkind in God's eyes. Will you agree to that?"

How hard it was. I would be more and more a cipher, a voiceless shadow. "I will agree to that. If you will also agree to intercede for my beloved sister."

"You drive a hard bargain, lady."

"And in return, my final foray into high politics," I replied, hiding my bitterness, "I will persuade the King to make terms with the Count of Champagne."

For a long moment we looked at each other, saint and sinner.

"I will beg the ear of His Holiness over the excommunication," Bernard agreed.

I took his offered hand, kissed his ring, controlling my creeping flesh at the touch of the scrawny fingers.

"Are we in agreement, my lord?"

There was no warmth in his face, but there was an appreciation. "You are a clever woman. I think it was Aquitaine's loss that you were not born a man."

"Thank you, my lord." I dabbed at my cheeks with the edge of my sleeve. It was the nearest I would ever come to a compliment from him. I decided we understood each other very well at the end.

"I will pray for you, Eleanor," Abbot Bernard said. "And I will speak with His Majesty."

"I am grateful."

Demurely, meekly, I left.

Bernard was as good as his word. As was I. That same day, the Abbot arranged a meeting between the two protagonists and I did my part to encourage Louis to attend and adopt a spirit of compromise. Peace was made, a chilly one but nevertheless a peace, between Louis and Theobald of Champagne, Louis returning all the territory he had seized. Louis appeared content with the promise of heavenly glory in return for his magnanimity.

What passed between Bernard and Louis over more intimate matters was outside my knowledge, but Bernard's prayers reached the ear of God. Louis came to my bed, presenting himself as if he had not been absent from it for more weeks than I could count. It resulted in an equally chilly—and brief—affair as his accommodation with Count Theobald, but Louis, under orders from on high, maintained an erection long enough to achieve the object of both our desires in less time than it took to say a Pater Noster.

Some weeks later, returned to Paris, I could break the good news. Louis was full of joy, and spent the night prostrated in my chamber, arms spread before my prie-dieu in grateful thanks.

"You have given me a child, an heir." He kissed both my cheeks.

"Thank God!" I replied, heartfelt, and prayed that it would be so.

The child grew within me to full term, as the court prepared to celebrate and rejoice. It was a strong and healthy baby, arriving without much fuss and a level of pain that was not beyond my tolerance—but a girl. I named her Marie in honor of the Queen of Heaven.

Louis kissed her forehead tenderly, astonished, so it seemed to me, that this was his child, rather than disappointed that I had not managed to produce the much-desired son. Clasping at the air with tiny hands, she was a pretty, undemanding child, very much Louis's daughter, her hair fair like his, her eyes light and intensely blue. I saw nothing of me in her as I handed her over to her wet nurse.

I regretted my lack of emotion. All I felt was an intense weariness and that terrible weight of failure.

One day, unless I carried a son, Marie would rule Aquitaine. Never France. The Salic Law made certain that no woman ever wore the crown of France in her own right, but my daughter would be Duchess of Aquitaine and much sought after as a bride, as I had been.

"You will love Aquitaine, as I do," I informed my child when I visited her. She lay in her crib, snatching at the play of sunlight on my jewels as I stroked her hair. "One day you will be a beautiful duchess." Her grasp on my fingers was surprisingly firm. Perhaps she was more like me than I had thought. "I pray that the man who wins you for his bride will be worthy of you, will bring you happiness." Had my own mother, of whom I had no true memory, wished this for me? I was astonished at the tears that stung my eyelids, and blinked them away.

As for Louis, he still needed a son as much as he ever had, yet showed no inclination to repeat Bernard's instructions to achieve it. He had mastered the fine art of evasion.

Sweet Virgin!

I rose from my empty bed and stripped off my shift to stand naked in the hard early-morning light. My hands told me what my looking glass was too small to reflect. My flesh was firm, my waist once again restored, my belly flat with barely a trace of silvered lines. My breasts were fuller—no bad thing, I decided. I was still youthful, still as beautiful as the April Queen. Still the object of desire to a man. My unbound hair fell like silk over shoulders and breast, enough to entice any man with red blood in his veins. I was as beautiful as I had ever been.

But as I shrugged into a chamber robe, I had finally to accept. Perpetual failure destroys all hope. Louis would remain obdurate in his need to seek salvation and I would always come a poor second. I would pray no more for his attentions. Loyalty and respect could be throttled to death for want of sustenance. Once I would have stalked him, determined to allow him no peace until he satisfied me. I stalked him no more. In my heart my marriage to Louis was at an end.

I received a letter from Aelith.

My dearest sister,

All my thanks are yours. How can I express my gratitude? Raoul and I have received the blessing of the Pope. We are restored to the Church. Our marriage is legal. I am so very happy. . . .

I could not read of such happiness and fulfillment, all that I lacked. I threw the parchment into the fire.

Chapter Nine

I went to Poitiers. In the autumn of 1145 when the days were still long enough and mellow with the lingering heat of the summer, the warmth of the south, of my own lands, beckoned. I left Marie with her nurses and traveled alone, with Louis's blessing. I doubt he noticed my absence. I set my course for Poitou, conscious of nothing but the years passing. I was twenty-three years old and had abandoned any hope of so basic and thrilling an emotion as lust. How would I recognize it? How could I know the blast of desire when I had never experienced it? I would go to my grave without my body being stirred by a man. *Take a lover*, Agnes still advised, but I would not. Love, I decided, was all a deceit, a crafty trick of the troubadours to warm a woman's heart and loins with longing for the unattainable, and so win valuable patronage for themselves.

"Love does not exist," bleakly I informed Aelith, who met with me on my journey and continued with me to Poitiers. "Physical desire is not worthy of a woman of intellect."

She was a grown woman now, confident, fine-drawn with the exigencies of the past months but gleaming with contentment. Dismounting in the road, I hugged her, joyful at being reunited with her. I think my emotions were decidedly unsteady, although that may have been a poor excuse for what I did—the choice I made that was far from good sense.

"Ridiculous!" Aelith laughed.

"How so?" I remounted. My emptiness was not the subject for laughter.

"Did I give up everything, even my immortal soul, for a warm friendship with Raoul?" The curl of her lip said it all.

"I don't deny the strength of your feeling," I admitted grudgingly.

"Yes, you do. Because *you've* no experience of it does not mean it doesn't exist. If you had even the slightest affection for Louis—which you haven't, and nor would any woman in your position—you would not say anything quite so stupid!"

Agnes, a willing eavesdropper, smirked. "I've said the same, lady."

Rattled, not altogether pleased, I touched my heel to my mare, encouraging her into a canter with Aelith following, to draw us out of earshot of interested listeners and smart retainers.

"I am not stupid," I said through my teeth.

"No. But you've never been in love, have you?"

I hunched my shoulders. "How will I know it?"

"You will. When a man touches you and your body responds. When even the caress of his eyes stirs fire in your blood. And I'll say this, Eleanor—anyone would think you were jealous of my good fortune."

Well, I was.

"Eleanor . . ."

I looked across at her to see the concern in her face and forced a smile. It was wrong of me to burden Aelith with my ill humor. I begged forgiveness, we were at one once more, but my heart was as heavy in my chest as a lump of overkneaded dough, my mood as sour as an Aquitaine lemon.

"Welcome, lady." My steward relieved me of my mantle as he escorted me to my rooms in the Maubergeonne Tower. "We have missed you here in Poitiers. Do you stay long with us? I will make your chambers ready to your requirements."

"I'm not certain. . . ." I unwound the veil that had kept the dust from my hair. I was surprisingly undecided, lacking any need or motivation other than to get out of Paris. I supposed I would travel on south, sounding out the loyalty of my barons, simply making my presence known, but Poitiers was so welcoming and familiar. The tower closed around me like a soft glove and I sighed with pleasure.

"The Seneschal is here in residence, lady."

"Oh?" Now in my private chambers, I dropped the veil, handed my gloves to Agnes.

"He has been here for some days, to hold a court of justice." The steward placed the mantle over a coffer before moving to open the shutters to let sunlight into the unused rooms. "There has been some noise of rebellion in the Limousin. My lord has stamped on it most effectively, I understand."

"Has he? That's good." Louis had appointed a seneschal to rule in my name—and his—in our absence, a sensible decision all in all, yet I felt a quick brush of irritation that I should not have the palace to myself and Aelith, but must play the role of hostess to the man. I did not want to converse and dispense hospitality. Rather I desired to brood alone.

The steward waited, bright eyed, accommodating. "Do you wish to speak with Count Geoffrey, lady, when he rides in? He'll be anxious to give his report."

Count Geoffrey, Lord of Anjou. I knew his name well enough. I had never met him, had no particular desire to do so. He had a reputation for military prowess but to my mind was little more than a robber baron, much like Louis's ancestors, descended from a long line of enterprising thieves, striving to make his mark in Europe by snapping up states that were not well protected. A pretentious upstart, so it was said, a dangerous man with an eye to every opportunity to consolidate his power.

I frowned. *Normandy* sprang to my mind, one of those opportunities snatched up by the Count. When Louis was too busy dealing with Theobald of Champagne to watch his back, this Geoffrey had marched his troops into Normandy and overrun it. Since then, the Count of Anjou and Louis had come to terms and Louis had confirmed his vassal status as Duke of Normandy, but I had seen no reason to encourage the man by making him Seneschal of Poitou as well, and had said as much to Louis—who ignored me and did as he pleased.

No, I did not have much of an opinion of Geoffrey of Anjou.

"Ask the Count to come," I requested as I washed my hands in a bowl of cool water, considering whether I really needed to see him, irritated that I must. The Seneschal was too important to law and order and the smooth running of Poitou to be cast off lightly. "Bring wine, if you will. And food."

Less than an hour later, a firm thump of boots on the stair heralded my seneschal. An oblique shadow on the curve, then a glint of metal and jewels as a figure moved through a sunbeam angling through a window, and came to stand in the center of the room.

I turned to face him.

God's Blood!

He was the most beautiful man I had ever seen. Before I could string two thoughts together, desire ripped through me—oh, yes, I recognized this longing, this need, sharp as a blade, for what it was. Here was no product of a dream to leave me dry mouthed and unfulfilled on waking, no romantic but nebulous image to sigh over from a troubadour's song. Here was a man: he lived and breathed and stood here in my solar. When he smiled at me, and bowed with such fluid grace, my heart leaped to thud against my ribs. In that moment I forgot Louis. I forgot my failure to entice, my loneliness and the restless emptiness of my life. I forgot everything but the starvation in my body, in my soul, everything but my wish to touch this man and for him to touch me. He filled me to the brim just by being there and looking at me as if I were the woman he coveted above all others.

Well! I hid every one of those thoughts, of course. I forced myself to breathe evenly and hold his gaze.

Lord, but Count Geoffrey was a bold man. He looked at me not as if I were his sovereign lady, but as if he would strip the silk from my body and ravish me on the floor. And by the Virgin, I wished for it too. There he stood, suffusing my solar with as much brilliance as the sun itself. Geoffrey *le Bel*. The fair, the handsome. At his heels an equally handsome wolfhound. It was as if all the air had fled from the chamber, and I had to struggle to breathe at all.

Had I lost my wits?

It was his presence that forced itself on me first. He was tall, taller than I, with the broad shoulders and lean athletic build of a trained soldier. He strode across the solar with such elegant ease, muscles fluid and shown to advantage in hose and knee-length boots of soft leather. And what a pleasure it was to see a man in a tunic of wool and silk, deep blue, trimmed and braided, showily impressive. Jewels glowed on his breast, on his fingers, clipped to the brim of his felt cap. Over all was cast a cloak of fine wool against the autumn chill, now flung back over one shoulder for ease of movement.

His face drew my attention.

Oh, he was good to look at. I had not known he was so striking a man despite his common sobriquet. Pleasingly clean shaven, he drew my lingering gaze to his mouth. Firm, with perhaps a hint of temper in its straight lines. And then a masterful nose and a chin that did nothing to hide the strength of his will. Confidence oozed from him as curds from a muslin bag.

Count Geoffrey halted, stripped off his cap with the telltale sprig of broom flowers clipped in the jewel—*planta genista*, from which his name Plantagenet derived—and bowed in a flamboyant manner. His hair was deep and glowing russet, trimmed short and mussed into disarray around his face, his complexion light, as so often matched such coloring.

I grabbed for composure, calling on the high blood of Aquitaine.

"Lady of Poitou." His voice was soft and deep.

"Plantagenet!" I lifted my chin at the yellow flowers, now drooping.

"As you say." His stern mouth softened in a smile. "You are right welcome."

"My thanks, Lord Geoffrey."

Suddenly incongruously, ridiculously shy before this man, I could think of nothing more to say. "A fine animal," I managed as the hound sank to the floor with a sigh, chin on paws.

"She is. And not yet grown to her full strength."

The Count's eyes were a clear gray with no subservience in them. His smile, deepening, was warmly intimate.

"We did not expect you, lady. We should have been prepared to welcome you."

"It was a sudden decision on my part."

I found myself holding out my hand. Count Geoffrey took it and raised it to his mouth, brushing my fingers with his lips, his eyes never leaving mine. His touch rippled over my skin, and I allowed my hand to rest there, enclosed by his long, elegant fingers. Until I pulled my hand away. How could I be so obtuse? So lacking in dignity as to stare at him as if I had never seen anything quite so desirable? Even more horrified, as I felt the flush of hot blood in my cheeks, it came into my mind that this arrogant man sensed my confusion when the quirk of his mouth gained a touch of malice.

"So your royal monk has allowed you to escape the confines of the Île de la Cité and travel alone."

How insolent he was, and yet I felt no animosity toward him. What impressed me far more was that he had fallen easily into fluent court Latin rather than his own Angevin French, and I had thought him no more than an ill-lettered lout, albeit a titled one. The Count of Anjou had received an education at someone's hands.

"I am Countess here," I remarked mildly, at odds with my galloping heartbeat, gesturing to Agnes to leave. It seemed that this was a day for preserving my privacy. "I travel when I wish."

The Count inclined his head. "I meant no disrespect, lady."

"And is your wife not here with you?" I could retaliate and punish him for his presumption. I knew full well she wasn't, and was not surprised when the Count's brow darkened into quick temper.

Everyone knew of the warlike Angevin marriage.

Matilda, daughter and only surviving child of King Henry the First of England, and thus by rights Queen of that country, was in England. I knew she would spend no more time than she had to with the husband foisted on her by her father against her will. Nor would the Count choose to spend his time with his undoubtedly important wife. She was the Count's greatest achievement so far in his climb to greatness, but it had not made for a comfortable coupling. Matilda, eleven years older than he and by repute a shrew of a woman, was fixed on claiming the throne of England, if only she could persuade the barons of that country that a woman could wear the crown as effectively as a man. I wished her well but could see little hope for her. The English barons were reluctant to take on a woman and would never accept an Angevin as their king, no matter how strong the claim of his wife. Instead they would rather give their oath of allegiance to Matilda's male cousin Stephen. His claim might be open to question but at least he was a man—and not an Angevin. So Stephen ruled and Matilda strove to snatch the crown from him.

"Does the Lady Matilda have no love for Poitou?" I asked sweetly.

Geoffrey's smile replaced the hint of the scowl, as if he saw my intent, but there was the edge of roughness in his reply. "She has other interests and is not here." Abruptly he changed direction. "Do you intend to stay long? There's good hunting to the north that I can recommend. Deer and boar are plentiful." His eyes gleamed with the thrill of the hunt. "And the wildfowl on the marshes are abundant, if you have an interest in hawking. The weather is set fair. . . ." Somehow he had taken possession of my hand again and led me to a low stool. "Will you stay, lady?"

I was conscious of nothing but his hand around mine, his fingers rough against my skin with calluses of sword and rein. And when I raised my eyes to his . . . they were smiling, as if they could read every thought in my head.

Take care, Eleanor! The warning whispered through my mind.

"Yes, I will stay," I heard myself say. Such an easy decision to make.

A noise at the door took our attention, followed by a shadow such as the Count had made, barred by the sun, and a scuffle of feet.

A young man emerged at the top of the stair, to stand momentarily below the door arch. A young man just escaping from the uncoordinated clumsiness of childhood, in transition from youth to man. Not uncertain or hesitant, he was nevertheless carefully watchful. I did not think he was a page. His clothes were too good, even though scuffed and showing signs of wear, and his demeanor held a touch of incongruous youthful arrogance immediately reminiscent of the Angevin before me.

Count Geoffrey barked a laugh. "Henry! You shouldn't be here. . . . But since you are . . ." He swung back to me, his face bright with pride. "My eldest son and heir, Henry, who will one day step into my shoes as Count of Anjou . . ."

I smiled a welcome but the youth did not smile back. Rather his forehead creased in a frown and his gaze darted around the room, taking in every detail.

"Come." I beckoned, and stood to encourage him.

Henry Plantagenet needed no encouragement from me. Loping across the room, he bowed with more energy than grace, then knelt at my feet, head bent. He had been well schooled. And how like his father—the same gilded russet hair, the same cool gray eyes, the same potent agility and energy. Two handsome, virile men. Henry might be young but he was already growing into his strength. Shorter than his father he might be, more stocky in build, but the Plantagenet print was strong on his features, in his hair.

"Stand up, Henry," I invited.

He did, but shuffled from foot to foot as if he could barely contain the energy that flowed through him. The hands that grasped his cap were large and capable, his appraisal direct and surprisingly mature. I felt its force with a frisson of amusement.

"You should make your apology for disturbing the lady," the Count growled, but indulgently.

"Forgive me, lady." Henry's eyes lifted to his father, then back to me. "I wished to see the Queen of France for myself."

His voice was his father's too. And his Latin polished.

"And now you have seen her." The Count cuffed his son affectionately on the shoulder. "So don't interrupt."

As the Count and I talked mundane matters of law and business in Poitou, I watched the Angevin heir out of the corner of my eye, my amusement growing. Constantly on the move, he strode to the window to inspect new arrivals in the courtyard below. He slouched in a chair to turn the pages of a book, lingering here and there, only to replace it and leap to his feet. His eye alighted on everything and anything of interest or novelty, and he picked it up, inspecting it, rearranging chess pieces on the board, inspecting his appearance in a looking glass but without much interest. An ivory-and-enameled casket brought by my grandfather from Outremer from his crusading days proved too much for him. With the point of his knife Henry dismantled the cunning hinges and clasp, then put them back together again.

He had an amazing, perpetual need to investigate and explore.

But when he descended on my popinjay, to ruffle its feathers, repeating his own name so that the bird might copy—it only squawked—the Count had had enough.

"Go away, Henry."

"Can I take the bird with me?"

"No!"

I laughed at the disappointment on his face. "Yes. Take it. But don't put it in a bad mood."

"I'll teach it to say Eleanor!"

With a blinding smile and a neat little bow, Henry turned on his heel and loped across the room, taking popinjay and wolfhound with him, only to stop by the stair and look back, one hand pulling at the animal's ears.

"They say she is the most beautiful woman in Europe. And she is."

Then he ran down the staircase, halting only to flatten himself against the wall as the steward appeared with the wine and a maidservant followed carrying a tray.

Count Geoffrey scowled after his son, then laughed. "Sometimes there's no restraining him. When he's not asleep he's on the move." His glance at me was sharp. "I'll add my own regrets for his manners, lady."

"I think you are proud of him."

"Of course. He is my son. And, before God, he speaks the truth."

Bright color rose in my cheeks again. The Count stepped aside for the steward to pour the wine, waiting in silence until it was done and we were alone again. Even so I was aware of his every move as he prowled restlessly toward the window, kicking a log more firmly into the fireplace. His son Henry was not the only one with an excess of energy. Finally he raised his cup in a silent toast to me. He didn't need to speak. It seemed I could read him as well as he could read me. The heat flared even hotter in my face.

"You'll need to settle in." The Count put down his cup. "I've given orders for hot water to be brought. Will you eat with me when you are rested? We will celebrate your return. Will that please you, lady?"

"Yes." Nothing would have kept me from it.

When he had left me, while the beat of my blood returned to its normal steady rhythm, I unfastened the clasp of the little casket, lifted its hinged lid. It worked perfectly. And then I laughed. On the chessboard, Henry Plantagenet had left the pieces at checkmate. The white queen was under threat from an opposing knight.

As the Angevin had promised, a banquet was prepared in the magnificent Great Hall. Given the short time to prepare it, it was admirable. Here were the banquets of my youth when my grandfather, Duke William, allowed his passions to run free. Color and music and laughter. Jokes and ribald comments married to courtly admiration. Succulent dishes stirred by the warm wines of the south. Dancing and singing. The softening dusk after a warm day with scents of lavender and rosemary. Everything to assuage the senses and welcome me home.

It should have been a delight. And so it was, yet I had to confess that I cared nothing for it except as counterpoint to the rioting in my blood, the churn of desire in my belly that destroyed my appetite. The rich sauces, the plangent song, even the caress of my silk skirts against my body fed my emotions so that I could barely contain them.

But I did. I was Countess of Poitou, Queen of France, and would behave as such. Did the Queen of France fall at the feet of the first handsome man who smiled at her and showed his hunger in his eyes, the caress of it in his voice? She did not. *Eleanor* might imagine the whisper of his breath over her skin. *Eleanor* might burn with a craving—and before God, she did so! The Queen set her teeth and kept her dignity.

But when we sat side by side at the High Table on the dais, looking over my vassals, who gave themselves enthusiastically to the food and wine, *Eleanor* had a tendency to replace *the Queen*. My barons might as well not have been there when Geoffrey's arm brushed mine as he offered me the grace cup.

What did we talk of? I had no idea. Art and literature, a little— he proved to be exceptionally well-read. His plans for Anjou. I think he told me about the skills of Alexander the Great as a battle tactician. He admired the achievements of my father and grandfather on the battle- field. Oh, he knew the way to my heart. He refrained from reminding me of how ineffectual a leader my husband was. He made no mention of the disasters of Toulouse and Champagne. *Vitry-le-Brulé,* as it had been sardonically renamed, did not hang in the air between us.

Nor did Louis. We did not speak of Louis at all. Nor, I recall, did Matilda encroach. We spoke nothing of our lives outside this moment in time.

So what was it that touched my heart more than all the rest? Count Geoffrey addressed me as an equal, not as a foolish woman who knew nothing but stitching and good works for the poor, who had no right to consider matters of government to be within her grasp. He asked my opinion on the state of Europe, on the power of the great eastern empire centered in Constantinople, showed interest in my views on the troubled, divided Papacy. He conversed with me, listened to me, weighed my comments. How long since any man had done that? Not since the death of my father almost a decade ago, and then I had been too young to give a balanced opinion.

Had not saintly Bernard damned me for such female impertinence in having an opinion?

The Angevin listened to my replies, his eyes intent on mine, and invited more. Did I consider Anjou to be an enemy of France? A threat to Aquitaine?

And I was entranced, so much so that I eventually clenched my hands into fists, afraid that I would let down my guard, allowing words and opinions to spill out as from a child who was encouraged by unex- pected attention. Such openness would be unwise. I struggled to keep my replies cool and measured. And I think I failed.

Geoffrey Plantagenet cast a spell on me that night. Far from the
ill-mannered lout I had anticipated, he saw to the comfort of those at
the feast, of Aelith, with such graciousness. He drew his son into a discussion of where we might hunt on the following day. Yet all the time
I felt the power of his concentration on me. He saw to it that I was fed
the choicest meats, that my cup was refilled.

Louis would not have noticed.

When Geoffrey offered me a platter of grapes from the south, his
fingers grazed my wrist. He did not look at me but I knew he wanted
me. I *knew*. . . .

"Well, now!" Aelith leaned close.

"Well, what?"

"Beware the Count of Anjou." Her eyes were bright and fixed on
the Seneschal as he conversed with the steward over some matter of
the provision of dishes. "He's hunting."

"I don't take your meaning."

"Oh, yes, you do. And it's not deer. *You* are the quarry."

"Then he will be disappointed."

"Make sure *you* are not the one to be disappointed, sister mine!" I
raised my brows but she grinned. "Shall I give you advice?"

"Certainly not."

"I'll give it forsooth. Take him!"

"As you took Raoul? Look at the mess that caused." And instantly
I regretted the words as Aelith flushed from chin to hairline. "Forgive
me." I squeezed her hand. "That was unpardonable. But I am not free
to follow my desires."

"So you admit to liking him?"

"How could I not? Liking is one thing. I admit to nothing else. Nor
will I act on some crude emotion that will only bring me pain!"

But then he danced with me. At Count Geoffrey's instruction, the
musicians struck up a simple round dance. He stood, offered his hand.

How could I refuse? Louis never danced with me.

We joined the other dancers and stepped the undemanding,
meandering measure. I knew the steps and the music—round dances
needed no sophistication, merely an ability not to fall over one's own

feet—and so could give my attention elsewhere. Not least to the elegant lifting of my long skirts and sleeves. And of course to the man who led me, turned me. And I reveled in it, this hot excitement of music and laughter. It was like the sweetness of honey in my blood. The heavy brush of his tunic against my thighs, the male scent of him, the heat of his body as we came close, all added to one surge of irrepressible delight. My breathlessness had nothing to do with the dance; nor did the flush in my cheeks when the music ended.

"My thanks, lady." He bowed low and touched his mouth to my fingers.

The heat prickled along my spine to center in my loins. "It was my pleasure," I replied with cool grace.

We returned to our seats. Count Geoffrey lifted his cup.

"A toast, lady. To our friendship."

"To our friendship."

I raised my cup to return the toast, and drank as I ignored the discreet nudge of Aelith's elbow.

He wanted more than friendship. So did I.

As we supped, one of my minstrels sang of the pain and pleasure of unrequited love.

When I see the lark moving its wings in joy against the light,
Until at last it forgets and lets itself fall,
By reason of the sweetness that fills its heart,
Oh, such envy comes to me of those whose happiness I see,
That I marvel that my heart does not melt away
At once with desire!

Anticipation shivered over me despite the heat of the room. Desire melted in my bones. Oh, yes. I would have that happiness for myself.

The next day we hunted, a group of us: Aelith, Count Geoffrey's knights and gentlemen, a crowd of hunt servants, on a bright day with racing clouds and a lively wind, the perfect day for flying the hawks. I had ordered up two of the descendants of my original white gerfalcons—perfect for bringing down cranes and herons—to be carried by our huntsmen. How long was it since I had flown them? I had forgotten how beautiful they were, how supremely fitted for flight and killing, as they stretched their wings and rattled their jesses. How magnificently elegant they were. Out of courtesy I offered one to Count Geoffrey.

"They match their owner in elegance," Geoffrey commented, but instead of accepting my offer, he summoned one of his own huntsmen with a bird tethered to a wooden perch.

"Oh . . . !"

It was difficult to find words. The golden eagle was indeed majestic, casting my gerfalcons into the shade. Golden eyed, it panted through its open beak, its talons flexing as if it could already sense its prey.

"I thought eagles were the preserve of emperors," I remarked, impressed but a little astonished at his presumption.

"They are. But what a waste." Geoffrey had a gleam in his eye as he smoothed his gloved hand over the fine feathers. His self-aggrandizement was a remarkable thing. "Only two emperors to monopolize so magnificent a bird. I think we can be a little flexible here. Why should I not fly an eagle in my own lands, where I am more an emperor than any other man?" He took the bird onto his wrist.

"I would fly the gerfalcon, lady." And there was Henry on a lively bay at my side, his voice creaking with adolescence, his eyes fixed not on the eagle but on my beautiful bird. His stare was no less fierce than that of the gerfalcon. Taking one of the birds for myself, I signaled to the huntsman to transfer the second bird to the boy. It settled on his wrist, talons tightening.

I gasped. "Your wrist!" I gestured to the huntsman a second time. "A glove, if you please."

"I don't wear a glove," Henry replied, his whole attention on the white raptor, stroking his fingers over her magnificent plumage.

"But she will mark you. Does it not hurt?"

A careless shrug was Henry's only physical response. "I'm used to it."

These two Plantagenets, father and son! Such confidence. Again

I was amused. Yesterday Henry had admired my beauty. Today I had paled beside the silver plumage of my hunting bird.

"My stubborn son, with a mind of his own." Geoffrey dropped his reins to clout him with his free hand. "I'm not so sanguine."

We flew the birds at rabbits and a heron that we flushed from the riverbank, then loosed the hounds to hunt hares set up in the meadow. The Angevins pursued them with enormous energy, riding as if born to the saddle, leaving the rest of us to follow in our own time.

I watched them with narrowed eyes.

"See, he is not hunting me at all," I remarked to Aelith, not altogether pleased. Geoffrey might have lit an outrageous need in me, but for the moment he was as much engaged with the hunt as was his son.

"Not at the moment, he isn't." She chuckled.

"I'll soon change that. . . ."

"Do you think so?"

"I know so. Since when is Anjou a match for Aquitaine?"

Suddenly, opportunely, a gamecock lifted from the grass almost beside my mare, taking wing with a harsh cackle and a clap of primary feathers. My mount shied, head tossing, eyes rolling. Then she was away and running. With a sharp cry I hung on, but she grasped her bit and pulled out of my control across the open pasture. I clung with knees and hands as I heard the pounding of other hooves.

"Hold on!"

I knew who it was, having seen him detach himself from the group who pursued the hare and spur his horse at a fast-approaching angle toward me. Now he bore down on me from the right, as my mare showed no signs of slackening her headlong flight, drawing level, reaching for the bridle just above the bit. As he drew his own stallion to a slower gait, he brought the mare close and under control, sliding an arm around me for support.

For a moment he looked down at me. For that moment his mouth was a breath away from mine. My eyes were wide on his and I could not look away. My fingers curled within the leather of his hunting jacket.

Lord, I wanted him. But common sense slammed back into me

with the force of a buffet from a shield. I slid my hands up to push firmly against his chest until he released me.

"Thank you, my lord." I brushed my hand over my sleeves as if to remove a layer of dust. "The bird startled her and I was careless."

"No harm done." He restored the bridle to my hands. "It would not do for the lady of Poitou to come to harm when under the Seneschal's care."

My heart thudded anew.

As we returned, stepping placidly toward the waiting party, Aelith coming toward us with a sly look in her eye, I slid the brooch with its sharp point back into the shelter of my glove. Poor mare. She did not deserve to be used so, but I was not in my right mind.

"I have never known a horse to bolt with you before," Aelith observed, wide-eyed.

"Nor I," I observed without hesitation. "There's a first time for everything."

The Angevin came to my solar to ask after me. Perversely I surrounded myself with my women and kept Aelith at my side.

"Are you recovered, lady?"

I remained seated in my high-backed chair, my feet on a footstool, my hair loose and only lightly veiled.

"I am well."

"You could have been injured, lady."

"You have little confidence in my skill in the saddle, my lord. I have ridden since I was a child."

"Your talent is clear for all to see. The fault must be with the mare—a mannerless beast." For the length of a breath I thought his glance held an unsettling skepticism, as if he saw my guilt, but then it passed—or he was better than I had thought at dissimulation. "I'll see you better provided for next time. Will you hunt with me again, lady?"

"If you wish it."

"The hunt is everything to me."

"So I see. Is the chase better than the final victory?"

"It depends on the quarry, lady. The end can be sweet indeed."

His face was stern, his meaning clear. And I at fault. Had I not led him into the conversation? I nearly dismissed my women. Nearly . . . But I did not. I was not so lost to discretion or awareness of the dangers. I needed to think.

But it almost destroyed me to dismiss him. The curve of his mouth as he bowed and went out held more than a hint of complicity. It would have been the height of good sense for me to leave Poitiers immediately and continue south. If I stayed—what would I do if he pursued the Aquitaine hare in earnest? Would I give in or would I resist?

Resist. Of course I would.

"I presume you have planned a campaign against this man?" Aelith asked quizzically.

"Of course. I am wooing Louis's seneschal to keep him loyal."

Aelith snorted.

Every day that I remained in Poitiers I woke to feel vibrant life race through my blood. Every night I detested my empty bed. The Count of Anjou kept close attendance and continued to catch me by surprise when one evening he took the lute from the minstrel, ran his thumb across the strings, and to a ripple of comment began to sing. He had a fine voice. Obviously the people of Poitiers had heard him sing before. It was a song I knew well.

Since, love, our minds are one, what of our doing?
Set now your arms on mine, joyous our wooing.
O Flower of all the world,
Love we in earnest!
Honey is sweet to sip out of the comb.
What mean I? That will I show, little one.
Not words . . . but deeds shall be Love's best explaining.

Finishing with a flourish and a self-deprecating grin, the Count handed the lute back to the minstrel while I, dry mouthed, joined in the applause. Oh, he was clever. Clever enough not to be too obvious.

Both subtle and gifted, he had delivered the sentiments of the song as much to my women and to Aelith as he did to me, but I knew to whom his intentions were directed. I knew!

I shivered and turned away from his challenging stare.

"Do you sing?" I asked Henry, to hide my blushes.

"No, lady." The croak in his voice was harsher than a raven's. As ever, his clever fingers were busy, investigating an engraved and pierced incense burner. He drew in his breath as he scorched his finger ends.

"Have you no liking for music?" I asked.

"I like it well enough, but I've no voice for it. I prefer to hunt and fight."

"He's young." Geoffrey laughed as he retook his seat. "He'll learn the way to a woman's heart, and that to be in her bed can be as satisfying as winning a battle."

"Have you found it so?" I was flirting. Damnably flirting.

"I have, lady. And I will again."

I expected him that night. I knew he would come, and had dismissed my women, claiming restlessness that would keep them awake. Aelith was the last to go.

"What?" I demanded sharply.

"Nothing—but . . ."

I was ill tempered with nerves. "You told me to take him. He wants me. Why should I not have him? I've taken no vow of chastity. If I leave it to Louis I'll never have a man in my bed again. . . ."

"Eleanor . . . !"

I covered my mouth with my hands. I had never admitted it—other than in my confessional to Bernard. Not even to my sister. The shame was too heavy.

"Does he not sleep with you?" she whispered, aghast.

I told her at last and hid none of my humiliation.

"Then if I were you," Aelith advised, at her pragmatic best, "I'd welcome the Angevin to my bed without a second thought. You want him."

"Yes." I wet my dry lips with my tongue. "Yes, I do."

"Then take him. Enjoy it," she whispered with a quick embrace. "You deserve more than a cold bed and a celibate husband. But don't fall for a child."

Wise advice. "Send Agnes to me, will you?" I asked as she left me.

We made preparations, Agnes's knowledge being vast and specific. "I'll not guarantee it, lady, but use it if you're set on this path."

She provided for me a plug of wool impregnated with sticky cedar gum, an old Roman remedy that was, she said, better than nothing.

Geoffrey Plantagenet did not come.

When I rose the next morning, tired and fretful, in no good humor, it was to learn that he had ridden out early, leaving no message for me, giving no reason for his absence. His son was gone too, so there was no chance of an interrogation, even if I would so demean myself. The Count of Anjou was away all day. Nor did he return to sup in the hall.

Was he not my seneschal? Did he not owe me an explanation?

Between anger and a strange relief, I forced down enough mouthfuls of roast meats so as not to draw attention. I could not bear the minstrels to sing but ordered up a coarser entertainment from a troupe of acrobats. A mistake. Even the lithe and sinuous jongleurs made me think of the Angevin. I retired early, dismissing my women, refusing Aelith's compassion. I did not want compassion.

I closed my door on a calm solitude I did not want.

And there he was. Smooth, charming, subtle. But now I knew him for what he was. A clenched fist in a gauntlet of the softest kid. His self-interest might be masked but it was there right enough beneath the damask tunic.

His bow was perfection. "I am vain enough to hope that you missed me, lady."

His absence had been quite deliberate. A cunning ploy, to play ducks and drakes with my emotions. I would not have it! We would play no longer. This seduction would be on my terms, not his. I would call the tune and he would dance to it. I walked toward the window that had yet to be shuttered against the night sky and looked out as if the stars filled my interest.

"Do we have business to discuss? Were you absent on my behalf?" I waited. "Well?"

"I sense your displeasure, lady." He answered evasively. "If that is so, I ask your pardon."

"It matters not to me where you spend your time, sir. As long as you fulfill your role of Seneschal, I have no call on your presence."

"I see I am in disgrace."

I heard his footstep, sensed his approach. He was standing behind me.

"Send me away if you wish it, lady."

I was playing with fire here and knew it, but I was so lonely, with such an urgency in my heart to know the feel of a man's body on mine. Not brief or perfunctory, not reluctantly. I wanted a lover who craved me beyond his own self-control.

"You deserve that I should dismiss you." I was cold.

"And why is that?"

"You neglect me. You absented yourself all day without my permission." So much for good intentions. I flinched at the admission I had not intended to make, but I kept my back turned against him.

"You think I left you willingly?" He managed to infuse his reply with a slide of regret.

"Did you not?"

"As your seneschal it is my duty to keep peace in your lands."

"And was your journey urgent?"

"Who's to say? I would not risk your safety."

"You have an answer for everything, have you not, Geoffrey." I used his name, deliberately.

"Not everything, Eleanor." It shivered through me. His breath was warm on my neck. And there, following it, the brush of his fingertips. "Send me away if that is your wish. But do it now. Before it is too late."

Oh, I knew it had all been contrived and he was a polished schemer. I also knew when I was beaten, and raised my hand to press his against my shoulder so that his palm was warm against my exposed flesh.

"Well?" Now his lips were against my throat.

"I don't want you to go." Had it not been inevitable from the beginning?

"Eleanor . . ."

Slowly he turned me around and, bending his head, placed his lips on mine. His touch was light, his clasp on my shoulders insubstantial, as if allowing me the choice to step away.

I did not.

Geoffrey's arms banded around me, his mouth hardened against mine, and I sank into the embrace. Louis's kisses had given me no warning of this. This was a long, dark slide of tongue and teeth, of ruthless possession, into a heat of blatant need in my belly and my loins. From there to my bed was no distance at all, where I discovered that I might lack the experience, but I had the desire and a sense of what would please the Count of Anjou. Moving with effortless skill, making me feel neither awkward nor inept, he loved me.

Pinioning my wrists above my head, he looked down into my eyes.

"Your monkish lover does not satisfy a woman of your temper. But I can."

I was swept along by his words. My skin heated, my breath caught, and my emotions no longer obeyed me.

That night the Angevin conquered Aquitaine.

I had had no idea.

Three weeks. For those three weeks I was Countess of Poitou, not Queen of France. I was a young unwed maiden again, not a married woman with a child. I was desired and indulged, flattered and beguiled with delicate pleasure. I was neither ignored nor rejected nor made to feel less than my worth. I was alive, under a breathtaking surge of excitement that I never wanted to end.

We rode, hunted, feasted, loved. I accompanied him when he rode to test the atmosphere in the neighboring lands. I sat with him when he dispensed justice. I learned much of him as a man, as a ruler. His justice was fair, tempered with mercy, but he was no fool. Those who threatened the peace of Poitou were punished under a heavy hand.

Louis and Matilda remained as shades on the edge of our perception.

At night he was my lover. Or we lay together in my bed in late afternoon, a stolen moment when the rest of the household slept or whiled away the surprising heat of the late-autumnal day.

"I think you will go soon," he remarked. He stroked his hand down the length of my hip.

"Yes. Soon. But not today." I was sated and drowsy.

"One thing . . ."

I lifted my head, intrigued to see him suddenly so serious. "What is it?"

"I'm looking for a suitable wife for my son. It's time he was betrothed."

Ah! So matters of state had crept up on us. Had I expected it? Perhaps I had.

"And have you someone in mind?" I asked carefully. I would not preempt the discussion I foresaw.

"You have a daughter."

"So I have."

"Would you consider a match between her and Henry?"

"Marie is less than one year old."

"A betrothal for the future, nothing more." Geoffrey's hand stroked down again, a slow, firm stroke, as his eyes held mine. "There are only thirteen years between them. There are eleven years between Matilda and myself." Suddenly he rolled and pinned me to the bed with his weight, his hands holding mine flat on either side of my head. "What do you think?"

I thought I did not like a marriage negotiation to come sneaking into my bed. Nevertheless I showed my teeth in a little smile. "So, my lord of Anjou, you have an ambition to be connected with the King of France?"

He did not return the smile. "I would not choose it—Louis is more my enemy than my friend. But this marriage would tip the balance in my direction. With Louis tied to an alliance, my power will be enhanced. And Henry's future secured." Suddenly, despite the intimacy of our position, his words revealed the ruthlessness that I had always suspected in him. "I'd make an alliance with the Devil if it brought me gain."

I breathed slowly, remembering my own assertion, so long ago now, that I would wed the Devil if it would keep Aquitaine safe. Geoffrey was staring at me as if he would will me to acquiesce. There was a cold ambition here, a calculation. Matilda, with her mind fixed on England, was not the only one to have an eye to the future. Suddenly the brightness of my chamber was dimmed as the sun moved beyond the window, and doubt, sharp toothed, bit at my heart. Was this why Geoffrey had wooed me, courted me? Was it to make me compliant toward an alliance?

"Eleanor? Do we make a pact?"

And I knew he had used me. I must step carefully in my dealings with Geoffrey of Anjou, circumventing any obvious traps. His will, his instinct for survival, was as strong as mine.

"Eleanor?" he repeated as he leaned over and kissed me very gently on the lips.

"You must ask Louis," I said, hedging a little.

"But would you stand against me if I requested such an alliance?"

I forced my mind to consider, to weigh the advantages. I willed considerations of policy and power to take precedence over my own ruffled feelings.

"No. I would not." I had no doubt that the Angevins would make their mark on the map of Europe. And for sure if Henry had inherited any of his father's charm and skill, he would make my daughter a more fulfilling husband than Louis had ever made me. "No, I'll not stand against you. I'll give such an alliance my support."

I saw victory in his gaze and was forced to turn my face away. I could not be sure that the pain that wrapped around my heart was not mirrored in my eyes, and it would not do for him to see it. I must show no weakness with this man.

"Eleanor, have I displeased you?" His voice was tender again. With one hand he cupped my chin and made me look at him. "I think I have. Let me pleasure you again. And myself." I looked again at his fine features, the fierce admiration in his eyes. I shivered. "I want you, Eleanor, and for now my desire and your delight take precedence over my son's future."

I would never trust him completely. I would be a fool to do so . . . but for now . . .

"Then show me."

Did those around us know? Did they suspect? No, I think not. We were discreet. No word of scandal hung in the air. We both knew the value of discretion and we were not so foolish as to be alone together in public. My women were present, often Aelith, often Henry. I was simply the Countess of Poitou enjoying the hospitality of her home and the experience of her seneschal. Rumor of a liaison between us would bring disaster down on our heads. An affair between those of high birth could be survived, but not for the Queen of France and the Count of Anjou.

It had to end. Aelith had already gone back to Raoul, with a wealth of gossip for his ears only. I must continue south to Aquitaine, and then back to my other life as Queen of France in Paris. Geoffrey must go to Anjou, where trouble was brooding and like to break out in rebellion.

We knew it must end, had always known, and we would not part in sorrow. No tears, no sighs, no longings. The troubadours would find no meat for their laments of unrequited love in my farewell to my seneschal. Our final parting was quite public. Our words of farewell, perfectly proper, could be queried by no one around us. The Count kissed my hand briefly before helping me into my traveling litter and placing cushions for my comfort. He handed me a package of documents, charters, and decrees appertaining to the government of Poitou.

"God be with you, lady." He stepped back and bowed, the sun gilding his russet hair. "I'll be in Paris by the end of the year. To discuss the matter of policy we spoke of."

"Excellent. It will be good policy, I think. I will advise the King of it."

Then he gave the office to start and I closed the leather curtains of the litter, almost allowing the package to slip from my lap, except that my eye was caught. The package contained a jewel. Not a ruby—Geoffrey had far better taste than Louis—and the scrawl that accompanied it was as incriminating as his public manner toward me was not.

> *I shall remember our autumn sojourn in Poitiers. My lovely Eleanor. I wish you well. I pray the fire in the heart of the emerald will remind you of our nights together.*

I studied the words and considered what I had done. I did not love the Count of Anjou. I had wanted him and had welcomed him without conscience, but I had not loved him. I had enjoyed him, relished his attention, gloried in the dominance of his body over mine—yes, all of those. But he did not own my heart. I think we were two of a kind, both selfish, both self-seeking. Aelith had given up everything for love. I would not give up everything for the Angevin. I had enjoyed what he could give me and I would miss him, but his absence would not ruin my life.

Unexpectedly a sob rose in my throat. I closed my fingers over the emerald, a magical stone to preserve the wearer from sickness and ailments of the mind. Perhaps I did love him a little. My heart was not totally free from anguish. I tucked the jewel into a little traveling coffer, resisting the urge to wear it on a chain against my breast. That would be foolishness. Nothing was to be gained from dwelling on what could not be.

And in a sudden little vignette, I recalled my parting from Geoffrey's son, the expression on his face.

He had been solemn, making his farewells with his customary good manners. In the business of packing all my possessions I had left a case of documents in my room. Forestalling Agnes, he bounded off to recover them and presented them to me with grace, despite his labored breathing, and a neat little bow so that I smiled my thanks for him. He did not smile back.

"Adieu, Henry," I said, holding out my hand.

He saluted my fingers. "God go with you, lady."

What was it I saw there? An unsettling acknowledgment, perhaps.

A speculation. Did he suspect my liaison with his father? I did not think it, and yet . . . I felt he was appraising me, and I could not read his conclusion. His lips were thinly closed, unsmiling, his eyes cool and even judgmental. It spoke to me of strong emotion under careful restraint. Whatever his thoughts, he was concealing them from me.

Did he dislike me, perhaps?

I gave a little shrug. It was hardly a matter for my consideration. "I wish you well, Henry, if our paths never cross again," I said.

"They will cross, lady."

"You are very sure. How can you tell?"

"I know it. It is meant to be." His confidence startled me.

On a thought, I gave Henry a present of one of the white gerfalcons, since he had admired them more than he had admired me. His solemn face split in a grin and he could barely thank me in his delight. How could I have thought him enigmatic? Henry was merely a boy with all the hopes and fears that youth suspends over our heads, like a bucket of cold water, to douse us when we least expect it.

Chapter Ten

The Cité Palace waited for me, a gray hunched beast to enclose me in its maw. The good weather had broken and the damp drizzle matched my mood. My chambers were clammy with the pervasive odor of mildew, as if I had been gone for longer than a matter of weeks. What extreme piety had Louis embarked on in my absence? Had he taken residence in a hermit's hut on the banks of the Seine? The King, I was informed, was at Notre Dame. I shivered as my life closed around me. Day after endless day in this dank warren of a palace stretched before me. My spirits were lower than at any time I remembered as my bones absorbed the chill. This was reality. This was my life.

Keeping my mantle close wrapped, I gave my women orders to unpack and dispose of my possessions, while I sat on my bed and looked at the emerald, and not for the first time since I had left Poitou. The glow in its green depths gave me no comfort, nor ever could.

"It'll not bring him back." Agnes was as plain-speaking as ever.

"No. And I would not want him."

Handing the jewel to Agnes, I instructed her to place it in my jewel coffer. I would not look at it again. I must turn my mind to my life here in Paris.

Still gripping the mantle to my chin, I visited the royal nursery to see my daughter. She had grown, a healthy child who clutched at my braids as she pulled herself upright in her crib. Her hair was still fair like Louis's, with none of the red-gold of mine, and her eyes had remained the clear blue inherited from her father. When I picked her up she whimpered a little. She would, of course, however much I might regret it. She had little knowledge of me.

"I think I have found a bridegroom for you, Marie," I informed her.

She stared back as if she understood, the tears drying on her cheeks.

"You will like him. He is called Henry and he has enough energy in him to set fire to the tapestries on your walls. Marriage to Henry will never be dull." She gnawed on my fingers with the suspicion of a tooth in her gums. "When you are older you will meet him. And when you are his bride you will leave home and all you know and love and go and live in Anjou. It is the lot of all women. But at least I can promise you that you will never be near-dead from boredom!"

For a moment I held her close, considering what the future might be for my daughter. Most of it, I was forced to acknowledge, would be beyond my control, but I was satisfied that Henry Plantagenet would never treat her ill. I kissed her hair, and then when Marie began to fuss I gave her back into the arms of her nurse.

Returned to my chamber, I saw that all had been put to rights. Now what? I would not sigh. I would not brood. Instead I would mark my return. I spun around to search out my steward and order a feast, with music and song. And there was Louis, standing in the doorway, sweat gleaming on his neck as if he had arrived in a great rush.

"Louis . . ."

I tried not to compare him with Geoffrey. Difficult not to. Impossible not to. Still playing the monk, Louis was thinner and less appealing than ever, his face marked with dark hollows beneath his eyes; in fact, he was almost gaunt. His hair was still shorn, jaw and cheekbones angular; I could see the tendons harshly prominent in his neck where it emerged from his hair shirt. I forced myself not to close my eyes, but still I looked away. Signs of saintly Bernard's extreme emaciation and total obsession were evident in my husband.

"Eleanor!"

The fervor in Louis's voice caused me to look back, to look carefully. Since Vitry, Louis was rarely fervent. Beneath the pale, strained features, there was an animation. An excitement. His eyes shone with some inner thought, the habitual shroud of self-loathing and abject penitence ripped apart.

"Louis. I have just returned—"

"Yes," he interrupted, advancing on me. "I have news."

There was even a flash of hectic color along his cheekbones. Something had stirred his blood and he could barely contain his words. Perhaps God and all His Angels had granted him a personal audience.

"Good news, I presume."

"The best."

He gripped my hands and leaned forward to kiss my cheek. His palms were hot, clammy. His lips against my skin burned moistly, as if a fever gripped him. I could feel the beat of his heart shudder through his body, and felt a pang of concern.

"Louis . . . are you well?" I asked, placing my hand on his forehead, then pulling him with me to sit on the edge of my bed. "You have a fever." I narrowed my eyes, making a more detailed examination of his body. Even clothed as he was, he was distressingly thin. "Have you eaten today?"

"No. This is one of my fast days. I fast three days a week."

By the Virgin! "It's too much. You are ill. . . ."

"No! Listen to me!" His hands squeezed my fingers until I hissed in pain. "It's Outremer."

"What about Outremer?"

I knew of it, of course, its history. Outremer, the name given to the Latin kingdoms established in the Holy Land, after the victory of our knights over the Turks in the First Crusade. My own family history was firmly connected with it. My grandfather had gone crusading there. Raymond of Poitiers, my father's young brother, had traveled there to be Prince of Antioch.

"It is in danger, Eleanor. Great danger." Louis's fingers gripped mine harder. "The Turkish leader Zengi has declared war. News has reached me." Now his nails dug into my flesh in his urgency. "An army of Saracen Turks led by Zengi has captured the city of Edessa. Do you not see? This opens the way for them to capture Antioch—and then the kingdom of Jerusalem."

That took my attention, of course. Raymond under threat of imminent attack.

"All the conquests of the First Crusade, all the victories, will be undone," Louis continued. "The Christian shrines will come under Turkish rule and we will be banned from them. . . ."

"Well—yes. But I don't see—"

"I should go." Louis announced it like a peal of bells, his voice ringing from the walls. "Think about it, Eleanor. Think of what I could achieve in God's name." The words tumbled from him. "I should raise a mighty army and go to their relief. I should deliver the Christian states of Outremer from the Infidel."

An invasion of the Holy Land? A new Crusade? My blood chilled. Louis's lack of success in warfare had been spectacular. The thought of him taking on the Turks filled me with horror. "But, Louis, you must think about this. . . ." I released my hands from his, cupping his shoulders, trying to make him concentrate on me, on good sense.

There was no reasoning with him.

"I *have* thought. I would make reparation for Vitry. I would make reparation for my sins." His voice lowered as if he were recounting a secret, leaning close to me, eyes glittering unnervingly. "I have always dreamed of carrying the Oriflamme of France, our sacred banner, to the Holy Land. When I was ten years old I made a vow to honor my poor dead brother Philip, who should have been King. I vowed to take the Oriflamme on a pilgrimage and place it on the altar of the Church of the Holy Sepulchre in Jerusalem. Here's my chance. It is ordained by God, and he will forgive me my sins. I will raise an army."

"Is it wise?"

"It is the way to my salvation."

Such conviction, but without hope of fulfillment, of course. "I'm sure that one day you'll find a way to your salvation, Louis," I soothed.

Such an outrageous plan. I doubted Abbot Suger would agree. I stroked his back as a mother might pacify her restless child.

"I'll do it, Eleanor!" Suddenly his arms were banded around me and he was kissing me, full of nervous determination, pushing me back onto the bed. "I can already taste the sweetness of victory," he murmured against my temple. "It's a magnificent idea."

"No, Louis . . . !" Holy Virgin! I did not want this.

"Yes! I will lead a new Crusade!"

I tried to push him away, and thought I had succeeded, but Louis simply stripped away his monkish robe, unaware of the ugliness of his mortified flesh. The abrasions from the hair shirt were things of horror. I could count every rib; the bones of his spine stood out in clear profile, while the jut of his hip bones was almost obscene.

"And you are as beautiful as the day I met you, Eleanor. I have missed you. You will give me inspiration for my Great Quest."

Oblivious to my shrinking flesh, Louis was kneeling beside me, over me, pushing up my skirts. I sank my teeth into my bottom lip, submitting to him because I must. Hands rough with need, he did nothing to rouse desire in me. A rapid, grunting possession that emptied his seed in me was the best that could be said for it. I dared not make the comparison between this and my body's delight in the Angevin caresses.

Louis did not notice my lack of enthusiasm. At least it was quick.

Pushing himself away, he retrieved his hair shirt and robe from the floor and shrugged into them, mercifully hiding his thin flanks and wasting flesh. He smiled at me. "I pray that you will bear another child, Eleanor. A son this time. If I do not return from the Holy Land, if I die there, it would be good to leave France with a male heir."

"Pray God I shall. I'll do my best." I pulled my skirts into order, cringing at the sticky remnants of his pleasure.

In truth I did not expect anything to come of Louis's new obsession, rejecting it as the product of a disordered mind brought on by too much fasting and long hours in prayer. I gave it no thought, and when my bleeding returned with its habitual regularity, I forgot the whole episode. Louis's prayers for a son had gone the same way as his vision of holy restitution, leading an army toward the gilded domes of Jerusalem.

I was wrong.

"My lords!" Clearing his throat, part exhilaration, a greater part nervousness, Louis rose to his feet. The Great Hall at Bourges swam with color and clamor: the remnants of feasting. Christmas Day. A day of joyous celebration.

"My lords!" Louis raised his hands to demand silence. He looked like a half-starved jackdaw amongst a flock of bright and keen-eyed hawks. Not even for Christmas had he made the effort to appear kingly, but wore a drab tunic with unspectacular decoration. When all eyes were on him, some interested, some skeptical, not a few disdainful, he made his announcement. "I have to tell you of the secret in my heart."

His face was flushed, but not from wine, his eyes flitting restlessly over his subjects. Here was Louis trying to sell his dream of a Crusade to his jaundiced barons. From within his robe Louis produced a document with a heavy seal. I tried to smother a sigh.

"This is from His Holiness the Pope." He glanced around to get the measure of his audience. They were not roused at the prospect, whatever it was. A number buried their noses in their cups and belched. "His Holiness exhorts me to raise an army and deliver the states of Outremer from the Infidel. He urges me to go on Crusade."

Silence. What did he expect? A shout of joy at the prospect?

Louis continued, eyes searching the sea of blank faces for encouragement. "I will launch a Crusade to liberate the city of Edessa from the Turks, and protect Jerusalem. I want you to join with me, to give me your knights and your silver and come with me. It will be a penance. It will bring us expiation for our sins. God will smile on us and grant us forgiveness."

Silence, apart from the clearing of a throat, the shuffle of feet, or a scratching hound.

God's Wounds, Louis! This is about as appealing as a dish of cold pottage! Give them a cause to fire their blood!

"We will go crusading to the glory of God!" Louis exhorted. "I have promised His Holiness that France will lead the conquest. Are you with me, my lords? You will pave your paths to Heaven and God's salvation."

The faces remained closed to him, Louis's vassals as well as my own from Aquitaine. I watched them, and read in them the same contempt that stirred me. Penance and salvation were no way to their hearts. Louis sat down heavily, at a loss.

"What will it take to persuade them of the rightness of this great cause?" he asked me.

Some faith in your ability to lead an army to victory would go a long way, I thought. *They'll remember Toulouse and Champagne. I'd not leap to follow you to Outremer.*

"Now, if I had the ability of your grandfather, Duke William . . ." Louis was muttering. "To move men to give their lives and pockets for the cause of the Cross."

"Duke William made it sound exciting," I responded with flat honesty. "You made it seem as enticing as an offal pudding."

"It is a holy mission! It is not frivolous, Eleanor! It is the chance of a lifetime!"

A chance of a lifetime.

Oh! An idea curled in my mind. A vision so desirable. Suddenly a vast horizon opened before me. An adventure, a gilded opportunity . . . An *escape!* My heart leaped, a single heavy bound against my ribs. Before I knew it I was on my feet on the dais.

"My lords." I had their attention, some astounded, some disapproving, all intrigued. "His Majesty speaks of the value to your souls. I would speak of something quite different." I could hear my voice—clear, feminine, persuasive. Certainly not weak. I looked around the hall, drawing these puissant barons to me. Oh, yes. I had their attention. I raised my hands, palms up in heartfelt plea. "I would speak to you of the earthly glory of such a venture. As you are all aware, Duke William of Aquitaine acquitted himself well in the Crusade. His songs tell of the bravery and magnificent exploits of the knights who gave themselves to the cause. Do you not recall? Their spectacular march through the lands of Europe, armor gilded by the sun, banners unfurled." My voice warmed, became more vibrant as I painted the picture I wished them to see. "Do you not recall the tales of their pride and superb achievements? Of the days of high adventure? Men still sing the praises of those first Knights of the Cross. Would you not wish for that? For your wives and children to know you too as heroes and adventurers?"

Their faces were no longer unresponsive. I had them in the palm of my hand.

"The lands of Outremer are richer than we can imagine. Look at the opportunity for those of you who yearn after more land, more wealth. My own noble uncle, Raymond of Poitiers, is Prince of Antioch. Who knows what earthly reward lies in store for any one of you. If the cost of such a venture troubles you"—I let my lip curl infinitesimally—"I wager you will recover your outlay ten times over. What is not to like in His Majesty's plan to take the Cross? Are you cowards that you will sit in France, on your estates, while others go crusading in your name? I call you to wealth and fame and everlasting glory in God's name!"

Even I was moved by my call to arms, but it was in my blood and the words could not be held back, even though I felt Louis's anxious circumspection.

I drew a breath as certainty grew in me.

I had not said the half of it yet.

"I too will go on Crusade," I announced. "I will ride at the King my husband's side." And then I dropped into the familiar *langue d'oc*, letting my eye rest on the faces of my own vassals. "I will lead my own to the Holy Land. Will you follow me, men of Aquitaine? Will you ride with me to free Outremer from these barbarians who would rob us of our right to stand at the site of Christ's birth?"

My mind was full of it. For me it would be a way out of the imprisoning life in Paris, chained to a husband who was no husband. My blood surged with anticipation.

I awaited a response.

"It is no place for a woman. To travel with an army."

One voice that I could not pinpoint, but the *langue d'oeil* was of the north. I raised my chin, raised my voice above the deep rumble of voices as the assembled barony considered my one weakness.

"Do you say?" I walked from my place at the table, brushing past Louis to stand at the very front of the dais, daring any man to challenge me. "No place for a woman? In my grandfather's day, he was joined on the march by the Margravine Irene of Austria, a woman as famous for her beauty as for her strong will. She raised her troops from her own lords and rode at their head. Am I capable of doing any less as a woman of Aquitaine?" I smiled down at my seated vassals. "I am young and strong. The Margravine Irene could give me a good few years when she raised her banners." A rustle of laughter. "My lords! I can outride any one of you here!"

A cheer rose to the rafters, swelling, reverberating as the idea and enthusiasm took hold.

"Will you follow me and take the Cross?" Now I strode along the front of the dais, kicking aside my skirts. "I will ride before you like Queen Penthesilea, who led her fabulous Amazons to victory, a female warrior, in the siege of Troy. I will ride before you like that warrior queen of old, leading you to glory. I have as much strength and courage as she. Will you follow me, men of Aquitaine? Men of France? For gold and land and everlasting fame in the songs of the troubadours?"

A moment of quivering silence. Would they do it? I found that I was holding my breath. Would they give me the weapon to strike the shackles from my wrists and restore to me my freedom?

"Deus Vult! Deus Vult!"

God wills it. The old Crusader battle cry. It hammered itself home against the walls from a hundred male throats. And I looked down and back at Louis where he still sat, hands loose on the table. He blinked at me in consternation. It was laughable, but I did not even smile my victory.

"There, Louis. You have your support for the Crusade."

And I had my escape.

Poor Louis smiled weakly, unsure whether my intervention was for good or ill.

Abbot Suger trembled with fury.

"You did not consult with me, Sire." He was barely polite. "You would take an army and a full treasury of gold out of France for a mission that is not guaranteed success?"

"God would surely say it was an enterprise worth the doing." Louis remained obstinate.

"God would be far better served if you remained in France, Sire, governed wisely and got a male heir to step into your shoes. Have you thought of the repercussions if you are killed in Outremer? Better leaders than you have met their end. It is far too dangerous for you to go, with the succession still so insecure."

He swung to face me.

"As for you, Majesty, how could you be so impolitic in this? You would leave your child of barely two years?"

"Do you accuse me of being an unnatural mother?" What pleasure it gave me to see Suger so inconvenienced.

"I accuse you of being thoughtless, Majesty. And as for Irene of Austria, you did not see fit to remind your vassals that she met an unpleasant death, trampled underfoot during a massacre."

I smiled caustically, sure of my ground. "No, I did not. I am a feudal lord. Who should raise my troops but I? Who should ride at their head but the Duchess of Aquitaine? What do you say, Louis? Do I ride at your side?"

"Perhaps it would not be safe, Eleanor. . . ."

Much the reaction I had expected. "Very well." I shrugged as if I did not care. "Then I will remain at home and rule the country in your stead."

"Ah . . ." Louis swallowed.

"No!" Abbot Suger flushed.

I almost laughed aloud. I knew I had won. I could see their fear writ clear on their faces. Who knew what I might get up to if left with the unfettered power of the Crown in my hands? It hurt me to see their fear, but it was a weapon I would use.

"I'm sure you can trust me to use your power wisely in your name."
I patted Louis's arm.

"Perhaps there will be an advantage in your coming with me after
all. . . . It would bind the Aquitainians to my army, of course. . . ."
Louis slid a glance toward Suger.

I closed my fingers gently around his wrist. "You need me, Louis.
Far better that I go with you."

The Abbot might be caught between a rock and a hard place, but
still he stuck to his argument. "You cannot both go and leave the
country without a male heir."

"Yes, we can." I smiled. "Perhaps God will bless us with another
child when we see Jerusalem. A son to rule France."

So Louis was outmaneuvered. It was decided, and Suger's arguments fell on deaf ears.

All I could see was the chance to spread my wings and fly. I had
battered down the walls of the Cité Palace. The ennui of my life was
swept away. Louis's military skills might be suspect, but with good
commanders at his side he would stand in Jerusalem.

I could not believe my good fortune. My belly was gripped with excitement; my blood ran hot under my skin. I was going to the Holy Land.

"Your Majesty." My steward stood at the door to my solar and bowed,
trying not to look askance at the piles of shifts and gowns and mantles
being made ready for the adventure that was still in the lap of the gods.
Louis obfuscated, Abbot Suger undermined my inclusion in the venture with every breath, but I was determined. I was going to Outremer.
So there I was on my knees in the midst of the chaos, one of my jewel
caskets open before me. Some decisions were too important to leave to
my women. "Majesty—you have guests. I have brought them here, as
His Majesty is otherwise engaged at Notre Dame. . . ."

I pushed myself to my feet, suddenly aware of the reaction of my
women as I did so, a twitter of birds in a cage as a hawk swooped
overhead. And turning, I understood. My visitor was not a man to be
overlooked. Neither one of them, it seemed, could be overlooked.

"The Count of Anjou, Your Majesty. And Lord Henry Plantagenet."

I had forgotten in the heat of crusading fever that this visit had been promised, and here were the Angevins come to court seeking a bride. For some reason that I could not name, I felt a cold hand of unease stroke the nape of my neck.

"My lord Count." I adopted a gracious smile, determined that my greeting should flow as cool as meltwater over ice. "You are right welcome."

As handsome as ever, Geoffrey of Anjou strode into my solar, smooth and controlled, raw power overlaid by elegance, exactly as I remembered him. But there was something more. . . . A flutter of apprehension disturbed my belly. The Count's expression was open and candid, but perhaps his eyes did not quite meet mine. And then he smiled directly at me—which did nothing to dispel my awareness of something awry. It reminded me that he was more than a master of deception.

There was the same attraction between us, of course. The Angevin's eyes sparkled with admiration. Beneath the nerves, my cheeks felt hot as fire. The desire was as strong as ever. How would I tolerate being with him in the same palace, yet distant from him? This was not my own indulgent Poitou; this was Paris. To indulge in bed sport in Poitiers was one thing; to continue it under the nose of Louis and Abbot Suger was quite another. There would be no assignations, no whispered words and intimate caresses here.

And perhaps I did not want there to be such intimacy. What had passed between us in Poitiers was over. I would not repeat my indiscretions.

Geoffrey took my hand, bowing formally over it, the slightest brush of his lips, all as was proper, with exactly the correct amount of deference. Oh, he was clever, the consummate actor, as if our previous knowledge of each other had been nothing more than one of business and negotiation, a seneschal with his overlord.

"Majesty. Forgive my intrusion." He was perfectly at ease.

But I would match him in this. My welcome was graciously formal. "There is no intrusion." I gestured to the steward to fetch wine as I turned to the younger Angevin.

"Henry. You've grown since I saw you at Poitiers. How long is it? Six months, I think."

"Majesty." His bow was equal to his father's in courtliness. Certainly he had grown. As well as height and a noticeable breadth of shoulder, he had acquired a distinct coordination of limbs and perhaps an adult gloss of confidence in those few short months. His mouth did not smile but his eyes held a gleam of mischief that put me on my guard as much as the Count's insouciance did. "I said we would meet again, lady."

"So you did. And here you are. I trust your gerfalcon is in good health?"

"Yes, Majesty." A grin dispelled his solemnity. "She hunts better than my father's eagle."

I laughed. He was still only a boy, still hunting-mad. Dismissing my women, I gestured that they should sit, as did I, disposing my skirts with éclat, my senses still stretched, fully alert. "We are preparing to journey to Outremer," I explained, indicating the upheaval around me, giving myself time to think. "Louis and I have taken the Cross."

"So I hear, Majesty." Geoffrey looked at me across the rim of his cup. "You are to be commended. A noble cause. And for you to accompany your husband on so dangerous a mission . . . Praiseworthy indeed."

"Indeed." I thought he mocked me, so, resenting such impudence, I chose to aim my own dart. No one mocked the Duchess of Aquitaine. "And you are not tempted to join us, my lord Count? In atonement for your earthly sins?"

"Christ, no! If I absent myself from my lands for more than a se'ennight, there'll be some enterprising brigand stepping into my shoes. I've no ambition to return to find myself a landless beggar."

"And I've got my eye on events in England, lady," Henry said, leaning forward, alight with enthusiasm. "My lady mother's supporters are at war with Stephen. It's my intention to lead them, to take the Crown for my own. . . ."

But the Count waved his son to silence. "I'm here to discuss the project I put before you in Poitiers, lady," he remarked without preamble. "I think I have your support, when I put my case to persuade His Majesty."

Had I not said I would support him? Something was afoot. And that same flutter of premonition held me back from the reassurance the Angevin wanted. "You must dine with us," I invited simply. "His Majesty will hear you and make his own decision."

"In my favor, I trust." The Count put down his cup, still half-full. His eyes lifted to mine, undoubtedly mocking. "It may be that your decision to go crusading, lady, has given me an unlooked-for advantage in my arguments."

"And that advantage would be . . . ?"

He shook his head as if it would be beyond my comprehension. "Not one that I wish to discuss where walls might have ears."

It was a mistake on the Angevin's part. I would not accept such condescension, and I tilted my chin. We were alone, so why not tell me his plans? In that moment, his handsome features illuminated in a glow of hard northern sunlight, I saw him clearly for what he was, as I never had in Poitiers: a self-interested rogue despite his lands and title, one who would snatch at fate and whatever was offered, without thought for any man or woman who stood in his way. Yet I knew he was still drawn to me. He would come to my bed if I made it possible for him to do so. Was that it? Was he waiting to see a way to my chamber?

Ah, but would I? Would I really do what he expected of me? If I did, that would put me under his power. And just how was he intending to use that power? *Beware!* The warning whispered in my head. There was a speculation in his gaze that I did not like, the close fixation of a cat deciding whether it was worth its while to pounce on a mouse.

I was no mouse. I would not be the means to any of Geoffrey of Anjou's ends.

"Then you must rely on that unexplained advantage to persuade my husband that your offer is in his best interests," I replied.

"I wait with impatience." Abruptly, Geoffrey stood, gesturing to his son that the audience was at an end, even though I had given no such indication, and they made their farewells as the steward waited to escort them to their accommodations. Geoffrey was as immaculately polite as on his entrance, his salute to my fingers just as lightly formal, but when Henry and my steward had gone on ahead, suddenly, as he had intended, we were alone in my solar. Polite formality vanished in the snap of fingers. The Count's hands grasped my shoulders, burning through the silk of my gown, and I was pulled hard against him.

My breath hissed my objection through my teeth but I controlled every muscle. "Did you wish to say more, my lord?" I asked sweetly, refusing to squirm, his mouth a kiss away from mine.

"Yes. I want you to add your voice to persuade the King."

"I have already said I'm not hostile to the match."

"No warmer than that? I think you might have an incentive, lady." His smile was outrageously seductive but still the warning hammered in my head.

"And that is?"

"It would not be healthy—for either of us, but especially for you, Eleanor—if Louis were to hear whispers of our weeks in Poitou. Our delightful sojourn in the Maubergeonne Tower. The woman in the liaison is always punished with a harder hand than the man."

I all but gasped, yet didn't. "Are you offering me threats, my lord Count?" I asked, smooth as the silk I wore and that his hands crumpled.

"Threats? No, lady. I'll not threaten, merely persuade."

He kissed me.

Damn him, he kissed me hard with a possession that stirred up in me all the remembered heat and color of Poitou. But beneath the sweetness of it, I tasted danger. It was tart and urgent. Beware indeed. If I was moved by honesty, I would say that fear slithered its path down my spine.

It was, of course, the height of court etiquette that Louis and Geoffrey should sit together at the High Table, side by side, the King of France flanked by one of his most powerful vassals. How unfortunate. Louis paled into a fragile candle flame, almost guttering into nonexistence beside the bright torch that was the Angevin Count. I sat at Geoffrey's other side, aware of every nuance, every slide of light and shadow. Louis urbane and unaware, always the innocent. Geoffrey all courteous charm and winning argument. And cunning deceit. Abbot Suger listening with pursed lips and a deepening frown, for what reason I was as yet unsure. He had not forgiven me for my championing of Louis's dreams of Jerusalem, but I did not think that I was the reason for his ill humor. And then there was Henry Plantagenet, dividing his concentration between the food on his plate and the discussion of politics, politics most frequently winning. His eyes darted from one to the other of the protagonists, dissecting, weighing, storing information.

Barely were we into the stews and frumenty of the first course than Geoffrey launched into his campaign. He was not a man to waste time.

"I have a proposal, Sire. My son and heir . . . I look for a wife for him. A wife with power and influence to match what, one day, will be his own."

Louis twitched his colorless brows in faint interest.

"In the fullness of time," Geoffrey added, "Henry will be Count of Anjou and Duke of Normandy, thus one of your foremost barons."

Louis continued to look vaguely unimpressed. Suger's ears pricked up and he pushed aside his cup and platter. In delicate discretion, I sat back and sipped the thin wine of Anjou, to let them do the talking while I remained vigilant. I became aware of Henry again. He was leaning forward. He too was alert, keen like a hound scenting a fox. When his eyes touched momentarily on mine, they were bright and involved. They lingered, widening, and I realized in that moment of recognition that there was more depth in this vivid young man than in his father, although he was certainly more transparent. With young Henry, I had the suspicion that what you saw on the serving platter was what you got on your trencher. An interesting young man. There was a control in him now that had not been present in Poitiers. I suspected his exuberant energy was the same, but now it was harnessed and his concentration was ferocious. Yes, he was restless at the enforced inactivity, his fingers pulling apart a piece of wastrel bread and rolling the soft dough into perfect balls of equal size, but his mind was wholly taken up with the discussion of his bride, and what that would mean for his future power.

Suddenly, astonishingly, a sharp bolt of some unnamed emotion held us. A frisson of something that was more than an understanding, more than a recognition. I did not imagine it. It dried my mouth and . . . I found myself frowning.

With an apologetic grimace and duck of his head, Henry Plantagenet gave his attention back to the exchange of views that had increased in intensity.

"Not only will my son inherit my estates," Geoffrey was continuing, "but through Matilda, my wife, he has a direct claim to the throne of England."

Louis was still unimpressed. "Except that your wife's cousin Stephen is securely on the throne of England, with a son to follow after him. I don't believe there will be many English lords who would raise their swords in the Lady Matilda's cause." He might spend an inordinate length of time on his knees, but Louis still had a finger on the pulse of power in the neighboring states, courtesy of Abbot Suger.

"Matilda faces difficulties; I can't argue against it," Geoffrey growled. "The English barons are reluctant to cede power to a woman. Unlike the sophistication of Aquitaine, where sex is no obstacle to power." He bowed his head to me, a glint in his eye. "But Stephen's claim stands on shaky ground. My son Henry has the legal right, and I think England will be open to the man with the weightiest sword. Would you care to venture with me, Majesty? To have your daughter wed to my son, and ultimately become Queen of England?"

Thoughtfully, Louis laced his fingers together and cast his eye over Henry, who returned the look, skin heating with the sudden attention.

"What do *you* say, Henry Plantagenet?" Louis asked him directly.

"I say that by the time the lady, your daughter, is of an age to wed me, I will be King of England."

I tried not to smile. Such arrogance, such assurance in his own talents. He had the confidence of a man twice his age.

Taken with the thought, Louis narrowed his eyes. "I think the suggestion has merit."

"And I think Her Majesty is not against the match."

Louis turned slowly, looking beyond Geoffrey to me. "Eleanor?"

"I was gratified to meet with Her Majesty in Poitiers when she traveled there," Geoffrey explained before I could consider a reply. His smile was as innocent as the skin on a dish of warm milk as he dropped the dangerous little pebble in the pool and waited to see how the ripples would form. "We had an exchange of opinion over the possibility—on more than one occasion."

"I was not aware," Louis said, a crease digging between his brows.

"Her Majesty was pleased to show me some of her favorite hunting grounds," Geoffrey explained. "We had excellent sport."

Well, now. My spine stiffened beneath the layers of linen and silk brocade as a quick shiver ran its length. The Angevin was deliberately playing with fire here, and I might be a brand for burning.

"You were in Poitou when Eleanor was there?" Louis asked.

"Indeed, Sire."

Louis's eyes snapped to mine, and I recognized what I read there. Had I not seen it before? Jealousy, as vital and green as the braiding on Geoffrey's expensive sleeve. So Geoffrey would make mischief for me, would he? It was no secret that Louis doted on me as a mother hen on her chick. The tale of Marcabru, my much-lamented, banished troubadour, had lost nothing in the telling. So the Count of Anjou would stir that pot of eels for me, would he? I continued to smile but anger—and not a little contempt—began to stir. How dared he sit there, juggling with danger, holding the truth over my head, threatening to allow it to fall on my neck like a fine-edged sword unless I sided with him. Would he do it? Would he uncover my indiscretion before Louis and the whole court?

Would he accuse me of infidelity unless I sided with Henry as a royal bridegroom?

I took a sip of wine to ease my dry throat.

No. No! Mentally I shook my head as sense took a grip. Of course he wouldn't. It would be far too dangerous for him—Louis's vassal discovered in sinful relationship with his wife. But he thought to threaten me with enough suspicion to cause me harm. Did he truly consider me so weak that I would support him in return for his silence? Fury flared again—that the man I had taken as my lover should put me in this invidious position, and even worse that it was of my own making. He would pay for it. I would make him pay. I summoned my resources and smiled at Louis.

"I went from Poitou straight to Aquitaine before I returned home, Louis, and so in the expanse of time I probably forgot so trivial a discussion with your seneschal. And yes, I believe my lord of Anjou mentioned his hopes over the marriage." I allowed my smile to encompass the Angevin, and lifted a shoulder carelessly. "But I suppose I forgot that too. No decision could be made without *your* consent."

"You did not tell me." Louis's face was set in obdurate lines.

I lifted a shoulder again, beautifully negligent. "When I returned you were taken up with an urge to go to Outremer. You could talk of nothing else. What point in discussing a marriage of our daughter, who is not yet two years old? I thought the plan had merit—an Angevin marriage for Marie, with the prospect of England as well." I smiled serenely at Geoffrey. "Now I'm not so sure. As you say, Stephen seems to have the upper hand in England."

It delighted me to watch a shadow of what could only be temper flit through Geoffrey's eyes, although his face remained carefully expressionless.

"I see advantages to the match," Louis said slowly, avarice replacing suspicion. "Marie as Queen of England . . ."

"I think it is far too important a decision to be made without deep thought, Majesty." For the first time Abbot Suger intervened, had he but known it, as my ally. I could have laughed aloud, but lowered my eyes to my softly clasped hands. "I think it would be wise to sleep on it."

Louis looked thoughtful.

"Excellent advice," I purred.

"Yes! I will pray for guidance." Louis smiled ingenuously at his seneschal. "Dine with us tomorrow, my lord Count. I will give you my reply then."

So he would hold me to ransom, would he? No one would do that, certainly not the Count of Anjou. And if he thought he would find his way to my bedchamber to renew his persuasion in person, he underestimated me entirely. Was this why he had seduced me in the first place? The idea flirted with my mind, refusing to let go. Had the conquest of his mouth and hands been simply to pull me into compliance with his plans for Angevin expansion?

My anger was so strong my hands shook as I threw a silver goblet against the wall of my bedchamber. The resulting dents in the precious metal gave me no comfort at all.

I had no idea where Geoffrey spent the night. If he sought me out at all, he would have found my rooms empty, for I spent the hours at Louis's side in Notre Dame in a night vigil. Yes, I actually did that. How slowly the minutes passed. How cold it was. I yawned and fidgeted and had to force myself to stay awake, but it was a valuable exercise. Louis and I prayed together for divine guidance in the matter of our daughter's husband. Surprised by my presence, Louis was warmly grateful and reassured of my loyalty.

Yes, I prayed, but not quite along the lines that Louis would approve. I spent those night hours in meticulous planning, and in a measure of self-blame over that turbulent autumn liaison when I had allowed desire to overcome good sense. I should not have mistaken the intentions of the Angevin. A queen must never put herself into the hands of a subject.

Returned to my chamber at dawn, I dressed with care and sent Agnes with a message.

"Tell my lord Abbot that I need a moment of his time. And tell him that it might be politic if His Majesty was kept in the dark—for the time being."

We had a most informative discussion, Abbot Suger and I, in

which a copy of a certain document exchanged hands. Abbot Suger's reluctant compliance became overlaid with enthusiasm. He made an unlikely ally, but in extremis I would work with God's thorn in my flesh.

I admitted to a sense of pride in my plotting. Declaring war on the Angevin, I would play to win. A pity that it would mean the end of Henry's hopes to wed Marie. He would have made an admirable husband.

We four dined privately—Geoffrey, Louis, Abbot Suger, and I. Should I mention that I wore emeralds? Not the single jewel of Geoffrey's gift but a heavy chain of gold set with more than a dozen of them, shining in baleful glory. I saw them take Geoffrey's eye. I was aware of a tension in him lurking below the well-mannered surface, and from the beginning he left me in no doubt of his intentions.

"Majesty. You are more beautiful than the songs of the troubadours." And then the sting of the snake's tongue. "You shine brilliantly in this dark setting, far more dazzling than when I recall you in the golden warmth of Poitou." How innocent of malice he appeared, hiding the venomous snake that would swallow me whole. "The emeralds become you, Majesty."

"Do they not. And so many of them! A gift from my husband on the occasion of Marie's birth." I smiled at the Angevin snake and then across at Louis.

"Eleanor is worth all the wealth of my kingdom." Gratified, Louis touched my hand. It took so little effort on my part to gratify him.

"The lady's reputation goes before her." Geoffrey leaned back in his chair, confident of his imminent victory. "The marriage, Your Majesty. Have you considered it?"

"I have. Prayed over it throughout the night, with Eleanor at my side." At Louis's words, I felt the slide of Geoffrey's sardonic expression in my direction. "I'm of a mind to give my consent."

"An excellent decision." Geoffrey all but rubbed his hands together. "Do we draw up an agreement, for when the infant is older?"

"No, my lord." It was the quietest of interjections from the Abbot. "The marriage is not viable."

Geoffrey froze. Louis looked startled, Henry interested. I feigned total ignorance.

"It is not appropriate that our Princess marry the Angevin boy." Still low and even, Abbot Suger's voice held the authority of Almighty God. "I will not countenance it, Majesty. Nor will the Church."

Irritation rapidly replaced Louis's amazement. "Is there a problem?"

"Yes. A problem. And after past history you should be aware of it, Sire."

"Speak up, man."

"It is Her Majesty"—Abbot Suger inclined his head to me—"and Lord Henry. A matter of consanguinity. They are related in the third degree. They share a common ancestor. It is too close for marriage between the two young people."

Louis's hands clenched on the table edge as if an arrow had pierced his gut; his voice was strangled in his throat. "I've had my belly full of consanguinity."

"Indeed, Sire!" Suger fixed him with a stern expression. "It would not be politic for you to cross Holy Mother Church—again."

"And this can be proved?" I asked in spectacular astonishment.

"Indeed, lady. Proved beyond doubt—by an eminent scholar."

Of course. Had I not informed him of the connection myself? What a valuable hour the Abbot and I had spent with the Bishop of Laon's document between us. Now I listened as the worthy Abbot explained with pompous exactitude that I was related to Henry Plantagenet by some distant connection back through Duke William of Normandy and his whore Herleva. Suger had learned his script well; his voice was clipped and assured, while I did nothing except continue to appear surprised.

Barely listening to the complicated lines of descent, I allowed my eyes to flicker to Geoffrey. He did not seem in any way disturbed by these revelations. For a moment he met my gaze and then smiled at Louis.

"I'll not dispute it. But dispensations have been sought and acquired for such in the past. Think, Majesty." He spread his fine hands on the cloth. "You are going Crusading. The journey is long and the dangers great. Life is cheap. If you don't survive the Crusade, your daughter is barred from the French succession through Salic Law. Now, if she's betrothed to my son, we might manage to weasel around such legislation. Henry and the little Princess would rule France and Anjou together. And, with God's will, England too in the fullness of time."

Again I saw the shine in Louis's eyes at the unfolding of such an extent of land. "France and England united. And Aquitaine, of course."

"No, Sire." There was Abbot Suger, reliable as ever, drawing Louis's attention back from the gleam of avarice. "No Angevin should be King of France. Get yourself a male heir, Sire. How would our barons accept the prospect of this manner of circumventing Salic Law? Rebellion on our hands—and you out of the country . . . Such a marriage is not permissible through the teaching of Holy Scripture. I don't need to remind you of it, do I?"

For a moment I saw Louis's face darken in anger against the hectoring tone of his minister. Now was the time for some careful intervention. I pulled on Louis's sleeve.

"My lord. If you are in any doubt over this . . ." I let a little smile curve my lips as I angled a glance at Geoffrey. *He thinks I am going to push Louis into Angevin arms. He thinks I'm going to throw my weight behind this increase in Angevin power. By God, I won't do it!* "I want only the best for our daughter. But you know it cannot be. Do you not realize where the strongest voice will be in opposition to such an alliance? Abbot Bernard himself. He has no truck with consanguinity. He will condemn it—and he'll condemn you too if you allow it to go any further."

Louis struggled with indecision and anger in equal measure.

"Does the King of France bow before the dictates of the Abbot of Clairvaux?" Geoffrey needled.

My fingers tightened on Louis's plain wool. "You know you must not become inveigled into the trap of consanguinity again, my lord. You remember how it ended last time."

Vitry-le-Brulé. Excommunication. I was very sure of my ground here. And for Louis? It was the final straw. His narrow features hardened and he all but choked the words.

"Vitry. Of course. I have decided, my lord Count. I will not give my consent."

Thank God. I had won. It had tottered on a knife-edge but I had done it.

To give him his due, the Angevin kept his disappointment well hidden. His nostrils flared, his mouth was thin lipped, but his reply was even. "I regret your decision, my lord." But I was in no mood for admiration. Time now to twist the knife. I would risk all on the Angevin's unwillingness to betray either of us. I would accept his challenge and prove I had nerves to match his. Did he truly think of me as a foolish woman, gulled into believing my reputation in danger?

"My lord of Anjou," I informed Louis dispassionately, "has expressed his reluctance to join the weight of his forces with ours in the Crusade. Perhaps you could add your voice to mine and persuade him?"

Pleased to escape the previous quagmire, Louis looked suitably shocked. "Not go to fight for Christ?" How desperately predictable he was. How easy to maneuver. "Every Christian lord should answer the call to take up the Cross."

Geoffrey inclined his head stiffly. "I must not. I have to protect my interests in Anjou and Normandy. If I take my troops to Outremer, I cannot guarantee peace at home—which would be in no one's interest. And I have my duties in Poitou—"

"I would have thought your family obligations would have swayed you, my lord," I interrupted.

Louis brows knitted. "What's that?"

"My lord of Anjou's half brother, Lord Baldwin . . ." How satisfying this was. If it came to duplicity, Geoffrey had met more than his match in me. "The Lord Baldwin is King of Jerusalem. And so will come under direct attack from the Infidel if we do not stop them." I looked at the Count, wide-eyed. "Louis and I go to safeguard my father's brother, Raymond of Poitiers, in Antioch. Would you not do the same for your brother? Would you not, in God's holy name, fight to keep your brother from possible death?"

The Count's fingers clenched around the cup before he eased them out. "I fear not."

"I think you should reconsider," Louis responded, now doubly shocked.

"I cannot."

It was only a hairbreadth short of rudeness.

"If Count Geoffrey is concerned for his duties as Seneschal of Poitou . . ." My concern was magnificent, my gaze lambent. I lingered on the pause, looking from Louis to the Angevin and back again. "We could appoint another seneschal if the Count wishes to take up his obligations in the Holy Land. . . . Do reconsider, my lord of Anjou. We would value your company with us. What is earthly power—a mere Seneschal of Poitou—in the balance with God's approval and the promise of reward in Heaven? There are other men I would trust with Poitou in your stead if you felt God's call."

At last I smiled directly into Geoffrey of Anjou's bland, furiously governed face.

What a beautiful, not-so-thinly veiled little threat.

After that, the meal came to an unsurprisingly abrupt end. The Count of Anjou's manner was tight with anger as he left the chamber with the briefest show of respect. I thought I had made an enemy there, but it did not disturb me. His son managed a more respectable bow and I thought his eyes sought out mine before he strode after his father to the door.

I would not comply, turning my back on the pair of them, nothing but two ruthless, self-serving wolves, with nothing to choose between them.

And yet I found myself regretting Henry Plantagenet's disappointment. Still, he was young and would find another bride who would bring him power and status, even if he did not achieve it for himself. I thought he would. It was a marriage I would have liked for my daughter, but not at the cost of my freedom to choose.

The outcome for me was entirely satisfying. How I enjoyed it.

The Angevins departed, with nothing to keep them longer. Returned to my cold existence, I was left to bury myself once again in crusading matters, with my own consanguinity lurking on the edge of my consciousness, pricking at me like a spur. Geoffrey's emerald? I took it from my jewel casket, handling it with distaste, then on a whim holding it out to Agnes.

"Take it." I smiled at the surprise on her face. "In recompense for all you do for me. It will go well with the russet of your gown, and I have too many jewels to wear."

I held it out on the palm of my hand, so that it glinted in the light with fire as only emeralds can. Then, before she could take it, I closed my fingers over it.

"Majesty?"

"No." I lifted a string of agates from the box instead. "No, these will be better. The gold and brown will be more becoming to your coloring."

As Agnes accepted with a curious glance, I replaced the emerald in the little coffer. I would keep it, but I would not wear it again. I would keep it as a warning against deceitful men who would use and manipulate me. I had come off best, but it did not do to be complacent. I remembered the boy's cunning placement of the chess pieces. A knight to take a queen? Never!

I would never put myself in so invidious a position again.

The end result, apart from Count Geoffrey's ignominious defeat, amused me, filled me with exhilaration. Eavesdroppers hear no good of themselves, so it's said. I wouldn't dispute it, but still I got my own way.

"Your Majesty!" Abbot Suger was addressing Louis as I stepped into one of the audience chambers, and he continued unaware. "I have reconsidered. I think you *should* take Her Majesty with you to Outremer."

"I thought you opposed me over it."

"I did, Majesty. Now I think it would be best for all of us if she were with you, under your eye."

"Well, if you think . . ."

"I do. You can't trust her at home alone. Take her with you, Majesty."

I pretended not to hear, and by the time I'd reached Louis's side, they were discussing some minor point of finance.

All in all a neat little victory. Over Anjou. Over Abbot Suger and Louis. I had achieved my objective, and I was going to Outremer.

With grateful condescension, I congratulated the Abbot on his appointment as our Regent in our absence. I suppose he deserved some recompense.

Chapter Eleven

*T*he Angevins were forgotten. The moment of my liberation grew closer, minute by minute. What a glorious adventure it would be. The bells tolled until their vibrations beat painfully against my ears like the throb of a military drum. Once again I stood in the abbey church of Saint-Denis. Once again Louis approached the altar, and as before the heat and emotion pressed down on us. Today he was clad in a black pilgrim's tunic, the red cross of the Crusader emblazoned on his breast, as it was on hundreds of others around me.

It was over twelve months since Abbot Bernard had preached the Crusade at Vézelay. How long did it take to muster an army and all its accoutrements? Far longer than any of us had expected. Now we were ready, the army gathered, the retinues assembled, the baggage carts pulled by oxen packed and repacked. Around me the church blazed with thousands of candles. Banners and gonfalons of the lords of France and Aquitaine shivered in the air. It was an awe-inspiring occasion—if only it would end and we could get on with it. At this rate, I would be in my dotage, my hair gray-streaked, before we set foot out of Paris.

In honor of the occasion the Pope, Eugenius himself—for Pope Celestine had managed to hold on to the Keys of Heaven for a mere five months before death struck him down—had journeyed across the Alps to give us his blessing, and there he stood before the altar to imprint our hearts and minds with God's holy presence. As tears flowed unchecked down Louis's cheeks—he had no sense of occasion!—as he trembled visibly with the emotion of the moment, the Pope lifted the silver chest containing the bones of Saint Denis and held the sacred relic for Louis to kiss. Then he handed to him the gilded pike of the red-and-gold silk Oriflamme, the sacred banner of France, to be taken to the Holy Land and placed on the altar of the Church of the Holy Sepulchre.

A triumphant roar broke from hundreds of throats. Louis wept copiously. Even I felt tears dampen my cheeks, mostly from relief that at last—at last!—we were ready to depart.

It had not been without a struggle. Pope Eugenius had damned the taking of fine gowns and cosmetics on crusade in the same manner as he thundered against whores and blasphemy. My example had been followed by my women and the wellborn ladies who agreed to accompany me, and how could we be expected to travel the hundreds of miles without some of the comforts and luxuries to which we were accustomed? Why should a number of ox wagons not be set aside for our needs? And of course we needed our tire-women. Could we be expected to wait upon ourselves? Was I extravagant? I did not think so.

"But so much clothing!" Louis had remonstrated with me when he saw my provisions for months on the road, his lukewarm attention drawn to the steadily increasing number of oxcarts by his two beady-eyed advisers.

They disliked me excessively. A feeling I entirely reciprocated.

Odo de Deuil, the less poisonous of the pair, was Louis's secretary, a monk from the Abbey of Saint-Denis, now appointed by Abbot Suger as Louis's chaplain for the duration of the Crusade to keep an eye on him, and I suspected on me. A self-righteous little man, he was under orders to write the official record of Louis's achievements for posterity. I swore he'd have little good to say about me even if my soul were washed whiter than snow. What possible use would he be to Louis in a war against the Infidel? What was Abbot Suger thinking?

Better to have appointed a knight, a man of experience in the field. I found it difficult to keep my contempt within bounds.

And then there was Thierry Galeran.

With this man I failed utterly to hide my dislike.

We were sworn enemies from the first moment we set eyes on each other. Galeran was a Knight Templar with some experience of Outremer, but limited to the raising and hoarding of Templar gold. Appointed as Louis's treasurer because of his previous connections along the route, Templar Galeran unfortunately lacked military insight. Furthermore, captured by the Turks at some time in his past, he had gained his freedom but had been gelded, and so, a man who was half a man, he had allowed his temper to sour. Abbot Suger saw in Galeran the perfect delegate to prevent any senseless frittering of money from the royal coffers. That was his official position, when he wasn't playing the part of Louis's watchdog, a role he took on only too well and to my mind gave precedence. He would keep me from Louis's side and Louis's ear if he could, considering me a malign influence. Ha! No eunuch would prevent me from speaking my mind. Galeran had a low opinion of women in general and me in particular—perhaps not surprising, when his own ability to satisfy a woman had been so thoroughly curtailed.

And here he was, with Louis, poking and prodding at my baggage.

"How can you wear so much?" Louis whined.

"Shall we not meet cold weather as well as the burning heat of summer when we reach the mountains?" I asked, knowing the answer. "So we need furs for one and veils for the other."

"But pallets with mattresses, Eleanor . . ."

"You don't expect me to sleep on the ground, do you?"

"No. No, of course not." Still, he looked aghast at the chests and bundles of equipment, lifting a silk tunic, allowing it to trail through his fingers. "So much . . . Is that a basin for washing?"

"Yes. And soap and napkins and towels."

"Perhaps Her Majesty should reconsider the amount she takes with her?" Galeran barely bothered to hide his reproof.

"Since when does Her Majesty take the advice of a gelded Templar?"

I observed crudely—and perhaps not wisely, waving him away. One could have a surfeit of Templar Galeran. "Do you really want the Queen of France to enter Constantinople looking like a complete rustic, Louis?"

Louis had retreated in ruffled defeat, Galeran remonstrating furiously but without effect.

Now before me, Louis held the sacred Oriflamme in his hands, but the dedication was far from over. I sighed and set myself to wait out the tedium, and my mind reverted to that day a year ago when we had received our crosses at Vézelay from Abbot Bernard himself. My heart leaped with the memory. I would never forget it.

What an amazing day it had been. A magical day to stir the blood. I had felt like a young girl again, carelessly, selfishly bent on my own pleasure. My spirits had soared to extravagant heights. My life force returned, my imagination flying free. Too free, some said, but what did they know?

It was a whimsy, of course, but a superbly planned whimsy. With the cross newly pinned to my breast, determined to spur on the faint-hearted, I whipped up the wives of my vassals for a quick and dramatic change of costume.

Dramatic? Louis did not see it in quite that light.

"In God's name, Eleanor!" He stared when he saw us, a strikingly colorful gathering, ready to mount and ride. For a moment his mouth opened and closed without further words. Then: "What are you doing?"

"Gathering support. What else? Look at them." I gestured to the ranks of knights. "How many here will slink off home as soon as your and holy Bernard's backs are turned? *I'll* get you your army, to sweep in victory through the Holy Land!"

"But this is a sacred occasion. By God, Eleanor! It's not a Twelfth Night play!"

"Of course it's not a Twelfth Night play! Do you not approve?"

Well, of course he didn't. "By God, I don't." It was rare for him to swear on God's name, and this was the third time in as many seconds. "It's not . . . not . . ."

"Have you forgotten?" I prompted his memory. "At Bourges—did I not say I would be Penthesilea and lead my Amazons? You did not disapprove then when your vassals cheered. And now you see the Queen of the Amazons before you."

"You make a spectacle of yourself!"

Which raised my spirits even higher. I laughed aloud for the joy of it and the sight of what I had achieved, with a little forethought. "Mount up, ladies. We'll ride and shame our men who hang back."

"You will not, Eleanor! I forbid it! It is frivolous and improper and not to be tolerated. . . ."

Louis's voice was soon lost to us as, riding astride in leather chausses, we spurred our white horses into the crowds of people who had come to hear Bernard preach the War of the Cross.

On that day, that occasion, we were nothing less than Amazon warriors, eye-catching in white tunics emblazoned with our red crosses. Our hair streamed free in the stiff breeze, mingling with the red plumes on our hats as we rode like the wind. Red boots completed the striking ensemble as we galloped through the crowds, wielding swords while calling on the reluctant knights and nobles to heed the summons. And those who turned their backs? We tossed spindles and distaffs and insults, shaming them before everyone.

Oh, I enjoyed it. Of course we did not ride bare breasted, as some would later claim in an effort to denigrate our participation and deliberately undermine my reputation. Of course we did not. How ridiculous that would have been. But if tunics and leather chausses made us men, then we were men, and not ashamed of it. What a symbol of freedom it was. What an impact we made on that stolid mass of waverers.

Louis had to concede my victory, if not graciously. "You behaved like a madwoman!"

"I behaved like a warrior—which is more than you did! And what was the result? Did we not rouse the reluctant, shame the coward, spur on the brave? You should be thanking me, Louis, for swelling your numbers. Not all are as enthusiastic about departing for Outremer for some unspecified length of time as you are!"

He stalked away in a thoroughly unholy temper, for was I not right? Emotion had flooded across the vast hillside like a storm wave. The demand for crosses had been so great that the saintly Bernard had been reduced to shredding his own mantle into strips to satisfy the numbers.

I sighed again as that bright memory faded under the cloud of incense and the endless drone of the prayers for our success. Now, finally, Louis was given the symbolic pilgrim's staff and wallet by the Pope, and there was nothing to keep us, except that Louis decided to delay again, to celebrate the feast day of Saint Denis to invoke the saint's protection. Well, I could tolerate it. What would one more week matter?

"So it begins." After sharing a final frugal repast with the monks, Louis had made his way from the refectory to the abbey guesthouse, where I was staying. White faced with strain, already exhausted, but still with fire in his eye, he refused the cup of wine I offered him, refused the stool I pushed forward toward the fire, but stood in the center of the room, blinking at the light from the candles. I thought he looked uneasy but it might have been a trick of the light.

"So it begins," I repeated. "Are you satisfied, Louis?"

"More than you could imagine." He smiled at me. He had obviously forgotten my Amazon moment. "Next year we will be in Jerusalem."

Surprising me, I felt a surge of unexpected tenderness for him. This was what he had worked for, for so long, and now it would come to fulfillment. Perhaps it would give Louis the ease his soul desired; perhaps I would see a return of the handsome youth I had wedded ten years before, not this troubled, careworn, anxious man who had to pray before he could make any decision. Perhaps this Crusade would be the healing draft he craved. He was a mere twenty-seven years old, but the religious life had added a score of years to bow his shoulders and imprint his face. Perhaps those years would fall from him if he could feel truly sanctified.

As if reading my thoughts, Louis fell to his knees before me, to cup his hands around my face. His smile was gentle, tender, reminding me of the days when he might have chosen to stay in my company, to ride at my side. To sleep in my bed. He kissed me lightly on the lips. The pressure of his mouth was warm and firm, in no manner unpleasant, and I leaned into it. Louis instantly pulled back with a shy smile. Did he need encouragement? I would humor him and let him set the pace for our farewells.

"So I leave tomorrow," I said. I knew the plan.

"You'll go on ahead. With your women and the baggage wagons and your own vassals from Aquitaine and Poitou. I'll follow on behind." Still kneeling, he enclosed my hands within his as if making a vow of fealty. "We'll meet up at Metz, where we'll gather on the banks of the Moselle."

And there, as I knew, we would join our forces with the German troops of Conrad, the Holy Roman Emperor who had, somewhat reluctantly, also heeded the Pope's call to arms.

"God keep you safe, Louis." My tender feeling toward him lingered.

"And you, my impetuous wife. I am not sorry you're coming with me. France will be safe in Suger's capable hands."

It felt good to part on such amicable terms. I kissed him again, and was urged on by the willing softness of his lips against mine. And because Louis seemed preoccupied—he ran his finger along the edge of my jaw, searching my face as if he had not seen me for a long time—I picked up the initiative myself.

"Will you stay here with me, Louis? Tonight? Our last night together for many weeks. There'll be no time for any private moments—perhaps until we reach Constantinople." I twisted my hands to link my fingers firmly with his. Surely he would see a need to stay. It might not be good sense to have me carrying a child when on crusade, but surely our last night should be one of celebration together rather than spent alone. "Stay with me, Louis." I gestured with a sweep of my hand around the comfortable room at the bright fire, the tapestried walls with their colors vivid even in the soft candlelight. The shadowed bed. "Stay with me tonight." I turned my face against his palm and pressed my lips there. He was my husband, and my duty should not be an unpleasant matter. He would not find me unwilling.

As if stung by a wasp, Louis shook me off, leaped to his feet, and took a step back.

"What is it?" I looked aghast as he retreated yet another step.

"I have taken an oath."

"An oath . . . ?"

"I've sworn to preserve my chastity when on crusade. Until I have stood in Jerusalem, in the place of the Holy Sepulchre, and been assured of God's forgiveness for my sins."

"Chastity!" I think I laughed. It was not a pleasant sound. "A vow of chastity?"

"I'll not indulge in bodily pleasures," he explained seriously, as if I might not understand him.

"Oh, I understand you right enough! So you've vowed to refuse my bed. I should have known!" I fought to quell the little knot of hysteria that threatened to expand and bubble over into some extreme emotion that I feared I might not be able to contain. Would I howl with laughter—or hit him? "And will I know the difference?" I sneered.

Louis stiffened in holy outrage. "You demean my sacrifice, lady."

I was beyond caring. The emotion transmuted into blind fury. "Sacrifice? And what about *my* sacrifice? You choose to live as a monk, yet you also chose to wed me. Or no—of course—you didn't. Your father chose that you should wed me. So if you take the vow of a monk, do you expect me to reciprocate and take the veil? Before God, Louis . . ."

His features were frozen. "I expect you to live as my wife, Eleanor. I expect you to honor my decisions."

"But I am not your wife, am I, except in name!"

"You are the mother of my child."

"And unlikely to get another!"

Louis's face flushed. "You should not say such things. I'll not talk to you about it."

"You will." I stood, advanced toward him. "We have no male heir, Louis! How many times do you need reminding? Does that not concern you?"

"You know it does."

"But you do nothing to remedy it. In God's name, Louis . . ."

"I shall spend this night in prayer. It doesn't become you to blaspheme, Eleanor!"

"It doesn't become you to dishonor me!"

I clenched my fists; then, when I felt the urge to strike out after all, I thrust them behind my back. As Louis took a step and then another toward the door, clearly intent on flight, I fought to rein in my anger and disappointment. Could he not even stay in the same room with me? He claimed he loved me, but such purity of love was an anathema. I needed a man who would hold me close. Who would talk to me of the trivia of the day and what we might do tomorrow. Who did not put God before me again and again. Who would look at me not as if I were a holy statue on a plinth but a warm-fleshed woman who could stir him to physical need.

"By God, Louis! You're so pure the light shines through you and you have no shadow."

"I'm sorry." He rubbed his hands over his face, then looked at me with what might have been grief. "I love you. I thought you would understand."

I had no pity. "No! I don't!"

"I need to feel cleansed. I've done some terrible things in my life. I have been excommunicated!" He still could not come to terms with it. "I was responsible for all those innocent deaths at Vitry. Those shrieks of agony lie on my conscience and trouble my sleep. . . ."

"In God's name, be silent! I've heard all this before."

"But listen . . . ! I feel that this chance to go to Jerusalem, to stop the Turkish onslaught, is God's path for me to bring me redemption. Christ was chaste throughout his life. How can I not subject my body to the same penance for a few short months? I thought you would understand, Eleanor."

"You are a fool!"

"When I have earned my salvation, I believe it will be God's will that we have a son."

I gave up. There was no arguing with him. "Of course you do." Weariness descended on me like an enveloping blanket. There was no moving him.

"I must go." He retreated to the door. "I'm expected in the abbey church."

"Then go. Go and talk to God. But how He will answer your prayers for an heir without some direct intervention from *you,* I have no idea!"

"You should respect my motives, Eleanor."

I turned my back on him. I could not look at him any longer. The monkish habit, the gaunt cheeks, the shaven head, they repelled me. "Do as you will, Louis. Spend the night with your precious Oriflamme and the oath to your long-dead brother. They mean far more to you than I." I could not stop the bitterness from flooding out.

I heard the door close softly and I was alone, and celibate for as long as it took Louis to get us all to Jerusalem. I wondered if Odo de Deuil or Galeran had had any part in Louis's decision to separate himself entirely from me. Perhaps not. He was quite capable of making it himself.

How angry I was. As much with myself as with my contemptible husband. How could I have ever thought that the Crusade could mend the rift that Louis created between us? How could anything mend it? He would remain a celibate at heart, and for the most part in body, until the day he died. And so, physically, through necessity, would I. I was too angry to weep.

I despised him. I washed my hands of him.

Nothing would be allowed to dampen my spirits. Cheering crowds lined the route the next morning when finally I threw off the dark restrictions of life on the Île de la Cité. I was twenty-five years of age, the beauty of my face and figure unimpaired, my authority over my Aquitaine vassals unquestionable. For the next months there would be no restrictions on my time and how I would choose to spend it. I was free of court life, of protocol, and not least of Louis. Constantinople beckoned with glittering gilded promise, the fabled city where the Byzantine Emperor Manuel Comnenus held tight to the last outpost of culture and tradition of the old Roman Empire. Where he and the Orthodox Christians worshipped under mosaic domes in defiance of the Muslim Turks who were already snapping at their southern borders. I could barely wait to set eyes on such rumored magnificence. Then on to Antioch, where Raymond held tight to his control and prayed for help. We would bring it to him. It would be a glorious victory. And finally Jerusalem! By the new year, in Louis's reckoning, we would be in Jerusalem. The adventure unfolded before my mind's eye.

What an impression we made, what a magnificent sight, this vast army inspired by its papal promise of driving the infidel Turks from the Holy Land so that we might worship freely in Jerusalem. The sun shone on helmet and armor, glinting off the hilts of swords that carried fragments of the true cross. Destriers fretted and stamped. Banners unfurled and lifted in the summer air, proclaiming the might of my vassals from Poitou and Aquitaine. I rode in their midst, their liege lord, my horse proud-stepping with its plaited mane, my saddle picked out in silver. My robes were as richly flamboyant as any I owned, embroidered with the royal fleur-de-lys. I smiled at my subjects as we passed. Still simmering with anger at Louis's intransigence, I was not sorry to be traveling without him.

"Pray for us in Jerusalem, lady," my people called.

I raised my hand in acknowledgment.

And Marie, my daughter? I had already said my farewells, accepting that it would be more than a twelvemonth before we were reunited. Not understanding, she had laughed at my solemnity, clutching at the fur of my cuffs when I looped a little silver cross on a fine chain around her neck. She would be well cared for.

My spirits were high, but doubts nipped at my mind as a terrier nips at the heels of recalcitrant cattle. Louis was certain of his calculations, his route, but could we trust him to lead such an army to its victory? His past failures scratched at my confidence. How could I have confidence in a dynamic leader of men when he insisted on keeping his pilgrim's gown? So vast an army of soldiers and pilgrims depended on us, and all those who hung on our sleeves. Servants and minstrels. Vagabonds and criminals and whores. Hunting dogs and hawks. The vast baggage train. Would Louis be able to get us all safely to our goal?

The thought made me shiver in the warm sunlight.

I made a silent prayer that he would surprise us all. Before God, he would need to.

Chapter Twelve

MARCH 1147

Nine Months Later

The port of Saint-Simeon outside Antioch in the Holy Land

Physically shattered, nauseously ill, I stepped from the squalid horror of the little round ship that had housed me for the past three weeks onto the solid quay of Saint-Simeon, the port of Antioch. With me there was no baggage, no horses, and no hope. Louis, of course, was there, and Odo de Deuil and Thierry Galeran—there had been more times than I could count when I had wished myself rid of all three of them. But there was no crusading army, victorious or otherwise.

What a sight I must have presented. Three weeks of storms and adverse winds and shattering sickness had left me almost as gaunt as Louis. My legs were shockingly weak. Unwashed and filthy, my gown and linens ragged and soiled after constant wear in the most loathsome of conditions with none to replace them, I imagined my face pale, lined with fear and exhaustion. My hair was matted with salt and itched, probably—by the Virgin!—with lice. At my lowest ebb, I had even considered taking a knife to the length of it. I had no looking glass to tell me the truth, nor could have borne to use it if I had. I would not have wished to see the wretchedness in my soul. I was desperately unhappy, my reputation in as many rags as my gown. It was an effort to hold my head high.

Nine months ago I had set out with such hope. The events I had lived through had been the stuff of tragedy. Never in all my life had I felt so utterly wretched as I did as I stepped from that ship.

Louis offered me his hand as I staggered on the unmoving dry land. I accepted his help, because appearances must be preserved in public, and there were plenty to mark our arrival, but I neither looked at him nor exchanged words of relief. I was beyond speaking to him. On that final day in France when he had rejected me by his sacred oath to keep his body pure, I had condemned him for a fool. Now I was beyond tolerating him to any degree. As soon as I was sure of my balance, I pulled my hand away. His treatment of me I considered deplorable, despicably unjust, far worse than mere physical rejection.

And it had all been done, appallingly, in full public gaze.

I strode ahead of him, pushing him from my mind. I'd had a belly full of Louis Capet to last me a lifetime. And of Odo and Templar Galeran. There was only one face I sought in the crowds that had come to welcome us.

Even so, I was vain enough to consider: what would these cheering citizens of Antioch see in me? Not the proud figure who had left Paris in a blaze of publicity, an Amazon on a white horse. Not the elegantly fashionable queen who had feasted and hunted and enjoyed the fabled luxury of Constantinople. Would they believe now that I was the Queen of France and Duchess of Aquitaine? I doubted it. I did not have more than one pair of sodden shoes to my name, and my gown hung on my bones like skin on the carcass of a scrawny chicken. My hair was a rat's nest of tangles, hidden, I hoped, by my less than pristine veil. I think I looked like a whore from the lowest stews of Paris.

The voices raised in welcome redoubled and I forced a smile to my lips. Perhaps my sore heart was soothed a little by the familiar chanting of the Te Deum by the choir, led by the Patriarch himself in festive robes. And as I felt my tense muscles begin to relax, I began to be aware of the warmth of early spring on my face. The storm clouds had retreated, leaving the sky the deepest azure and the hillsides covered with flowers, their spicy scent drifting on the light wind. Just like Aquitaine. Just like home in Poitiers and Bordeaux.

The memory of what I had left behind brought me close to tears.

And there in the midst, walking toward me, was Raymond, my father's brother. Raymond of Poitiers, now Prince Raymond of Antioch, as magnificently striking, head and shoulders above the crowd, as my memory of him. Indeed, his new authority burnished him in gold.

"Eleanor!"

He had no eyes for Louis. None for Louis's damned advisers. He looked at *me*. He walked straight to me, such balm to my soul after weeks—months, even—of my being excluded from Louis's endless, pointless negotiations with those close to him. Closeted hour after hour with Odo and Thierry Galeran, my miserable husband had not once asked my opinion, yet he was quick to castigate me for the collapse of his plans. Now I was greeted as if I mattered.

Louis and his minions might not have been there.

"Eleanor. My dear girl. We feared for your safety. How you must have suffered." Raymond's welcome rolled over me, wrapping me in comfort in the soft accents of the *langue d'oc*.

"Ah, Raymond. I am so pleased to be here." I almost wept.

He opened his arms and I fell into them, and, unable to fight against it, I did weep on his shoulder. All my hopes when I had left France—for adventure, for victory, for sheer pleasure in the day-to-day travel—all had been destroyed under the weight of Louis's stupidity as much as by the military skill of our enemies. And I was being held accountable. But now my ordeal was over. This was home. Raymond's kiss of welcome on my wet cheeks healed my immediate wounds.

My nightmare was at an end.

Nightmare? It had been no mere nightmare, to fade with wakening. It had been a never-ending torment, as black as the pit of Hell.

It had all gone disastrously wrong. Oh, we had started out bravely enough, celebrating our journey across Europe, glorying in the spectacle we made, the flower of western Europe. Hunting and feasting. Enjoying good weather and new surroundings, marveling at the wonder of Constantinople, where we were entertained and cosseted in luxury at the Emperor's court. Then Emperor Comnenus's hospitality wore thin in the face of our vast army camped outside his city. Might our invasion not stir the Turkish rulers into uniting against him? Far better to play divide and rule with the Infidel, he urged Louis. Better to plot and scheme, setting one Turkish lord against the next to keep their mutual desire for conquest from focusing too readily on Constantinople. When Louis rejected any such policy of compromise out of hand, our Byzantine host ushered us rapidly on our way.

But should we have gone; were we not warned? Had there not been a complete overshadowing of the sun, the sky darkening to black night, as we left Constantinople? An omen, our troops muttered with fingers circled against the Evil Eye. Perhaps we should delay our departure. But Louis refused to be diverted. Were we, bearing the Oriflamme of France, not protected by God and His Holy Angels? Ha! So much for Louis's intimate knowledge of God's plan for us! We should have acknowledged the night-black morning when the sun was lost to us as a dire prediction, and acted on it, for what was to come could not have been worse.

It was Louis's fault, of course.

Seven months after we had set out so bravely, Constantinople behind us, we were still untold days from Jerusalem, still floundering in the mountainous regions of Asia Minor. The German Emperor Conrad and his forces had gone on ahead. And Louis? Despite our numbers being bolstered by Louis's uncle, the Count of Maurienne, and a tidy force of knights, Louis's spirits were dangerously low. For five days he sat and fretted, debating whether to rendezvous with Conrad or sit tight and wait for news of him. Anyone of wit could see that our army was eating its way through our limited food supplies while the days passed and winter loomed.

Louis's ability to lead men, always uncertain, seemed to disintegrate into indecisive idiocy with every day. I did not remonstrate with him. He would not listen to me. I'd have told him to take hold, to get the army under way and push ahead with all speed. What point sitting tight and making no progress? But Odo and Templar Galeran were the only ones with access to the royal ear, and they whispered caution. How would they—one a narrow-minded, scribbling priest, the other nothing more than a miserly, venomous clerk—know anything of relevance to pursuing a military campaign? Under their influence, Louis became as useless as a cracked jug. When he heard of Conrad's defeat at the hands of the Turks, and the total destruction of his army, he was struck dumb with grief. And when Conrad struggled back to our camp with the most vile head wound that all but robbed him of his wits, Louis burst into a bout of noisy tears that embarrassed us all.

Stupid, stupid man!

We needed leadership, not raw emotion. We needed the advice of knights and fighting men, not men of the Church. And did Louis turn to his barons and knights? Did he turn to his uncle Maurienne or my own experienced vassal Geoffrey de Rancon, who could have given him some seasoned advice? No, he did not. I had to leave the tent in disgust as Louis wept and fell to his knees to beg God for guidance.

Finally, at last, we struck camp, taking the route south along the coastal lowlands—a reasonable enough choice—but nothing would persuade Louis against halting again to celebrate the Christmas festivities. How could we mark Christ's birth when on the march? By God, would the Holy Child have cared, as long as we got to Jerusalem? It proved to be a desperate decision. Louis's choice of campsite was simply bad. Torrential rain beat down on us. Gales brought terrifying floods that swept away our tents, our weapons and equipment. Precious food was spoiled or lost. Men and animals drowned or were battered to death on the rocks. Instead of a glorious celebration it was ruination.

It became impossible for me to even speak to Louis with any show of respect.

After the devastation of Christmas, he decided to press on to Antioch without delay, taking the direct route through the mountains, which of course condemned us to the slowest of progress, with winter at its most inhospitable. I will never forget the misery of it. I will never forgive him for it. The mud that sucked at the horses' feet, the impossibly steep gradients, almost too much for the horse-drawn litters in which I and the women now traveled. The thick leather curtains failed to keep out the constant rain and sleet. Every day we were set upon by Turkish raiding parties, and all the time we retched at the stench of decomposing bodies of the massacred Germans who had already taken this route and failed.

Was Louis even aware of our plight? Oh, he prayed interminably for our success. He sent off letter after letter to Abbot Suger, pleading for money, but never did he give the army the commander it needed. In a misguided spirit of unity, he divided responsibilities amongst his barons, each night designating a different commander for the next day.

Disastrous!

And what use was Louis in facing Turkish raiding parties, with their fine arrows and sharp swords, when he turned his horse aside to visit yet one more wayside shrine? If he prayed at one, he prayed at a score. I was full to the brim with contempt. I seethed with frustrated anger.

We paid the penalty for Louis's terrible decisions. How we paid, many with their lives. And I? I paid with my reputation. Never will my good name recover from the stain of what happened at Mount Cadmos. Mount Cadmos. Still I shudder at the name, a cataclysm that will be engraved on my heart and on my soul until the day I die. Those who recall Eleanor, Duchess of Aquitaine, even when she is dead, will damn her for it.

I was not to blame. How could I have been?

Here's how it was.

Louis had sent ahead the vanguard of the army, my own Aquitainian forces, under the command of my vassal Geoffrey de Rancon and the Count of Maurienne. I accompanied them, leaving Louis to bring up the rear with the main body of Frankish troops that escorted the mass of unarmed pilgrims and many of the women, as well as the baggage. We were, by his orders, to set up camp on a plateau before the next mountain pass, to wait there for Louis to join us, a position that both de Rancon and the Count quickly found to be quite untenable, windswept and open, with no water source or protection from either the elements or raiding Turks. We had learned from experience that we could never relax our guard: an opportunitic Turkish force could sweep down on us without warning, causing untold damage. So since daylight was still good, the two commanders agreed to push on through the rocky pass to a sheltered, well-irrigated valley beyond, suitable for a camp. I could see nothing but good in the plan. Yes, I agreed to it, if that made me guilty of what was to come. There, in our well-protected camp, we spent a night waiting for the main army to join us.

And it did not.

Looking back, I see it as a long night of dread, the news that reached us the worst possible. Louis had chosen to camp before the pass, on the dangerous plateau that we had abandoned. Safe as we were that night in our strategic encampment, Louis's Frankish troops, disastrously exposed and defenseless, were not. Surely at least one of his more shrewd commanders must have advised him of the fatal weakness of his position. If he did, Louis did not listen. The attack that de Rancon and Maurienne feared had come to pass. Without warning, a Turkish army had swooped down on the plateau and cut our main army to pieces.

Fearing for Louis's life, I prayed through those dark hours until my voice was hoarse, my knees sore. He did not deserve to end his life by a Turkish sword. All we could do was wait until the remnants trickled into our camp. As day broke, I stood with de Rancon and Maurienne, searching every face. And with daylight Louis rode in, slumped on a borrowed horse and guided by a monk who had found him wandering aimless and lost. Almost falling from the animal, he staggered over to where I waited for him, hands outstretched in greeting, tears of relief drying on my cheeks.

"Louis! Thank God!"

Chest heaving, swaying from exhaustion, Louis wiped a smear of mud and blood from his cheek and temple.

"Come with me," I urged. "Let me . . ."

He swept aside my hands.

"God damn you, Eleanor!"

I was struck dumb. Surely I had misheard?

"You're to blame for this, Eleanor." Louis's voice was cracked with fatigue, but he made no effort to control its volume. "You and your damned Aquitainians. You and de Rancon!"

It took a moment for his words to make their impact. There Louis stood, blood-smeared, swaying with fatigue but shaking in anger. A tense little group gathered around us: Odo de Deuil, Galeran, de Rancon, the Count of Maurienne.

"You have caused my army to be wiped out," he raged. "You have destroyed my hope of reaching Jerusalem. . . ."

Had I not spent the night in prayer for his safety? Any concern I might have had was fast vanishing. "I have done no such thing!"

"Who would de Rancon take his orders from but you? Whose advice would he seek? He's your vassal, by God! It's your fault!"

"This is nonsense!"

"Yours was the authority, Eleanor. . . ."

"Don't be ridiculous, Louis. *You* put de Rancon and Maurienne in charge. They were perfectly capable of making their own decisions. It was none of my doing. They gave me their military assessment of a difficult situation—and we acted on it. Should I have refused to listen? It seemed eminently sensible to me."

Louis did not listen. "You should have waited for us—as I ordered."

"On a wind-blasted, unprotected plateau? You must be mad. . . ."

I was under attack; the culpability for the whole debacle was being leveled at me. At first I could hardly believe it. Then when I felt the bite of the words, and was so angry I could barely search for a suitable defense, it was an anger of cold control. Deadly cold. To be so rebuked, in public, by my own ineffectual husband. And without any just cause. Pride stiffened my spine and I drew my courage around me at the barrage of accusation.

"Your actions left the rest of my army unprotected. I needed your men, Eleanor! If you had camped where I told you to camp, and we had joined forces, the Turks would have been driven back," he accused. Then with a snarl: "I note that *your* vassals—the troops from Aquitaine and Poitou—survived unharmed at the front."

"For which you should be thankful," I retaliated with icy calm. "Without them you would have barely a hundred knights left to your command."

"You made the wrong decision, Eleanor!"

De Rancon tried to halt the tirade. "Indeed, Sire. I made the decision, not Her Majesty."

Maurienne made to agree but Galeran silenced him with a gesture, turning his flat stare from me to de Rancon. "He admits it. He disobeyed orders, Sire. As a warning to the rest of your knights, de Rancon should be hanged for treason."

Hanged? I could not believe what I was hearing.

De Rancon paled, muscles tensing in shock. "I made the best decision, Sire."

"I agree, nephew," Maurienne added weightily. "The plateau was a bad choice."

"You'll not hang one of my vassals," I snapped.

But Louis was beyond reason. "Thousands killed. Our baggage train plundered. Innocent pilgrims cut down. Horses and equipment lost . . ."

"For God's sake, Louis. If you're going to apportion blame, then take some onto your own shoulders."

Louis ignored me but strode to de Rancon to deliver a fisted blow to his shoulder. "You disobeyed orders, sir. No, I'll not hang you—but I don't want you with my army. You'll go back to Poitou."

"You can't afford to lose any more commanders, Louis," Maurienne warned.

"I can't afford to keep those who disobey my orders." Louis swung back to me. "And in future you'll keep your fingers out of military matters, madam! Now get out of my sight! All of you. I need to pray." He began to stalk to my tent, his own lost with the baggage train. "All lost. Everything. If I fail it will be on your shoulders, Eleanor."

"I am not guilty."

"You must repent, Eleanor." His condemnation carried harshly on the morning air. "You must beg God's forgiveness for your terrible sin, as I did for Vitry."

I will not! I will not! I am not at fault!

The words screamed in my head as I took refuge with my women, my belly churning in turmoil. Was I guilty? I refuted it; I would always refute it. Yes, I gave my consent, but I acted on the military experience of de Rancon and Maurienne. How could I anticipate the terrible repercussions? All I knew was that I was chosen for the scapegoat, in disgrace, my reputation trampled in the mud of the mountain pass where our knights and soldiers and pilgrims lay dead.

Unfair! Unfair!

Yet I would hold my head high. Not to do so would be to accept guilt.

I spent a difficult night. Even my women treated me with a strange sort of silent reticence. The rumors of Louis's bellowed accusations had resounded around the camp and lost nothing in the telling, and Agnes provided me with any detail of my misdemeanors that had passed me by. She was not reticent. I had weighed down the baggage train with the inordinate, selfish load of my possessions. I had left the main army stranded and vulnerable by ordering my vanguard to cross the pass. I had placed my own safety and comfort before that of the knights and troops and pilgrims who followed me. I had caused the death of the women who had chosen to travel with me, but had elected to journey at the rear.

So now I knew why my own women would not meet my eye.

Eleanor was guilty. Eleanor must bear the weight of the dead. Did not her own husband so accuse her? My skin crawled at the injustice of it.

"I can't believe Louis would put me in so invidious a position," I stormed at last when I could vent my fury without an audience.

"No, but I can believe it of that Templar snake!" Agnes brushed my hair with long, angry movements. "That's where the blame lies."

"You can't exonerate Louis. He would listen to Galeran before me!"

"Galeran fears you. He wants power." The stroke of the brush became heavier. "He fears Louis's love for you. He'll destroy it if he can."

I was not mollified. "What sort of love is it that accuses and shames without evidence?"

I rose next morning determined to plead my cause before Louis and his War Council. I would be heard. I would not be ignored. Louis and his knights must give me a hearing. For my sake and de Rancon's

I must put the record straight. Surely Louis, after a night's sleep and more reasoned thought, would listen to me.

Did I expect to be included in Louis's councils? I should have known better by now: Weighty decisions of state were not the preserve of women. Thierry Galeran, of course, stiff legged and snarling, barred my way into the pavilion, and Louis refused to see me. Short of an undignified scuffle at the entrance, I had no choice but to retreat. Such anger burned within me beneath the humiliation. I could taste it, bitter as bile. I had been cast to the dogs by my own husband, my reputation stripped bare, to be squabbled over and torn apart by the gutter riffraff of Europe. If Louis refused to see me, who would listen to my vindication? There would be no vindication. How could he humble me in this way, his wife? How could he put me to shame before those of lesser rank?

Galeran's smug complacency disgusted me. His influence was surely in the ascendant.

Never had I been brought so low.

If I had to choose the moment when I knew that I could not tolerate this sham of a marriage, perhaps this was it. That my husband would denigrate me without foundation, listening to the slanders of those who bore me ill will, treating me like a woman rather than a ruler in her own right with as much authority as he. I knew I would never forgive him as I walked away from that pavilion, knowing that I had been rendered powerless.

I recall I accused Thierry Galeran of being no better than an emasculated cur, snapping to protect its master. The Templar would never forgive me for that. Unfortunate, as it turned out.

That was not the end of it. Our shattered army limped out of the mountains to the nearest port, the town of Attalia, where we found no relief but instead weeks of unspeakable horror. Already we were half-starved. With the loss of our baggage train, lack of food threatened our very lives quite as severely as did the Turkish attacks. Even now my belly revolts at the memory, of being reduced to eating the rotting flesh of dead horses and mules. Some knights bled their horses to gain sustenance by drinking their blood. We lacked clothes, even shoes.

My hands and feet blistered, my lips cracked, my clothes fell into rags around me.

"We will regroup in Attalia," Louis predicted.

He was wrong, of course. Storms battered us. Food continued in short supply and was expensive, as the local Greeks determined to make their fortunes from us. Yet only three days away, so short a journey by sea, lay the golden city of Antioch. All we needed were the ships to take us there. The local fishermen rubbed their fingers at the prospect of crusading gold falling into their pockets.

"I'll not pay the price!" Louis fumed. "Four silver marks for each passenger—on top of the cost of each vessel! I'll not pay it."

"Do we have a choice?" I asked wearily.

"Of course we have a choice! Galeran says we can't afford it. With God's help I'll beat them down."

God was beyond persuasion. Five weeks of haggling, with Antioch nearly within our sights. Five weeks of indescribable torment. Dysentery broke out amongst the troops. The stench of death and bodily waste enclosed us—and then the first outbreak of plague. Death stalked us, while Louis refused to pay and we sat there in Attalia.

Enough! In God's name, enough! I sought out Louis, who was as usual praying with Odo de Deuil, Count Maurienne looking jaundiced, Galeran standing guard at the door. Without a word I pushed past him, daring him to draw the sword in his scabbard.

"We can't stay here, Louis." I didn't wait until he struggled to his feet. "It's intolerable. Our army is dying on its feet."

And, taking me aback, Louis smiled. "I know. We leave tomorrow."

"Thank God! We've enough ships to move most of them. . . ."

"No. We march." What? *March?* "I'm determined on this, Eleanor." The fervor was back in his eyes. "We'll march in the footsteps of the first Crusaders. Their valor is remembered today—and so will mine be. We shall achieve glory in Heaven."

"A hazardous journey of two months on foot when we could be there in three days by sea? You must be insane."

"I'm assured of God's blessing. If we die it will be as martyrs for a righteous cause."

God's Bones! I was beyond valor and martyrs. I felt the strongest impulse to strike Louis's self-satisfied, self-righteous face. Did he not understand? What mad dream of martyrdom did he hold to? My mind was made up.

"No!"

"I don't understand." At least I had wiped the smile from his face.

"Then let me explain, Louis! I'll not march with you," I stated. "If you persist with this madness I will leave you and go by sea. What's more, I'll take my own vassals with me."

"But the cost . . ." Galeran gasped. "No, Sire . . ."

"Cost? What are four silver marks compared with a man's life?" My voice rang clear, fired by a sense of rightness. "Our troops who can pay will do so. The rest will remain here until we can make other arrangements."

"You would not. . . ." Louis looked aghast as I threatened to rob him of the major portion of his army.

"Try me!" I showed my teeth in a smile that was not a smile. "If you march, you go without the men of Aquitaine and Poitou."

Louis fell into an agony of indecision. His fingers writhed; his teeth bit into his lower lip. Such weakness! Such unforgivable weakness. Such lack of either compassion or common sense.

"You are forcing my hand," he muttered.

"Yes. I am. Tomorrow I sail for Antioch. We should have been there days ago!"

Maurienne smirked. Galeran scowled. Odo raised his eyes to Heaven for guidance. And in the face of my obstinacy Louis's resistance collapsed. We were barely on speaking terms when we took to the little fleet of round ships.

It was a nightmare of a journey.

Storms descended, bringing with them all the fear of shipwreck and grim, unrelenting seasickness. Three weeks it took us, under winds that drove us off course. Three weeks in which Louis lamented the loss of his dream to follow in the footsteps of those who had captured Jerusalem. He offered me no comfort, only a continued fretting that my decision had lost him an army on the slopes of Mount Cadmos.

By the time we reached Saint-Simeon, I could no longer bear the sight of his strained features, his bent shoulders, the unending drone of his prayers. He did not even show concern for the thousands of unfortunates who could not pay the passage and had been left behind in Attalia to starve or die of plague.

"I forbid you to approach your uncle over this matter," Louis lectured me. "*I'll* see to the rescue of my army. Do you hear me, Eleanor?"

"Yes. I hear you, Louis. Do it soon, before they all die."

If we were barely on speaking terms when we left Attalia, we were not at all three weeks later when we finally arrived in Antioch. I fell into Raymond's open, welcoming, compassionate arms.

Chapter Thirteen

" **W**elcome, lady. Everything has been made ready for you. Come and regain your strength. Rest, now. Be at ease."

His voice was as rich and smooth as the oil from the olive trees that had lined our route, as succulently sweet and melting to a frozen heart as a cup of hippocras on a winter's eve. Raymond helped me to alight from the cushioned traveling litter he had provided for me, into the sun-filled courtyard of his palace. He smiled at me and I smiled at him as bright memory rushed back.

Raymond of Poitiers, my father's young brother, who, landless and ambitious, had taken himself to England as a young lad, where he was reared and trained for knighthood until King Fulk of Jerusalem invited him to travel to Outremer and become ruler of Antioch. Raymond's visit to us in Aquitaine en route for that honor, when I was barely twelve years old, had left a lasting impression. Only nine years older than I, yet already a man to my young girl, he was tall, immensely strong, and ridiculously good to look at. And he could sing. . . . I recalled the velvet-warm vibrancy of his voice as he sang the troubadour's verses of love and devotion of a man for a woman. Sometimes he was audacious enough to sing them to me. I had watched him as he honed his knightly talents in the tiltyard, battling with sword and mace. On horseback he was a dream of long-limbed grace, of power, of polished skill. Raymond laughed and danced and played foolish games. For those few short weeks, he entranced me, before disappearing as fast as he had arrived, all energy and vital life, like a magic creature from a troubadour's tale.

Oh, yes! I recalled Raymond of Poitiers. I had not forgotten him, this epitome of gilded knighthood. And now here he was, in the flesh, welcoming me into his home.

"This is wonderful!" It was all I could think to say as I looked around, astonished at the wealth, at the sheer luxury. All the fears, and that terrible sense of isolation that had dogged me for days, now calmed to leave me enfolded in the softest of pleasure.

Raymond smiled and took my hand to lead me up the flight of shallow steps. "I think it will remind you of home. Of Aquitaine."

"Oh, it does. It does." I did not wait to see if Louis followed me. In that moment I did not care if I never set eyes on him again.

"Let me introduce you." A young woman was waiting at the top of the steps, her hands lifted to take mine. "My wife, Constance."

I knew of her, daughter and heiress of the late King Bohemond of Antioch. We kissed formally, as required.

"My husband's family is welcome here," she said.

Clad in flowing Eastern robes, a small, fair young woman with soft blue eyes, a little younger than I, she smiled shyly before leaving us.

"My wife keeps to the ways of the seraglio," Raymond explained.

So I was left to experience this manner of living in Raymond's care. The sunshine touched my head, my shoulders. It was as soft and dulcet as a southern spring in the castles of my childhood. On the ten-mile journey from Saint-Simeon I had cast back the curtains to look out in wonder. I had not expected so magnificent a city, or the instantly recognizable trace of Greek and Roman foundations as I had known in the cities of Aquitaine. Antioch unfolded before me like a precious book as it gripped the terraces on the slopes of Mount Silpius, quite magically shimmering in the light. So beautiful it was. If I did not love my own Aquitaine so much, I would choose to live here, I decided in that moment. No wonder Raymond was captivated by it. No wonder he was in fear for its survival at the hands of the Turks. Hanging gardens, tumbling from terrace to terrace, perfumed the air, as did the tall sentinels of pine woods. Orange and lemon groves hemmed us in, their heavy perfume intoxicating.

And then the city. As we entered under the arched portal, it promised comfort in colonnaded villas, its streets paved with marble, a pleasure to walk along. All protected from those who wished us ill by great walls and watchtowers.

All now under threat, however impregnable those defenses seemed. It broke my heart to think that this beautiful city would be overrun if Turkish aggression was not halted. But now was not the time for such heart-tearing. Indeed, I was too weary for it. Here was friendship and quiet pleasure and the easy tolerance of family. Mount Cadmos with its failure, its hurt and rejection, seemed a thousand miles and an equal number of years away. For the briefest of moments as I stood on the steps, I closed my eyes and let my feverish mind rest.

"You look weary, Eleanor." Raymond drew me into the first of a series of cool audience chambers. "You look as if you have traveled far and hard."

"How flattering you are!" My cracked lips managed to smile even as I felt the burn of tears. "You have no knowledge of how far and how hard it has been." His concern struck deep and I was forced to blink. I must be more tired than I had thought.

"You'll soon recover your beauty. What better place than this?" It wrapped me around, as smooth as the silk of the new robes laid out for me on my bed, as soft as the swan's down of the pillows provided for me. Without fuss, without drawing attention, Raymond handed me a square of linen to wipe my eyes.

"I can think of nowhere better." I touched his hand in gratitude.

"I trust there are accommodations for my knights, sir," Louis broke in, his voice cold, his Latin clipped. And I realized that Raymond and I had slipped into the *langue d'oc* through ease and habit. Rude, but not intentional.

Louis had not even noticed that I was so weak as to weep in public.

"Of course." With the slightest apologetic smile to me, Raymond now gave his attentions to his noble guest, returning to educated Latin. "Forgive me, Majesty. If I have been remiss, it is only that your wife's health gives me concern. But now I see that she needs only rest and time." He gestured to a waiting servant to present Louis with a cup of wine. "I make you as free of my hospitality as my dear niece. Your knights have all been allotted accommodations in villas and palaces as befits their rank. You may stay and enjoy what we can offer you as long as you need. Certainly until you have recovered from your ordeal."

Churlishly, Louis refused the wine. "We cannot impose on your hospitality long."

"We can stay for a little while." I tried to draw the sting of Louis's discourtesy. "Our knights and foot soldiers need to recover."

But I earned only a sharp response from Louis. "We must press on to Jerusalem."

"Undoubtedly you must. And we will talk of that." The perfect host, in no manner disturbed, Raymond snapped his fingers to summon a waiting steward. "Show His Majesty to his quarters." Then he turned back to me. "Now, let me show you to *your* rooms, Eleanor. They have the most magnificent view to the north toward Trebizond. . . ."

I was considering not the views from the palace but Raymond.

He had grown, filled out into manhood since we last met, as fair as I recalled and even more impressively regal, and I saw in his sun-kissed skin and hair, in his patrician cast of feature, in those intense blue eyes, the noble blood of Aquitaine: the troubadour, the wily politician, the flamboyantly handsome warrior lord. Warmth flooded back into me from my crown to my toes.

I walked with him to my rooms, senses adrift.

It was like a dream. A sensual, scented dream. With the windows—superbly glazed—now open to the warm air, I bathed in aromatic water, lulled by perfumed candles. Servants moved silently to bring me fruit and sweetmeats from a fragile porcelain dish, and a goblet of wine chilled with mountain snow. Potions and salves were brought, redolent of herbs, to anoint my wind- and rain-cracked skin. After Mount Cadmos and its aftermath, the glamour of Raymond and his court overwhelmed me. I sank into it, wallowed in it, luxuriated in it. Some of my wounds healed with the fragrant water that ran into the bowls.

I sank to my nose in the water in a mosaic tub as I admired this room I had been given. Frescoed walls had a charming frieze of musicians and dancers who leaped and capered, and for my own pleasure a serving girl strummed softly on a lute. When I rose from the tub to a servant waiting with the finest of linen, a silk gown was provided for me, soft footwear and a jeweled band to hold the transparent veil, material so delicate that it slipped through my fingers.

I had never experienced such unabashed luxury.

From my window where I leaned, hands spread on the warm stone, I looked out to the view that Raymond had praised, dominated by Mount Lebanon. There in the valley, tiny figures in the distance, were the strings of camels that followed the caravan routes to bring Antioch its wealth. A fortune in spices and dyes, silk and perfume and porcelain.

Drawn by the sight of cool greenery, I made my way into the garden to sit amongst the flowers. There, later, Raymond found me.

"That's better." Sitting beside me on the cushioned stone bench, stretching out his long legs in elegant ease, he touched my cheek with gentle fingers, tucked back a curl of my hair that was rapidly drying in the sun and escaping from my veil. "I had forgotten how lovely you are. Or how intense your hair is when the sun shines through it." He let one of the tresses curl around his finger, memory smiling in his eyes. "I remember calling you a vixen when you were a red-haired child."

"So do I. It infuriated me."

"Now you have become a beauty. How long is it since we last met?"

I pursed my lips. "Twelve years or more." I tried to laugh, and failed. "I was but a child—careless and ignorant and still unwed." Even I heard the bitterness in my voice.

"So you were."

He drew my hand through his arm, stood, and led me to the balustraded edge, from where we could look across the expanse of palace and gardens, golden stone, soft greens, and the riot of exotic flowers. There was a silence between us, as if Raymond waited for me to decide to speak, if that was what I wished. And so, lured by someone who had a care for me, I did.

"I am no longer careless and ignorant." Raymond's quiet interest invited confidences. "The last months—the last years—impossible! They have made me aware of . . ." I could not put my thoughts into words after all.

"You are not content."

"No."

"Not even as Queen of France, with a daughter of your own."

"No."

"Will you tell me?"

"How can I be expected to be content when . . ." I closed my lips and shook my head.

"It would be no burden for me to listen to you."

His smile, his gaze, were all compassion. It was too tempting. But I would not. It would be too easy, and there were so many things I dared not say.

"Forgive my moodiness, Raymond. It means nothing." I buried my sorrow deep and turned my thoughts to the future. It was more than a pleasure to have an intelligent man willing to listen to me, to talk to me. "This lovely city . . . Do you truly fear for your existence here?"

"Yes. I do." A line appeared between Raymond's brows as he followed my lead from personal to politics, but still he allowed it without comment. "The Turks are becoming aggressive."

"Is their leader not dead?"

"Zengi? True enough. But there will be no respite. His son, Nureddin, is a worthy successor. And they now have Edessa." He pointed into the distance toward that invisible city. "It was a major loss to us and it opens us to attack. And after that? What's to stop them from making a successful advance against Jerusalem?"

"You're hoping Louis will lead an attack against them, to retake Edessa?"

"It's my hope. If his purpose here is to safeguard the Holy City, it would seem eminently sensible. Edessa is the key. Retake that, and Antioch and Jerusalem can breathe again." Raymond led me to another carved stone seat—how well the garden was furnished—and motioned for me to sit. "But can we persuade your husband? What do you think, Eleanor? You know him better than anyone." He looked down at me so that I had to look up, squinting into the sun. "Can he be persuaded to use his forces in the name of Christ against the Infidel and beat them from my door?"

As I raised my hand to shield my face, I decided to be honest. What point in raising Raymond's hopes when Louis could be fickle and impossibly unpredictable? "He may do so. If you can persuade him not to stop at every shrine along the way. Louis is fixed on saving his soul, and it takes an unconscionable length of time." I was even more honest. "But to turn away from Jerusalem? Louis may not see how it lies to his advantage." I frowned. "It will also depend on what Galeran thinks."

"Does Louis not listen to your advice?"

"No. He banishes me from his councils to prevent being seduced into listening to me! Galeran guards his master's privacy and his thoughts."

I was horrified at the emotion that colored my voice, but here in this paradise with a man who would not judge or condemn me, I was not afraid to speak the truth.

"Then we'll have to see if we can detach Louis from his guard dog, won't we?" Raymond said. "Surely between us we can tempt him with the glory of conquest."

As if the mention of his name had conjured his image, Louis emerged from one of the buildings below us, to stride through the gardens without seeing their magnificence and disappear through another doorway.

Raymond sank onto the stone beside me, smiling ruefully. "I see that His Majesty has refused my offer of clothing more suited to his standing."

I laughed. The embroidered silk-and-damask robes that clothed Raymond with such opulence had of course been rejected by Louis. He still wore the pilgrim's garb he'd arrived in.

"The robe was given to him by Bernard of Clairvaux," I explained. "Thus it is sacred to him."

"But not very clean! In the short time since you arrived, my servants could have done no more than brush away the worst of the filth of your journey. Is it possible that he considers dirt and lice a sign of sanctity?"

"For a man who wears a hair shirt, of what importance are lice?" And I found it easy to laugh again, enjoying the mockery of Raymond's raised brows. Until I felt Raymond's eyes narrow on my face. I grew suddenly self-conscious—and looked away as if one of the colorful finches that flitted through the bushes had taken my attention.

His next words stole my breath. "How do you live with a man like that, Eleanor?"

He must have seen the despair in my face, however hard I tried to hide it, for his hand was on mine. I felt the warmth of it, of some unexpected level of attachment. And I felt obliged to pull my hand away.

"I won't have your pity," I said.

"Nor do I give it. Only my admiration. Tell me, Eleanor."

I swallowed against the sudden lump in my throat. "How do I live with him?" I sighed as I was forced to face it. "In God's truth, I don't know."

"He is not a husband for such as you."

"I don't think our suitability was an issue when Fat Louis arranged it. My father's decision to give me into his safekeeping meant that I had no choice. But what girl does?"

"And Fat Louis had an eye to your acres."

"Of course. The destiny of all heiresses. I cannot complain, can I?"

"Does he make you happy?"

"No. But happiness is not everything."

"Then does he make you sad?" Raymond persisted.

"Yes. Oh, yes."

"I can't believe he beats you."

Raymond's attempt at humor promptly shattered my defenses. The words I had not intended to say fell from my lips. They were demeaning. Humiliating. Had I not found it almost impossible to tell even my sister Aelith? But here in these magnificent gardens, all my senses compromised with heat and perfume and a compassionate listener, I spoke them aloud.

"No. Louis does not beat me. He does not touch me. Not to any degree, at least. It astonishes me how many days he has been able to discover in the Church calendar when what passes for intimate relations with his wife are frowned on by God!" I gripped my hands together to prevent myself from saying more, and again failed. "Even when God permits, it's not an experience to gladden my heart! So no, Louis does not make me happy. It is no marriage."

A little silence fell between us.

"So his monklike habits are deeper than that robe he insists on wearing," Raymond observed after some thought.

"Yes. And at present he won't come near me. He's taken a vow of chastity until he reaches Jerusalem. Even then I don't hold out much hope."

"By Christ! What a fool he is." It was balm to my soul. "How did he manage to get even one child with you?"

"Because Abbot Bernard told him he must persist, to get a male heir for the throne." I fought unsuccessfully against the bitterness that coated my reply. "Louis must have been eternally grateful that I fell for a child as fast as I did. We still don't have a son but he seems to consider his duty done. He won't touch me. Not that I care—I don't love him, you understand." I tried to unravel my complicated feelings. "I don't *want* him, you see. But I am forced to live like a nun. I am not fitted to such a life. I am hedged around by formality and ritual in that cold place in the middle of the gray waters of the Seine. How do I bear it? How do I live like that for the rest of my life? And I really need to carry a son. . . ."

"Eleanor . . ." Raymond leaned close and kissed my forehead. "I am so sorry."

"He does love me," I admitted in fairness. "In his way. Louis cares, you see, and that makes it worse. He showers me with gifts. He never upbraids me for the style of life that he frowns on. I have created my own Aquitaine so that I'm not too homesick for music and conversation and festivity. Louis disapproves but his disapproval is silent mostly. Until Mount Cadmos, that is." My voice caught in my throat as I remembered. "He blamed me for that. I'm sure you have heard. I expect the details reached you before we did. . . ."

Raymond nodded, adding dryly, "The Turks were keen to herald their victory over the Christian invaders, and they were nothing if not explicit." He paused, narrowing his eyes at the voluptuous greenery around us. "Your losses were vile, Eleanor."

"And Louis would not even let me put my case. So I became outcast."

"He was probably afraid you would show his commanders where the true fault lay—with a man who is incapable of leading the proverbial horse to water, much less a vast army of Crusaders and pilgrims into hostile territory."

"He has never won a campaign or a battle," I admitted. "Did you know that?"

"There you are then. You are not to blame, Eleanor." Once again tears ambushed me, and I dabbed at them with my sleeve. "I think you are lonely. And you don't even have Aelith to act as confidante."

"No. And now even my women are cold since so many of their friends died on that mountain. My heart is sore for them. . . ." And since the emotion refused to be contained any longer, I covered my face with my hands and wept.

"Dearest Eleanor . . . don't be distressed. . . ." Raymond took me in his arms with such tenderness and let me weep against his shoulder, his arms strong and infinitely supportive. It was as if a dammed torrent had been released. I wept for the death of so many of our number. For the apparent futility of our journey, and for my own unspeakable position, whilst Raymond murmured and stroked my back. The soothing words and actions made me weep even harder until I emptied what seemed to be a vast ocean of grief. Until I was reduced to a hiccupping exhaustion.

Raymond's question surprised me.

"Will you spend the rest of your life with a man for whom you have no respect?"

It jolted me out of my self-indulgence. Was the answer not obvious?

"I have no choice. I am no different from any woman forced into a marriage that does not please her. The fact that I am Duchess of Aquitaine is irrelevant."

"The fact that you are Eleanor, and a woman of some remarkable spirit, might have every relevance. If you ask my advice . . ."

Footsteps interrupted, the slap of a pilgrim's leather sandal against the warm paving. I turned my ravaged face away from the intrusion.

Slowly Raymond released me and stood. "Your Majesty."

So it was Louis. Who else? I wished it might be anyone but him to see me like this. Raymond placed himself between us so that I could blot the remaining tears with my ill-used sleeves.

"Come and sit with us. Eleanor is distressed. She has been telling me of your tribulations in the mountains."

To my relief—the aroma of unwashed cloth being suddenly paramount—Louis did not sit but stood, arms folded. "We all suffered. It is a trial sent to us by God, for us to bear. And we should bear it, with fortitude." Looking up at his hard words, I saw that he frowned at me, as if he found my grief a matter for his displeasure.

"And I will help you bear it in any way I can," Raymond spoke gently. "I regret your losses at Mount Cadmos."

"It should not have happened. My orders were disobeyed."

"Perhaps it was not the wisest route to take—through the heart of the mountains in the winter months. It's dangerous at the best of times, as I know, and with the Turks at large, what better place to stage an ambush." My heart warmed that he should come to my support, when no one other than the ill-fated and now absent de Rancon had challenged Louis. Even the Count of Maurienne had been lukewarm when he saw Louis's obstinacy. But here was Raymond, my champion. "You walked into that ambush. Your advisers did not know the land, the terrain. That is where you should look for your culprits, if you would cast blame. You should look to your advisers who sent you there in the first place."

"We would have presented a stronger force if my wife's vassals had camped where I had instructed!"

"You know your advisers better than I. The monk Odo de Deuil and Templar Galeran." To my delight, Raymond infused his voice with the lightest hint of scorn. "They would not be my choice—but every man to his own. And I hear they keep Eleanor from your tent."

Raymond waved aside Louis's attempts to object. "I would have thought a sovereign leader of a vast proportion of your forces, as Eleanor undoubtedly is, would expect to have a voice in your councils. But that's for the future and for you to decide." He took Louis's arm, his face perfectly bland so that Louis was unsure whether he had been an object of mockery or commiseration.

"For now, let me show you my city. I did well, did I not? From a landless knight to the glory of Antioch? Let me lavish all that I have on you. And perhaps we can provide a new pilgrim's robe for you. . . ."

Raymond was as good as his word. Every sumptuous luxury was laid at our feet, banquets to tempt our jaded appetites, tournaments to entertain. Music and chess and drafts to stir our minds. Jewels and garments to replace those we had lost. When the gardens and the magnificent rooms of the palace palled, we hunted with leopards and falcons. Or I did, with Raymond as my host and companion. Louis declined. He could not refuse to eat with the Prince of Antioch without appearing uncivil and churlish, but he rejected the rest, burying himself in feverish planning with Odo and Galeran, as he had when we were on the march. If I wished to see him, which I didn't, I had to go to him.

But I did, when the despicable news reached Antioch.

Louis sat at a table, documents rolled and scattered in front of him, lines of figures under his fist. He stared unseeingly at them, but looked up when I entered. For a long moment he stared at me, eyes bleak, before he turned away to scowl at the view from the window.

"I've heard." I wasted no time. "You did nothing to help them, did you?"

Louis surged to his feet, to stride across the room away from me as if he would escape. I followed him, giving no quarter.

"They are all lost to us. All those brave souls we abandoned in Attalia. You forbade me to ask Raymond for aid. You said you would organize their rescue. Did you not pay for the ships to return and transport them here to join us?"

"No. I could not. Think of the cost. And I am still so far from Jerusalem. Such a project would have beggared me."

"How could you have left them there . . . ?" I could not disguise my horror; nor did I greatly try.

Suddenly Louis whipped around and strode back to the table, thrusting past me, dashing the lists of figures from the surface with a sweep of his arm. "I don't have the money. I demanded it from Suger but there is none. And now my army is in pieces." Snatching up a final column of numbers that had escaped his fury, he tore it into pieces and cast it to the floor. "All I see is failure. I shall never fulfill my vow. . . ."

"And that is all you can think about when you left your army to the mercy of the weather and the Infidel?"

The courier had been graphic. All our abandoned troops in Attalia were gone, either starved or dead of the plague, while those who lived were enticed by the Turks with offers of food or an outright threat—convert to Islam or die.

Louis's eyes blazed with fury. "They deserve no sympathy from me. Hundreds of them converted!" His mouth twisted as if he would vomit from disgust. "They took the Cross, they accepted the holy symbol from the hands of Bernard himself, and at the first obstacle they went over to the Infidel! By God, they did not deserve to be rescued."

"I think they had little choice. We had abandoned them."

"I should have stayed to lead them by land." His anger descended into the habitual refrain of maudlin despair.

"Then you too would be dead!"

Shaking his head, Louis thrust his foot against his chair to send it hurtling onto its side, the cushions scattering. "I shouldn't have listened to you. A monstrous debacle."

So I was once more to be the whipping boy. But I was stronger now, and Raymond had done much to restore my confidence. I would not be downcast. I would not take on this burden.

"I'll not be blamed for this, Louis. I would have saved them."

But Louis fell into a silence, his eyes focused on the floor, reminding me vividly of those weeks in Paris when his mind had become completely taken over by the depth of his sin at Vitry. This was not the time for him to fall into a melancholy that would freeze him into an inability to make any decision other than to spend every night on his knees before God.

I struck his arm with my hand.

"Louis . . . ! For God's sake . . ."

"Go away, Eleanor. . . ." He looked around with distaste at the opulence of the room, with its hangings and gilded furniture. "I must talk to Odo. The sooner we leave here the better."

At least he was thinking, planning. It was the best I could hope for. "I expect you'll tell me when you've made your decision." My scorn was heavy.

"Yes. I'll tell you. And I tell you this." Face pale, mouth set, he turned foursquare and his eyes focused on me at last. "I consider your intimacy with your uncle unfortunate."

"My *intimacy*? I hunt with him, eat with him. . . ."

"You talk to him. You're always talking to him. What do you talk about?"

"All the things *you* will not talk to me about! Politics. The Turkish threat. The safety of Antioch and Jerusalem. You won't—and Raymond will. You can't find fault with me for that, Louis."

"I don't approve. I forbid you to discuss French policy with him."

"Forbid me? By what right do you forbid me?"

"As your husband."

"If you acted as my husband I might listen to you. Since you do not, I will spend my time as I choose. And if I wish to discuss affairs of war and politics with the Prince, my own blood—then so I will!"

I thought that would be the end of it. It was not. Louis took a deep breath and blurted out the accusation.

"I don't like the rumors I hear, Eleanor."

I was alert, all senses come alive. But I remained as cool as a glass of sherbet, my eyes commanding his.

"Which rumors?"

"You are too much in Prince Raymond's company." At the last his gaze slid uncomfortably from mine. "You are too intimate with him."

It made no sense. "Louis—you are a fool!" I announced.

Louis's lips tightened with disapproval. He stalked past me. I rejected his ridiculous words. I had more important things to think of.

How do you live with a man like that? Will you spend the rest of your life with a man for whom you have no respect?

Raymond's questions, even though I had answered them, would not leave me. They remained, like burrs under a saddle to irritate. They disturbed my sleep, stalked me through my waking hours. They troubled me.

Or did they? Did they not light a tiny flame of hope? And in the leisure hours in the heat of the day in Antioch did I not breathe on that little flame until it glowed and the idea began to emerge as a bright phoenix stretching its wings from the flames? Sometimes I thought it impossible. In other moments—well, why not? It was entirely possible if I made it so.

The fact that you are Eleanor, and a woman of some remarkable spirit, might have every relevance.

So I worried at the idea, like loose threads on the worn cuff of a gown. I must think and plan.

"Lady—you should be aware . . . court gossip . . ." Agnes hovered.

"Of what?" I hadn't time for empty tales and false chatter.

"They say that you and the Prince . . ."

"Raymond's court has nothing better to do with its time than to indulge in idle speculation. Lies and artifice—either a figment of Louis's disordered imagination or Galeran's poisoning tongue. I'll not hear it."

"As you will, lady . . ."

Once, I would have asked her, "What do they say of me?" Once, I would have listened to her sage advice, but now my mind was too caught up in my grand scheme. So I thought and planned, until every argument was worked out in my mind, clear as the reflection in the Venetian looking glass that Raymond had provided for my use.

For a little time I was diverted when Raymond summoned his War Council. I was not invited—in matters of government Raymond could be as intransigent as any man—and so was forced to glean information from the violent aftereffects. It was not difficult. The palace was awash with opinion and conjecture, not least because within minutes of the Council's meeting, Louis and Raymond were at each other's throats.

Raymond's plan of campaign, which I well knew, was to show Louis the wisdom of diverting the crusading army from its progress to Jerusalem, and launch instead an attack on the Turkish strongholds of Aleppo and Caesarea. With the Turks distracted and weakened, it would be an easy next step to recover Edessa and thus save Antioch from Turkish inundation. And Raymond's strongest argument, to appeal to Louis's principle objective, was that to drive the Turks back would in the long term strengthen Jerusalem.

Louis had balked like a stubborn mule. Jerusalem was his goal and that was where he would go. My own vassals had sided with Raymond, but their inclination was ridden over roughshod. With terrible conviction and total blindness, Louis declaimed that he would not deliberately shed the blood of his enemy until he had completed his pilgrimage to Jerusalem, to lay his standard on the altar and be washed of his sins. Then he might consider Raymond's vulnerability, but not before.

Stunned, Raymond had retaliated in an unusual show of anger.

"God's Wounds! If you are not prepared to help a fellow Christian, then you may as well leave tomorrow. What point in your staying when you would close your eyes to my plight, and that of every man and woman in this city?"

"I am aware of your plight, but I don't consider it to be immediate."

"Then God help you if you are ever forced to witness a city sacked by the Turks."

The Council had ended in a tumult of bad blood and I was left to count the cost of the inevitable consequence of my decision: battle and wholesale slaughter. The knowledge turned my blood to ice in the heat of the day. More than once, looking out from my window toward the distant invisible domes of Jerusalem, I considered the wisdom of my choice. But better that my Aquitainian forces help Raymond to defeat the encroaching Turks than that his troops be cut down, the women and children defiled, their homes burned, and the fine city of Antioch laid waste. I faced the choice I had made with regret, but I would stand beside Raymond, whatever the cost, as would my own commanders.

And at the end of it all? I would be mistress of my own destiny.

After the Council's collapse, Raymond seethed. I had no idea what Louis did. Raymond was the one I went to.

"It would have to be a holy miracle to get that damned husband of yours to see beyond his immortal soul!" Raymond's anger had cooled, but not greatly.

"Not a miracle." I smiled disarmingly. "An ultimatum. I want you to recall your War Council. And this time I will be there." I waved him to silence when I saw the objection of a man who still saw a woman's place as the kitchen, the solar, or the bedchamber spring to his lips. "You should have invited me to the first one. I should not have *needed* an invitation."

"It is not customary."

"Is it not? I will be there." I laid my hand on his sleeve and weighted my voice with authority. "Call the Council, Raymond."

He studied my face—would he refuse?—then nodded once, a sly glint in his eye. Of course he would agree. Was Raymond not a military man, a skilled tactician, awake to every opportunity? "I don't know what you're planning but you are a clever woman," he observed with the calculating grin reminiscent of the young man I remembered. "And a beautiful one. I will do it, because you ask it. We'll see if Louis can be forced to bend with the wind."

Yes, we would indeed see. I could barely wait.

I delayed my arrival at the War Council to enjoy the effect as I walked into the room, as Raymond rose, to lead me to the chair that had been placed for me at his right hand. There was a rustle of interest around the table. Louis stiffened, fingers closing around the cross that lay on his breast, probably for strength to withstand me. Galeran's narrow features were harsh with condemnation. Odo de Deuil looked contemplative, as if deciding whether to write about my uninvited presence, or if it might be better to gloss over what might become a vituperative occasion. The rest of Louis's knights were uneasy. Only my own vassals showed any pleasure in my appearance.

"I have allowed my niece to attend because she requested it," Raymond announced, suitably enigmatic.

I smiled at him, at the Council, inclined my head graciously, and took my seat.

"Well?" Louis made no concession whatsoever to my appearance but, eyes sliding first toward Galeran, addressed Raymond. "There's no need for this Council. I've given my answer, and have put into place arrangements for us to leave for Jerusalem immediately. I've made my case perfectly clear. . . ."

I wasted neither time nor breath.

"You have refused to help him, haven't you?"

Louis's mouth thinned, predictably. "This has already been aired. What need to ride over the same ground again? I don't even understand why you're here, Eleanor. . . ."

"Hear me, Louis." I raised my hand. "I reject your decision!"

"To what end? I leave for Jerusalem immediately."

"And I don't agree."

I looked at Louis, at the unhealthily sallow skin, the tightness of it over his sharp cheekbones, the dart of his restless gaze. And I saw the infinitesimal twitch of a muscle beside his eye. *He fears me*, I thought. *He fears what I might say, what I can do.* And Galeran too was uneasy, his jaw set hard. My anxieties and strained emotions of the past weeks vanished. Latent power surged through my blood.

I smiled at Louis as if I would put his mind at rest.

Louis sighed; his voice gentled. "What do you want here, Eleanor? What can you add that hasn't already been said? I will do what is necessary for both of us." I could feel the tension lessen in the room as he reached across the board to take my hand. "It is not seemly for you to put yourself forward and . . ."

I looked at his hand, palm up on the table in open demand, Louis expecting me to place my hand in his in feminine compliance. And I did. I saw Louis exhale in utter relief. And then, when he smiled encouragingly at me, I launched my attack.

"It is my *right* to be here—and I have made my decision, Louis.

Here it is for you to consider. *I* say we give our remaining forces to the aid of beleaguered Antioch. The Prince has asked for our help, and before God we should not refuse him. If you are determined to set your face against him—a disgracefully selfish action, to my mind—then I can do nothing to alter that. But this is what I can do." I hesitated, just for a moment, to draw out the tension, enjoying Louis's discomfort. "On my own authority I will give my own troops from Aquitaine and Poitou to Raymond's cause."

"What?" Louis snatched his hand back as if it had been suddenly scratched to blood flow by a soft and purring kitten. "What did you say?"

"If you march for Jerusalem, I'll not go with you. I'll remain here and put my forces under Prince Raymond's command."

"You will not. . . ."

"And how will you prevent me?"

Louis's voice sank to a whisper that hissed in the silent room. "You would destroy any final chance I have of getting to Jerusalem. You know that to remove your men would tear the heart out of what's left of my army."

"I know."

"You would disobey me!"

"Not necessarily. I think you should reconsider Antioch's position. When Antioch is safe, then you are free to go on to Jerusalem."

With a sweeping glance, I assessed the faces that looked back at me. Some aghast. Some intrigued at this battle of wills. My Aquitainians nodding in agreement. I had the whip hand and everyone knew it. Louis had no choice but to acquiesce. He would give in; Antioch would be safe. I felt the slide of Raymond's gaze, felt the appreciation in the curve of his mouth.

"God's Balls!" Louis was on his feet, leaning over the table toward me. "You'll not do it, Eleanor. You'll not defy me."

I stood too, and Raymond. In the same moment my Aquitainian captains were on their feet. Suddenly the atmosphere in the chamber was intensely volatile.

"It's *his* influence, isn't it?" Louis's stare at Raymond was vicious.

"It's the self-seeking ambition of a man who has lured you into his power by fair means or foul!"

"Foul means . . . ? Don't be a fool, Louis!" I felt Raymond stir as if to take issue, his hand automatically moving to the knife at his belt, and put out my hand to stop him. I'd misjudged Louis, thinking he would bow before a stronger force. I saw the anger begin to build, the violence that could sometimes race out of control, as the ill-fated de Lezay had once experienced. But I would not back down. "Surely any commander of insight would see the good sense of Prince Raymond's plan of campaign—to attack the Turks in their own base, to drain their strength. But if you choose not to see it . . ."

It was as if I had struck him. Louis loped around the table, clumsy in his urgency, to lurch to a halt so close that his foot crushed the embroidered hem of my gown. "Insight be damned! You'll not stay here. You'll come with me when I leave, even if I have to tear you away by force!"

Like the crack of a whip his hand closed on mine as if he would drag me from the room, but Raymond's reaction was even swifter, gripping Louis's wrist, fingers white so that Louis winced and cried out, letting me go.

"Tear her away from here by force, man?" Raymond snarled. "Have you gone mad?"

I took a breath, stunned by this show of open violence, yet still with enough presence of mind to take a step between Louis and Raymond.

"My lords . . ."

"Take your hands off me," Louis demanded.

"You'll not force her without her consent," Raymond flung back. "Is she some common kitchen slut to be ordered by you?"

"She's my wife and will obey me."

"I will not leave Antioch," I declared.

There we stood, a three-cornered knot of savage hostility at odds with the sophisticated surroundings, our audience looking on openmouthed.

"Are we to have this debate in public?" Louis, unbecomingly flushed, lashed out at me. "It's my right to demand your presence with me.

I'll not brook your refusal, Eleanor. You'll not dictate terms to me. You are my wife and you will obey me."

What a day for ill-judged statements. For a long moment I appraised my husband. The furiously working mouth and staring eyes, the clenched fists and monkish attire. This was the man to whom I was tied. By God, it appalled me, but my control was superb.

"Your wife? Yes, I am. I consider it my misfortune."

Was this the moment? Should I do it, should I act on the compulsion that had been building and growing within me? My mind flew back to that far-distant day when I had visited the Bishop of Laon. It was as if I stood in his room overlooking the green-banked river rather than here in the arid heat of Outremer. What would it take to be separated from this man who demanded my obedience? This man who had destroyed any vestige of affection or respect or loyalty in our marriage? I knew the steps, but dared I take them?

Everyone was looking at me. How long had I been standing in silence, listening to the Bishop of Laon in my mind, following his pointing finger on the manuscript under his hand? When Galeran shuffled up, and with a hand to Louis's shoulder, leaned to whisper in his ear, when I picked up the words ". . . wife . . . humor her . . . later we can remove . . . ," my decision was made.

Humor me, would he? My memory of the content of the clever Bishop of Laon's document was prodigious. I raised my voice so that everyone in the room would hear and there would be no doubt of my sentiments.

"Yes, I am your wife, and as such, under your dominion, my lord. But the days of that dominion are numbered."

"What's this?" Louis was puzzled, turning a frowning look from me to Galeran, as if the Templar might read my mind. "I don't understand."

I felt my heart beat against my ribs with a terrible anticipation. Dared I do it? Yes, I did dare!

"There's no misunderstanding, Louis. You heard me. Here, in this Council, I state my case. I want our marriage to end. I demand an annulment."

Chapter Fourteen

"*W*hat?" Louis jumped like a cat.

There was a silence, like that following a shattering thunderclap. A silence that could be felt on the skin, that could be tasted with the metallic bite of blood. Once again I took in the reactions of the men who sat at the table or stood at my side. Raymond was as startled as the rest, but I caught what I thought was admiration in the brief inclination of his head. No admiration in Galeran—his features flattened with hatred. The Count of Maurienne was frankly astonished. Odo gulped in sudden anxiety. Only my own vassals vibrated with a lively interest in this unforeseen development. And Louis . . . *poor* Louis! By God, I prayed I wouldn't have to think that ever again. Well, Louis was simply perplexed, with a burgeoning shadow of fear in his pale eyes.

"An annulment?" he croaked. "But you cannot. . . ."

"Oh, I can."

"Eleanor . . ." As if he had pulled on velvet and ermine robes to cover the black wool, Louis struggled to regain his regal dignity. It was an impressive display of stiffened spine and rigid shoulders, but unfortunately entirely superfluous and too late, far too late. "You are my wife and Queen of France. On what possible grounds can you demand an annulment?"

"On legal ones."

"Legal?" Almost visibly cringing at this public discussion, Louis attempted to take my arm and draw me aside from the Council. "We have a daughter together," he whispered. "How can we have an annulment?"

I would have none of it. "Our marriage is still illegal, Louis."

Louis's face was stamped with utter bewilderment. Or was it? He knew exactly the legal state of our marriage. Then I saw a tiny flicker of fear . . . and drove home my advantage.

"We should never have been wed at the outset. Don't pretend to me that you don't know! Even Abbot Bernard warned you of this. I was there—I heard him. We are related in the fourth degree and there was no dispensation."

Face as white and drawn as a corpse, Louis looked from me to Raymond, and back again. "Is this *his* advice?" he demanded.

"No. I don't need advice. Here are the facts. By the law of consanguinity our kinship makes it unlawful for us to be man and wife. Is that not so?"

Unable to find a rapid rebuttal, Louis swallowed hard. I launched into my argument. I was well prepared. This was my moment and I would make the most of it.

"It is the truth. We both know it. You are my cousin through four generations. Consanguinity is not new to you. You supported Vermandois and my sister on those grounds. Henry of Anjou was refused as a husband for Marie for the same reason, so there's no arguing against it. If you chose to close your mind against it all these years and deny its existence—well, that doesn't change the fact of our illegal union." Energy infused my words as I watched Louis almost physically retreat from the force of my arguments. "You know it was wrong—and we have suffered for this sin committed by your father, who sidestepped the dispensation in his greed. It's my belief that my failure to bear a son is due to God's displeasure. I have to presume I shall never carry a male child with you. You need a son for the future safety of France, Louis. If we gain an annulment, you can wed again and get an heir."

Our audience was agog. So much washing of royal soiled linen in public. More than a few throats were cleared.

"What's more . . ." Here was my most lethal arrow. "If you hold me to a marriage that is sinful, you are placing my immortal soul in jeopardy. As well as your own!"

Louis's clenched fingers opened and closed convulsively. His eyelids flickered with uncertainty. "No. I won't do it."

I ignored this, pressing on with my case at my most accommodating. Could I not afford to be? "I will give up my rights as Queen of France, of course. And until it's all settled between the two of us and the Holy Father in Rome, I will remain here, under my uncle's protection in Antioch."

"You cannot agree to this, Sire!" Odo could barely find the words, his voice perilously close to a squeak.

"It's not possible." Galeran's portentious accents.

"Why not?" Raymond had cast himself back in his chair to watch the out-playing, but here he chose to intervene. "It seems to me that your magnificent wife has it all worked out, Louis. If it's a matter of the law, can you argue against it? Do you fear to lose her lands? I agree Aquitaine and Poitou will be a sad loss for France, but if your immortal soul is in the balance . . ."

I cast Raymond an arch look and a smile, but turned to make my way toward the door. I had nothing more to say, had I? I had laid my case superbly.

"I'll not agree," Louis's querulous voice followed me.

"I don't think you have a choice, my lord," I replied over my shoulder.

Louis was still standing as rigid as one of the stately palm trees of Antioch, his mouth a seamless line, as I left the room.

"Eleanor! Wait!"

Louis followed me, of course, as I strode along the open-sided loggia with its lambent light. I did not slow my steps. If he wished to continue the argument, he would have to keep to my pace. I would match my steps to his no longer.

"Eleanor . . ."

There he was at my side, then stepping in front of me when I made no move to halt.

"This hurts me. I love you. How can I agree to what you ask?"

I saw tears gather in his eyes and was forced to look away. Galeran and Odo de Deuil could have him, with my pleasure. I would be free of him.

"I have always loved you."

Now I stopped. "Love?" My lip curled. My belly curdled at his tears. This weak, silly man who thought he could serve as the husband I needed! I had given him too much of my life, but no more. Grabbing the front of his robe in my two fists, I shook him to make him understand. "Perhaps you do love me, if it's some sentimental emotion that demands you shower me with presents. It's not my idea of love. What is love—if you can exist for longer than a year with no desire to actually touch me? I was not meant to live my life as chaste as a virgin. I am young and my blood races with life. I want a man's hands to awaken me to passion, a man's body to be roused with desire for me. What I don't want is a furtive scramble that leaves my flesh cold and unresponsive." Horror at my outspokenness chased across Louis's austere features, but I did not let up. "I feel no physical response to you, Louis. And after your treatment of me, I have no other feelings beyond disgust. I don't want this life. I wish to end it." I stepped around him and resumed my sprightly stride. "Nothing you say will make me change my mind, so don't try. And if you consider my argument, you'll see the value of it for yourself."

"But an annulment?" He pattered behind me. Louis, of course, would never understand. How could I ever think he would? "The ignominy of it—the King of France forced into this position. The humiliation . . ."

I whirled around to face him. "Is that all you can think about? Your humiliation? It's no better for me."

"I know, but—"

"You don't know! You don't know anything! We don't have to actually tell the world that you don't sleep with me, Louis! Now, that would be humiliating!" Temper surged, adding force to my intent. "We don't have to air our differences in public for the inns and whorehouses to gossip and laugh over. It's so easy—a mere legal matter of consanguinity. Nothing more. Nothing less. Our marriage can be ended in cold-blooded legality, and save face for both of us."

"Eleanor, can we not—"

"No, we can't. Whatever it is. You need a male heir, and I'm unlikely to give you one as things stand. I want my freedom from this prison of your making."

I could almost see the thoughts jostling in his mind. Still, as I continued toward my rooms, he would not let me go and I knew he would placate me, flatter me, anything to stop me from shouting my demands to the four corners of the earth.

"I will consider it, I suppose."

Just as I thought! "Good! You consider it, Louis, but don't take too long over it."

"I'll need my counselors and my barons to agree, of course."

How slippery he could be. "Why do you need to ask their permission? Are you not king?" I turned and faced him at the door to my quarters. "Do you not have the power to dictate your own life? Surely you're answerable to no man."

"Yes, I have the power. But I will still ask Abbot Suger's advice."

"Do as you will, but our marriage is at an end. And unless you agree to come to Raymond's aid, I will withdraw my forces from your command and act independently. The decision is yours, Louis."

I opened the door at my back.

"Eleanor . . ."

"What now?" The vitality was leaching from me, leaving me surprisingly exhausted.

"Why now, Eleanor? Why after all these years?"

Why, indeed? I looked at Louis Capet, Louis my husband, King of France, and had no very clear answer. And then saw the man who stood there, hand on my sleeve, a plea in his voice. I saw the dust-begrimed feet in the clumsy leather sandals. The plain woven robe with the heavy cross that banged against his hollow chest when he moved. The rounded shoulders and scanty hair, the death's-head from years of fasting and abstinence, with shadows as deep as red wine beneath his eyes. Skin as pale as wax, as if the blood beneath ran cold as ice. How was it possible for a man to be so colorless after months of crusading? The hands that clutched and gripped . . .

And I knew the answer.

"Why do I want an annulment, Louis? Because I cannot bear to live with you one day longer."

I entered my room and closed the door in his face as if I were closing the door on my marriage. I felt victory throb through my blood. I had done it. I had made my desire public. Now I must pursue it to achieve my salvation. Oh, I was presumptuous in my glee. I saw full well the obstacles that faced me. Louis would fight me tooth and nail. But I would persuade, argue, fight: I would do whatever it took to break this foul bond.

Louis could not leave me alone. In the palace, in the gardens, at leisure in my own rooms, even in the meadows to loose the leopard, there he was at my heels. If I heard the approaching slap of his wretched sandals once, I heard it a dozen times. He hounded me, soft and persuasive like summer rain, Galeran invariably in his shadow.

"Don't say it," I stopped him before he even started. "Don't say that I'll see sense."

Unendurable. Insufferable. The taint of Galeran was on his skin. I could almost hear the Templar's brutal advice. *Go and persuade her. She's only a woman. Take her a gift of eastern jewels to win her over.* I turned my back on Louis and the chest of gaudy gems he had placed before me.

"I see sense *now*, Louis. I don't need gifts; I don't need persuasion. You should be putting your mind to helping Raymond save Antioch. And if you think to change my mind over our annulment with this tawdry gesture—you won't do it."

"His Majesty is anxious to continue his journey to Jerusalem." Galeran bowed with a slimy pretense of respect.

"His Majesty is perfectly free to do just that—if his conscience can bear his betrayal of the Prince of Antioch."

"There'll be no annulment," Louis howled. "Do you hear me?"

"I think they hear you in Jerusalem."

Suddenly he was shouting, his words ricocheting off the arched walls of the sun-filled courtyard, all control gone. "How dare you hold me up to ridicule before the whole world? As for helping your precious Prince . . . He disgusts me. His lifestyle—the abomination he has created here. Why should I put myself and my forces in danger for him? I owe him nothing. All I see is a licentious court, immoral and louche, tolerating such debauchery as intermarriage with Saracens and acceptance of their religion. Listen—even now . . ." He stabbed his finger toward the sound of the call to prayer beyond the window. "He's been seduced by the East—a popinjay in silk slippers and loose gowns more suitable to the seraglio. No, I'll not help him. And nor will you and your forces! I forbid it!"

I shrugged elegantly, seating myself on the stone edging of a little pool.

"You're a selfish woman, Eleanor. You've undermined my Crusade at every step of the way."

I trailed my fingers in the warm water, disturbing the golden fish that swam to the surface in search of food.

"Your behavior here in Antioch is deplorable. . . ."

I laughed aloud, leaning forward to see my reflection.

"By God, Eleanor!" Louis's fury was magnificent. "They are saying you behave like a whore!"

"A whore?" Now I looked up, but in no way disturbed. "Do you believe every silly rumor you hear? Are you going to ask me about Saladin? What do you think, Louis? Does it have the ring of truth? Or is it some fabulous fiction worthy of my troubadours?"

"There! You see? Are you never serious?"

It was a magnificent tale. Seduced by the subtleties of the East, I, Eleanor, had supposedly cast my eyes around for a more suitable mate than my bloodless king, and lit upon Saladin, an eminent Turkish leader. When Saladin, equally enamored, had sent one of his galleys to whisk me away to a life of Saracen luxury, I snapped at the chance, abandoning my forces and embarking in the dead of night.

But Louis was warned by a serving wench. And picture this . . . My brave husband threw on his garments and rushed to stop me just as I was setting my foot on the galley. Louis took my hand and led me, unresisting, back to my chamber, asking me why I was running away. Such love and devotion from him, to rescue me from a fate worse than death.

Raymond had roared with laughter when he first heard the calumny.

"It's a monstrous tale," Louis said, outraged.

"Particularly if you consider that Saladin is a child of twelve years!" I couldn't subdue a peal of laughter. "I think I called you a rotten pear, Louis, and claimed to love Saladin more."

"It's not fitting that the Queen of France should be held up to ridicule," Galeran intoned in pompous disapproval.

"It's not fitting that His Majesty or his ministers should listen to such filth," I retaliated. I had had enough. "Let the gossipmongers have their fun."

But beneath the laughter I was angry: with Louis that he should even pretend belief in so outrageous a slander; with Galeran that he should dare to take me to task.

With a cursory gesture, Louis motioned for Galeran to leave us alone together. "Is your reputation strong enough to withstand the rumors that your relationship with the Prince is . . . inappropriate?"

"Not again, Louis." I yawned.

"They say you share his bed."

My hand itched to remove the sanctimonious disapproval from his face. "Do they? And do you believe them?"

"I've seen you together. He touches you. He kisses you. He walks alone with you."

"He cares for me. His kisses are not intimate."

"He is your father's brother, Eleanor. It is immoral!"

I stood, unmoving, as I absorbed the imputation. So that was what they were saying, was it? And Louis had believed it sufficiently to repeat it to my face. The itch became more than I could bear. To my shame, I struck out, to leave a red weal on the pale skin of his cheek. I did not temper my strength.

Louis flinched but did not retreat. "Do you deny it?" he demanded.

"No. I neither admit nor deny anything."

"You will moderate your behavior, Eleanor. . . ."

"Do you think?" I smiled. "I am no longer answerable to you, Louis."

So they said I shared Prince Raymond's bed, did they? The gossipmongers, the trouble stirrers, my enemies. They whispered incest and scandal. They would destroy my name, coating it in the blackest of filth. For so is incest, the worst of perversions, the lowest depravity.

Would I commit such a sin?

Apparently I would. I did. Oh, the rumors were right enough! But not until after Louis's accusation. I was guilty as accused and I stepped into it with my eyes open.

Raymond, Prince of Antioch, with all the glamour of an Eastern potentate in appearance and in fact, became my lover. How seductive is absolute power wielded with confidence and finesse. With one snap of his fingers his will was done. One glance of an eye or lift of a brow and his minions ran to do his bidding. And how beautiful he was to my jaded eye after those weeks of fear and hardship when death threatened from every side. Oh, yes, I was seduced. I fell willingly under the spell of his subtle courtship.

Ah, Raymond. You lured me into fatal indiscretion.

I loved him; I adored him, my senses overpowered by his sheer physical presence. Did I know it was wrong to allow desire to rule? Perhaps I did, but I made no apology for my intemperate emotions. How could I not feel the power of his presence, respond to it against all the teachings of Holy Church, or even of good sense? I had been raised to political awareness, but one smile and the gleam in those dark blue eyes and my political wisdom shriveled into dust at my feet.

He had thirty-six years under his belt and was truly a magnificent animal, more handsome than any man had the right to be—but not the hard russet gloss I had known in the Count of Anjou. Oh, no.

Raymond was large and golden, a virile lion of a man. And such physical strength as he had. I could not imagine Louis—or any man—able to halt a destrier by the simple clenching of his thighs. Hercules, Raymond was called with affection, and so he was, a handsome Greek hero to shoulder twelve labors and emerge with a triumphant crown.

I'll not blame Louis for my fall, but what woman wed to a shadow of a man with no steel in his scabbard would not have given more than a passing glance to Raymond of Antioch? He was everything Louis was not, an adventurer, a reputable warrior, a charmer of women, a skilled horseman, as his minstrels were forward in telling. My heart leaped as they sang of his hunting, his exploits against the Turks. Beneath the power, his manners were sophisticated, his demeanor gentle and courteous, as smooth as the Oriental silk of his robes.

Louis had been quick to denounce Raymond as nothing better than a degenerate owner of a seraglio, yet there was no gluttony or drunkenness or debauchery at Raymond's court. Raymond was surprisingly abstemious. Unless it be counted against him when, to honor me at a banquet, golden nets suspended above our heads were released, to shower us with scented rose petals, floating down on table, on marble floor, on shoulders.

Raymond's eyes, disarming in their directness, invited me to enjoy the foolishness, the deliberate extravagance created just for me—and I fell into the romance of the occasion as into a bottomless but softly cushioned pit. I swear Raymond was capable of wooing the angelic host down from Heaven.

Louis retired, silent in his censure, petals caught incongruously in his hair.

So much for romance. Ah, but should I have gone to Raymond's bed? It was the magnificent Roman baths within the palace that proved my final undoing, if I wished to believe that I needed to be seduced. Tiled, heated, with the music of splashing water from a myriad of fountains, the main bath was large enough to swim, for those so inclined, comfortable enough with silk-cushioned seats for those who would take their ease. It became my custom to luxuriate in the warm waters in the late afternoon with wine or sherbet and sugared sweetmeats, the servants dismissed to grant me privacy. There I would lie back on the steps in a loose bathing robe, the silky water caressing my limbs.

I had not seen Raymond since the War Council when he strolled in to join me.

Did he know I was there? Certainly he did.

"An impressive performance, Eleanor!"

"It was, wasn't it!"

Despite the smile, there were lines of strain beside his eyes and mouth that I had not seen before—doubtless the product of the growing threat to his lovely city—as he lowered himself to the poolside with a groan. For a moment he simply sat; then he scrubbed his hands over his face and smiled at me. Without a word, and without any self-consciousness, he stripped off his robe and, naked, eased into the water beside me, where he stretched his arms along the sides of the bath and sighed deeply.

"I don't think I could ever return to the West," he said, head tipped back against the warm stones, hair curling out into the water. "Cold winters. Ice and snow to freeze a man's balls. There's too much comfort here."

"All Eastern rulers run to fat. So I've heard." Was my encouragement of him indeed reprehensible?

"So I, too, have heard." He sighed in the warmth. "And what do you think now, Eleanor? Having seen one in the flesh?"

He smiled with deceptive sleepiness, turning his head so that I caught the glint of sharp blue beneath his eyelids, and I regretted my ill-considered flirting. Conscious of the transparency of my garment, I swam away to the other side. Was I sure of this? Was this what I wanted?

"You have left me, delectable Eleanor," Raymond mourned. With delicious grace, he poured wine and held out the cup to offer it to me with a crook of his finger, so that I swam back. Taking the exquisite glass, the warm water lapping discreetly over my breasts, I sipped, watching him over the lip of the cup.

"Louis's preparations to leave are moving apace," he said, surprising

me with the sudden change in direction. Were we here to discuss matters of policy? "By the end of the week."

"I know."

He tilted his chin. "Are you, then, determined to stay?"

"If you'll have me."

"Oh, yes." He leaned to kiss my temple. "My lovely Eleanor. You'd
stay here with me forever if I had my way."

What would your wife say if I did? I admit to giving no thought to
Constance. Leading a retired life as she did with her women, I saw little of her, not at the feasts nor the hunting parties, nor even strolling in
the gardens. Occasionally I visited her in her strangely sequestered life,
astonished that she should accept it with such unquestioning equa-
nimity. What, I wondered, did Constance do with her time? Her little
son, Raymond's heir, was already in the care of tutors, and her two
infant daughters had their own separate household, in the tradition of
the West. There was no solace for her in their company. Constance's
life was bound by the walls of her shaded rooms and the pursuits of
stitchery and music. It seemed an intolerable confinement to me, and I
pitied her. But then, Raymond's wife had known no other life.

Poor Constance. She had no conversation and little interest in the
outside world. She'd have been better, I thought, keeping an eye on her
handsome husband.

"I think I might stay," I replied.

With a toss of his head to spray an arc of drops into the water, Raymond drained his cup. "No, you won't. I know you too well. Aquitaine
sings in your blood. You'll find an excuse to go home."

"You know me far *too* well. After only eight days." I drank the rich
wine of Antioch and sighed in pleasure. "It seems a lifetime."

"A lifetime . . ." Raymond took the cup from me and placed it on
the side. "Come here." Linking his fingers with mine, he pulled me
gently through the water until I stood before him, swaying to keep my
balance. Fingers drifting down my arm, barely stirring the air between
us, he kissed me between my brows, then transferred his lips to where
my hair curled damply at my temple.

He sniffed.

"What?"

"Whatever you've used on your hair is magical," he murmured. "I swear you're a witch."

"I use no spells."

"No?" His eyes were quizzical on mine, and very solemn. "I've been faithful to Constance until this moment—even in my thoughts. But now . . ."

I shook my head, feeling a sudden bolt of panic in this moment that truth stared me in the face.

"Come with me . . . ?" Raymond invited.

A question, rather than a demand, allowing me the ultimate choice. Before God, I could not put the whole weight of blame on his shoulders. Without a word I went with him. To a robing room, a comfortable divan clothed and cushioned in silk. What passed between us there should remain unwitnessed, unsaid. Enough to say that my Prince of Antioch reminded me of all I had known, and astonished me with much I did not.

"We would be damned for this," I said when I had the breath to speak at all. "We would be condemned."

"We would be damned and condemned for all manner of things. Are we not free to choose our sins?"

It was wrong. It was, of course, however I might try to excuse what we did together, however much Raymond might persuade me that we did no wrong, that we hurt no one. *Incest.* An unpleasant word, gathering to it all the condemnation and vituperation of those who held to the high tenets of Christianity. Once I too would have condemned it, and still would in my more honest moments, but when Raymond closed his hand around mine to lead me from the pool, I forgot everything but the welcome of his embrace.

To me, what we did together was out of love, harming none. To Louis it was a cardinal sin, punishable by the Fires of Hell.

But what would God's judgment be?

Raymond might be too close to me in name, in blood, but I had no knowledge of him as family; nor was he of an age to be in authority over me. We were alike in all things, the reflected half of each other. The blood of Aquitaine ran true and drew us together.

When I was finally called to stand before the Almighty on the day of my death, what would I say?

I was my uncle's lover.

Would He damn me to everlasting Hell for it? Had He damned my grandfather for adultery? My grandmother for her betrayal of her husband and family? Surely He would judge what was in our hearts, Raymond's and mine. Not evil or viciousness. Not cruelty or revenge. No, God would not strike me with His wrath. He would touch me instead with His compassion. His tears would mingle with mine. He would understand when I finally stood before Him. I knew it.

It was, after all, merely a matter of degree, was it not? So close with Raymond to be called incest, a damnable offense. Close enough with Louis simply to bring the legality of my marriage into question, but not to damn me to everlasting perdition.

If Raymond had been my cousin, there would have been no objection.

See how well I could formulate an argument to my purpose.

My only regret: that Raymond had a purpose of his own. Oh, I had no doubt that he loved me, that he desired me, but he wanted to secure my influence, the power of my forces, and what better way than through my bed? Not like the Angevin, secretive and hard edged, but open and warm. I knew from the beginning what Raymond wanted from me, for he never hid it. Nor did it mean he had no true affection for me. We loved each other honestly, with genuine care, knowing that we would be condemned but considering it of no account.

Why did I allow myself to tread that dangerous line?

Perhaps I'd lost my mind in the mountains of Cadmos and the horrors of Attalia. Just a little. That's all I can say in my own defense.

Did I think of Constance? No, I did not. Not once. Perhaps for that I deserve to be condemned.

I was asleep—until some sound, some movement in the air, pulled at my consciousness. I opened my eyes, lay still. Nothing. My room was empty, dark, so it was not even near dawn. Perhaps it was a roosting bird stirring in the gardens—the windows were open to admit the cool air. I closed my eyes.

A slide of a booted foot. The rasp and chink of mail. Someone was in my room. Slowly I sat up, my heart beginning to beat hard.

"Agnes?"

The shadows moved.

With a sudden spurt of fear I grasped the handle of the knife I kept beneath my pillow—a misericord—the deadly, thin-bladed dagger that could be slipped between the joints of body armor that the crusading knights carried to deliver the coup de grace if they were ever in danger of being taken prisoner by the Turks. After Mount Cadmos I had taken to keeping one close.

"Who is it? What do you want?"

The blade suddenly gleamed along its length in the light from a partially shaded lantern. I tightened my fist, raised it with intent to strike.

"Damn you!" An oath quickly cut off. "Oh, no, you don't. . . ."

A flurry of movement and my wrist was seized in a hard grip, the blade plucked from my fingers by a mailed fist. Saracens come to murder me? Their attack on Antioch a terrible reality that had already begun? But why no melee of fighting? Why no outcry from Raymond's guards or from the crusading forces?

"Not a word, lady, if you know what's good for you!" The same harsh voice of command hissed in my ear.

I had no intention of obeying despite the fear that curled in my belly. "Let go . . . !"

The mailed hand was clapped over my mouth to stop my crying out; then the folds of a heavy cloak dropped over my head and wrapped around me as if I were a parcel of cloth for delivery. I thought a rope was wound around the outside to pinion me securely, to bite into my flesh. I was helpless, immobile, a prisoner in a dark and airless prison, reeking of wool and sweat. The fear bloomed to fill my lungs, my throat. Surely I would suffocate. I had to concentrate on shallow breathing. I must not panic. I must not use the air needed to fill my lungs.

I was lifted, carried clumsily, roughly, clutched and shaken when I struggled.

"Lie still, damn you." A snarl of a whisper. "Be still if you don't want to suffer more." And because I was indeed helpless, I lay still as I was carried from my room. Since I understood the orders, it was not the Saracens. I felt no better for the revelation.

I knew when we had left the palace by the change of footsteps from marble flooring to stone paving. Then I was dropped onto cushions covering a harder surface that moved beneath me. A litter or a palanquin, I thought, hearing the strike of shod hooves and feeling the distinctive sway. The cloak was loosened to allow me air, but the ropes were left in place. Even so, the busy sound of military activity reached me, the rasp of voices, quietly but clearly giving orders.

Abducted!

I lay on my side, hot, sweaty, and terrified, unable to move other than to roll—to no advantage unless I wished to fall blind from the litter—and considered.

I could imagine only one man who would undertake this assault, and I knew exactly where the advice had come from, even the hand that had guided the practicalities of my imprisonment. I might have recognized the solid body that restrained me, the voice that threatened me if I'd had my wits about me. And what could I do about it? Nothing. All I could do was lie in this stuffy shroud and endure it as the litter began to move. My heart began to settle to a steadier beat and my breathing eased. I no longer feared for my life. My death was not the object of this chain of events. And the perpetrator?

Louis, of course.

Since I would not go to Jerusalem of my own free will, Louis would ensure that I did so under duress. Without clothes or possessions, or my women. Doubtless we would be reunited at some point in the future. Who would have believed him capable of such trickery? But such unscrupulous deceit was entirely within the scope of Thierry Galeran's odious planning.

As fear drained from me, fury raged to replace it, and I lay and fumed, pulling ineffectually at the ropes. Galeran had dared to set hands on me, had dared to carry me off without my consent. Galeran, that paid minion, had forced me, Duchess of Aquitaine, against my will.

I had not even been given the opportunity to make my farewell to Raymond.

The hours passed, dark emerging into light. The litter lurched and swayed without compassion. I simply lay and endured.

When the sun rose and we were at a distance from Antioch, just as I expected, Louis saw fit to release me. Lifted from the litter, I was carried into the pavilion erected temporarily as Louis waited for the rest of his forces and mine to catch up with us. God knew what he had told my commanders. At this point I did not care. My anger had reached vast proportions.

Silent and resentful, head throbbing, I stood as the ropes were loosed and the cloak unwound, and there was Louis standing in front of me, his face a mask of frozen disapproval. He looked at me, lips twisting in distaste at my dishevelment and dusty night robes, which were all too revealing. Without a word he took the cloak, dismissed the man who had unwrapped me, and, deliberately at arm's length, he held out the heavy folds to me.

"Put this on. You are not suitably dressed. Your garments will arrive soon and you can put your appearance to rights."

So he did not wish to touch me. I took the mantle but let it drop to the floor, refusing to look away from Louis's denunciation. I refused to cover myself as if in shame.

"My appearance is the least of my worries, Louis. You can hardly blame me for it. It was your doing."

"Do you expect me to apologize, Eleanor?"

He did not look sorry. In fact, he looked amazingly satisfied. Here was a confident Louis I rarely saw, and I reined in my own temper. Anger would not help, and I needed to know his intentions.

"You have treated me like a chattel," I remarked as calmly as I could.

"Do you deserve any better?"

"It was my wish to remain in Antioch. You knew that."

"I could not allow it. I had to remove you for your own good. Once we are settled in Jerusalem the rumors will, I pray, die a natural death."

"Remove me for my own good . . . ?" Control was becoming more difficult, and my breath caught on the enormity of it.

"Do you not hear what they say of you? Or were you so steeped in sin that you closed your mind to the vicious rumors? Galeran made me aware—"

"That toad!" I spit. "It was all his idea to abduct me, wasn't it? You'd never have thought of that on your own."

"All I know is that it would be better for you if you did not remain in Antioch. . . ."

"How magnanimous of you! To have my well-being so much at heart!" But I recognized that there was no arguing with him. "What happens when we reach Jerusalem?"

"You will remain under my surveillance."

"A prisoner?" I felt a flutter of alarm.

"If you wish." How inflexible Louis had become. Between us, Galeran and I had driven him beyond his usual dithering. Here was a firm conviction, a determination that astonished me. "I shall keep you under armed guard if I have to, to preserve what reputation you have left. As for our marriage . . ."

"Will you give me an annulment?"

"This is not the time to discuss it. Nor are you in a position to ask favors of me."

"Favors? I ask no *favors*. Only my rights . . ."

"You will stay with me in Jerusalem," he continued as if I had not spoken. "We'll not talk about what happened in Antioch—we'll pretend this unfortunate little incident never occurred. You'll see, Eleanor, when sense prevails, that my actions were for the best."

How typical of him. How horribly typical. To close his eyes to what he did not like, to refuse even to speak of my sin with Raymond out loud. And with Galeran to bolster Louis's self-righteousness I could not see my way forward. All my plans had gone awry. Louis was refusing an annulment and I no longer had the weapon of the control of my forces to hold over him.

Damn him! Damn him to Hell! But I knew I must be careful, very careful now.

At last he moved toward me, stooping to retrieve the cloak, placing it around my shoulders as if I were an invalid in need of care. And no, he did not flinch from touching me. His words were gentle, so gentle I felt an urge to strike out at him again. I did not want gentleness from him.

"You have lost your way, Eleanor. I will look after you. You will stay here, in this pavilion, until your garments and your women arrive. Then you will robe yourself suitably and bear yourself with dignity before your Aquitainian forces."

How damnably condescending!

"You will find that your captains are no longer willing to follow blindly where you order. Your behavior has condemned you in their eyes."

He could not have made my situation more plain. I shrugged and cast myself down on a divan to wait. I had no choice, had I? When, later, clad demurely in silks and fine linen as befitted my status, I left the pavilion to watch my troops approach, nothing could be clearer than that my captains could not meet my eye. Among my forces rumor at my expense had been well spread, thoroughly stirred to such a pitch as to put me firmly in disgrace. It did not take much guessing as to the owner of the viperous tongue.

I was alone and powerless. Dependent on Louis.

Time for thought as I traveled in my solitary litter. Time to apportion blame. It was all my fault, of course. I had committed the sin, if that was what it was. I had made the choice—and so I must accept the consequences. Taking Raymond as my lover had been unwise, at best. I would admit to that, even if I would not accept Louis's accusation of depravity. But now my foolishness had become a sword to be used against me, with Galeran's hand on the hilt, to wound me and sully my reputation forever.

So what about practicalities? What was my plan now for the future? To remain with Louis? It had been made spectacularly clear to me that any planning had been taken out of my hands. My belly lurched, and not with the sway of the palanquin.

I set my mind to feverish decision making.

With so few options, on one point I was unshakable: I would have to go to Jerusalem because Louis had decided I must, but I would not stay there at Louis's pleasure with my name on the lips of every crusading knight in torrid speculation. I could not bear it. Once there I would hire a vessel—I had the money and the authority—and I would return to France, to Aquitaine, where I would remake my reputation. I would rid myself of Galeran and Louis.

In my own lands I would make my reputation shine again.

Yes, that was what I would do. I was determined on it.

There would be no mending of my reputation yet for a while. My residence in Jerusalem proved far longer than I had either foreseen or hoped.

And why?

I could not believe I had been so thoughtless, so blind to consequences. But I was: I had taken no Roman precautions. How should I, when that single sultry afternoon with Raymond was not premeditated? How willful is the body when one would wish most to subjugate its natural impulses. How ironic that my reluctant womb should fall prey to Raymond's masculinity.

Foolishly, carelessly, impossibly, I had fallen for a child.

Chapter Fifteen

A child. And with Louis in his chosen state of holy celibacy he was not the father. I carried Raymond's child. In that one heated, pleasure-filled afternoon in the bathhouse of the palace at Antioch, where we had knowingly and willfully committed the Great Sin with rare enjoyment, Raymond had got a child on me. I had given no passing nod to any consequences beyond the thrill of the moment. Now the consequences had to be faced, as they must when Fate unwinds the skein of life, and not only by me, but by Louis also. So the King of France expressed to his army his wish to remain in the Holy Land above and beyond the demands of his Crusade, to celebrate Easter in Jerusalem in the most sacred Church of the Holy Sepulchre. Well, so he might, but he had a clutch of more worldly motives, not least a profound desire to be rid of my embarrassment. How could he even contemplate returning to France with me full and rounded with Raymond of Antioch's child, Louis smiling sourly as if the child were his?

When I told him, his reaction was so predictable as to be ridiculous. Did he condemn me in righteous anger? Did he damn me for a whore and a harlot? Neither. At least, not on that occasion. Instead he placed me somewhere between a fallen woman and a leper; in the softest of voices, without recrimination, he offered to pray for my delivery from eternal damnation and for the soul of the bastard child. I think I wish he had railed and roared his fury at me instead. But he could not. My fertility pointed too forcefully at his own lack.

"Have you considered my request for an annulment, Louis?" I asked mockingly when he paid me a dutiful visit to ask after my health, entrenching himself distantly on the threshold. Was it not the obvious path forward? "You have had enough time to weigh the good against the bad. Do the scales not lean heavily in my favor now? Do you want a whore as a wife?"

For the first time since my unwelcome news Louis's eyes focused on the swell of my belly beneath my loose robes. Louis and his royal household had been lodged with great ceremony in the Tower of David as guests of the Patriarch of Jerusalem, but not I. I had been hurried away to be accommodated behind the latticed screens of these sumptuous but secluded rooms under the aegis of Melisende. Louis need see me and the burgeoning result of my sin as infrequently as he chose. Now with evident disgust his gaze slid from my expanding waist to take in the luxurious fittings of the room, the hangings, the furniture, the soft light. The flagon of ale and jeweled cups were a gift from Queen Melisende of Jerusalem. The low music of the lute in the background should have soothed. Instead, mouth set, without speaking a word, he strode across the room, ripping a folded manuscript from the breast of his robe and handing it to me. It was much traveled, I noted as I opened it, and Abbot Suger's careful ecclesiastical script leaped from the page. I read rapidly through the polite introductions, the refusal of more money, and homed in on the one passage that was guaranteed to sway Louis.

> *As for the matter of an annulment as broached by your lady wife. Consider this, Sire.*
>
> *The loss of her dower, the great inheritance of Aquitaine and Poitou, that the Aquitaine lady brought with her to your marriage, would be highly damaging. If you agree to let the lady*

go as she requests, and if she remarries and has sons to stand as her heirs, the Princess Marie will be deprived of her inheritance. Just as your own Frankish kingdom will feel the loss of so vast a territory.

My advice, Sire—this must not be. You must refuse her demands. If she remarries, taking her dower with her as she must, consider the strength of her future husband. A circumstance not in French interests. It would be a grave mistake on your part, Sire.

Certainly you must do nothing to weaken your position until you return to France. In my opinion, the Duchess of Aquitaine must remain your wife at all costs.

Nothing there for me to misunderstand, all as plain as the ink. The Abbot saw my value in terms of land and power, as it had always been. And I was to be kept tied and bound to the Frankish kingdom—and to Louis—as helpless as a hog trussed for market.

I was not to be released.

I reread it to give myself a little time, then cast the letter aside onto the divan.

"You have not told him of the child?"

"By God, I have not!"

"So you refuse an annulment."

"Yes." Louis had retreated again to the window. "I refuse. Abbot Suger says I must. And before God I still love you, Eleanor. I always have, and always will."

There was Louis, all his confidence gone, strangely reduced and even more diffident than usual, with shoulders bowed and eyes restless and unstill, whether from his own failures or my own predicament I could not tell. God's ultimate blessing before the altar of the Holy Sepulchre had not worked its miracle in his unquiet mind, and his expedition against Damascus had heaped further failure on him.

Had I not mentioned Damascus? How could I forget? For at the same time as I had turned my thoughts inward to this child, Louis had launched a fatal attack on Damascus, only to be driven into ignomini-ous retreat. Fleeing before victorious Nureddin, leaving uncounted numbers of Crusader corpses in his wake, Louis had returned to me with my inconvenient burden and entire lack of repentance. For a moment I felt a breath of compassion stir on my skin. I had not given him an easy life, had I?

"I love you, Eleanor. Does that mean nothing to you?" he asked. At last his rage broke free like waves breaching sea defenses. "You commit-ted adultery with your uncle. Incest, by God! You let him fuck you!"

In the world of military vulgarity in which we had lived for so long, rarely was Louis quite so vulgar. So I matched it, because I was in the mood to do so. My compassion was as short-lived as a mayfly snapped up by a spritely wagtail.

"Yes, he did. And very effectively."

"Slut! Whore!" He did not measure his words. "To give yourself to the brother of your own father!"

How sordid he made it sound, but it did not harm me. I winged my arrow through the opening he had provided.

"And are you and I any better?"

"There's no comparison, by God! We're cousins in the fourth degree! Not uncle and niece! You have no shame."

"No. I do not."

"I cannot lift my head in public."

"Who's to know the truth?" I advanced on him, so that he took a step back. "Will you accuse me of it in public? Will you take me before the courts? What will you do, Louis? Have me whipped through the churchyard in penance? By the Virgin, you're more of a fool than I thought. And I will not comply. I will deny it. I'll not have you drag my name through the gutter to appease your own pride."

"The penalty for a queen committing adultery against her lord is death," Louis spluttered.

"And you would not dare. You would have war on your hands before my head hit the stone and my blood puddled around your sanctimonious toes," I sneered. "Aquitaine and Poitou would rise up against you."

"You deserve any punishment I mete out."

"Then give me an annulment, Louis. Is that not punishment enough?"

"I will not! I wish it had not come to this." He covered his face with his hands, looking more like a flea-bitten whipped hound than ever. "And don't think of foisting the child on me. I'll not have it. Better if the bastard dies, Galeran says. He thinks . . ."

So Louis had told Thierry Galeran, whose hatred of me burned like a torch in the black of midnight.

"Don't tell me what Galeran says and thinks." I was now eye to eye with Louis, and he stepped back again. I could imagine the vicious words, could practically read them in the taut ropes of tendon in Louis's throat as he swallowed convulsively. *Kill it. Smother it at birth. Poison it. Bury it in an unmarked grave. And its mother with it!* Anything but bring shame on the King of France through the actions of his wife.

I think Louis thought I would strike him, as I had once before. I had raised my arms, hands clenched into fists. But I would not. Striking Louis would not stop him from listening to Galeran's naughty mischief.

"Get out!" My voice echoed satisfyingly off the plastered, painted walls.

Louis marched from the room, anger shimmering around him, leaving me to my solitary thoughts, the chains that imprisoned me growing heavier with every day.

A year I spent in Jerusalem. The longest year of my life, a year of loneliness and bitterness and loss. Louis would have had it a year of humiliation and repentance if he'd had his way, but I would not. Regret, yes; repentance, never. For all those months in Jerusalem, as the child ripened and grew in me, I rested and ate well. I recovered my looks and the flesh that had been stripped from my bones in the aftermath of Mount Cadmos. My skin and hair glowed in the warmth. I knew I had never been so beautiful as I waited to see the path of my troubled future. I should have felt isolated. My own women were barred from me, except for Agnes—Louis's dread of gossip, of course—so I was served by the silent and soft-footed girls of Queen Melisende's household. And yet in some inexplicable way, in this world of women, which was almost a seraglio, I became resigned to my temporary fate, even though I was shut away from society and played no part in the events that followed our arrival. Within my mind and my heart there was a still, cool smoothness, like a perfect pearl from one of the oysters of the River Garonne, which lapped the walls of my city of Bordeaux. In all that time I never demanded my release. Perhaps the filigreed window screens and guarded doors gave me the solitude I needed as the child grew.

So it was a strange time, as if I were suspended from life, a creature in hibernation. I was given no public role and, in the circumstances, how could I seek it? Did I appear at Louis's side at the formal entry into the city by the Jaffa Gate? Rather I was hustled away. Did I see him lay the Oriflamme of France on the altar of the Holy Sepulchre and receive the absolution he had so longed for? I did not. Nor did I hear the shouts of joy that welcomed Louis as hero and conqueror. If I had, I would have screeched with the irony of it. The Great Council of Crusaders at Acre, attended by all the great and good, passed by without my presence.

It was as if I did not exist. "Was my absence noted?" I asked Agnes, more out of curiosity than anger at my banishment.

"They gossip!"

Well, they would. What treasure my enemies would find to mine from my lack of public appearance.

"You are in disgrace," Agnes added.

"Because of Mount Cadmos?" I asked.

"Yes."

To be expected, of course. "Because of Prince Raymond?" I would rather not, but . . .

"That, too. You could not expect to keep it secret, lady."

"The child . . . ?"

She shook her head and I sighed with relief.

"Some say you tried to stick a knife in Galeran," Agnes said with an appreciative smile.

"Untrue. Unfortunately." I smiled too.

There was little for me to smile about in these arid months, as our once magnificent Crusade fell into ruin around us. If my mind had been on the military glory of France, of Aquitaine, the final disintegration of our once proud army would have struck hard. How could I have dragged my sire's and grandsire's reputations in the dust with such ignominious defeat? With money and resources running low, morale even lower, without any clear leadership from Louis, our fine forces, in the nature of unpaid and discontented soldiery, abandoned themselves to fornication and robbery and every sort of wickedness.

How we were all shamed. It was too painful to contemplate.

Why did I not leave? Why did I not demand my freedom, as I had in Antioch, when I was brave and confident? Why did I not hire my own ship and return to Aquitaine, as I had planned? I could not. My isolation was as much self-imposed as demanded by Louis. My resilience waned as my belly grew.

And Raymond? I neither wrote to him nor sent a courier—although I could have found some means to smuggle out a message. I never told him of the child. I could not and saw no purpose in it. But I would love his son or daughter because it was his blood and mine. Aquitaine blood, rich and rare, and so to be cherished.

Idly I considered the future of my child, raised discreetly in some loyal household in Aquitaine. If a male child, he would be trained as a knight; if a girl, she would receive an education as extensive as my own. And no, the child would never be passed off as Louis's. I would make provision; I would take responsibility. And then, when the child was grown? Then I would see . . .

As the days passed, my mind recovered its sharpness and I planned. Eventually I would leave this place, for this soft imprisonment would not last forever. I was tied here because of the child. But when it was born I would be free to order my own affairs.

And what then?

I began to plot and plan, to consider and arrange. Who would help me point Louis along the path I wanted? Who could demand Louis's obedience more strongly than any other, even more than Galeran or Abbot Suger or even Holy Bernard? Who would speak with God's voice?

I knew the answer. There was such a high power.

The anticipation strengthened me through those endless months.

Odo de Deuil gave up on writing his history of the Crusade for Abbot Suger's delectation. Enough was enough. Louis's humiliation at Damascus gave him pause for thought. My own unwritable sin tipped the balance finally and paralyzed his hand as it tried to move across the page. At least I had that to be thankful for.

The child would be born at the turn of the year. As early as the first days of November the first pressure of pain woke me. Nothing to concern me, I was told, only a twinge, a cramp, a knotting of muscles. It was too early and the pains gentled—I was mistaken in my fear after all. I had grown soft in my captivity, my sinews lax from lack of exercise. Agnes, whose uncompromising presence I insisted on in the midst of the seraglio beauties, assured me I would carry the child to full term.

Not so. My body betrayed me.

Even now I recall the viciousness of it. The heartbreak of it. Sharp bites of pain forced me to my knees. The waters stained my skirts, puddled on the tiles. I cried out in agony and, I admit, in terror.

It was hard for me, much harder than when Marie was born. A hell- ish nightmare of sweat and strain, of mingled fear and despair seized my mind as my thoughts reverted again, when they could escape the confines of my afflicted body, to the loss of the stillborn child during the second year of my marriage. I prayed. I called on God's name. I beseeched the Holy Mother in her mercy. Surely God would not pun- ish me.

But perhaps He would, for my sin.

I cried out, clutching the rosary that Agnes thrust into my frenzied fingers as the pain overwhelmed me, its claws agonizingly sharp. Hot as the jaws of Hell; cold as my isolation in my extremity. I was nearer to despair than I had ever been in my life. Why struggle, if God had put the mark on me for my double sin of adultery and incest?

Agnes was with me throughout. She was the only one I wanted. Hers was the hand I gripped when I had no more energy to give to this birthing.

"Push, m'lady. Don't give up now. Don't let Galeran have his way!"

And I didn't, because in spite of everything, I wanted this child.

The baby was born, slithering from between my thighs with amazing speed at the end, as a long day slid toward dusk, but the child did not draw breath. Small, blue of skin, lifeless. Nothing so much as a skinned rabbit.

It was a girl. A daughter.

"Give her to me," I demanded.

"Indeed, lady, I think you should rest. . . ." Agnes was already enfolding the lifeless figure in silk.

"I want to hold her."

Too early. Too weak to live on her own. Yet, unlike my first child that had not lived, she was perfectly formed, beautiful, fair and translucent. The corners of her mouth curved softly inward as if she treasured a secret, her eyelashes so pale as to be near invisible. Her hair was nothing more than wisps of gold.

Poor, pretty creature. She was already gone from me. I did not kiss her, for I dared not. I would have loved her for the blood of Aquitaine doubly in her veins. I would have loved her for Raymond's sake. Dry-eyed, I gave her back to Agnes.

"Perhaps it's for the best, lady."

"For the best?" I blinked at her, for the moment not understanding.

"Convenient. It would be a difficult birth to explain. With His Majesty's oath and all."

Convenient for Louis. I could not speak. Grief robbed me of any words but I could not weep. It was as if all my emotions, my heart and my mind, were frozen to ice, despite the suffocating heat.

Louis did not come near me. Nor did I expect it. He let me do as I pleased.

What to do with my daughter's tiny body. A hasty burial, drawing no attention, would have been wise, perhaps, or an interment in some unmarked grave. I cringed from it even though my thoughts were difficult to harness to their task. *I* would decide. Not Louis, not Galeran. I used the powers still left to me, and the French coin that in enough quantity would buy any man. A priest was summoned who, for a pocketful of gold, would swear that the child drew breath at the first and cried out so that she might be worthy of baptism. I would not commit a daughter of Raymond, Prince of Antioch, to the horrors of Limbo, shut out of Heaven throughout eternity.

Philippa. That was her name.

For Raymond's mother, my own grandmother.

I did not see the child again as I decided what I wanted. She would be embalmed with spices and sweet unguents to preserve her frail flesh, then swaddled and encased in silk and leather, as fine as any cradle and covering. Another purse of gold paid for the passage home of one of my household. On my instructions, and without heralding the news to anyone, he took ship for Europe, and I charged him with taking my daughter to be buried in the graveyard beside others of my family at Belin, where I was born. She would rest there and know the same warm sun, the light aromatic breezes and the birdsong that I had known. She would have her final resting place in Aquitaine. One day I would find my way to her grave.

It crossed my mind—as it must: I cared more for that lost child than for my healthy, living daughter, both flesh of my flesh. Why should that be? Philippa was a true child of Aquitaine—perhaps that was it.

It was a time of heartbreak for me. It surprised me how the grief infused my whole body and would not let go. For the first time in my life I could not look forward. I could not *think*. All was dark and full of misery. I could not sleep but sat and stared blankly. Yet I could not weep.

I would draw a veil over that sad time.

But I knew my enemies would not. Since when is any event appertaining to a queen kept secret?

We left Jerusalem in March of the following year, with a mere three hundred as the remnant of our original magnificent force, sailing west from Acre. Three hundred men out of an army that had once been numbered in tens of thousands. So few were we that we all fit into two small vessels, bound for Calabria in southern Italy. And what had we achieved? Jerusalem might still be secure, but for how long? Nureddin and his Turkish allies grew stronger by the day, openly ridiculing

French efforts to defeat them. The reputation of France was trampled in the dust.

Although my body had recovered rapidly from the birth, my mood had not and I was a broken reed, following with a draining lethargy Louis's instructions to make ready to depart. But I was not so broken that I would consent to share accommodations with Galeran. Nothing! Nothing would make me consent to stay trapped in the same confined space as the man who might have plotted the death of my child if God had not forestalled him. Nor would I travel with Louis. I had nothing to say to either of them, so I feigned illness. It was not difficult to do, so low in spirits was I, to the very depths of my soul, that it was almost beyond my powers to rise from my bed. So we traveled separately, I with my household in one vessel, Louis and his advisers in the other. A little victory, even if a petty one.

I think Louis was relieved. He looked positively cheerful.

Thinking back, I see that the voyage was as much a time of fear and horror as the one that had carried us to Antioch. Surely God and His Angels were against us. Ill winds and storms tossed and buffeted us until we were blown off course, and my vessel was soon parted from Louis's. Did I fear for my life? I don't think I did, shrouded as I was in a melancholy as thick and deep as the clouds that hemmed us in. We seemed to make a circuit of the Mediterranean, to every godforsaken spot on it—and then to some He had not even discovered, putting into port even on the Barbary shores of Africa, even taken captive by Byzantine raiders until we were rescued by Sicilian galleys. It all meant nothing to me. I was adrift, wallowing in misery and what could only be self-pity. Never was I so guilty of succumbing to such weakness.

Eventually, finally, I made landfall in the Kingdom of Sicily, where Louis awaited me. Meeting me on the quay when I walked unsteadily ashore, he fell on my neck with tears of joy for the answer to his prayers. God had saved me, he announced. I had been reunited with him at God's will. He kissed my brow and assured me that all would be well.

I submitted, as unresponsive as a bolt of cloth. What a miracle a few months of separation had made. It seemed I had been restored to the royal favor.

I could not respond. It was beyond me. I did not care.

We were received with honor, Sicily being a Norman kingdom, where King Roger opened his gracious hands to us and provided all the luxuries we could have asked for at his elegant court at Potenza. Seeing my exhaustion, he demanded nothing from me and allowed me to retire immediately. I thanked him. All I wanted was to close my eyes and blot out what life might hold for me on my return to the dread Cité palace.

Then, without warning or apology, before I had even taken occupation of the well-furnished rooms, King Roger paid me a private visit.

"I have news," he said. "From Outremer. And a letter has been brought by courier for you." A serious, stolid man, King Roger regarded me with somber eyes. "I think you should sit. It is not good news, lady."

So the news first. I sat, sliding the letter into the slashed sleeve of my gown. King Roger wasted no time. What point in attempting to soften news that cannot be softened?

"The Prince of Antioch is dead, lady."

I gasped. I struggled to draw another breath. "What?"

"The Prince is dead. I thought you would wish to be alone when you heard."

For a moment, before the truth of his words hit home, I wondered how much King Roger knew of my liaison, that he should make this opportunity to tell me alone. But, of course, that was not his reason. Raymond was the brother of my own father, and I saw compassion in the Norman's face. It was right that I should be told first, and in private.

And then the words made sense.

They were a mailed fist to my belly.

Raymond was dead. My magnificent golden hero, my lover, no longer breathed the same air as I. How could it be? How could his love of life, his vibrancy, have been snuffed out with no more of a ripple than when snuffing out the flame of a candle? I had not known. How could I not have known it?

"Tell me," I commanded calmly, though I was in a mind to shriek my grief and loss.

So King Roger sat himself beside me and told me, in the baldest and most critical of terms, because that would be the least painful way. Raymond was killed in a foolish, ill-considered campaign against the Saracen leader Nureddin. My gloriously courageous but foolhardy Raymond had refused a truce with the Turks when it was offered and had attacked a massive force with only a few hundred knights and a thousand foot soldiers. A brave attempt, King Roger admitted, but not feasible. The sheer bravado of the attack, so typical of Raymond, who believed himself invincible, went beyond common sense. My beloved Raymond was surrounded, slain by the stroke of a Turkish sword as exhaustion laid him low. And then . . .

"Tell me!" I insisted when Roger's flat description faltered.

"They struck off the Prince's head and right arm."

Ah! I could not speak.

The Sicilian King was not finished. How brutal it was. "His head was set in a silver case and sent to the Caliph of Baghdad," he finished in a rush. "I'm told it's displayed there over the city gate. There is huge rejoicing. Allah's most formidable enemy dead. They held him in high regard, even though they killed him."

"But why did he do it?" My frenzied demand filled the room, my voice harsh with grief. "Why would so able a commander run such an imprudent risk?"

King Roger shrugged. "How to know? Fear for his city? No ruler would condemn his city to be sacked by the Infidel. Perhaps in his mind the Prince was driven to desperate measures simply to hold the Turks at bay."

And I heard the words Roger did not say. I added them myself. "Because my husband refused to lend his forces—and mine—to protect Antioch."

Roger's eyes fell before mine. Thus I knew the worst.

"Thank you," I managed to say. I drew my veil over my head. Over my face so that the King would not see the effect of his news in my expression. "Blessed Virgin! Why did he have to die?"

"It is in the nature of heroes to die at the height of their powers, lady. We must celebrate his greatness as we mourn his passing."

"But I cannot celebrate."

Sensitive to my loss, King Roger withdrew.

So I mourned him. I did not weep for so brave and foolish a warrior, because that is not what he would have wanted from me. If tears were to fall for him, perhaps Constance would do the weeping. It was her right. Instead of shedding useless tears, I put the blame for Raymond's death where I thought it lay: Louis's callous refusal to help him had cost Raymond his life. Louis's abduction of me had prevented me from giving my Aquitainians to Raymond's use.

And perhaps if I had insisted on returning to Antioch from Jerusalem . . . perhaps I, too, could have made a difference.

And now Raymond was dead.

It made the loss of his daughter even more unimaginably tragic. I had nothing left of Raymond but a bright memory of ten magical days spent in that golden oasis he had created in Antioch.

"Sweet Jesu! I hope you have a conscience!" I had no tolerance for Louis, and so accused him moments later, even as he shook his head in rebuttal. "However much you deny it, your hands are drenched in Raymond's blood. I hope God can forgive you for it, Louis—for I cannot."

Louis refused to reply. We never spoke of it again.

I was crushed with sorrow.

Where was the proud, confident Duchess of Aquitaine? Not here in Potenza, that was certain. The woman who sat in her borrowed rooms was buried under a weight of guilt and loss and unhappiness. Nothing but emptiness. Eating, sleeping, even thinking seemed beyond me. Until Agnes crouched beside me, her hands closed around mine where they lay limp in my lap, and squeezed hard.

"Lady. Look at me. Listen to me."

I gazed into her concerned face, surprised by the command in her tone but not particularly stirred to obey. And Agnes, dear Agnes, enfolded me in her arms and rocked me like the mother I had never known.

"It might be good to weep," she said softly.

"I cannot."

So we sat silently, until I struggled for release and Agnes turned me to face her.

"This is no good, lady. You have to be strong. If you do not . . . do you live under Louis's subjection forever? Do you let Galeran win?"

"Louis will not release me."

"No, he won't." I blinked at her honesty. "He's weak and stubborn, both in equal measure, and Galeran has his hands on the reins. When you are returned to Paris there'll be no respite—it will be Abbot Suger who resumes control. No, the King won't release you or your lands." Her hands gripped even tighter. "Not unless you do something about it."

"What can I do?"

Agnes released me and stepped away with a fine sneer inappropriate in a tire-woman. "You're as weak as a mouse! Where's the woman who came to Paris and took us all by storm? Where's the woman who cajoled and wheedled and bullied until she accompanied her husband on Crusade? Who demanded an annulment in the middle of a War Council? Is she dead?"

"I think she is," I remarked dolefully.

"So they talk, gossip, rip apart your reputation. Will you let them do it? Will you sink into a trough of misery? I had thought better of you, lady. Even Queen Adelaide had more spirit than that! What's more, if you continue to languish in so pitiful a manner, you'll lose your looks!"

Well, that got through to me, the banality of it. I tilted my head. "Well?"

Agnes fell to her knees beside my chair. "Listen, lady. Galeran has Louis's ear again."

"When does he not?"

"He tells the King to discipline you, to take you to task. To force you to travel on. He says your illness is a trick and that His Majesty should order you to resume your journey home."

"Does he?" I felt my mind stir with mild resentment, the first time it had roused in any direction for days.

"We are in Sicily, lady."

"And so?" I found I was looking down at my gown, my shoes, really seeing them with some surprise. Had I chosen to wear this gown?

Its weight and dark mourning hue displeased me. How could I have allowed the ends of my hair to become so dull through the exigencies of travel and neglect? I rubbed them between my fingers, unable to suppress a grimace. How dull the glowing color had become. My hands were less than soft, my nails ill tended.

"We are in Sicily! Do we go on to Italy, to Rome?" Agnes demanded. "What would Prince Raymond tell you to do?"

Ah . . . My mind snapped back from the deficiencies of my wardrobe and person. How difficult it seemed to stir my thoughts to life. But no longer. As if a window shutter had been opened to let in the first blush of dawn, I was beginning to think again.

"Rome? I'm not sure."

"Ask His Majesty. No—tell him! Tell him you must go to Rome. For the good of your soul. He'll not refuse you."

Like the mist clearing in the heat of the sun, my abandoned planning began to reorder itself. I looked at Agnes and smiled for the first time in longer than I could recall, the muscles of my face stiff with disuse. "I should beg an audience with the Pope, shouldn't I?"

"Most definitely!"

I had forgotten. How had that been possible? It had been my intent when I had schemed and plotted through that long incarceration in Jerusalem. The Holy Father would support me against Louis, and Louis would be forced to listen. Pope Eugenius would outrank and outargue Abbot Suger any day. How could I have let my plans slip through my fingers for so long? It was time—well beyond time—for me to take control, to order my life again, to drag my mind back from the brink of what had seemed to be inconsolable despair.

"And, lady"—Agnes was holding a document—"this fell from your sleeve. I put it aside for you. It is still unopened. I think you should read it."

The letter. King Roger had given me a letter. Who would send a letter to find me here? Nothing that would not keep. There were more urgent matters to arrange. Louis would discipline me, would he? Take me to task, would he . . . ?

"It has the lions of Anjou on it, lady."

"Anjou . . ." Now here was an unexpected communication. "Give it to me." I snatched it up.

To Eleanor, Duchess of Aquitaine, Countess of Poitou.

Well, that was clear enough. I opened it with sudden urgency, eyes racing down the single page. Considering the time and effort spent to get this to me, it was very short.

I send this in the certain hope of it finding you. Roger of Sicily is a family friend who can be trusted.

News of your desire to end your marriage has reached Anjou. You'll not need me to tell you that this will make you vulnerable. If you should find a need for the protection of a strong arm from a man who has always admired you, I am he. I can be your eyes and ears, as alert as your magnificent gerfalcons.

My admiration for you has not lapsed over the years.

As I studied the writing, the scrawled signature, I laughed aloud at the outrageousness of the offer, my voice rusty with the effort. A strong arm. Eyes and ears. Just what was the meat in this offer? Then I concentrated on the author. Not Geoffrey, as was my first instinct for so personal a letter. Nor in the neat, educated hand of a clerk. Instead, in a hurried style and quite idiosyncratic, with strong uprights and lacking any embellishment, the well-formed words galloped across the page. And there the final flamboyant signing.

Henry Plantagenet.

And then a scribbled footnote, even more hurried, as if he had abandoned the earlier formality to write what was in his mind.

More to the point, every ravenous power seeker will be sniffing at your heels when you are unwed. You need me to stand for you. If you consent, I promise that you will not regret it.

Despite my misery, I laughed, and remembered. Another life, another place. How many years ago now since I first saw him in Poitiers? Four years? The boy with russet hair and gray eyes, precociously aware, already bidding to be a warrior. A youth with blood on his wrists where my hawk's talons had dug in because he refused to wear a gauntlet. And then later when he had sat at the council in Paris to discuss the possibility of a royal wife for him, watching, weighing, assessing. He would be a young man now, capable of a cool appraisal. I recalled my acknowledgment that here was a rare intelligence. And I remembered all that uncontrolled energy as he investigated a pierced incense burner, singeing his fingers as he did so.

So Henry Plantagenet had written this letter, offering to be my hawk. He would stand for me. An enigmatic statement that left much to the imagination. Was that all he was offering? Who would be the hawk, blinded and controlled by hood and jesses? Who would be the master? This was not an offer to take without due consideration.

But should I be considering it to any degree?

I reread the extraordinary request, absorbing the truth in it.

> . . . *every ravenous power seeker will be sniffing at your heels when you are unwed.*

I had been protected all my life, and so busy snatching at my freedom that I had not truly considered what I would do when—if—I was at liberty to return to my own lands.

I would be the perfect target for a well-planned abduction and a hasty marriage to any ambitious knight who saw me as his road to greatness. Was that not the reason I had been so precipitately wed to Louis in the first instance, remaining incarcerated in Bordeaux until he came to fetch me with all the power of a French escort, for fear that I might be ambushed before I could reach Paris? The man who took the Duchess of Aquitaine to his bed, willingly or by force, would be fortunate indeed.

So if I could escape from Louis—*if* . . . I scowled at the opulent surroundings; if I could escape from this damned marriage—what then? Who would protect me from the jackals that would circle to pounce and take possession? I would have a pack of them on my heels before the ink on the annulment was dry.

The golden lions of Anjou grinned at me from the seal. Was this nothing but the puffed-up confidence of youth, entirely implausible? Unless Count Geoffrey was behind the offer. Now, there was a thought that did not please me. But if so, why hide behind his son? And I did not think it had the essence of Geoffrey. It was far too direct. Geoffrey would wait, bide his time, then swoop when I was at my weakest. This was a very direct proposal.

From a mere boy!

How old would Henry Plantagenet be now? He described himself as a man, not a boy. Determination sprang up from the bold, black script on the page. How intriguing. To take the trouble of sending a message across Europe, to put himself at my side. And what a turn of phrase he had.

I folded the parchment, hooding my eyes from Agnes. "Put this in my jewel coffer," I said, and felt the desire to determine my future resurface, thundering through my blood with enough force to make me catch my breath. I rose to my feet, issuing orders. A tub. Hot water. Perfumes and lotions. My clothes shaken out, my jewels laid out for my inspection.

Within the hour I was restored.

A servant led me to the chamber occupied by my husband.

"Eleanor . . ."

He struggled from his knees before the prie-dieu, a guarded expression on his face. Thank God neither Odo de Deuil nor Galeran was hovering in the shadows. I curtsied. I hid a smile at the startled winging of his brows. There had been little respect between us of late.

"I have a request, my lord."

Louis looked as if he would rather I hadn't.

"I want to go home. And I want to go to Rome first." Louis's brow wrinkled. "I want an audience with His Holiness the Pope. I wish to stop in Rome."

Louis steepled his fingers to his lips. "Abbot Suger wants us to get to Paris as fast as possible. There are rumors of discontent at home. . . ."

Which I very well knew. I had spent the last hour in taking more than control of my life. If my own reputation had been damaged, Louis was wholeheartedly blamed for the failure of the crusading enterprise. His vassals were murmuring loudly about dishonor and the reckless waste of money, rattling their swords and threatening rebellion. I widened my eyes with a magnificent pretense at anxiety.

"It's been well over two years since we left, my lord. Will two more weeks make any difference? Abbot Suger is a capable man."

"I don't see the need to linger in Rome now."

So I lied. I perjured my soul. Why not? I would never forgive Louis for his cruel role in Raymond's death. "I wish to make repentance. I have sins on my conscience."

Magic words. Immediately Louis's features softened. Oh, how soft, how gullible he was.

"Eleanor. My dear wife. Of course. His Holiness will give us both his blessing. He will grant us absolution of our sins. And then when we return to Paris, we can look forward—to our future together."

"Thank you, my lord. I knew you would understand."

He walked forward, placing his hands tentatively to cup my shoulders. When I steeled myself not to pull away, Louis kissed me tenderly on my brow.

"Of course I understand. You have been unhappy." I prayed he would not conjure Raymond's name between us. "You are so high-spirited, it draws you into dangerous currents. It has always been so. But God will know what is in your heart and give you His comfort. As I will give you mine. The past will be wiped clean and we will walk forward together in God's holy light, both of us restored to His salvation."

He kissed me again on the lips.

I escaped before I might vomit over his sandaled feet.

We left for Rome with an escort from King Roger. His teeth glinted in a smile that was almost a grin as he handed me into the swagged and cushioned palanquin.

"I trust the letter from the Angevin brat was of interest to you."

My brows rose. Angevin brat? Was he being deliberately provocative? And what did the King of Sicily know of it anyway?

"Family connections, you know." Roger kept hold of my fingers and raised them to his lips, a charming formality, then added with utmost seriousness: "If he offers help, don't reject it out of hand."

"And how do you know he offers me help? What help could I possibly need?"

"Only you know that, lady." He signaled for the escort to move off with a distinct gleam in his eye. "Henry Plantagenet will go far, I predict. If not always comfortably. He'll be worth watching."

"He's very young."

"Angevins mature quickly, lady! Watch yourself!"

"I have no intention of doing anything foolhardy!" I replied, inexplicably ruffled.

King Roger smiled.

Before I left Potenza—how I hated Potenza!—I gave money for perpetual Masses to be said for Raymond's soul and prayed that God would not judge him too harshly. He was a man of much charm and not a little talent. How could I not have loved him? I tried not to think of his naked skull encased within rigid silver, adorning the gates of Baghdad. I tried not to think of the carrion eaters swooping to peck at the rotting flesh.

Some days I was still sick to my stomach.

But now I looked forward. The image of Henry Plantagenet slipped through my guard—until I banished it. I would be under the control of no man. I had almost fallen foul of his father, who had wooed me for his own ambitions. I would not do the same with the son.

And then I found myself smiling again within the sumptuous enclosing curtains as a long-distant memory burst into my mind with great clarity, of when the young Angevin had taken my popinjay with the promise to teach it to repeat, *Eleanor*. He had done no such thing. When the troublesome bird was returned to me, it enunciated with great clarity, *Henry*, followed by a squawk that might have been, *Plantagenet*. And continued to do so until I banished it from my solar.

Chapter Sixteen

"*My* children. Such troubles as you have faced together." Pope Eugenius, a small, rotund cleric with the bright, smiling features of an ingenuous cherub—and a similar potential for malice, I suspected—held out his hand bearing the papal ring. We knelt to kiss it—first Louis in a disgusting flurry of bent knee and spine-cringing respect; then I followed suit, trying not to shudder at the sensation of fat, damp fingers on mine. His Holiness was not abstemious in the matter of diet. Nor was he well-informed of the need for frequent washing. The heavy perfume did not quite swamp the reek of uncleansed silk and skin. I held my breath and touched my lips to the grubby jewel with marvelous respect. This meeting would be my salvation.

Not being welcome in Rome, part of the ongoing dispute over who might actually be in possession of Saint Peter's keys, Eugenius had agreed to receive us in his palace at Tusculum, south of the city. It had a lovely aspect, clinging to the northern slopes of the Alban Hills, enclosed with gardens and trees—except that it reminded me of a soft green mirror image of Antioch, and I closed my eyes to its beauty.

I was resilient. I would let nothing—and certainly not this fat little cleric—stand against me.

"We have looked for this meeting ever since your messenger arrived to beg an audience," Eugenius said, beaming at Louis. "I know your efforts in the Holy Land were not crowned with success, but God sees the intent in the heart of every Crusader. You are indeed blessed. Come . . ."

With a swirl of his noxious robes—he dressed the part in gold and purple, whether his status was in debate or not—Eugenius led us out onto a shaded terrace, where we sat, accepting the goblets of wine provided by obsequious servants. The foul scent was less obvious here in the open air. I filled my nostrils with the pungency of cloves in the spiced hippocras, which was not particularly to my taste but was better than the stink of the unwashed papal garments.

"To have worshipped before the Holy Sepulchre. Magnificent! To have stood in Jerusalem . . ."

I let His Holiness ramble and murmur in admiration as I sat and sipped the wine. Louis nodded and agreed as the unctuous voice filled every space. Such a powerful, rolling voice for so small a man. So far I had said not one word. But when I did, every word would count.

"And I think your journey to Sicily was not without its trials, my son. We have heard that—"

Even Louis had had enough.

"Our time here is short, Holiness." I saw the quick slide of Louis's eye in my direction. "We need the benefit of your experience. And your intercession. It has been in my mind to proclaim another Crusade—to achieve what we failed to put right. I would ask your advice, Holiness. . . ."

By now I also had reached the limit of my forbearance. The two would be knee-deep in plotting another disaster in Outremer if I allowed it. With a little rustle of distress I placed my cup down on the stone ledge beside me and leaned forward, hands raised in open plea. I played the gamut of despair, eyes wide with sharp distress, voice catching with emotion.

"Indeed, Holiness. My husband has his own concerns. But I need to speak with you. I seek your advice. It is a matter of great urgency to me. In fact, without your intercession, I fear for my soul. . . ."

Pope Eugenius's eyes narrowed slightly in suspicion. Then he remembered to smile.

"Of course, my daughter."

"Alone." I held his bright gaze.

"Then so you shall."

Sweet Virgin! How I despised God's Representative on Earth!

He kept me waiting until the following day. I might have insisted but I used my time well. How to make my approach? With Abbot Bernard I had moved from cold rhetoric to impassioned, overabundant emotion. What would move this fat little cleric other than self-interest? Why was it always necessary for a woman to persuade rather than command? When I finally made my obeisance before him in his private chamber, I was still in a morass of indecision. My evidence was indisputable. Had I not had a whole year to plan this meeting? But how to present it—I did not know, now that the moment was upon me.

As I knelt I breathed deep, despite the stink, to still the trembling in my belly. He would not refuse me. He would see the justice of my plea. My heart tripped and jumped. Victory was in my grasp at last. I would weep over his soiled papal slippers if I had to.

"Tell me what is in your heart, my daughter." Eugenius raised me, kissed my cheek with false fatherly affection, and led me to a cushioned window seat. "I see you are in some torment. I assure you, it cannot be as bad as you think. Tell me all."

So I did.

Eyes downcast like a woman in sorrow and utter frustration, I touched on the illegality of my union with Louis through consanguinity. I lingered on my failure in twelve years to produce any child but a girl who would never rule France. Did His Holiness not realize that over the past two hundred years, no Capetian king had ever failed to produce at least one male heir? Yet Louis and I had failed. It was God's punishment. It must be—a punishment for a marriage that should never have come to pass. Fat Louis had sinned, making no attempt to gain a dispensation for our rushed union, and so we—Louis and I—paid the penalty. And so would France if Louis did not have a son; I finished on this most vital of points. I slid over the fact that Louis had a brother who could quite easily step into his shoes and was probably able to rule far more effectively.

Eugenius sat, head tilted like a gaudy magpie eyeing a nestling. I had kept his attention but could read nothing in his bright gaze.

"I have something to show you, if you would look, Holiness. . . ."

"Then do so, my child."

From my sleeve I drew out and unrolled a document written out in my own hand, as detailed and explicit as my memory could achieve from my long-ago conversation with the Bishop of Laon, the generations of Aquitaine and Capet that united their children, Louis and Eleanor, within the forbidden degree. I offered the scroll and Eugenius took it, but his eyes never moved from my face. Impossible to tell what went on behind that masterfully smiling mask.

"It is all most explicit, my child. What would you have me do?"

Could he not see what I wanted? I smoothed over the jagged edge of impatience. Would this slimily complacent cleric make me, Duchess of Aquitaine, beg?

"This document maps the illegality of my marriage, Holiness," I urged. "And here"—I produced another elderly scroll with the flourish of a jester releasing Louis's disastrous flock of singing birds from the contents of a pastry subtlety—"is the well-considered opinion of our own Abbot Bernard of Clairvaux. Our erudite Abbot has already spoken against our marriage. He thinks it should never have been made."

A powerful weapon. His Holiness was not averse to turning to the holy Bernard for advice. I watched the effect, once again unsettled as His Holiness barely glanced at the letter, his eyes returning to mine as if he would dissect every thought in my head.

"I am not unaware of the opinions of Abbot Bernard." He placed both documents neatly together, lining up their edges as if therein lay the answer to the problem.

This was not working! Why could the man not be swayed by the weight of legality? So if I must beg . . .

"I feel my failure, Holiness. Every day, every hour. I cannot live with it. Can you imagine what I am made to suffer through no fault of my own? My lord needs a son to inherit his throne and feels our lack keenly. He puts the blame on me, because his counselors tell him that the fault is mine. Do you realize the life I have been forced to lead?" I stretched out my hands, beseeching his pity. "I cannot live like this longer, Holiness. I cannot believe it is God's will that I suffer for a sin that is not mine."

"I agree, my daughter." He rose and walked to his prie-dieu, where he knelt, lifting his eyes to the crucifix before him, leaving me to sit in terrible uncertainty. Then he pushed himself ponderously to his feet and smiled across the room. "I see my way. I must restore God's peace and contentment to your heart."

My heart leaped with hope. "God's peace can be restored to both of us only through a restoration of legality. An annulment. I beg your consent, Holiness, to put this marriage aside. For both our sakes, and for France."

Real tears were wet on my cheeks. So much hung on this one decision. So much. If it went against me, what would I do? To remain bound to Louis for the rest of my life was more than I could bear. My tears flowed more freely.

"I beg of you, Holiness." Yes, I begged him for my separation as tears dripped to blot on my carefully prepared vellum that Eugenius had discarded. The lines of consanguinity that tied me to Louis through our ancestors blurred and ran until they were all but indecipherable.

Eugenius nodded. "It is certainly a matter to be considered. Come here, my child."

Once more I knelt before him, determined to leave no stone unturned.

"You should know, Holiness, that my lord refuses an intimate relationship with me."

"Indeed . . ."

"Another child is impossible unless Louis can—"

"There is no need to say more. You have suffered so much. God will have mercy on you and bless you." I felt the touch of his hands as I bowed my head. "I admire you, Eleanor. You have presented a powerful case to end this union." His voice was warm; he had used

the intimacy of my name. He would do it! Thank God! Silence filled
the room, broken only by the twittering of finches outside in the close-
fitting branches of a towering cypress. The hands lifted from my head.
I looked up in gratitude, the tears drying on my face. The Pope smiled
at me. "I have seen your evidence and heard your passion, my child.
You are not at fault in any of this. There is no need for your conscience to trouble you, or to fear God's continuing punishment . . .
but I think you have misunderstood. It is the duty of a wife to cleave
to her husband."

Cleave? I should cleave to Louis?

"It is not in your interest, nor in that of His Majesty, for you to be
set apart. There is no illegality in your marriage."

Was he a fool or misguided? Did he not understand? How could
he simply abandon the facts I had placed before him?

"Your troubles can be healed, my daughter. Your marriage restored."

Hope fled out of the window to join the mindless twittering of the
birds. "He does not come to my bed. How can it be healed, restored?"

Eugenius shook his head in a smooth tolerance that promptly set
light to my anger. "You have to be compassionate, daughter, to the
strain of your husband's leading the Crusade. His holy vows of celibacy should be commended, not held up for criticism."

Commended? My irritation was swamped by fury. "I'll not com-
mend him for his neglect of me! He rarely touched me even before he
grasped the Cross!"

"You are a high-tempered woman, Eleanor. You must pray for self-
control." Now my blood ran from hot to cold. How could it be that he
made me sound like an importuning whore rather than a neglected
wife? "And perhaps now that the Crusade is over—"

"It has been over for twelve months! Our marriage is not tenable!"

"You are wrong, Eleanor. Abbot Suger thinks it is."

Suger! The name sounded like a death knell to all my plans. What
had Abbot Suger to do with this?

"And Thierry Galeran also advises me that, once returned to the calm atmosphere in Paris, you will regain your dignity as Queen of France and accept your marriage."

And Galeran! Regain my dignity? How dared that lowborn upstart comment on my dignity?

As if a page in a book had been opened before me, I saw what I had so disastrously overlooked. Louis had sent on a courier to arrange our audience here at Tusculum. He had sent Thierry Galeran, who had used his time well to drop poison into Eugenius's ear. Of course he had, and Eugenius had not been slow to listen and be swayed by his favorite Templar.

"Galeran argues for the marriage to stand. Both he and Abbot Suger understand your situation very well. I have listened to them and I will lean in their favor in my decision. That's not to say that you don't have my compassion, my child. But I think you are wrong. I will not give you the annulment you ask for."

I could barely breathe. It had been a lost cause from the very beginning. They had destroyed my arguments, Suger and Galeran between them, cutting the ground from beneath my feet by their oh-so-smooth and understanding compassion for my *situation*. Eugenius had never had any intention of listening to me. He had known from the beginning that he would refuse. If I had had my dagger to hand and Galeran before me, I swear in that moment I would have gutted him. There was no point in kneeling before this weak-willed, ineffectual Pope who would be manipulated by such a creature as Galeran.

I stood, smoothing down my skirts, willing composure over my shaking limbs and features, and addressed him in frigid accents.

"I assume that both of your esteemed advisers—when daring to discuss the personal matter of my marriage—mentioned the immense value of Aquitaine for the Kingdom of France." I was pleased to see color rise to His Holiness's receding hairline. "I assume they informed you that my lands were far too valuable for Louis to lose over the mere whim of a woman to achieve her independence."

"We discussed your need for Louis's protection," Eugenius replied with terrible simplicity. "How else would you keep your lands intact? It is not practical for you to be unprotected and alone."

The validity of my arguments counted for nothing. They never had. Tears pricked behind my eyelids again, but this time from fury, and I refused to let them fall.

"You must accept that I know what is best for you," Eugenius simpered with ill-concealed victory. "If you will kneel again we can pray together."

I would not. "I don't want your prayers. I want an annulment."

"But your husband does not. He loves you. Is that not a blessing, my daughter?"

"A blessing? Louis's childish infatuation is a chain around my neck!"

I managed a curtsy, ensured that it dripped with disdain, then strode from the room, striving not to slam the door. I left my evidence—what use was it to me now? The houses of Aquitaine and Capet were cast on the floor at Eugenius's feet and I left them there. Anger shook me.

I consigned Suger and his interfering to the Fires of Hell. Along with Galeran and his vicious poisoning. And Eugenius . . . They were all in it together.

Nor was Louis without blame. I ran him to ground in one of Tusculum's little antechambers, with its view over gardens and distant hills, where he stood in a window embrasure, poring over a list of figures with Galeran.

"What have you done!"

I gave no recognition to Galeran; nor did I moderate my voice. The papal guards at the door remained stolidly unmoving.

"I suppose His Holiness refused." Louis looked mildly astonished at my passion.

"Of course he did. He'd no intention of doing anything other. He played me for a fool, pretending to listen and then . . ." I shut my teeth with a snap. "I'll not speak of it with your creature picking over every word like a vulture over a carcass."

"I have your best interests at heart, lady." Galeran was impossibly, unforgivably smug. He even smiled at me. "And the interests of France. We cannot afford to lose Aquitaine and Poitou. And you are too dangerous to be left free. Any one of our enemies could covet your lands. . . ."

"Dismiss him," I ordered Louis without a glance at the Templar.

"But, Eleanor—"

"You heard me."

Louis did, hunching his shoulders against an imminent storm if he refused.

"What did you say to that misbegotten, self-satisfied hypocrite of a Pope?" I demanded as Galeran retreated.

"Only that I want another holy war to . . ." I saw that his hand was clenched like a claw on the document and read his guilt there.

"Damn the Crusade, Louis! What did you say to him about us?"

"That I love you."

"What use is that, to either of us?"

"It's true. His Holiness asked me—"

"Are you so . . . so witless, Louis?" I snatched the scroll from his hand and flung it to the floor between us. "Did you not tell him that we need an annulment? Did you not demand it from him? You are the King of France. His position is not so strong that he can fly in the face of your wrath."

"I told him I wanted a son. I asked for his blessing." By God! Hopeless! "His Holiness said that you too had expressed your grief that you could not carry my heir."

Of course I had said it. It was the only argument I could use. That did not mean that I wanted it. I never wanted to share a bed with Louis again. I wanted to scrape the filth of Paris from my feet and wave Louis farewell. There he stood, old before his time, fingers trying to flatten the scroll he'd rescued from the floor. Even now, he was looking beyond me to see if Galeran was lurking within earshot, so that he could be summoned back to continue to tally the figures for a new Crusade.

There was nothing here for me to love or respect.

"God's Bones, Louis! Have you no sense?"

* * *

My baggage was packed and we would leave at daybreak for Paris, but I could not sleep. Wrapped in a loose robe over my shift, my hair unbound on my shoulders, I could find no way past Eugenius's obstinacy. Should I appeal to Abbot Bernard again? I glowered at the invisible gardens beyond my window.

A sound at the outer door took my attention. Low voices whispered.

Then Agnes said, "A servant is here." Her disapproval was sharp. "His Holiness wishes to speak with you before you leave. What does he want at this time of night? Couldn't it wait until tomorrow?" She picked up my cloak and stood waiting.

I was not of a mood to stir myself to hear one more piece of kindly advice to put myself in Louis's care, subdue my own intemperate nature, and set myself to a life of unparalleled boredom in the Île de la Cité. After Outremer, with all its heights and depths, Paris beckoned with the promise of a dungeon cell.

"The servant is waiting, lady," Agnes chivied. "He says to go now. His Holiness does not stand on formality."

"At almost midnight!"

I allowed her to bundle me into the mantle, a veil around my hair.

"I am to come with you," Agnes said as she wrapped herself in her own cloak, and the servant nodded.

I did not care greatly. The sooner I got there, the sooner I could accept whatever soft-voiced imprecations Eugenius would direct at me for a holy marriage, and return to my bed.

We walked through antechamber after antechamber in what were clearly Eugenius's private apartments until our guide opened a door, bowed discreetly, and ushered me into a study with table and books and exceptional hangings. So, a room for audiences and business. It was softly lit with wall sconces and filled with the fragrance of costly wax. And there was Eugenius, gleamingly silk-clad in papal robes despite the hour. And beside him, in the act of rising to his feet from his knees, Louis, looking no more pleased than I at being summoned at this ungodly hour. Even he was in a chamber robe rather than his black habit, although I thought I saw the hint of a hair shirt at the open neck.

I ignored him.

"My daughter. So pleased . . ."

Eugenius bustled forward, hands raised in greeting, face alight with what might have been construed as innocent pleasure, except that my hackles rose. There was something not right here. Nevertheless I knelt and kissed his ring. One must not treat God's Elect in too cavalier a fashion. One never knew when one might have need of him.

"Holiness," I murmured respectfully.

He raised me to my feet, keeping my hand in his, drawing me with him toward Louis, who shivered like a stag at bay.

"I wish to bless you once more, before you depart." Eugenius seemed even more sprightly and cheerful than usual. "I have only one final piece of advice for you young people before you journey on to Paris. You were joined as one in holy matrimony in the eyes of God, and I believe it is His purpose for you to remain so. It is good that your lands are united under one ruler, is it not? It seems to me that your problems can be solved by one simple step." He beamed. I felt apprehension walk its chilly path down my spine beneath my night robe. "Give me your hand, Sire." Now he was stern with implacability.

Louis obeyed, eyes wide and watchful, darting between my guarded face and Eugenius's determination. For a moment we stood there in strange alliance, the Pope holding both our hands. The chill in my body became even colder. It seemed to me that we were puppets, maneuvered and manipulated in whatever manner God's Chosen One desired. Unless one of us refused and put a stop to it.

One of us. It would not be Louis. He would hop in whatever direction this priest desired. I tensed in Eugenius's grip, which clearly he felt, as his fingers tightened around mine.

"May God bless and keep you safe from all sin and wickedness, my dear children."

Then, lifting our hands, he placed Louis's on top of mine within his own, enclosing them in greasy dampness, as if we were about to be wed all over again. Panic danced over my skin. Did he truly think that such a piece of mummery would heal the rift? It was in my mind to snatch my hand away, but he held on, his plump fingers surprisingly strong.

"You need a male heir." He inclined his head to Louis. Then to me: "And you, my daughter, believe it is God's will that you have failed to bear a son, a holy punishment for a marriage you consider to be outside the law." He shook his head so that his jowls wobbled. "Not so. I have prayed long and hard about this. I have the answer."

Nerves rioted over my skin. I heard the soft scrape of Agnes's feet behind me as she shuffled. Louis seemed to be thinking hard. Was he part of this? I thought not. He looked as uncomfortable as I. As for Eugenius, his expression was as keen as my misericord dagger, now lost to me, yet he laughed softly, entirely pleased with himself, as if he were about to shower us with priceless gifts that would grant us eternal happiness. Releasing us, he turned away toward a door in the far corner of the room, moving swiftly for a man of his girth.

"Come now. I will show you."

He opened the door and preceded us into the room beyond. I followed as Louis stood aside to bow me through.

And I stopped so quickly that Louis trod on my hem, my heel. I did not feel the pain.

If the previous room was the essence of comfort, this one was sumptuous, a masterpiece in polished wood and mellow stone, the walls covered with priceless silk hangings glowing as brightly as did the Pope in their midst. The windows were shuttered against the night and drafts, with illumination from two branches of fine perfumed wax candles. A magnificent arched ceiling above all enabled the angels carved on the hammer beams to look down on us with trumpets raised to their lips.

It was a dramatic scene, set with care. Set with complete duplicity. I should have known Eugenius for the cunning fox he was.

"I hope you approve, my children. All the furnishings were brought here from my own chambers." He made a gloatingly self-satisfied gesture with his hand. "I thought you would enjoy this after the privations of your journeys."

The room and the luxury it offered might have taken my attention. But it was not that. Oh, no, it was not that which gripped me by the throat.

It was the bed.

In the center of the room was a vast bed hung in gold and purple silk that was heavily embroidered in gold thread. A papal bed. A royal bed. As ornately carved and embellished a bed as any I had ever seen. And far larger.

A bed in which to conceive a child.

"You need a child, a son for France. Here is the opportunity, under my aegis. God will not turn a deaf ear, I assure you."

Eugenius beckoned us forward. Behind me, in the doorway, I heard Agnes gasp. Louis stood like a statue at my side. I was speechless with anger at the duplicity, but also with fear.

I had been tricked. I was trapped.

If His Holiness was disappointed at the lack of overt appreciation, he hid it well, continuing to reassure us as he smoothed down the already smooth coverlet with his hand.

"Look on this as the first night of your marriage. You are full of hope and admiration for each other. Put aside your differences as you put aside your clothes. God will be magnanimous."

I found my voice, but it was more reedy than I would have hoped. "I will not. . . ."

"But, lady, you begged my intervention," Eugenius murmured, as sly as a stoat. "This is the very best I can give you. You will be reconciled and—as my prayers reach the Heavenly Throne—made fruitful."

My wits scattered and my feet seemed frozen to the floor. Louis proved to be no help at all. With a ragged murmur of abject thanks he fell at Eugenius's feet with bowed head. Then, rising, he stripped off his robe and the dire hair shirt, exposing his unimpressive assets. He slid between the silk covers, looking at me expectantly.

Leaving me standing adrift and alone in the center of the room.

I won't do it. I'll not be used like this.

Eugenius looked expectantly in my direction. "It would be my greatest achievement, lady, to reunite two such attractive people and restore them to God's grace. I know you'll not deny me."

My whole body shrank in denial. My mind scrabbled, helpless in the toils of papal certainty, Louis's obvious delight, and my own disgust. How could I allow this? To be put to bed like a virgin bride. The Pope took my suddenly inert hand to lead me to the bed as Louis folded back the covers, exposing his skinny ribs and flanks.

I swallowed against the ball of revulsion in my throat and dug in my heels. I should decline politely—no need to make a scene—and make my exit, leaving Louis looking foolish and Eugenius disappointed.

Leave now. Before it's too late.

Or I should storm out, order up the horses and my palanquin, dress, and flee this calculated trap, anything but remain here with this dreadful anticipation on the two male faces.

Yet I did not.

"Come, my daughter. Allow your woman to disrobe you."

I looked across at Louis, who sat as apprehensive as the bridegroom of twelve years before, the silk lying across his thin chest revealing the rapid rise and fall of his rib cage, his eyes anxious on mine.

He thinks I will refuse. He fears I will reject him and make of him a fool.

"What stops you, my daughter?" The papal voice in my ear was as wickedly persuasive as the serpent in Eden. "Here is your husband, waiting to show you his love and devotion."

No!

"You are his wife. His Majesty can command your presence in his bed, my dear."

The words lay like slime on my skin. Louis ran his tongue over his lips, fingers clutching at the papal sheets.

Suddenly all my choices seemed to vanish. I would have to do it. Pray God that Louis could not perform, even at the instigation of God's Anointed. As soon as we were alone, I would change his mind. I might not persuade the Pope over consanguinity, but surely I could quench Louis's ardor.

Outwardly composed, every muscle controlled, my mind set to accomplish what my body deplored, I let my cloak shrug from my shoulders into the waiting hands of Agnes. I let her take my loose veil. I slipped my feet from my soft shoes, leaving them where they lay, then turned to allow Agnes to unlace my chamber robe and remove my shift. Head high, chin lifted, I stalked to the bed, making no attempt to hide my body other than with the natural cloak of my hair that brushed my hips. Never had I been so thankful of its concealing. Eugenius's eyes were far too prurient for my liking. I slipped in beside Louis, making use of the silk covers. And there we sat, ridiculously, like children waiting for instruction.

Hysteria ruffled my composure but I dared not allow it to surface. Beside me I could feel Louis tremble against the banked pillows. I must not laugh. I must not weep. Eugenius picked up the vial of holy water, to scatter it over the bed and the pair of us. Then he knelt at the foot, his triumphant face uplifted in fervent prayer.

"Let us pray together, my children." Beside me Louis bent his head, his lips already moving. I closed my eyes, clenched my hands tight, and willed it all to go away. "Almighty God. Here are your children, at odds with each other. I would make intercession for them. Heal their wounds. Grant them love and affection. And make them fruitful. Amen."

"Amen," repeated Louis.

I could not speak.

Eugenius, his mission accomplished, struggled to lift his corpulent body to its feet and bowed to us, cheeks still damp with the tears of victory.

"Make good use of this moment, my children. It is holy and must not be squandered."

He left us, Agnes following, trailing my garments in her arms, looking back with disquiet.

"A holy moment." Louis repeated the exhortation and grasped my hands as if he would waste no time. "It's what we wanted, Eleanor. A new beginning."

"Don't play with me, Louis." I shivered in terrible apprehension.

"Play? I'm deadly serious."

"This is not what I wanted—it's the last thing."

"Eleanor, you don't know what you want. *I* know what will make you happy." I could see the fervor building in his eyes. "We can be healed in God's love and forgiveness."

"When you've spent the whole of the past year damning me for my adultery with Prince Raymond?" There! I could not say it more plainly. Some of the fervor died. "An annulment would suit us both very well. Don't let His Holiness persuade you otherwise. You have only one daughter."

But I had lost him. The mention of Eugenius had been a mistake. The fervor flamed again.

"No, my love. My dear wife." I cringed at his endearments. "His Holiness sees it clearly. We are meant to be together. We must do as he says, and we will be blessed in the eyes of God. We took vows!"

His hands were on my shoulders, dragging me close.

"Are you going to hold me to my empty vow, Louis? On the word of an old man who is probably outside that door even now, with his ear—or eye—to the keyhole, rubbing his hands at making the King of France obey him, even to taking a woman to bed?"

"Yes. I am going to hold you to it."

And he would, by God. With a quick, violent action, twisting away, I made to slide from the bed. Louis's hand snapped firm around my wrist.

"No, Eleanor."

"Let me go."

"I won't. You are my wife, and His Holiness has directed us to sanctify our marriage in the eyes of God. We will do it." And he tugged me back between the silken sheets.

His grip was strong, and then his mouth hot on mine. Stirred by God or bloodshed, Louis could perform as any man. I felt his need hard and ready between us as he dragged me close. His fist wound into my hair.

What happened between us in that bed? I won't say. I won't think of it. Louis was under orders from God and so could not refuse despite my distaste. A holy rape, all in all. Except that would be unfair to Louis, who used no force. In the end I simply submitted to the overwhelming odds. Why did I allow it? I don't know, other than that I was seemingly robbed of all strength in the face of Eugenius's scheming, the late hour, and a sense of profound inevitability.

I should have run screaming from the room!

Instead I submitted. Yet throughout Louis's God-driven endeavors I prayed to the Virgin to protect me from conception. If by some miracle Louis was able to do what he had failed to do more than twice in the whole of twelve years, and if that child was a son, then I was trapped in this marriage.

Forever.

Consanguinity had proved to be an empty vessel.

My prayers became even more fervent as the weight of Louis's thin flanks pressed me to the papal bed. Eugenius's encouragement had stirred Louis's manhood magnificently, and his thrusting was more prolonged than in the past, his groan of fulfillment harsh with one-sided satisfaction. It was unfortunate that he felt a need to complete the deed with his eyes closed and his lips moving in rapturous prayer. My flesh was unmoved. I lay like a stone effigy on a tomb until Louis was finished and he rolled aside to kneel at the prie-dieu and pray. Did he never stop? Did God ever close his ears at the same persistent voice? Then he returned to the bed, kissed my lips, and fell almost immediately asleep, his cheek pillowed on his hand like a child.

I lay awake until dawn in utter dismay.

"Take me home," I ordered Louis when he awoke with nauseating gratitude. "I wish to leave today." I could not stay one more moment in this villa that had seen the destruction of all my plans.

Pray God Louis's royal seed failed. Pray God indeed!

Barely had we reached Paris—some two and a half years since the day we had left it—than the ill health that had plagued me on the journey to Sicily struck again. Robbed of energy and appetite, I was afflicted with a deadly lassitude, my spirits as low as the fur-lined shoes that were once again a necessity in this ice-cold fortress. How I longed for the soft kid slippers of Outremer. Not even a reconciliation with Marie could restore me. Five years old now, she was a fair, sturdy child, bidding to become a beauty, but she did not know me, running to her governess as soon as I released her, the beads of lapis I had brought her from Antioch, chosen to match the blue of her eyes, discarded in favor of an old and much-loved doll. She prattled endlessly about her pony, a gift from Louis, when I tempted her back to my side. Regret drove a sharp blade into my heart. Marie had not missed me, and it hurt, even though I knew I should be grateful for it. She was a precocious, healthy child, and I must ask for nothing more, accepting that she must learn to live her own life, as I had had to do. When I left her she smiled at me; it eased my pain a little.

I felt no better for the visit.

Outside the Cité Palace the Seine was solid with ice, the bone-biting winds cutting through the streets, whistling through the windows of my chambers despite the shutters and glazing, despite Abbot Suger's refurbishment of them for my return. If he thought to worm his way back into even the slightest degree of cordiality with me after his deceitful conniving with His Holiness, he failed. I might have once used the Abbot as an ally to thwart the Count of Anjou, but it would take more than a roomful of hangings, however fine the stitching, to win my forgiveness. Suger had merely gilded the bars of my prison. I would never trust him again.

My limbs ached and nausea gripped my belly.

"You don't need me to tell you what's wrong with you, lady!" Agnes hovered, holding a square of linen as I vomited into a bowl for the third time since I had risen from my bed.

I groaned.

I suffered.

Sweet Jesu!

The only relief from my misery lay in that I did not have to tolerate Louis's abominable sense of triumph as well. Glowing with incipient fatherhood, he instigated another pilgrimage to the destruction that was Vitry-le-Brulé, to plant a grove of cedar trees brought back from Jerusalem as a symbol of his contrition. I hoped the inhabitants, the families of those who had been burned to death, appreciated the gesture.

Incarcerated in the Cité Palace I trembled with helpless fury. Pope Eugenius's prayers had reached the Heavenly Throne, and God was listening. My courses had stopped. Louis's royal seed had damned well prevailed against all the odds.

"The Queen is brought to bed. The birth is imminent! Thanks be to God!"

The announcement echoed around the palace, from mouth to mouth.

I shuddered and whimpered as the familiar clenching, tearing pain took hold. Familiar? This torment was worse than any before, attacking mind as well as body. If it was a boy, an heir for France, these walls would hold me fast, like a novitiate enclosed within a convent until the day of her death. If I gave Louis a son, he would never let me go. He would have his heir and Aquitaine, and nothing I could say would move him from his noxious jubilation.

"The birth is imminent. The birth of the Capetian heir."

Even I could hear the blast of trumpets, the joyous announcement from so many throats, above my screams of pain as the child fought for release.

It was not an easy birth. The hours seemed to stand still. Louis sent his heartfelt thanks in unwarranted optimism, and gave orders for a Mass to be said in praise of the arrival of his son and heir. He sent me a jewel. Another jewel.

I groaned and pushed, sipped red wine laced with some baleful substance to deaden the pain, and submitted to the ministrations of Agnes and Mistress Maude, the royal midwife appointed by Louis to ensure my safety. Or so I liked to think. If it came to a choice between me and a male child, I wasn't so sure where Louis's priority would lie.

The pain was bad, but the relief of finally reaching this point was indescribable, for the months of my pregnancy had been indescribably dire.

Since the day I had informed Louis that his efforts—and those of the Pope—at Tusculum had been successful, I had been hedged about. Everything depended on this child. My life was not my own. I was twenty-eight years old and had become a mere vessel to carry the heir to France. Suger had prayed over me. Louis had lavished me with useless gifts as my body swelled. My hands and feet had become blocks of ice in the bitter temperatures when the Seine froze around us, as if to hold me and the palace still.

My beauty waned; I knew it even though I refused to turn to the reflecting glass, my hair dull and lank without the sun, without the warmth. I wanted to go home to Aquitaine.

"Let me go. You could come with me," I urged Louis. "We can stay in Poitiers. I can give birth there just as well as here."

"We can't."

I had not expected such a blunt refusal. "I would like it. Indeed, I would."

"No." He was preoccupied. I had not noticed.

"Why not?"

Louis took a turn about the room. "There's a rebellion. . . ."

"I didn't know. You didn't tell me. . . ." I was short on patience, and remained single-minded. Rebellion of a parcel of Frankish barons was the last thing on my mind. "Can you not crush it from Poitou as effectively as from Paris?"

"It's the Angevins," he said bleakly.

"Oh?" That took my mind momentarily from my ills. "What are they doing?"

"The Count of Anjou has ceded Normandy to his son Henry. Neither of them—father or son—has bothered to pay homage to me as his overlord for it, or even ask my permission. It's deliberate defiance and I can't ignore it. I see what they're doing—do they think I'm blind? They're empire building, setting up a power to rival mine. But I'll not have it!"

He refused to elaborate further, but my political mind absorbed the possibilities, the dangers, glad of something to distract it from my belly. So the Angevins were challenging Louis for preeminence, casting around for new territories to seize and consolidate their standing in Europe. Empire building in truth. Henry, in the fullness of time, would be Count of Anjou, Duke of Normandy, and, if he had his way, King of England too. How old was King Stephen? I wondered. At least fifty years. Without doubt Louis had reason to feel insecure and nervous. If Henry of Anjou could take the Crown of England in his mother's name, he would be a very powerful young man.

Shuffling my detested bulk in the only chair that gave me ease in those final weeks, I tapped my fingers against the carved fleur-de-lys on the arm. Except that King Stephen had a useful son in Eustace, Count of Boulogne. England would not be for Henry's taking. Henry Plantagenet might have to look elsewhere for his empire.

Hmm. My thoughts were well engaged now.

So was that it? That intriguing letter that had waited for me in Potenza? It made me reassess. Was it all part of the scheme to strip Louis of as much power as possible without direct conflict, Henry making use of me as craftily as his father had attempted to do? Since the young Angevin lord could not be certain of England, did he have his eye on Aquitaine? I wouldn't wager against it. I thought he might have an eye to anything for his taking.

Henry Plantagenet will go far, I predict. If not always comfortably.

King Roger's words seemed likely to be fulfilled, but Henry Plantagenet would get nothing from me that wasn't to my advantage. I was beyond playing games. I'd already had my fingers burned. Were all men such selfish bastards, intent on their own power?

"I've sent an army to our border with Normandy," I heard Louis muttering.

"Are you sure that's a wise move?"

"What would you have me do? Close my eyes and let the Angevin power grow? We'll stay here in Paris. Not much longer now, my dear Eleanor."

"Holy Virgin!"

How I abhorred his bracing tones. He eyed my swollen belly with avarice but, seeing my fingers tighten around the cup of warm wine, at least chose wisely not to touch me.

"I'll keep a night vigil for you."

"You do that, Louis."

As the child kicked against my hand, I cursed Pope Eugenius, Louis, and all men indiscriminately, and in a fit of petulance, when Louis had gone and I was alone, I struggled to my feet to open my jewel casket. Removing the single sheet of parchment, I consigned that strange little note from Henry Plantagenet to the fire without a second thought, watching the flames curl and consume it.

I was alone.

I cursed the Pope, Louis, and God in equal measure.

In one brief respite in those bleak days, Aelith braved the ice and cold to come to me. We fell into each other's arms—as much as I was able as my girth strained against the seams of my gown.

"Why are you still so beautiful?" She hugged me as we wiped ridiculous tears from our cheeks.

"I'm not."

"And why are you so fretful?" She peered closely at me. "You're unhappy," she stated immediately. "Tell me about it."

And I did. Everything. I held nothing back.

She was my sister, and sisters do not judge each other. As I had not upbraided her over Raoul of Vermandois, so she did not respond with horror. Or if she did, she hid it well.

Her compassion was balm to my soul as this child struggled to take its first breath in this world.

The pains increased and I was caught in a shadowy world of relentless agony and fear, peopled in my mind by those with an interest in the outcome. Pope Eugenius, nodding benignly, sure of his state of grace and his direct pathway to God's ear. Louis, of course, his lips moving in prayer. *Of what use Aquitaine without a son to inherit it? God send me a son!* And Galeran, stony faced, hostile, daring me to produce a girl child.

The child was born.

"Tell me."

Agnes and the midwife had their heads together as they wrapped the baby in soft linen. Its lungs worked well. I had no fear for its life.

"Tell me." My voice was cracked, my throat as dry as if I had ridden through the desert after Mount Cadmos.

They approached, carrying the child. All I could see was the fluff of fair hair and one aimlessly clutching red fist. Mistress Maude looked stern. I caught a flash of emotion in Agnes's eye.

"Well? By the Virgin! Will someone not tell me? Or do I read your silence as my failure?"

They turned back the cloth and Mistress Maude thrust the child toward me. It squalled on an intake of air. Well formed, active. Fair haired as I had thought. I stretched out a finger to touch the perfect cheek, to outline the miracle of the tiny ear. The relief within my belly bloomed, impossible to measure.

"Not what we had hoped for, Majesty." Mistress Maude managed to express her disapproval in those few words.

"A girl!" Agnes said the obvious.

"His Majesty will be disappointed," confirmed Mistress Maude.

"But not Her Majesty," murmured Agnes when Mistress Maude was out of earshot. "A miracle, I would say."

Surprisingly I wept, holding the child. For relief. For joy, for was she not my daughter, blood of my blood? And, above all, in her I had the key to the chains of my imprisonment. For all his petitioning of the Almighty, Pope Eugenius had been beaten. I had borne another girl. Despite my hurting body, my emotions soared. My dower lands remained mine and Louis had no heir to step into his shoes. Louis was once more overshadowed by the black cloud of his failure to advance the male line of Capet. It was perfectly clear—if he remained wedded to me he would never achieve his ultimate desire.

And how he felt it! Louis wore a path to the High Altar in Notre Dame. There was no outburst of festivity, no bonfires, no feasting. No medals to herald this royal birth. All such arrangements were hastily canceled.

She was a pretty child. I did not feed her. She joined Marie in their own establishment with wet nurse and governess and body servants. She was called Alix. I considered, all in all, that I had fulfilled my duty to Louis Capet. I swore I would bear him no more children.

"What now, lady?" Agnes asked.

I had no idea. In all my dreams of freedom, the sticking point was Louis, but I was not disheartened. The trap that had been set for me by Eugenius had failed to hold me. I had sprung it. I would escape yet.

Chapter Seventeen

*W*ell, now. This should be interesting. They marched down the center of the Great Hall, the booted feet of the Angevins and their entourage advertising the mood even if the bristle of swords and spears did not. They were not here to be conciliatory. The scratched bows, curt and graceless, were barely polite. How could they be when they had been at war with Louis along the border between Normandy and France for the past twelvemonth, off and on?

"Your Majesty." Louis's steward tried to hide his anxiety, but his smile wobbled. "The Count of Anjou."

"Well, we're here, Majesty." Count Geoffrey's stance left us in no doubt of his uncompromising mood. "At your request."

Request? They had been summoned. And Geoffrey of Anjou was not prepared to make an effort at friendliness. Even their attendance had been in doubt until this eleventh hour, before Louis had threatened a renewal of hostilities.

The question was, of course, why had they come at all?

Louis, seated formally beside me, was limp in his chair, face ashen and unhealthy, his hands in a death grip on the chair arm. I turned my face away. It continued to astonish me how often my husband sank into a fever and took to his bed when faced with a strong challenge. This time he'd almost fled the battlefield, leaving it to Abbot Bernard to try to patch up the damage. My lip curled as much as our guests' did while Louis squirmed like a butterfly on a pin. Even if he had appeared in regal splendor to cow the unruly Plantagenets into obedience, rather than as this gray and ill-tempered object only recently emerged from his sickbed, nothing could take away the impact of the Angevin contingent. Nor of Louis's Seneschal of Poitou, Gerald Berloi, a proud man, a formidable soldier, now weighed down by heavy chains that he dragged the length of the hall between two Angevin men-at-arms. He looked like some trussed and bound animal taken in a hunt, a boar most like, about to be dismembered.

Groaning at a hefty nudge in the back, Louis's seneschal sank to his knees under the burden of the metal looped over his shoulders. The Angevins ignored him.

So Geoffrey of Anjou had come to court.

I let my gaze travel over this man who had once lit fire in my blood. Geoffrey had aged in the handful of years since I had last seen him. He was still a handsome man, still upright and elegant with a soldier's bearing—I doubted he would ever change—but there was gray in his bronzed hair, and I thought the lines in his cheeks were deeper. Nor was there the intimate smile in his eye as he acknowledged the inclination of my head. He had, thank God, no wish to remind me of our past liaison. Neither charm nor mischief lurked there, rather a formidable coldness.

Interesting, I thought, my attention fully engaged. For behind the controlled facade was anger. Indeed, I realized, the facade was barely controlled at all.

Not surprising, given the circumstances.

What would Louis do with this flagrant defiance—an armed force all but filling this vast chamber and his seneschal in irons? I knew what I would do. With wine and food and soft words, I would soothe the ruffled feathers of this brood of raptors until they came to my hand. That was what I would do—but as yet I did not have the power.

Not yet. But soon.

"My lord of Anjou. You took your time getting here."

Typical of Louis, he ruffled the already hunched feathers even further. Count Geoffrey raised his chin and braced his legs. He was out for blood.

My eye moved from the Count to the three who flanked him. One I deliberately overlooked for now, but concentrated on the two I did not know, both on the edge of manhood with a distinctive Angevin cast to their features and the same tall, rangy build of their father. How true these Plantagenets bred. The elder—this one would be young Geoffrey, I supposed, Count of Nantes—his bright eyes taking everything in, was a handsome youth except for an unfortunate narrowness to his attractive features. I would not trust any one of them, I decided, but certainly not Geoffrey. And then a younger lad. William. I'd made it my business to know this family, for many reasons. They had come to court in force.

The heat, oppressive, excessively humid as it often was in September in Paris, pressed down on us. We all sweated in formal robes or leather and mail, but it was more than the heat that made the temperature in the room rise and perspiration touch my top lip. The third of the trio who supported the Count I knew. I was aware of him even when I did not look at him. As he was aware of me.

The Count of Anjou yanked on the chain to force the Seneschal to his feet, to stagger forward.

"That is my seneschal!" Louis's outrage was vast.

"I know who he is," Count Geoffrey snarled.

"How dare you treat a noble prisoner, and my own appointment, in that manner!"

Louis's hands now clasped and unclasped around the carved lions' heads. To his left, dark and brooding, stood Abbot Bernard, looking to have no real hope for a lasting truce here, despite his efforts.

"I dare when he attacks my lands. Did you put him up to it?" I hid a smile at the lack of respect in the Count's demand. "Your damned seneschal erected a castle on the border between Poitou and Anjou at Montreuil, and from there he's been harassing my lands every time my back's turned. And it took a year of my time and far too much money to take it by siege. I demand reparation for the damage done to my people, my lands, and my honor."

Louis could not take his eyes from Berloi, who was a horrific sight indeed: filthy, ill-used, wrists and ankles chaffed and rubbed raw, his undershirt and chausses in rags, his face showing signs of recent violence, with a swollen eye and cut lip barely healed. Here was no evidence of soft imprisonment as befitted a man of birth and rank. The Angevins played by different rules.

"You imprisoned him like a common criminal," Louis accused again. "A man of noble birth!"

"You're lucky I didn't hang him from his castle gateway for his sins." The Count wheeled on Abbot Bernard, who had so far remained silent. "And don't think to threaten me with your damned hellfire and excommunication. I can see it writ on your face. If my holding this man prisoner is a sin, I'll embrace excommunication. There's blood on his hands—the blood of my own people—and I'll stand before God and argue the rights of my case." He swung back to Louis. "I want justice from you, my lord. And I'll have it! That's my final decision on it."

"And mine," Bernard fired back, "is that you'll be dead within a month if you challenge Almighty God! Blasphemy! The reek of it is enough to damn your soul to Hell."

"I care not!" Geoffrey sneered. "You black crows watch and wait to pick over the entrails of honest men in the name of God. You've no jurisdiction over me. I'm no puppet of yours to dance to your tune."

The defiance thrilled me. This was war. Abbots Suger and Bernard had done their best to hammer out a truce, but I could see the Angevin temper was up, fire-bright, and Louis was in a fractious mood.

"You've no right to besiege my seneschal in his own castle."

"I do if it's used as a base for attack."

"Nor have you the right to bestow Normandy on your son."

"I have every right."

"Not without my permission, you don't."

"My will is my own in my lands."

"I am your liege lord. You answer to me for Normandy."

From bad to worse. Berloi groaned in agony, gray faced with pain and fatigue.

"For God's sake," Louis snapped at last. "Let my seneschal sit."

Count Geoffrey hauled him upright again with the chain. "Not until I have a judgment from you."

"Nor until you acknowledge me as Duke of Normandy, Sire."

A new voice in the argument, heavy with respect, low and with a rough edge—it was a voice that took command. When he had last come to court he had remained silent until spoken to. But no longer. My eyes slid to its owner. It had been difficult to keep them away. And so I allowed myself to take cognizance at last of what had become of Henry Plantagenet.

The Seneschal's all too vocal sufferings faded away, and my surroundings retreated as my focus changed and centered on the man who had dared to write to me when I was lost and bereft.

If you should find a need for the protection of a strong arm from a man who has always admired you, I am he. I can be your eyes and ears.

Henry Plantagenet. Henry, now Duke of Normandy. Henry, would-be King of England.

I appraised him thoroughly, marveling at his bold self-belief. What if I had rejected him, shown the letter to Louis? He would immediately have been branded a traitor, with Louis breathing fire and swearing revenge. Had it even crossed his mind? I thought it had not, and even if it had, he would not fear Louis. A threat from Louis to this man would be as limp as a pennon in a damp breeze.

"I am now Duke of Normandy, and accepted by my barons," he said in that same forthright manner. "I'll not be your enemy, Sire, but neither will I step down."

A challenge, no less. Here was a man much like his father, and yet not. The russet hair was the same, surprisingly close cropped, unlike the prevailing fashion, the clear gray eyes that watched and assessed and pierced—I recognized those. And the physical energy that all but shimmered around him was at this moment carefully reined in, with a bright gloss of authority. The hand that gripped the sword hilt at his belt would seize and hold just as firmly as his father and his forebears had done to carve an undisputed territory for themselves.

But there were differences. Geoffrey might still be the lion of the Plantagenets, but the heir to that authority was already making an impression. Henry had grown into his strength since he had so thoroughly destroyed the wastrel bread when considering my daughter Marie as his future bride. He was not overtall, and I thought he would grow no taller—if I stood, I decided, our eyes would be on a level. His shoulders and chest were broad and well muscled, thighs firm with power. He had the look of a soldier as he stood with legs braced, a man who preferred to spend his life outdoors rather than in the Council chamber or the Great Hall. I suspected that he had to fight hard for patience, for tolerance of those whose wishes did not run in tandem with his own. I watched as that confident stare latched onto Louis, and knew that Henry Plantagenet would happily take my husband by the neck with those capable hands and shake him, like a terrier with a rat, until he complied.

Even more noteworthy—he had not once looked at me, yet I felt the direction of his interest as if he had touched my sleeve. I had to swallow hard against the tremor that began deep in my belly.

Henry's hand, white knuckled, tightened around his sword hilt as Louis shifted under the combined scrutiny of the Angevins. Would I be willing to put myself into those hands? Would Henry be impatient and intolerant with me? The lad who had flown my falcons had gone forever. Perhaps diplomacy would never be an easy talent for this young lord. I thought he would speak direct from the heart without dissembling.

A movement caught my attention again.

Count Geoffrey was beckoning, and took a scroll from Henry. Striding forward, he unrolled it and slapped it down before Louis on the table behind which we sat, with Henry flanking him to hold down one edge as Geoffrey stabbed at it with impatient fingers.

I looked with interest. A map. The lands of the Capets, the

Plantagenets, and my own vividly colored by some enthusiastic scribe in reds and greens and blues, and I was aware of how vital my own lands were as they stretched from Poitou all the way south to the Mediterranean. No wonder Louis was reluctant to let me go. No wonder Abbot Suger and Galeran had formed a bulwark against me.

"Here's your proof. This is mine. And this yours—Poitou. This is your seneschal's castle, newly built. It encroaches on what's mine." The finger almost drilled a hole in the parchment. "It's deliberate provocation."

"My seneschal had every right to protect my land. He can take whatever means necessary."

"But, my lord," Henry observed, soft voiced. "Poitou belongs to the lady."

A hiccup of suspended breath.

"So it does," I replied before Louis could stop me.

"Do you approve of this, my lady?" Henry tilted his head, now regarding me with unabashed interest. No, he was not a youth but a man full-grown, with an impressive skill at homing in on the salient point. "Do you agree to illegal encroachments made from your lands?"

I was taken aback. That he should ask me. And even more that he should wait for my answer, brow quirked in inquiry. And to my discredit, it had been so long since I had been asked such a question, I was slow in deciding the most politic reply.

Louis lurched to his feet. "*I* am Count of Poitou. My seneschal does *my* work—as you yourself did in earlier days. You will release my man immediately—and you will back off."

"Have him," Count Geoffrey consented as Henry pushed Berloi to his knees again, where he promptly slid to a heap on the floor. "But back off I will not, and no threats from your pet vulture there will make any difference. My son is Duke of Normandy. I'll have your recognition of it. If not, I'll resume hostilities. There'll be an army within your borders within the week."

Louis's face twitched at the ultimatum. "I won't agree."

"Then it's war."

I put my hand on Louis's arm before he dug the hole any deeper, knowing that Henry watched me still.

"I'll await your decision," Count Geoffrey stated. "But not for long."

"Majesty." Henry bowed. "My lady." His gaze held mine just as long as it needed to. There was unfinished business between us. Business barely started.

The Angevins stalked out in a black cloud of resentment, leaving the suffering Berloi on the floor. Louis collapsed back in his chair as clamor rose around us, the stunned court exchanging disbelieving glances. But whereas Louis looked deathly, the exchange had stirred my blood, rekindled my defiance. All the fire I had lost in my fatal clash with the Pope was suddenly stirred from ash to flame. I would manage a meeting with the young lion before they left court. The only question was where. Where could we meet that would not draw attention?

The irony of it was—our assignation was arranged by Henry Plantagenet, not by me.

I met him on my knees before the High Altar in Notre Dame. Not necessarily a private place, with monks attending to their duties, nor the one I would have chosen, but the hour was late, the air cold despite the heat of the day, and the chancel blessedly empty, a sanctuary from prying eyes and ears. What would any interested eavesdropper see and hear? The Queen of France petitioning the Almighty for the health of the King. The Duke of Normandy bending God's ear for a favorable resolution to the threat of war between France and Anjou. Louis, thank God, had retired again to his bed, drained of energy.

Henry Plantagenet entered like a strong wind blowing through the door. Striding in, moving swiftly down the length of the nave, short cloak swirling around him with the force of his movement, he genuflected before the silver cross on the altar, then rose to come to kneel beside me, hands clasped on the altar rail.

His eyes were piously fixed on the gleam of silver and wax, as if in prayer.

Nor did I look at him.

Every inch of my body sensed that this meeting was vitally important to me.

The silence settled around us, dense as a winter snowstorm. Unnerved I might have been, but I would not break it. Let the Angevin speak, if speak he must. The anonymous eavesdropper would have gone away, resigned to our lack of communication.

"We need to talk."

His voice was soft, not a whisper but barely stirring the air, yet it reached me. I waited to see the direction he would take. What an enterprising man this was. What would he say to me?

"The stronger I am," he observed, as if debating the direction of his foreign policy with one of his captains, "the more chance I have of winning the support of the English barons and taking the crown of England from Stephen."

"And taking England is paramount to you."

"Yes. It is."

Not once had he acknowledged my presence by even a glance. Between us stretched at least ten hand spans of space, yet my skin prickled with awareness of him.

"It's my inheritance, you see," he continued in the same conversational mode. "It was never Stephen's. It's mine, as it was my mother's— and I'll not sit back and let a usurper rule it."

I thought for a little while, inhaling the silence. If Henry Plantagenet had his eye to me, so had I to him. However I might wish to argue against it, my position as a woman alone was untenable. I needed a man at my side and I knew that I needed *this* man. Even in this chill place, even with our deliberate distancing, it seemed that the air was charged between us.

"You offered me your help if ever I was in need," I said at last. "Did you mean it?"

"Yes." Unequivocal.

"Do I understand, then, that you have an interest in Aquitaine?"

"Of course. What man would not?"

"How uncomfortably honest you are."

"What point in dissembling? I know you want an annulment. And if you get it, it opens up a treasure trove of possibilities."

"Or a bloodbath."

"True." Slowly he turned to look at me, full-face. I knew he looked at me, but I did not reciprocate. "I would risk it. It's in my mind to get what I want."

"Ah! But what do *I* want?" I saw every point in dissembling. It would not do for me to appear too eager. This must be on my terms. "I'm not at all sure that I want to end Louis's authority over me, simply to hand it over to you," I said. "What would be the advantage for me in that?"

Henry's reply was direct to a fault. "You want your freedom. You want the restoration of your authority and your independence. And you need a man who'll ensure that it's not snatched from you as soon as you achieve it by some nonentity of a baron with neither integrity nor a brain to reason with, who'll tumble you into his marriage bed without your yea or nay."

"And you have both integrity and wit?" I could not resist.

I could feel the force of that stare through my linen. "I am no non-entity of a baron!"

So! "There's no guarantee I'll get the end to this marriage." I pursed my lips. "Louis still totters on the edge of a decision."

I sensed the derisive quirk of Henry's lips even though he was once again facing the altar. "Surely a woman of your talents can persuade him."

I played my hand close. "Abbot Suger and Galeran don't agree."

"An old man and a eunuch!" Impatience now, a hint of temper. "Louis is in no position to refuse. Don't let him. More than anything he needs a son, and God's not smiling on your union. Louis detests his brother so much that he almost vomits at the thought of passing the crown sideways."

Which was true. Henry's summing up was masterful. But still I would not appear too compliant. Compliance was not in my nature, and I would not throw myself in fervent gratitude into this man's hands.

"Louis will not listen to me if he's distracted—if you and Louis are at war, for example."

"We'll not be at war." My brows rose in disbelief, which he must have sensed. "Believe me. My father will come to terms with Louis."

"Do I believe that?" Count Geoffrey had given off no aura of peacemaking.

"Look, Eleanor . . ."

Now his face and his whole body, were turned fully to me, no pretense at prayer, and I responded at his use of my name to return his gaze. The urgency in him and the directness of him were utterly compelling. An awareness rippled along my skin as if he had stroked it with a finger. Or was that too smooth a response to him? Was it not more like a hook embedding itself in my heart? I didn't want it—but I could not deny it. I could almost sense the honeyed taste of him on my lips.

". . . once you're free, you're fair game for any riffraff, common or noble, who'd chance a throw of the dice. I could name a whole parcel of them, and some not a score of miles from where we kneel in this diabolically cold place. Why in God's name did I choose to meet you here . . . ?" In a quick gesture he rubbed his hands over his face as if to dislodge the cold, ruffling the short strands of his hair. "Do you want that? To be a prisoner in all but name, either walled up in one of your own fortresses, or wed to some nobody who'll rule from the protection of your skirts, giving not even a nod of recognition to what you might want? It's like a game of chess, with all eyes on the queen. And any ragged-arsed pawn will chance his arm if that queen is unprotected and open to rape, pillage, and forced marriage."

Henry had a vivid if crude way with words. "You warned me of that in your letter," I observed mildly, my mind racing, revolted by the picture he painted yet knowing it for the truth.

"So I did." He chuckled softly. "Do you still have it?"

"I burned it."

"Burned it? Well, it wasn't a love letter, so I suppose being female you saw no need to keep it."

He was smiling. I had the strangest sensation that we were flirting. But suddenly his words were not tender; they were aggressive and they disturbed me with their presumption.

"God's Eyes! Why have you not pushed for the split before now, woman? Don't tell me you've any respect or affection for him. More like to have respect for the lad who cleans out the privies. Louis has as little backbone as a worm. And about as much wit . . ."

I laughed, my breath echoing strangely around us. How little he knew of my situation, the pressures on Louis to hold firm. How typical of a man to level the blame at me. It was, I thought, time to exert my authority.

"I have not pushed for the split, as you put it, because Abbot Suger is Louis's backbone, and the Abbot still says no. And the matter of my safety concerns me. Why wouldn't it? Do you think you can protect me from these vultures that would snatch and wed me without my consent? And don't call me *woman*!"

"Of course I can protect you, *lady*."

His confidence could have been arrogance, yet I thought it was not. He simply believed in his own powers to take and hold, without question. Even now he was looking at me as if I were an idiot to question either his right or his ability. The urgency was back, this time in his clenched fist on the altar rail.

"Get your annulment, Eleanor, and come to me. Of course I want your land—I'll not deny it and I'd be a fool if I did. But look at what I can give you one day in return—a vast empire stretching from the coast of Normandy through Anjou to Maine and down to the south of Aquitaine. Here I'm offering to toss it into your lap. Would you refuse it?" His voice rose until he realized where we were, what we were about, and he forced it to drop. "What can we not do with such an empire? And if England falls at my feet . . ."

Stop! Stop! Is this marriage? I had determined to keep this negotiation, if that was what it was, tight in my fist and here I was carried along willy-nilly like a . . . like a twig in a whirlpool. Did I want this? Did I truly want to step, as I had said, from one curb rein to another?

Well, it would all depend on whose hand held that rein.

The man moved abruptly, flexing the muscles in his shoulders, stirring the air again so that the candle flames flickered. Energy pulsed from him, touching me, enveloping me. From the corner of my eye I caught the flex and clasp of his hands on the rail, as if he would rather clasp them about my person and carry me off. The heat in my belly increased. I might not be averse to such a show of strength, and yet . . .

I frowned at my folded hands. "What are you offering me? Are we talking of marriage here?" I asked bluntly.

"Yes. What else would we be talking of?"

"You did not make that clear in that letter."

"It was not the time. Now it is."

I glanced across to him. His voice, his words, might be implacable, but his face held a striking serenity. He saw no obstacle at all to his plans, unless I proved to be the obstacle by refusing him. I suspected he would nag and worry at me until I surrendered—if he didn't carry me off and wed me by force. So he enjoyed plain speaking. I would give him plain speaking.

"Does it not trouble you that I have failed to carry a son?" I asked. "That in all the years of my marriage, of all my children, alive or dead, there has not been one male child? I may prove to be unable to give you an heir. Does that not disturb you?"

His glance snapped to mine. "By God, no. I'll do better with you than that excuse for a man you've lived with for more than a dozen years. How could you stand it? I'll do better. We'll have sons together, Eleanor."

And he smiled at me.

The words, the smile—so sensual, so possessive—drove like a sword into my body. My heart thudded against my ribs. Somewhere as the years had passed Henry had acquired a ruthless mouth as well as an inflexible will. The bones of his face had emerged, skin tight and surprisingly elegant over cheek and jaw and a powerful blade of a nose.

"Here's the plan . . ." he stated.

And he had a plan—all worked out, by God!

"You get your annulment, Eleanor, and ride as fast as you can to Poitou. You tell no one; you don't advertise your departure; you don't waste time. But you send me a message—word of mouth only, by a courier you can trust—and I'll come for you. I'll wed you before anyone knows any better."

Never had I been issued so many instructions. Nor did he even consider that I might balk at such a flight cross-country. "Louis will never allow our marriage." I hesitated, clawing to keep reality in my vision. "As your liege lord he must give his permission."

Henry Plantagenet merely shrugged, an overt defiance that tempted me to laugh again. "I don't give a damn for the King of France's permission. This is between us—and God." He waved a casual hand toward the figure of the pain-racked Christ on the crucifix. "Do we have a pact, woman?"

The stare that fixed me was predatory and I could not look away. Did I have any choice? Not that I could see, and not if this Angevin had his way. Did I want to refuse? All was still uncertain, but in that moment my mind settled. I needed this man's protection, and I wanted him. By some strange alchemy as our eyes held, I felt my heart beat in unity with his. In harmony? No, I thought, perhaps not. *Harmony* was not a word I associated with him. But we were of a mind. Two halves of a whole, I decided fancifully. Henry Plantagenet was the man I wanted. I shivered with the enormity of the decision.

"Yes," I said. "We have a pact."

"Excellent. One thing—have you thought? You'll have to give up your daughters." Still his eyes bored into mine.

"I know."

"Louis will keep them."

"Yes."

"And I doubt he'll let you associate with them if you wed me."

"No."

"But I'll give you sons."

Although not a word of love passed between us, it was a wooing in its way. The honesty was blistering, breathtaking.

"What next?" I asked to cover my reaction.

"Leave it to me." His expression softened a little. "Why do you smile?"

I lifted my shoulders in a parody of his gesture. "Will you leap to seize any chance, Henry Plantagenet?"

"If it brings me an advantage, I will," he replied promptly. "I'll not ride roughshod over the law, but if the victory's there for the taking, then I'll grip it hard." He closed his fist tightly. "It's my great-grandmother's blood. Not as highly refined as yours, lady, but undoubtedly bold. She—Herleva—was a lowborn tanner's daughter from Falaise who took the Duke of Normandy's eye and made sure she kept it, until she bore him a son and he arranged an advantageous marriage for her to a man of status. Now, there's a willful woman for you. Are you willing to ally yourself with the gutter sweepings of Europe?"

Enticed beyond all good sense, I committed myself. "As for gutter sweepings"—I wrinkled my nose, shook my head—"no, but I'm willing to ally myself with you."

Henry pushed himself upright, and waited until I too rose to my feet. He did not help me, as Louis would have done with wearying solicitude, as if I were a weak woman in need of a supporting arm; as Raymond would have leaped to do with glorious chivalry. This Angevin waited to give me my own space and time, despite the impatience that made him fold his arms and look sternly at me as I shook out my sleeves and arranged the folds of my skirts. Oh, yes, I would keep him waiting. When I stood, finally, facing him, he hefted his sword from its scabbard at his belt.

"Don't flinch. It's not your blood I'm after. I think you still don't trust me altogether, lady. I'll just have to prove to you that I don't make promises lightly." And he pressed his lips to the simple undecorated cross hilt. "I swear by God that I'll protect you, Eleanor, with my sword, my honor, my name."

How impressive. How solemn he was in this oath that came from the depths of his soul. And I believed him. He did not make promises that he intended to break. Still, for my own sake, I was of a mind to appear cynical.

"Does God guide your actions, or self-interest?"

"I don't see them as incompatible."

"It's a heavy oath, with a fine ring to it."

"I like to make a good impression. My father taught me that, if nothing else."

The vestige of a grin, a gleam in his eye, stirred an inner whisper:

Beware. Henry Plantagenet was a devious man after all. Yet he surprised me when he transferred his sword from right to left, and held out his right hand to me—and he must have read that surprise in my face.

"To seal our agreement, lady."

I placed my hand within his and felt it close around mine. A man's way to seal a pact, hand to hand, palm to palm, an agreement of equals. It was a strong hand, dwarfing mine, the callus of sword and rein rough against my fingers, the gold shank of his ring digging in. I liked it. I liked the gesture. My hand felt as delicate as a songbird within his protection. As, I knew, he had intended me to feel. I thought I would get on very well with Henry Plantagenet, as long as I did not trust him! His fingers tightened around mine.

"I'll make you Queen of England," he promised, as if it would tip the scale of my decision.

I was not so sure. England. What did I know about that northern kingdom, other than that it was an uncivilized and barbaric place, worse than Paris with its lowering skies and constant rain? But to be Queen of England . . .

"Do you doubt me?"

I shook my head, admiring his skill at making the impossible seem entirely possible. I laughed softly as a memory returned with sharp clarity.

"King Roger of Sicily called you the Angevin brat," I remarked.

"By the Eyes of God! Did he indeed." Henry was surprised into a bark of laughter, the bright sound echoing up into the arches; then he sobered just as rapidly. "No. That's not me. That's Geoffrey, my brother, who's still a mannerless lout. My advice—don't trust him! Now *I* have come of age."

Then with nothing more than a brusque little bow, he thrust his sword back into its scabbard and strode up the chancel, leaving me standing. He stopped at the stone-carved screen and swung around.

"Until Poitou, Eleanor."

"Until Poitou, Henry."

He turned away.

"Henry . . . !"

He looked back over his shoulder.

"How old are you, Henry Plantagenet?"

"Nineteen years."

Nineteen years! Eleven years between us. Silence stretched between us, a moment suspended in time. Until he turned away, but not before I registered the curve of mischief on his mouth.

I watched him go, to disappear into the shadows of the nave until even his footfall disappeared. The force of him, the swagger, the outrageous confidence. Not once had he touched me other than that one clasp of hand, but I felt his presence with me still, wrapped around me like a velvet mantle on a cold morn. Still so young, yet he had ordered my life and pointed my direction in it.

Would I give myself over to a man of nineteen years?

Yes. Yes, I would. King Roger's Angevin brat had grown up. He had stirred my cold heart.

At least he'd had the courtesy not to return my question.

In the remaining days of the Angevin delegation there was no obvious working out of terms. So much for Henry's assertion that there would be no war. Count Geoffrey expressed his intention to leave, even though there was nothing between him and Louis but hard words. The Count demanded a final audience with Louis, who was irritable at being interrupted from his prayers.

"What use in this?" Louis grumbled. Geoffrey scowled. Henry gazed blandly into space. "I'll not recognize your son as Duke of Normandy."

Count Geoffrey cleared his throat. "I will offer terms. I want peace." He produced the map again, unrolling it with distaste. The words were wrung from him. "I'm willing to pay to get it, and to end hostilities between us. My offer—that I give up the Norman portion of the Vexin in return for your recognition of my son as Duke of Normandy."

Now, if I had had to guess the basis for an agreement between the Angevins and Louis, it would never have been the Vexin. As a stretch of territory it was notorious for warfare, a much-disputed piece of land stretching between France and Normandy and coveted by both. It had been snarled over, in fact, for more years than I could count, like a tasty bone between two starving curs. France held the south, Normandy the north. And both, in the interests of border politics, wished to annex the whole.

So Count Geoffrey would give up the Vexin, would he?

"The Vexin?" Louis was as startled as I. "You'll give up the Vexin?"

The only one not openly astonished was Henry, whose hooded eyes gave nothing away.

"I want peace," Count Geoffrey said.

"And you'd hand over the Vexin?" Louis reiterated.

"So it seems," Count Geoffrey snarled.

"Then I accept," Louis replied before the Count could change his mind, "and I'll thank God for it."

Louis held out his hand, meeting Count Geoffrey's reluctant one.

For one brief moment Henry's glance touched on mine. So he had persuaded his father. Count Geoffrey might detest it, but Henry would have his way.

Well, we would see.

I was sorry to see him go.

"A miracle," Louis announced almost gleefully. "I prayed for this."

"Then God answers your prayers."

"It must be so, to change the Angevin's mind."

Ha! God had very little to do with it.

It is never good policy to make plans for the future and expect them to materialize. Two weeks later, unexpected news: Count Geoffrey was dead of a virulent fever after swimming in a river to relieve the heat of the day on his return to Anjou. I was sorry. Despite his unscrupulous wooing of my affections, I had good memories of that sojourn in Poitiers when the Count of Anjou opened a closed box of delights for me and taught me the pleasure that could exist between a man and a woman.

Louis cloaked his satisfaction in a High Mass for the Count's unworthy soul. Holy Bernard claimed inner knowledge of the Count's punishment for reviling the Lord's name.

I was simply regretful.

So now what? His death opened quite another box, one that proved not to my disadvantage. The old lion of Anjou was dead, and into his shoes would step the young lion. Henry, Count of Anjou, Duke of Normandy, now with no curb on his power or his direction. Henry would rule. My future suddenly seemed bright with possibility.

Even at home Fortune was angling her capricious face to smile on me. Within a matter of months, in January of the new year of 1151, Abbot Suger was dead, the one voice that was raised so eloquently to the bitter end to keep Louis from setting me free. He died peacefully in his sleep and that voice was silenced at last, Almighty God taking him to His bosom for all his good deeds in Louis's name. And thank God for it. I would now hound Louis at every step and there would be no one to drown out my demands. There was still Galeran, of course, but I ignored him with smiling arrogance and set my sights on my quarry.

The tide was running strongly for me at last.

At Matins I knelt at Louis's side in Notre Dame as the choir lifted its voice to Heaven in joyful praise.

"In God's name, Louis, give me an annulment."

Louis closed his eyes and covered his face with his hands.

At supper, when Louis picked at the fish during Lent.

"Why will you not consider it? There's nothing left in this marriage for either of us."

"We are man and wife in the eyes of God and the law." He gobbled the mess of salt cod as if it were his last meal.

"The saintly Bernard doesn't see it that way." I considered a spoonful of the harsh, unspiced flesh, then rejected it.

Louis, too, pushed aside the portion unfinished, eyes bleak. Much as those on the cod's head on the serving platter. "I can't do it. You'll make me a laughingstock."

"Better an annulled marriage than no male heir," I stated under cover of the mournful wailing of a group of traveling minstrels who did not deserve my patronage.

His face paled. I had him there. I was destroying his appetite and had no compunction.

In his audience chamber, I approached as a supplicant with Alix in my arms.

"If this is the last child I carry for you, your brother will inherit your throne."

"I know what you want. My answer is no."

I smiled serenely. "You know it is so. Your brother can't wait to snatch the crown. He watches every breath you take, and prays it will be your last."

"I won't do it, Eleanor. The Pope blessed our union."

"But I am incapable of conceiving a son."

When Alix let out a high-pitched female shriek of infantile wrath, Louis flinched.

In his bedchamber, I sat in wait for him to return, pale faced and gaunt, from a night vigil.

"Is Aquitaine worth all this, Louis?" I asked.

He shut himself in the garderobe and groaned as if his bowels were gripped by a flux.

I pursued him to the stables, where he inspected a favorite horse.

"Majesty . . ." I was conscious of the listening grooms.

"No!"

"You louse, Louis! I'm out of all patience with you!"

In the Great Hall. I steeled myself. I would not relent. If I could not rest with this marriage, Louis must not be allowed to sweep the problem behind the tapestry either. And here was Galeran at his shoulder, deliberately summoned to stiffen Louis's spine. Even better.

I marched across to them.

"Grant me an annulment! I will have it!"

Louis turned to look at me, eyes unnervingly expressionless.

"Louis . . . !"

"Then have it."

No, his eyes were not expressionless. They were full of misery.

"What?"

"Have your annulment!"

"Do you mean it?"

"Yes. Have I not said?"

"But, Majesty . . . !" Galeran plucked at his sleeve, lines of agitation suddenly digging deep from nose to mouth.

"Enough!" Louis pulled away with quick temper. "I know the arguments against it. I know what I'll lose."

"Half your kingdom, Majesty . . . !"

"Do you think I don't know? I've had enough of it. You're right, Eleanor. It's God's will. Have your annulment. Before God, you've worked hard to get it!"

"But you'll lose Aquitaine," Galeran almost wailed. I watched his efforts to force a rebuttal on Louis, and rejoiced at his defeat as Louis turned on him.

"Do you think I don't know it? Of course I do, you fool. But what is Aquitaine to me if I don't have a son to inherit it? It's a choice created by the Devil to torment me." And to me, his voice thin in querulous anger, he spoke at last the words I had all but despaired of hearing: "We can't live together any longer. Take your freedom. Go back to Aquitaine. I'm done with you."

It had come at last. And so swiftly I was astonished. I could barely believe it.

"I will. Gladly. You'll not regret it."

"Yes, I will. I'll lose an empire. I'll lose face. But have your annulment." He snatched his arm again from Galeran's clutches. "Leave me alone. And *you*"—he glowered at me—"can go and crow over your victory."

Louis stalked into the church to prostrate himself.

I was breathless, a constriction around my ribs. But my mind was not at ease. In all these weeks of my wearing away at Louis's defiance, I had heard nothing from Henry Plantagenet. Not one word. Did our pact still stand? For all I knew, he might be in England, engaged in a lengthy campaign. Would he still come to my aid if I found myself under threat?

Oh, I knew he would. I had to believe in his promise.

One step at a time, I told myself. I would get my annulment and take refuge in myself to Poitiers. Then I would face the new Count of Anjou.

Chapter Eighteen

We ended our marriage, Louis and I, formally in a court of law, at Beaugency on the Loire in March of the Year of Our Lord 1152. All the years of my marriage brought to an end as if they had never been. My independence and my inheritance returned to me in my thirtieth year, at a stroke of a pen on vellum. All was legal and weightily judicial. And cold, cold as the ice that encrusted the edges of the river, Louis, flanked by his sour-visaged men of law, as unemotional as if casting judgment on a squabble over fishing rights.

I listened to every point. So fast. So smooth. So plain. There were no surprises. I was granted my annulment on the grounds of a consanguinity that had never received papal dispensation. Louis and I were related within the fourth degree, which was forbidden, and which had been known since the day Fat Louis had schemed to get his son a rich windfall. So my lands were restored to me, although I must acknowledge my allegiance to Louis as my overlord. I could expect no less. My daughters were deemed legitimate despite the dissolution—and given into Louis's care.

We were both free to remarry, although I must ask Louis's permission.

Must I? I felt a tremor of anticipation as this restriction was duly noted.

And that, with our joint signatures, as if by magic, was that. Finished. All ends tied, sealed with their official red dollop of wax. Did I feel even the slightest regret? None. If I never set eyes on Louis again, I would not lament. But as for my daughters . . . Had not Henry Plantagenet warned me? A price had to be paid for this separation, as I had always known, for Louis would not let Marie and Alix go. I had already parted from them, deflecting Marie's bright curiosity in where I was going and when I would return. Alix was too young to understand. They had not seen that this was forever, but I had. I prayed that with maturity they would understand why I had left them, and would not condemn me for my rejection.

"You will grow to be beautiful young women, and I will never know you," I said. "Never forget that Aquitaine is your true home, as it is mine."

My final words. I kissed them and walked out of their room before I might weep.

Now I stood and looked across the table to where Louis still sat. Although he had given his assent as if it had meant nothing to him, I knew better. He hated it, detested being forced into this position. I could sense him mentally tossing the conflicting interests from one hand to the other like an inexpert juggler, afraid of which one might drop to smash like an egg on the floor. Every choice for him was an anathema. Give up a vast tract of land—or condemn himself to having no male heir by me. Condemn me for adultery with Raymond and keep the land—for I would be forbidden to remarry and Aquitaine would pass to Marie. On the face of it an excellent idea. But that was no way forward, for adultery would also condemn Louis to remaining unwed until my death, and without a male heir for his kingdom. He could imprison me for my supposed sins—but our marriage would remain and he would still be tied to me.

No escape, Louis, no escape in any direction other than annulment.

Now it was done, and to my satisfaction. And if Louis thought to bind my future actions—well, we'd see about that. Did he think I would accept him as my liege lord? Did he really think I would ask his permission for any direction I would take in my life? To ask his permission to remarry?

I shook out my skirts and walked with deliberate calm to the door, the damask brushing smoothly against the stone, but excitement sparkled in my blood to the very tips of my fingers, so much so that I had to prevent myself from running from the room. I felt like a young girl again, without responsibility, without commitment, even though I had resumed both with my newly restored authority over Aquitaine and Poitou. I was free to return to Poitiers and take up my rightful place.

At the door I stopped, turned at the last, and I curtsied to my liege lord. Rising slowly, I stood and simply looked at him across the room, knowing deep within me that this would be for the final time. There he sat, pale and emaciated as the driven monk he wished to be. His beautiful hair thin and shorn, his face deep-lined, he was an old man despite his lack of years. He stared back at me without acknowledgment of my leaving.

What did he see, I wondered, that reduced him to silence? A woman silk-gowned and bejeweled for the occasion, her hair as rich as it had ever been, her skin flawless, her beauty without question, and now her power restored to her. I felt that power surge through me in counterpoint to the glitter of anticipation of an unknown future. Louis no longer had a responsibility to me, nor I a duty to him. And I smiled.

Fifteen grim years of marriage. Finished.

My smile was not reciprocated. Louis's scowl was that of a thwarted child.

Within the hour I left Beaugency for Poitiers, tightly surrounded by an escort of my own men. Before I left I made a few necessary adjustments to my garments and sent word to Henry Plantagenet.

I knew that I had never been as vulnerable as I was at that moment.

I rode. Fast. My escort was pared down to the barest essentials. No palanquin or litter on this journey, but fast horses, frequently changed. Even Agnes was left behind, for speed was of the essence. I knew the dangers. I might keep my movements secret, but news of my impending freedom would be spreading like fire through the undergrowth in a summer drought. As I drew near to Blois, determining to request food and lodging within the sanctuary of the abbey, the memory flooded back, myself a young girl in flight from Bordeaux on the day of my marriage, Louis urging me on toward Paris for fear of revolt and imprisonment from my vassals. Now I fled back to Aquitaine, to safety, with no man at my side.

Alpha and Omega.

I felt the unquenchable excitement again, the breathless exhilaration. My small escort of Aquitainians hedged me around; within two days I would be safe inside the Maubergeonne Tower in my capital. In Poitiers I could defend myself, staring down from my ramparts at any fool who thought himself capable of taking me by storm. No one would stop me.

And then I would see if Henry Plantagenet was man enough to fulfill his promise. And if Henry should find that he had better things on his platter—well, so be it. I might prove that I did not need him after all.

I urged my escort on, the towers of Blois in sight through the gathering dusk.

Freedom beckoned, as glittering as my own ducal diadem.

It was too good to be true. Perhaps Blois was not the wisest of routes.

"Ambush!" Raoul, my captain, warned.

Theobald of Blois no less, second son of the Count of Champagne, Louis's old adversary, barred the route, lying in wait with a force of men and the kidnap of my person in mind. He was an ill-advised young man with visions of grandeur but with a far stronger force than I possessed. How he would crow if I fell into their hands. My reins were slick between my fingers as I imagined my fate: a forceful abduction followed by a cold-blooded rape and a hasty marriage to give Champagne control of Aquitaine.

And where was Henry Plantagenet to save me from such a fate?

Totally invisible! Damn the man! I set my teeth against the flood of disappointment that he should have failed me. My mettlesome stallion had fallen at the first obstacle.

But did I need him? My lips curved into a tight smile as I rapped out my orders. I had had the presence of mind to employ outriders who had spied the waiting trap. So, warned of Theobald's plan, turning my back on the lure of the soft comforts to be found in Blois, I fled on through the night, trusting myself in pitch blackness to a leaking barge along the Loire into Touraine. A wet and dangerous journey it proved to be, without lights to draw attention, but Touraine seemed safe, one of Henry Plantagenet's possessions. Perhaps it was a good omen. Wily Theobald never came within earshot of me. I admitted to feeling smug at outwitting him, and my spirits rose. If I could escape Louis, I could outrun and outwit the jackals.

I sent out scouts again as we rode on south to cross the Creuse at Port des Piles, an easy fording place, knowing that this would be the spot if any man had a mind to it, a perfect setting for a full-scale ambush. We slowed as we approached the river, moving stealthily, halting frequently to listen. We heard nothing but the ripple of water, the wind in the reeds, the call of some night bird. Nothing more. Once across, my own lands would be within my grasp.

"Do we cross now, lady?" Raoul asked, low voiced and tense.

After the night of rain the river was fast enough to deter all but the foolhardy, lit infrequently as clouds scurried over the waxing moon. The pale faces of my men glimmered around me. A rustle of undergrowth off to our left made us all start, but it was just a hunting animal. There was nothing to be gained by waiting, I decided. I dared not wait.

"Cross now." I laughed softly, swallowing my sudden apprehension, brought on by uncertainty. Yet where were my scouts? They had not returned with bad news or good. . . . I couldn't wait. "We'll soon be home. Safe from any predator."

I did not hear Raoul's reply, for a deluge of sound swamped us, the violent crashing of horses' hooves and the thrust of heavy bodies through undergrowth. My mare threw up her head and snorted as I pulled on the rein, but there was nowhere to go. From every side came armed men to hem us in. Around us I saw moonlight glint on mail and helmet, on drawn sword and boss of shield. In front of us the only escape—into the water—appeared dark and unfathomable. It was too dangerous to ride into it at a gallop where one misstep would result in being thrown into the fast-running current.

We were trapped.

Then impressions came thick and overwhelming, even as panic skittered along my nerves. Too large a hostile force to withstand, too well organized to defeat, too well armed, but the plan—thank God— must be one of kidnap rather than massacre or we would all have been cut down already. And, as I saw, there was no attempt to hide their identity. Sure of their victory, they came at us in confident array, the badge of Anjou clear in the moon's revealing light. A hand seized my bridle; a mailed arm tightened around my waist to keep me still. My men were disarmed in little more than a skirmish, all over in the time it took for me to recognize my captor. There he sat, handsome features illuminated beneath his metal helm as the moon emerged, holding his mount in check to direct operations with a sweep of his arm. By God! I knew I was in real danger even if my life was not threatened. If Theobald of Champagne was unprincipled, any man of Angevin blood was doubly so.

"You bastard!" I snarled, struggling against the knight who held me, furious at my own blindness in falling into this trap. If he had been closer, I would have struck his laughing face.

Geoffrey of Anjou. Short in years and long in ambition.

"Henry's Angevin brat!" I spit at him, recalling Henry Plantagenet's condemnation of his younger brother as a mannerless lout. "What have you done with my scouts?"

"What do you think?" He flashed a distinctly feral grin.

"You are despicable!"

"And you are highly desirable. Welcome home, lady."

His parody of a bow disgusted me. "This will never be my home."

"Do you say? I think you're not in a position to dictate where your home will be. I have a priest waiting for us at my castle at Chinon." I saw the gleam of his teeth in a self-satisfied smile. "You'll be my wife before the sun rises. And then I'll be Duke of Aquitaine."

Such overweening arrogance. Such bloody assurance! "By God, you won't."

"And who's to stop me?" The smile vanished. The young voice creaked with bitter jealousy. "You're my compensation, Eleanor. I didn't get much from my father's death. I was promised Anjou and I didn't get it—thanks to my damned brother. Do you know what I got? Three castles! Instead of the whole of Anjou!" And now the smile returned, as untrustworthy as a snake. "So I'll have you. Since you're available . . . and in my possession."

"I'll see you in Hell before I—"

But at a gesture from my abductor, the hand belonging to the knight who held me was clamped over my mouth to cut off my objections.

"Quiet! Be still!" he growled.

I struggled no more. I had enough experience of the Angevins to know that young Geoffrey would have no compassion for me. They seized what they wanted. Within minutes we were rounded up, hustled back from the river, and in a closely guarded formation we were urged into a smart trot, heading, I supposed, for Chinon, where my marriage bed awaited courtesy of a renegade priest who would not question the bride's willingness. Nor would this be a marriage with guests and family. I was helpless. I could do nothing but comply, so I wasted no effort in worthless resistance. My mind seemed to be equally frozen, incapable of making any decision. I must wait until we reached our destination.

But if the bloody Angevin thought my rape and submission would be easy . . .

A shouted command brought us up short.

"God's Wounds!" Geoffrey swore.

Dark shapes, more racing shadows, the glint of moon on an entirely new thicket of sword blades. A furious descent of horses' hooves from our flank. The hand left my bridle as my captor drew his sword. I was suddenly free, but no less bewildered. Another attack, by the Virgin! Not an ambush but a preemptive strike. And so different. No banners or pennons. No tabards to clothe mail with determining emblems.

This force was sinister in its facelessness. No words were spoken—how ominous that was—but I sensed the tight control by the nameless lord who sat his stallion on the edge of the melee, motionless but carefully watching, one hand fisted on his hip, face covered by a closed helm. This abduction took as little time to accomplish as my earlier capture. A brutal fight ensued with some bloodletting, until Geoffrey of Anjou and those of his troops who were still standing scattered, leaving me and my escort at the center of my new captors. A different hand snatched up my bridle and without a word I was swept off at a fast gallop despite the uneven ground and poor visibility.

Handed like a basket of turnips from one abductor to another, by God! And I had no choice but to ride like the wind to my unknown destination.

I clung to my saddle and concentrated hard. I was not brave. Fear rode me, sharp spurred, without mercy. I was no longer certain that my life was not forfeit.

How long we rode at that breakneck speed I had no idea. Then we slowed, deliberately, and pulled to a halt at a parting of the ways to regroup. Gulping air to regain my breath, I took stock. My own men, it seemed from what I could make out, were safe but unarmed, surrounded by this efficient little unit and under no illusion but that resistance might invite the kiss of a slim blade between the ribs. Free but not free. Fear continued to assault me without mercy, my misery made infinitely worse by a storm of rain that drenched us within seconds, by the now moonless darkness, and by the deliberate disguise of my abductors. My exhausted limbs trembled at the unspoken threat.

A knight rode up beside me on my right. "A rough night, lady." He spoke in a laconic voice I did not know.

"Who are you?"

"Only a man grateful to be able to rescue you."

I was out of all patience with guessing games and almost blind with fatigue. "Rescue? It's in my mind that I've fallen from the hands of one bloody robber into the clutches of another, with nothing to choose between you. At least I saw the face of the Angevin bastard! I don't see you having the courage to show me yours!"

A rich chuckle carried through the rain, off to my left. I turned my head but could make out nothing of the man except a distant solid shape. I rounded on the man beside me again.

"What now?" I snapped.

The knight looked across toward the silent watcher, nodded, and again addressed me. "Now we make a run for it, before young Geoffrey takes a second bite at your person."

Again a grunt of laughter to my left.

"Where are we going?" I tried, as my mare leaped forward into a gallop, my rescuer's hand sharp on her flank.

No reply. We rode on as if the Devil himself were at our heels, changing horses as necessary. Nor did I receive any further communication until I saw the towers of a substantial fortress looming in the gray dawn, and with it the reality of imprisonment. Was this where I was destined to live out my life, at the hands of a man who had snatched me up like a trophy of war?

Later, when I could, I laughed at my inability to recognize my surroundings. Bone weary and frightened out of my wits, riding blindly through a solid curtain of rain, I had not identified my own home. Home! For this was Poitiers. I, the basket of turnips, had been delivered home. As my whole entourage, escort and captors alike, clattered into the town, then into the courtyard in the shadow of the Maubergeonne Tower, relief turned my weary limbs to water as my brain struggled to make sense of the events of the past hours. Here were my steward and my servants approaching to greet us, laden with trays bearing bread and cheese and cups of hot wine, when I had been expecting a cold restraint, an enforced marriage, and an undesired consummation. Here was comfort, warmth, and blessed familiarity. I slid from my equally exhausted animal, needing a conscious effort to summon all my strength, and for a moment I was forced to hold tight to the saddle, eyes squeezed tight and breathing deep, stiffening my spine. Only when I was certain my legs would hold me did I turn and face the man who had caused me such fear. Now I would have some answers. My suspicions were fast becoming certainties. I would still demand to know why.

As dispassionately as I could, I surveyed the scene, a milling bustle of armed men and horses, my captors making the most of the food and drink with enthusiasm and laughter at the expense of young Geoffrey, neatly foiled. My own escorts, now released, were gulping the wine and as perplexed as I.

"By the Eyes of God!" My head snapped around. "That was hard work. Damn Geoffrey for a fool—and an inefficient one at that!"

Well, I recognized that voice, the oath.

"Thirsty work too. Find me a mug of ale, if you will. . . ."

Who else could it possibly be? Who would sweep me up with such insolent assurance? Who would now be making himself at home in my own damned courtyard?

He walked toward me and bowed with more respect than his brother had shown me. He was clad in mail for hard riding and danger, indistinguishable from his men except for the confident assumption of authority. He had removed his helm and tossed it to his squire and was scrubbing his still-gloved fingers through his sweat-matted hair. He was as filthy and rain-soaked as I.

Henry Plantagenet looked me up and down.

"Very nice."

I stiffened.

"Your unusual garments are almost flattering. I'm surprised, but I suppose I shouldn't be."

"It's practical."

"I've never seen you quite so . . . unwashed, lady." He grinned. "Nor so inappropriately dressed."

Color rushed to my cheeks. My escape from Beaugency with all its attendant dangers had been no place for feminine skirts. But now, dressed in male attire, in tunic and leather chausses, sweaty and mud spattered, my hair stuffed unflatteringly into a felt hat, I was suddenly, embarrassingly uncomfortable under that quizzical stare. And angry that it should matter so much to me what he thought.

"So you got my message, I see," I remarked. "A pity you could not have acted on it sooner."

I buried my discomfort under a show of temper. I was tired to the bone. We were both tired—but you would not have thought it to look at him. Not for the last time I suspected that it would take more than a whirlwind ride across his dominions to exhaust the man.

"No, I did not get it. Your courier must have gone astray. It happens." Now stripping off the gloves, Henry slapped them against his thigh, dislodging clods of earth from his mail and boots. Then his eyes pinned me; his tone became accusatory. There was no humor in him now.

"What were you thinking? You knew the dangers. Did you not think to travel with a stronger escort?" His face was stern, the stark lines giving him a hard maturity. He had no compassion for my travails.

"I thought to travel fast. I didn't expect to be waylaid not twelve hours after my annulment!"

"You should have expected it. You're not a fool!"

It had been a long two days. I felt emotion build in my chest and I was perilously close to tears. For a moment I daren't speak.

"It's to your advantage that I had news of what my enterprising brother was planning," Henry continued.

"How fortunate for me!" I managed.

"Nothing to do with good fortune. I make it one of my priorities to keep an eye on Geoffrey."

"So I find myself ambushed by both of you."

His chin tilted with superb arrogance. "You don't seem very grateful for my rescue, lady. You'll fare better at my hands than Geoffrey's, I promise you."

My control was back in place. "You don't have a tame priest in your saddlebag, waiting to tie the knot, do you? Should I be grateful for being treated like a . . . like a haunch of venison?"

"A prettier cut of venison I've rarely seen! I thought I treated you with all consideration, lady!" Henry seemed taken aback at my lack of gratitude, a blankness descending on his features, and I was not sorry. A lingering residue of fear still churning in my gut, I was in no mind to be conciliatory. Why the haste, why the damned secrecy, when he already knew my mind? Had we not made a pact in Notre Dame? Had I not invited his interest now that I was free? I felt the heat of anger begin to warm my blood again.

"I suppose I should expect such cavalier treatment at the hands of an Angevin!"

A spark of temper lit my rescuer's eyes too. "I know exactly what's due to you. When you wed me it will be in the full light of day, lady, not in some hole-in-the-corner event. I've more finesse than my brother. I'll have you know I've covered a lot of distance in an impossibly short time to keep you from Geoffrey's greasy clutches. Three fine animals foundered under me and I regret their loss. Perhaps I should have left you to him."

"And let Geoffrey become Duke of Aquitaine? I think not. And why the need to keep me in suspense once you had rescued me, I can't understand!"

"It pleased me."

"To see me in your power? To see me at a disadvantage?"

"If you like." To my pleasure, the muscles in his jaw and throat were taut. "Be content I didn't throw a bag over your head! Perhaps I should have done just that, to keep your tongue from sharpening its edge on me!"

I had wounded his smug satisfaction. Good! My own anger settled to a simmer of mere irritation.

"Why the cloak and dagger with your brother?" I demanded, intrigued as I remembered.

"Because I might have need of Geoffrey's support at my back at some point in the future. I didn't consider it worth antagonizing him over something so inconsequential as the waylaying of a woman!"

"Inconsequential!" I took a breath to reply—my anger had leaped into flame again. As I detected the gleam in his eye and saw that he was goading me, I resorted to the most edged courtesy I could manage.

I was proud of it. "I'll give orders, my lord, for you and your men to be cared for."

"No need, lady. We're not staying longer than an hour. All we need is hot food and ale, and fodder for the horses."

And I saw that my steward had already begun to find stabling and roust up the kitchens. Henry Plantagenet had an air of command about him, even in my own home. He reached to snag a cup of warm ale from a passing servant and took a hearty gulp, wiping his mouth on his sleeve, then held my eyes with his, and they were deadly serious.

"What now, Eleanor—no-longer-Queen-of-France?"

"I'll not discuss it here," I snapped ungraciously, then remembered. "I'm sorry about your father's untimely death."

"Yes. Unexpected, as you say." He took as step toward me, holding out the cup of ale. "We can't delay discussing what next, Eleanor."

"I know." I disliked his peremptory attitude. A shiver shook my whole body as the cold wind swirled around the courtyard.

"Drink." He nudged the cup into my hand.

I shook my head, deliberately wayward. Henry promptly retrieved the cup—"Well, if you won't, I will!"—drank it to the dregs, then took my fingers and kissed them in a surprisingly gallant gesture. Until I snatched my hand away.

"Always gracious and charming." He grinned.

"Perhaps I am when I've not ridden through two days and two nights without rest. Now go away and see to your men."

"Is that how you reward your rescuer?" He was already striding across the courtyard.

"Yes. Until I've put my appearance to rights."

I found myself addressing his back and was more than conscious of my travel-stained, unorthodox, and unfeminine state. I left him and marched to my rooms in the Maubergeonne Tower. I heard him laugh behind me, although I thought it held more irritation with me than appreciation of any absurdity. It infuriated me, but the exhaustion had quite vanished from my bones. Once more I felt full of energy, of anticipation.

"I swear you're as wily as a bag of ferrets." Later, my appearance put to rights, I renewed my attack. "The Devil take you, Henry Plantagenet! Abducting me, terrifying me half to death . . . !"

"I don't recall your being terrified!" he responded, in no manner discomfited, lounging against the closed door of my chamber. "Furious, yes, but in fear, no. Have you ever been afraid, Eleanor? I doubt it."

I scowled at him. Once, in the past, I recalled thinking that Henry was unsubtle. I could not have been more wrong. Here was the king of ferrets that could fool the rabbit into hopping into the poacher's bag as if at the invitation of a close friend.

I had bathed, dressed—for some illogical reason I did not want to remain in male attire—and my mood had improved. I had considered very carefully. I would let him take the initiative. I would like to be wooed—so let him do the wooing. I would like at least to think that I was an object of desire rather than a necessity in a political alliance.

Yes, yes, I had agreed to marry him when we had knelt together in Notre Dame—but that was when Henry's support had been crucial for an undertaking fraught with personal danger. Now I was safely back in my own fortress and could make my own decisions. Nothing was engraved in stone. Unless I wished it to be. Unless I really did want him.

And I did. I'd make him pay for frightening me, shake him a little out of his composure. But I wanted him—and now I'd have him. As he had said, I was no fool. To keep Aquitaine and Poitou safe, I needed Henry Plantagenet.

Henry had made no attempt to clean up. Still in his mail, he brought with him the pungent aroma of sweat, horse, and dust—but his annoyance with me was in abeyance. He laughed, eyes bright with some keen emotion as he took in the changes I had made in so short a time. My gown was pearl-stitched cream damask layered over pale silk, more appropriate for a formal reception than a confrontation with an opportunistic, upstart warlord.

"Very fine! I've rarely seen such a transformation. From drowned rat to a pearl of great price." He bowed. "A finer pearl I've never seen."

"Like the haunch of venison?" I snapped, unsure whether this was Henry's brand of mockery at my expense. But no. I could read admiration in that open stare. So he could be gallant. Where had he learned that little trick, that a compliment would take him a long way to a woman's heart? From Geoffrey or Matilda? I recognized his father's elegance of phrase with not a little discomfort. How many women, I wondered, had Henry practiced on? Dozens, if rumor held true, yet still I liked the compliment. I turned away, conscious of the burn of my cheeks, grateful for the slide of rich silk and fine linen to add to my dignity. What was it about this man that touched me so closely? I walked to the window to see my courtyard warming in the early-spring sunshine now that the rain had passed, the enclosed space bursting with horseflesh and men in mail. Henry followed me without compunction, leaning against the carved sill to look down.

"This is a fine place," he observed. "I remember it—we had good hunting from here."

"Are you considering it for your own possession?" I slid him a glance. "Not without my permission, you won't. The Devil take you and your scheming!"

"I think he already has."

Before I was aware of it, he straightened and stepped close. His breath was warm against my cheek, stirring my hair against my temple. He stood so that he could view my profile, so close that I deliberately kept my eyes on the view, even when he lifted the jeweled end of my ribboned braid and wrapped it around his fingers.

"The Devil and I came to terms long ago." He inspected the carved finial that restrained my hair. "After all, it's said I'm descended from Melusine."

It meant nothing to me, although he announced it as if it were a matter of some weight. Who was Melusine? Henry was watching me as a kestrel watches its prey. But I would be no prey of his. I kept my mind on his words rather than on the fluttering in my belly.

"And are you?" I asked. "Is she another ancestress like Herleva?" The Angevin had a tendency to brag about the women in his family.

"So the stories say." He leaned back against the stonework but kept my braid loosely held. "A distant Count of Anjou—one of the many indecipherable Fulks, I expect—took a beautiful wife, Melusine. No one knew her background, her family. She brought no land or wealth, no important bloodline that any could trace, only the fortune in jewels around her throat and her beautiful face. Fulk insisted on marrying her, against all advice."

"As he would." I smiled, lured by his soft voice. It sent a shiver down my spine.

"She was so very beautiful, you see." Releasing my hair, he rubbed his knuckles across my wrist, but his eyes were still on my face, always watchful. Where had he learned such skill in the years since I had first seen him loping up the stairs, here in this very palace? Here was no callow youth but a man seasoned with sword and with wit and the ability to charm when he chose to use it. It crossed my mind that this was the wooing I had wanted, in Henry's own particular way.

"So Count Fulk wed the fair Melusine and she carried his four children. They were blissfully happy—except for one small matter."

"There's always one." I felt myself flushing under his scrutiny.

"Of course there is. Melusine stood dutifully at her husband's side in church—but refused to remain during the elevation of the Host in the Mass or to take the blessed sacrament. No matter how the Count remonstrated with her, even to using a whip about her sides, she would not."

"A whip? I advise no man to try that against me if I displease him."

"As I wouldn't dare." His grin was mischievous. "Besides"—Henry shrugged, ever the pragmatic—"it did no good. Melusine refused. Fulk's suspicions grew. In the end he decided to outwit her by ordering four of his knights to stand on her cloak, to prevent her leaving." Henry released me to raise his hands in graceful mimicry of the priest. "As the priest elevated the sacrament, Melusine turned to go—and eight mailed feet crashed down onto the edges of her mantle. So what did the enterprising lady do?"

"I've no idea."

"Struggling from the cloak—she left it in a heap on the floor—she grasped the hands of two of her children and flew shrieking out of the window."

I smiled. "Never to be seen again."

"Exactly! Have you heard this story before?" He chuckled as I shook my head. "And thus she was, as proved by her flight, the daughter of Satan." His glance was sly. "You don't believe me, do you?"

"I've heard taller tales. Do you believe it? That you are descended from the Devil?"

"Why not? We're all red-haired, with a temper to match, enough to scorch the tapestries on the walls when the mood's on us. I make no apology for it. It is so. You saw Geoffrey's behavior. Is that the action of a sane man?"

"Obviously not."

"You should take it as a warning when you're wed to me, Eleanor. The Devil's in us for certain. When you're my wife, there will be times when you'll wish that you were not."

Ah! We had reached the crux of the matter with great speed after the diversion into Angevin geneology. And perhaps even that had had its purpose, as a warning for me. Henry, as I was learning, did not let grass grow under his feet.

I did not reply immediately.

"Now what's wrong?" Henry's frown was suddenly fierce. "I see no difficulties."

"I am to wed you." I needed to say it, as if the words spoken aloud would make it clear in my mind at last that this turbulent man would be my husband.

"Undoubtedly. We agreed in Paris." He was deadly serious. "It was decided on a handclasp. As soon as you were free of Louis you would put yourself under my protection. And that means marriage, to my mind. I thought I made it clear enough. You'll be no whore of mine, but my wife, legally bound."

And so I would.

"I swore an oath. I'll not break it, Eleanor."

No, he would not. We were made for each other. And yet . . . I would like to know that he wanted *me* as much as my dominions. The question was, of course, would he ever tell me that? Even if I asked outright?

"I wondered if you might be reluctant. And thought this might persuade you," he said suddenly. Henry fished in the leather purse strapped to his belt to lift out a gold collar set with opals. Dangling it from one finger so that the light caught and gleamed on the strange stones, he regarded me speculatively. "What woman can refuse a jewel?"

"From the neck of the magnificent Melusine, I suppose."

"Clever girl! Where else? The fleeing Melusine left her cloak and her fortune on the floor of the church."

"And you carried so priceless a family heirloom all this way through Normandy and Anjou on an attack and abduction?"

"It was in no danger. I was not about to fail, was I?"

As before, his self-assurance robbed me of breath. As did the touch of his hand on mine as he took hold and rubbed his thumb over my palm, a strange little soothing gesture. My heart leaped. Why could it not be still?

"Do you still have the cloak?" I asked inconsequentially, pleased with my ability to sound disingenuous.

"I'm afraid I don't. The moth will have its way." A smile of great charm lit his features. "But this bauble has been kept safely—although not many of the Angevin women have chosen to wear it. It is not to everyone's taste."

No. I could well imagine that. It was a true collar of a Byzantine pattern such as I had seen in Constantinople: heavy, solid, with interlaced ropes of gold and flat plaques. The opals too lay flat, surrounded by pearls. It would require a woman of some stature to show it to its best advantage. And a brave one to wear opals. Stones of ill omen to many, they were feared and shunned. I smiled. I would not fear them.

Walking behind me, Henry placed the collar around my neck and latched the fastener. He allowed his fingers to drift along my skin. The gold lay cold and inert at first, then warmed and rested intimately along my collarbone, over my shoulder and breast.

"Well, lady? I'd say it was made for you." As he stood behind me, his hands cupped my shoulders and his lips grazed my nape above the clasp. I had been right: He was as tall as I, perhaps a little taller. "Does it persuade you?"

"It might." My tone remained light, but my cheeks burned even hotter.

But it was not the opals or the gold that drew me. Not the fanciful tale. Rather it was his touch, and the gleam of his eyes, as bright as the gems. I could feel every print of his fingers, the heat from his large, capable hands through the stuff of my robe. My blood was as hot as fire.

"When will we wed?" I asked.

"When I've the time."

It was hardly flattering. But practical, I supposed. I knew in that moment that as Henry's wife, I must accept that I would not always come first with him.

"What's wrong?" His lips pressed and slid along the side of my throat to my ear. "Something else? How can a sensible woman find so many difficulties where they don't exist?"

"I don't know." Nor did I. Female perversity, I supposed. *Do you desire me?*

"I'll protect you, you know."

"Is that all?" *Do you have any feeling for* me? *For me as a woman?*

"I'll use your money and your power." I felt the sardonic curve of his mouth until it was replaced by the nip of his teeth as he bent to caress my neck again.

"I know you will."

"But I'll give you an empire."

"Hmm." His tongue slid along my shoulder to the edge of my gown. My eyes closed. "I will like an empire."

"I know you will." His teeth nipped again. "I want you, you know."

Ah . . . "You want me."

"Yes."

Not good enough. Suddenly, as swift as an arrow, I wanted more than that. I tipped my head to look back at him, but all I could see was the dense growth of his hair as he concentrated on my collarbone.

I closed my eyes in pleasure but still found the voice to ask: "Is this a statement of lust and possession, Henry?"

There was no hesitation. "I'll love you, of course."

My eyes snapped open. "Love me?"

"Yes. Did you think I would not?"

Slowly he turned me so that I faced him and I could see myself reflected in his eyes. I did not doubt his words for one minute. In his own way he would love me, and it would be an impatient, restless way—but still it would be love. An answering beat struck in my chest as I acknowledged that I would love him too—in my own fashion. We would not always be as one in our future together, but the connection between us was strong. Too strong, perhaps, for comfort.

I held my breath. Was that what I was afraid of? The uncontrollable longing to belong to him on whatever terms he handed out? If I loved him, I would have to fit with the pattern that Henry demanded in our life together. Could I accept that? I did not think I had a choice.

"Wed me, Eleanor."

There it was. No soft request but a demand.

I breathed out slowly, balanced on the edge of prevarication. I smiled and he knew my mind.

"Good girl! It's all decided." Henry's face was suddenly full of light. "Does it appeal, my beautiful Eleanor? To be the Devil's consort? After pious Louis?"

"It's an interesting proposition." Automatically I raised a hand to touch his cheek, as if I had been doing it all my life.

And the grin was gone. Henry caught my wrist in his hand. "By God, Eleanor—I'm as hard as a rock." Without thought of my discomfort from the imprint of his mail, he crushed me to him, lifting me to my toes, the fierce ownership in his grip, in his voice and face, leaving me in no doubt of his need. His mouth was a mere inch from mine. "I'd better go. You'll wed me when I return. And I'll not leave you a second time without a promise of my intent. Your lips would seduce a eunuch, by God! How I resisted tasting them in God's presence in that damnably cold cathedral in Paris I'll never know." Henry's features were stark with desire. "I've shown remarkable control so far, haven't I, lovely Eleanor? No more. You are mine, my magnificent Duchess of Aquitaine!"

He kissed me, mouth on mouth, a kiss of passion for the first time. Firm and cool, his lips were assured, parting mine so that tongue touched tongue with, at the last, the promise of fire to lick through my blood. How astonishingly like the man that kiss was. Forthright, possessive, dangerously potent. A statement of fact. I belonged to him now.

"Don't start to think of excuses as soon as I've ridden out of your gate!" he admonished, raising his head and dropping me back on my feet. "You know I won't take no for an answer."

I was afraid I did know. His lips seduced like the Devil for sure.

Yes, I would be the Devil's consort.

I saw him out into the courtyard where his men were already mounted, disappointed that he must leave so soon but not prepared to beg him to stay. If he had business that took precedence, then so be it. I looked up into his vivid face when he had swung up into the saddle, and knew there was one subject we had not touched on and that I should raise—reluctantly, but it could not be left unsaid. I did not think Henry would damn me for my honesty in this. I took hold of his rein above the bit, holding his stallion still, although with care for my toes.

"Did your father know of your plans to wed me?" I asked abruptly.

"Yes. I told him. That's why he gave up the Vexin. Snarling his objections but accepting my argument in the end."

As I had thought. "I just wondered. . . ."

"I know what you're wondering." He stretched out his still-ungloved fingers to touch my cheek, an unexpectedly tender gesture. I arched a brow, trying to read his face but failing, so his reply shook me. "My father told me I shouldn't wed you—because his own relationship with you had been . . . God's Wounds! Why be mealymouthed? Because you'd shared his bed. Or he'd shared yours, since it was here in your castle."

"Oh." So there it was, out in the open. "Did you believe him?"

"Yes. I have always known."

Ah! I felt the blood heat in my cheeks. "Does it matter to you?"

"No. I don't see my father as a rival for your affections. If our past lovers are to step between us, Eleanor, you'll have a whole crowd of them from my side to tolerate. I've taken no vow of chastity."

The stallion's restless sidestepping gave me respite from finding a reply.

"Did you love him?" Henry asked conversationally.

"No."

"Did he seduce you?"

"Not that either. I went to his bed willingly."

"I suppose you had your reasons. Any woman wed to Louis would have reasons to take solace elsewhere. Now my father's dead—and you're promised to me." His eyes bored into mine. "Since we're stripping each other naked . . . there were other rumors, Eleanor—from Outremer. From Antioch."

Of course he would have heard them. My throat closed on any possible words of explanation and I resented that I should have to make any explanation of what had occurred between myself and Raymond. How easy it would be to destroy this fragile relationship between me and the Angevin.

"My enemies enjoyed the opportunity to embroider every move I made," I managed.

"Rumors have a distressing tendency to spread and contaminate, like the stench of bad meat," Henry said, his tone as arid as Aquitaine in high summer, as if he had not even registered my hesitation. "I'll not ask you again about Antioch, Eleanor. It is in the past and is of no importance to me. Nor, I think, to you."

My throat eased in relief.

"But now you're mine," he added. "And don't forget it."

Henry gathered up his reins. What a complex man he was. Sharp and brusque, it was not the parting of a lover—but, of course, we were not lovers. I would have stepped away but abruptly he closed his fingers around my wrist and leaned down. For a moment I thought he might kiss me, but he would not, not in public. Our association was not yet for public knowledge. Instead, eye and voice fierce, he whispered in my ear.

"You'll be safe here. Keep your gates closed. I'll come for you when I can." Releasing me, he moved his fingers to rest on the gold collar that still encircled my neck. "I'll be back! Keep the faith, Eleanor."

Then he was giving his horse the office to move off. Henry Plantagenet, my betrothed, was gone without a backward look, and I wore the Devil's collar around my neck.

Chapter Nineteen

ive weeks. Or was it six? I closed my gates, set my guards, sent out my scouts. If another presumptous baron chanced his arm to take me prisoner, it would take a full-blown siege to do it.

And nothing from Henry Plantagenet. No message, no letter, not even a helpful rumor. I knew what kept him from me. Plans for his imminent invasion of England were well advanced, and Henry was not the man to let them stand still. As soon as the planning to transport men and provisions was complete, and the weather calm and suitable for campaigning, the invasion would begin. It was April—what better time to launch an attack, with the summer months ahead? What would be his priority? Me or that distant crown? I did not like the obvious reply to the question. Every morning when I rose I watched from the battlements. Every evening when the palace settled into its nightly routine, I took up the same vantage point, but only for a handful of minutes. It would not do for my people to see their Duchess malingering when she had only just returned to them.

I set myself not to think of him.

But my anxieties built as the weeks passed with still no news. There was no guarantee that I would see him again before he left to cross the

sea. And what then? If he made a foothold in England, if he defeated
Stephen in battle or came to terms with him, what would the outcome
be from that? Would not an English wife be a more astute choice for
a claimant to the English throne? I feared she would, and cursed the
unknown lady.

Promises and gifts of gold collars were one thing, political necessity to win a kingdom quite another.

And, of course, Henry might always meet his death on the battlefield. . . . Or his ship could founder with all lives lost. . . .

Alone, I fretted. No one knew of our agreement; nor was it safe for
me to talk of it. That much I knew. To share a secret was to put it into
the public domain. Even when Aelith came to join me, I felt unable to
whisper my secrets as I might once have done. Agnes, reunited with
me, in dour mood and with caustic questioning on my need to wall
myself up in my own castle, was no recipient of my doubts and fears.
All was too uncertain, too dangerous. If our intention to wed, to unite
Aquitaine with Anjou and Normandy, reached Louis's ears, he would
move heaven and earth to stop us. An immediate invasion of Normandy by the King of France would put all Henry's plans in jeopardy.

But why did the man not write to me? Why leave me in suspense?

Aelith complained that I was not good company, and when she
threatened to leave me to stew in my own ill humor, I took myself in
hand. What point in fretting over so much that was outside of my control? I was my own woman. I was ruler of Aquitaine, and it was time
I acted as such. Gone were the days when I would be barred from the
councils of government. Gleefully I turned my mind to annulling all
the acts and decrees made by Louis, issuing charters in my own name
to underline my autonomy. It did my heart good to revoke the grant
of the forest of La Sèvre to the Abbey of Saint-Maixent—and then
promptly restore it in my own right, for my own gratification. How
inconsequential in the scope of my marriage to the Angevin, but how
amazingly satisfying to see Louis Capet's name removed and replaced
with *Eleanor*!

It took my mind off the possibility that my acquaintance with Henry
Plantagenet might have come to an untimely end before it began.

After some heart searching, leaving Aelith in Poitiers, and against Henry's order, I took a private visit to the château of Belin near Bordeaux, where I was born, and where a child called Philippa, a child who barely drew breath, was buried in the graveyard, as I had instructed. It was a simple stone, recording only her name, for who but I would visit this sad place? I wept with my veil pulled over my face. For the lost infant, for myself. And for Raymond, Prince of Antioch.

That was the last time I allowed myself the luxury of tears for what was past. I set myself to look forward, for better or worse.

"There's a force approaching your gate, my lady," my steward informed me, six weeks after Henry Plantagenet had deposited me within my courtyard, as the late-spring dusk of May sank rapidly into night. "Not big, but showing no device. Do we keep the gates shut? It's late to leave someone benighted, but they're not announcing themselves. . . ."

"Keep the gates shut."

I did not waste energy or words in pretending ignorance. I had known of his approach, not because he sent me word—of course he hadn't; he would not see the need—but my scouts had informed me of his approach with a small force of Angevins. It had given me time to consider my welcome, and I did not feel welcoming.

Oh, I knew what the outcome would be. What woman in my position would not? Yet I was of a mind to be difficult. I was fascinated to see what he would do. After a lifetime of the entirely predictable Louis, Henry Plantagenet was a blank scroll.

So I kept the gates closed against him. He could hardly expect me to open them to some nameless force after dark, could he? *Keep your gates closed*, he'd said. And by God, I would! Of course, it was pure mischief on my part, mixed with sharp anticipation, the heady brew of honey and spices stirred into hot wine, enough to make the blood sing. I suppose I was testing him. What *would* he do? Go back to Normandy and dissolve our agreement? No, for I was too valuable to him. Settle in for a siege? Beg or threaten? Cajole or scowl? I knew I would find out on the morrow.

From my vantage point on the battlemented gatehouse, well concealed, I watched his arrival in the minutes before all was hidden in dark shadow. No mistaking his figure at the forefront of his soldiers on the familiar bay stallion. Mail covered by a long surcoat, head covered by coif and helmet. He dismounted. Removed his helmet, handed it to his squire, and pushed back the coif. Seeing the gates shut in his face, he stood four-square, fists planted on hips, and observed my fortress. He rubbed his hands over his face, spoke to the man at his side. And then he laughed.

I expected him to at least send his herald to announce his arrival, even to demand entrance. Henry took one more long look at the closed gates and unresponsive guards and did nothing except turn his back and issue a series of sharp orders. Within the hour a small camp of tents and horse lines had been erected on the open space before my gates.

For the rest of that night we heard nothing of importance from the Angevin camp, but plenty of noise. Of the soldiery settling in, of singing and raucous laughter as barrels of ale were broached—and where had *they* come from?—as the campfires were lit and the scent of roasting meats drifted across the space. I expect my cattle and sheep had paid the price, along with my cellars. Later, women's laughter was evident. I closed my ears to it. Henry could do as he pleased.

After supper I went to watch again, Aelith with me.

"So it's the Count of Anjou, is it? Why has he come?" she asked from her position of ignorance at my shoulder.

"Who's to know?" Glad of the dark as the moon slid behind a cloud, I could feel her eyes on me.

"Eleanor, you're not thinking of making an alliance with him, are you?"

"Would it be so bad?"

"I don't know." A long moment of thought followed that I would not break. "Eleanor, you're not thinking of marrying him, are you?"

I kept my counsel.

"You are, aren't you? Eleanor! All he wants is Aquitaine!"

"I know."

"And you would take him on those terms? An adventurer?" I noted she did not say he was too young. "Would your vassals accept him?"

"Yes. It won't be easy, but they will. He'll win them over. But I won't wed merely for a strong sword arm and an army."

"Do you love him?" She sounded aghast at the thought.

I tilted my head. "Do you remember when you decided you wanted to wed Raoul? And nothing could stop you?" I replied obliquely.

"I remember."

"And you would not turn aside, even when it took us into war and the horrors of Vitry—not that you would have known of that, of course, but the warnings of war were stark enough."

"Yes. I remember." I felt the defiance in her even after all the years that had passed.

"Why did you do it?"

"I loved him. I knew we were meant to be together."

"Yes. And that's what I think about Henry Plantagenet. I don't know about love as you might recognize it, but there's a bond between us—we're destined to be *something* together; of that I'm certain." I smiled. "Would you do the same again, Aeli? Knowing the outcome?"

"Ah! A clever trap for me to fall into." She shook her head a little.

"No trap. Just the truth. If it were me, and the object of my affection was Henry, I think I would risk my life and my reputation to keep him."

"So you will wed him." Aelith did not sound convinced.

"Yes."

Her smile was wry. "Be it on your own head. I wouldn't want that man in my bed. He's too opinionated by half. I wouldn't risk one broken fingernail for him."

Oh, but *I* would. I'd risk more than that.

"You need a long spoon to sup with the Devil," Aelith continued, turning from the seething encampment.

"Then I'll make sure I have one." I laughed. "A deep one at that. And you're wrong," I informed my critical sister, as we trod carefully down the steps into the courtyard. "He doesn't just want Aquitaine." I couldn't stop the proud curve of my lips. "He wants me as well."

Next morning I expected the arrival of Henry's herald, bedecked in gaudy red-and-gold Angevin lions, to make Henry's greetings and request entry. And I would meet with him, as a gracious hostess, and open my gates. My terms, my timing. How foolish—but magnificently pleasurable.

Not so.

The three obligatory blasts of the herald's trumpet shattered the early-morning quiet, so early as to get me from my bed. The sky was barely paling. I wrapped myself in a velvet chamber robe, slid my feet into slippers, and headed for the gatehouse, but not before a further series of earsplitting blasts. And as I sped up the steps to the battlement walk, breath catching, the trumpet was replaced:

"Eleanor!"

A roar of a voice.

"Eleanor! Get yourself out here!"

No herald, no blast of a trumpet this time, but Henry, hands clamped around his sword belt, bellowing our private concerns before the whole of my household and his troops. Above his head the Angevin banner lifted aggressively in the sharp breeze. He was regarding me much like the lions passant guardant flapping above his head. How remarkably the clarity of his voice carried, and how embarrassing—if embarrassment was a state I was prepared to acknowledge. At least he was unnervingly succinct.

"At last. Would you lie abed with an invading army at your door, woman? Open the damned gates!"

"Good day, my lord." I looked down on him, heart thudding, and not from my efforts to get there. "Talk of the Devil?"

I saw his answering grin.

"No time for pleasantries. Time's short. I've an army waiting to sail for England."

"And you made time for me? I'm honored."

"Only just. If I'm mistaken in you, Eleanor, I'll leave within the hour. I've already struck camp."

And so he had. Damn him.

"All agreements between us are off. Trust a woman to be tricky," he bellowed, while I clenched my teeth, sensing the ripple of interest through our growing audience. "And I'd be grateful if you'd return Melusine's gold. If you don't want it, I know a grateful lady who does."

"Only one?"

At my side Aelith giggled.

"Just throw it down."

"No."

I think Henry grimaced.

"I'll not be back, lady. If you're in need of protection, my brother Geoffrey will be pleased to come to your aid. I'll send him word."

"Don't you dare!"

Thus a standoff, superbly created by the pair of us. And a ridiculous piece of mummery it was too. I think we both enjoyed it, both knowing full well that Henry wouldn't leave me. And I wouldn't let him go.

I ordered the gates to be opened.

From that moment I knew who would hold the upper hand in our marriage. It might not please me, but I accepted it.

The result? A breathtaking descent, a whirlwind, a storm, my courtyard filled with Angevin lions on tabard and pennon almost before I had made my way down the steps from the outer wall. Yet I kept him waiting long enough to acquire a veil and filet and an elegant overtunic in patterned damask.

"My lady." Henry handed his mount over to his squire.

"My lord." I curtsied.

"Good to see you took my advice and kept your gates closed against robbers and thieving rabble! Very commendable, Eleanor."

I think I flushed. He was mocking me, I knew he was mocking me, but his face was as grave as a stone mask.

"You could have let me know—my lord." I was wonderfully gracious.

"I didn't know myself. My supporters in England are urging me to invade before the rank and file lose patience and turn back to Stephen. I haven't long, Eleanor. But I did make time for you." I liked the glint in his eye. "A cup of ale would be acceptable."

I led him to my solar, where he sank into a cushioned chair, to the detriment of the embroidered covering from dust and horsehair. He looked entirely out of place amongst the cushions and soft hangings and my women, who fluttered predictably.

"What have you been doing with your new independence?" He stripped off his leather riding gloves, frowning at the forefinger of one of them, picking at the loose threads. So he would talk politics. I followed his lead, intrigued.

"Removing any trace of Louis from Aquitaine."

"Which I'm sure you enjoyed."

"I enjoyed every stroke of my pen on every new charter! As Louis's wife I was forced to do what Louis—or Abbot Suger—wanted, and was given little voice in their decisions." I smiled, but with a warning for Henry Plantagenet in my mind. "Here the authority is now mine again. I am sovereign."

"I'll remember that." He looked up from the glove. "D'you think they'll take to me?"

"No. You'll have to win them around." Whether he did or not, I knew in my heart my days of autonomy were numbered. "And your barons? Will they approve of this match? Will they show me respect?"

"By God, they will! Or they'll feel the edge of my sword." He leaned back, completely at ease. "Besides, how should they not? Look at the wealth you bring me. There'll be some voices raised against your reputation, but most will see the sense of not crossing me."

I laughed. There was no guile in Henry, at least for today.

"Tell me about England."

"It's ripe for the plucking," was all he'd say, hinting nothing of the real force that drove him to claim his inheritance, or the dangers of his enterprise. "I'll not be defied in this, you know. Stephen wants his son Eustace to be crowned King now, to ensure his future inheritance." Henry grunted a laugh. "It needs papal permission, and His Holiness, quite sensibly, is keeping his head down."

As he spoke, he picked up the glove again. Then beckoned to the nearest of my women, Florine, whose attention was divided, and not evenly, between her embroidery and our conversation.

"My lord?"

"A needle and thread, if you please."

Flustered, Florine handed over the needle and thread already in her hand. Henry regarded it quizzically.

"I'd rather not stitch this in green. Or in silk . . ."

"Forgive me, my lord. . . ."

Henry took the ocher thread she offered instead and began to stitch the hole in the seam of his glove with considerable aplomb and not a little skill. My women looked aghast. I was amused. Agnes, now standing at his elbow with a cup of ale and a platter of cheese with a heel of flat bread, found it impossible to keep a still tongue.

"We have servants to do such tasks, my lord. Or any of my lady's women."

"But I can do this just as well." He continued to apply the needle, rapidly stitching up the loose seam. "As I was saying, in England . . ." He looked up as the quality of the silence around him struck home. His teeth showed in a sudden grimace of understanding.

"So you disapprove?" He looked at me. "It's Herleva's blood. As a superior tanner's daughter, Herleva's skills were manifold. And I inherited them. I'm not ashamed of it."

Agnes looked askance.

"Why the curled lip, mistress? The Lady of Aquitaine has the same blood as I. Solid stock was Herleva, and I'll not hear otherwise." He completed his stitching, biting off the thread with sharp teeth, and returned the needle to its owner. "There—as good as new." He took a mouthful of ale but waved aside the food. "I'll eat later. Now I must . . ." His eye focused on me. "I see you are wearing my gift, lady."

I put my hand to my throat. Melusine's necklace, of course. The opals had a distinctly baleful quality, but today they seemed to glow warmly in the early light. "It never leaves me." I think I smirked. It had been a last-minute thought, after my veil and filet, but there was no reason for Henry to know that.

"Then, lady, we have business to discuss. And even less time, since you kept me waiting overnight. Is there somewhere we can exchange plans—in private?"

He stood up, thickset, powerful, filling the room with his energy. It would have been impossible to refuse him. I led him to my private chamber.

"What is it you wish to discuss?"

"My rights." He closed the door firmly.

"Rights?"

"Of betrothal. They're binding. And I'm claiming them now."

Henry was already stripping off his attire—tunic, boots, hose, chausses all dropped and scattered on the floor—with impressive speed and complete absence of self-consciousness.

"Come here!" he ordered.

"And if I don't?" I struggled to reply, resenting his authority. My breath was suddenly caught in my throat, my body slick with desire, my flesh sensitive to his presumption that I would obey. Henry naked, determined and aroused, with a lift to his chin and a glint in his eye, was a sight to entice any woman.

"You will." Henry smiled. "You were made for me. And I for you. You are my beloved and I am yours."

Poetic his words might be, but he waited for me no longer. Covering the ground between us in a heartbeat, Henry took me unawares and his mouth was an urgent demand against mine, his fingers a brand through my gown into my skin.

"You won't fight me, will you?" He lifted his head, so close that I could see my own reflection, tiny but perfect, in his eyes. "At this eleventh hour?"

I hadn't the breath to reply at all, nor the will to resist. He dealt with my garments with the same admirable application as he had stitched the glove, every lace and tie and ribbon dealt with until I was as naked as he. Except for Melusine's collar that lay warm and heavy around my throat.

I felt the flush in my cheeks as he looked at me.

"Duchess Eleanor, you are my undoing."

"I thought you had exemplary control, my lord." Shivering with nerves, I was deliberately formal.

"Let's see."

He stooped, arms sliding to waist and knee so that he could lift me, a flex of fluid muscle, and suddenly I found myself pinned to the bed without mercy, my wrists locked tight in his fingers. Mercy? I needed none from this man. My blood was aflame with need.

It was an education for me at the hands of a master, an opening of a book I had never read. Perhaps I should have resented his mastery, his sheer bloody dominance over my body, but I did not. I felt as if I were at the center of a campaign as Henry applied his skills in warfare, honed on the battlefield, but now used with the same intense dedication to possessing me. Cunning deployment of his mouth and fingertips distracted me and stole my breath. Stealthy advance tricked me into yielding. And when I had no will of my own, his furious attack and refusal to retreat, driving on to an inevitable conclusion, ended in overwhelming invasion. Such heat and fire. They consumed me.

"I wasn't in control," he said when he could, taking the weight on his elbows, pressing kisses along my throat where Melusine's necklace still lay.

"Neither was I!" My wits were scattered.

"I think I should try a different approach. . . ."

"I can't. . . ." My limbs were as weak as those of a newborn lamb.

But Henry's kiss was as soft as a whisper. Who would have thought the Angevin had such patience to stroke and soothe? Such thorough attention to detail he had, as every inch of me was caressed and stirred to life. I was thoroughly stalked, captured, and destroyed over and over again, this time by a miracle of tenderness, by a man who proved to have every weapon in his armory.

But then, as my body glowed and my mind struggled to grasp the pleasure, I rethought Henry's approach. Perhaps it was not a military conquest, after all, rather a sumptuous feast of which we both partook, a banquet that we shared with equal enjoyment.

"There, you see." He groaned; even Henry seemed to have run out of energy. He lay on his back, arms spread. "Aquitaine finally submitting to Anjou."

I pushed myself up to sit beside him. "Anjou looks in retreat to me. . . ."

His laughter was strong. "Kiss me, Eleanor. . . ."

And I did. More than once. And discovered that Henry's energies were unflagging.

You are mine, he had once said. *And don't forget it.*

After an hour in my bed with him, I was not likely to do so.

"Do I measure up?" he asked impudently at last, sprawled at my side.

"In which area?" I could be as arch as any woman in the correct circumstances.

"In any you like."

I smoothed my hand over the interesting array of scars on his shoulder and torso that I had already discovered, mementos of a lifetime of lively combat. Oh, but he was impressive, with the smooth musculature of an athlete. And forsooth, he had no modesty. Why should he? His possession of me had been both lengthy and magnificently all-encompassing.

"You exceed all my expectations," I admitted. "I think I have been waiting all my life for you."

"The feeling's reciprocated. You're a beautiful woman." His hands were cradling my face so that I could not look away, the directness of his gaze overwhelming. "I believe I love you, Duchess Eleanor. I thought I did. Now I'm sure."

Now, *that* I had not expected, spoken with such an intensity of feeling, and it drove me to reply in kind, in honesty. "I've waited a long time to hear a man say that." I was shocked at the sudden imminence of tears.

"From a man you can love?" Henry demanded.

"I might," I hedged.

Henry laughed. "You give nothing away, do you? But I think we are both satisfied with each other." Henry kissed me enthusiastically. "You do realize you might just carry my child, my love. You have to wed me."

But when I expected a repeat performance of Henry's assault, he sprang out of bed.

"Where are you going?"

His reply was muffled as he pulled a tunic over his head. Already he was searching for hose and chausses. "Get up, my love." He sat to pull on his boots and looked across at me. "Get your bishops and friends and family and witnesses to the cathedral, Eleanor, and we'll marry."

"Now?" Sweet Jesu!

"Why not? Can you think of a better time?"

When Henry loped from the room, shouting for his squire, I took a small ivory-backed looking glass from beneath my pillow and stared at the reflection. I looked for a long time, until the softness of eye and mouth, the riotous tumble of hair, the delicate flush embarrassed me. It was not right that an hour in the arms of the Angevin should weave such magic. Hearing returning footsteps, I slid the looking glass back out of sight.

"I don't believe you're having second thoughts!" Henry lounged in the doorway. "Get up, woman, and get dressed."

Still shaken, I did as I was told.

And here we stood, waiting for the Bishop to make his ceremonial entrance.

"I presume you didn't ask Louis's permission for this, as your liege lord?" I asked Henry, who fidgeted at my side.

"No." He was a man of action but few words, as I was fast discovering. His brows rose. "Did you?"

"I did not."

We were waiting in the vast nave of the cathedral of Saint Pierre for the Bishop, having taken him by surprise. We had taken everyone by surprise, so it was all in the way of a scramble. No one was dressed for so momentous a union and celebration, certainly not the bride and groom. Henry had managed to dispense with his mail but was in hunting leathers. My gown had dust along the hem and my hair was in hasty and uneven braiding. In fact it was no celebration at all, merely a much-desired culmination of a secret agreement set in motion when

I was still a wife. Yet I had gold and opals around my throat, courtesy of Melusine.

"Legally," I continued, "without a male protector, I am Louis's vassal and must therefore ask his blessing if I marry."

"Bugger that!"

I choked on a laugh. "Louis would forbid it."

"By God, he would! I would forbid it in his shoes. His loss, my gain. Look at what we'll hold together, my love. All the land from the sea in the north to the Mediterranean and the Pyrenees in the south." The smile on his mouth slid into a sneer. "The King of the Franks—such an inconsequential kingdom in comparison—must be quaking in his pilgrim's sandals."

"I don't suppose we have a dispensation from the Pope either?"

"No."

"Being related in the third degree as we are."

"Yes, we are. And no, we haven't. What does it matter?"

"The Pope still considers me a true wife to Louis."

"He'll be disappointed then." Henry turned and frowned at me. "Where's that damned bishop? I suppose you did inform him?"

I nudged him in the ribs. "His Holiness might excommunicate us."

Henry shrugged. "I don't think the Almighty has enough time to be interested in our matrimonial affairs."

Here was a man after my own heart. How different from Louis, who quaked at the prospect of divine disapproval.

"Don't worry, Eleanor. I didn't think you were a worrier! I don't give a pig's eye for a dispensation." Henry took a few steps forward, then back to me, disarranging the procession as everyone moved out of his way, his voice suddenly echoing up into the vaults. "I'll not want an annulment. You'll carry a son for me—a whole clutch of them—and there'll be no grounds for an annulment."

I sighed as his laughter rippled in the air. I had the feeling that my life would become even more public when I was wedded to Henry.

"You're very confident."

The old anxieties of my past failures rose up to choke me, but

Henry grasped my wrist to demand my full attention from the scurry of clerics around the High Altar.

"Tell me honestly, Eleanor. How often did Louis honor you with his attentions?"

"As little as he could." I lapsed into sotto voce as Henry raised his expressive brows. "And in at least the last decade, only when commanded by Abbot Bernard or the Pope."

"Really? By God!" Nothing sotto voce about this. I could feel the pricking of ears around me, but Henry was oblivious. "Who'd have thought it? A *decade*? You poor girl. I'll make it up to you." His grip slid to my hand to link his fingers with mine. "Nothing will part us, you know. No one will take you from me. I wanted you and I've got you. Nothing will stop me from ruling the most powerful empire the Western world has ever seen. Or from my having you as my queen, at my side. You're mine and you'll stay mine."

I stopped worrying as we made our way to where the Bishop at last waited for us, a startled but resigned expression on his face.

When it was over, when the Bishop had mumbled through the requisite words, as if he feared the Pope might be listening from one of the roof beams, when we were finally wed with the good wishes of our small but interested congregation . . .

"What will you wager?" Henry demanded, his hand enclosed around mine, and with a smile altogether malicious.

"On what?"

"On the fact that we'll be at war against Louis within a se'enight."

I didn't take the wager.

Two weeks of married life. Henry gave me two whole weeks, although by the end of it he was itching to be about his affairs and I knew I could not keep his attention.

What did I do to entertain the restless new Duke of Aquitaine and Count of Poitou?

Hunting and hawking for the most part. Argument and discourse— mostly argument. He was not a man of regular hours or meals. I swear, he would eat on his feet if I allowed it. I would never get a banquet showered with rose petals from Henry. Or a peacock subtlety breath-ing fire for my entertainment. Meals were something to be consumed with speed, to turn one's mind to more immediate matters.

We spent an immeasurable amount of time in bed.

Henry continued to pursue his siege and conquest with vigor. I think I learned a thing or two about attack and retreat, to my own advantage. Henry proved to be a lover par excellence.

If I had taken Henry's wager, I would have lost it. He was right, of course. The first advance against us was Louis's summoning of Henry to present himself to his liege lord in the Cité Palace to answer the charge of treason. Henry's response was entirely predictable.

"God's Eyes, I won't do it. Does he think I'm a fool? Once in Paris I'd find myself clapped in a dungeon. Louis'll have to do better than that."

Henry tore the summons in half and cast it in the fire.

Louis did do better.

The rumors, as Henry had once remarked, filtered in to us in Poitiers, as pernicious as rotting flesh and equally unpleasant, stirring a running and indiscriminately lewd commentary from Henry. Louis set himself to building alliances to isolate us—"God rot his balls!"— joining hands with anyone who had a bone to pick with me or my argumentative husband. We heard of the growing web of enemies without much surprise, although Louis's acumen was new to me. Some clever dealing was going on here, which smacked of Galeran. Eustace of Boulogne, son of King Stephen, who had all to gain if Henry died on a battlefield, was the first to sign up—"Well, he would, wouldn't he, the turd!" Henry's brother Geoffrey clasped hands with Louis, sim-ply because it would put Henry's nose out of joint, and I expect he'd been promised more castles to add to his meager tally of three—"That bastard always scuttles up like a louse in a seam, just when you think you've crushed it!" Henry thumped the wall with his fist. With them joined the two sons of our old enemy the Count of Champagne, Henry and Theobald, the same Theobald who had tried and failed to abduct me. Now both of them, to tie them firmly to Louis's side, were craftily betrothed to my infant daughters Marie and Alix. "I'll kick the balls of the whole sodding lot of them!" Henry declared.

I laughed. How refreshing to be addressed like a man, rather than a weak woman to be banished from all matters of policy. And it took my mind off the sharp stab of hurt that Louis should make such calculating use of my daughters against me. This seemed like a betrayal and touched my heart with irrational sorrow. Who knew better than I that a woman of rank had no choice but must accept the demands of power and diplomacy? Louis had deliberately offered them, children still, to bind Henry's enemies to France in an unholy alliance. My daughters must accept this as their fate.

I turned my face away—I would not let Henry see my grief—but perhaps he did, and found time amidst the logistics of war to prove his possession of me. He might talk to me man-to-man, but in bed I was all woman to him.

"Louis has got more sense than I gave him credit for," Henry stated, his mind reverting to the immediate as soon as his appetite—and mine—was slaked and his heartbeat beneath my cheek returned to its normal steady thump. "When we have a son, Eleanor, my love, he'll get Aquitaine and your daughters will lose it. By shackling the Champagne lads to his daughters, Louis has given them every incentive to put a sword through my gut before I can impregnate you."

"Then I'd better pray they'll fail," I retorted dryly, not entirely pleased with my role in this bid for power. "And that your efforts to procreate are rewarded."

"You don't need to pray, dear heart."

After another spectacular display of masculine energy, Henry took his troops and abandoned his new wife.

"Come and pray with me," I invited Aelith.

"For what in particular?"

"That Louis's habitual fever when faced with stiff opposition sends him home before he and my husband can come to blows on the battlefield."

"And for Henry's safety."

"That goes without saying."

I prayed harder than I'd ever prayed in my life, and commissioned a window to be placed in the cathedral to commemorate my marriage. There Henry and I, depicted in a mosaic of vividly hued glass, a blast of color as strong as his will and mine, knelt in solemn adoration to present the gift of the magnificent glass to Saint Pierre. I knew Henry would not object. He might even admire the window if he returned to Poitiers and stayed with me long enough to notice it.

The progress of war reached me third- or fourth-hand and caused me little anxiety. It was a brief and rapidly concluded affair. When Louis, as expected, led an army into Normandy, Henry advanced to meet him, which immediately put Louis, fever ridden, into retreat. With a fast revenge in mind, Henry went on to lay waste to the Vexin, snatching up two of brother Geoffrey's castles, spurning the last only because there was no time to lay a siege—and leaving Geoffrey hopping mad but ineffectual. After that, nothing was left bar the shouting. Louis succumbed to his righteous fever, signed a truce, and fled to Paris. My prayers were answered. Geoffrey begged some sort of forgiveness, which Henry accepted with sardonic humor and little faith that his brother meant it. The Champagne contingent skulked below their battlements, and Eustace retired to his lair in England.

A tidy little campaign, all in all.

What had Roger of Sicily said? Henry Plantagenet was going far.

My new husband might be going far, but his route never seemed to find its way in my direction. I sat at the High Table in Henry's palace in Angers, where I had moved my household at Henry's request, as a good wife should. I did not even have my beloved Poitiers for consolation. Still he did not come. So the succulent dishes congealed, neglected before me as I wallowed in my troubadours' bittersweet sentiments of love and rejection.

Alas, I thought I knew so much
Of love—and yet I know so little.
For I cannot stop myself loving her,
From whom I shall never have joy.

Plangent chords. The lute sang in the hands of a master of the craft. The angelic voice wrapped its pure notes around my heart.

Before her I am powerless—and really not myself at all
Since the moment she met my gaze in the mirror
Which put me in her thrall.

Heart-wrenching words. They touched my need and I almost wept with the intensity of the emotion, if I transposed *she* to *he*. For Henry *left* me. Frequently. Lengthily. How could he *do* that, and I a bride? I was bereft.

He managed a miraculous four months with me at the end of the year, when we made a progress through Aquitaine to introduce him to my Aquitainian vassals as their new lord. Winter months when sun filled my heart, and Henry was of a mind to be understanding of my barons, who resented an Angevin ruling over them—although not as much as they had resented Louis. During all that time, Henry had kept an affable smile and a friendly approach to my vassals, who were at best suspicious, at worst hostile to a new lord who might bleed them dry to fund an invasion of England. He hunted and hawked with them, drank a vast amount of ale with them, and wooed them to his side. I was impressed.

And then we came to Limoges. A prosperous little town, one of my own, proud of its impressive, newly contructed walls and a fine new bridge over the Vienne River.

If I recalled the events in Limoges in bloodred detail, so would the inhabitants of Limoges.

We had pitched our tents and pavilions outside the walls, prior to our making a formal entry to greet the burghers, who would declare their oaths of allegiance. That day, after celebrating Mass, we would feast and mark our arrival in informal manner with the great and the good, the wealthy burghers and clerics. A meal was served; platters and dishes were carried in from the camp kitchen; wine was poured liberally; minstrels sang. We traveled in style despite the inconvenience of canvas in wet or windy weather. Our guests from the city were seated along the board to toast our union and our felicitous arrival. Henry, deep in conversation with one of the worthy burghers, picked up his knife . . .

And stared. So did I as I followed his preoccupation, and saw what Henry saw.

The platters on the trestle were few, their contents spare. I counted the dishes: no more than a dozen, and all of a humdrum nature. A stew of coney with onions. Fish that might have been salmon. A thick pottage of cabbage. Beside me, Henry's stare turned to a glower.

I beckoned to a servant. "Are there no roasted meats? Send in the rest, if you will. This is no formal banquet. . . ."

"There is no more, lady," he croaked.

Henry skewered our steward with a glance. "Send in the cook, if you please." The soft accents did not correspond with the tightening of his lips, the white shade that settled around his mouth.

The cook, a portly man of rare reputation and skill in my kitchens, bowed low, and lost no time in the telling, hands raised in apology. "How can I show my skills when I don't have the wherewithal, my lord? The burghers of Limoges have failed to provide me with the customary supplies due to their liege lord. This is all we have."

Henry's eyes traveled along the table to search out the Abbot of Saint-Martial, who sat in self-regarding splendor, the jewels on his fingers winking.

"Explain, sir." Although unnervingly mild, Henry's demand hung in the air.

"We fulfilled the letter of the law, my lord." The Bishop had a terrible smugness. I trembled for him.

"Whose law?"

"Our feudal duty to our lord, the Lady Eleanor. Supplies are due from us for her comfort and sustenance." Unfortunately the abbatial lips curved into the smallest of smiles. "When the lady is lodged within the city walls."

"What?" Henry's voice grew softer still. He leaned forward, the better to hear.

"Since the Lady Eleanor is domiciled in a tent, not in the castle, and thus outside the walls, we are not duty-bound . . ."

He was foolish enough to make no attempt to hide the deliber-ate intransigence. I was taken aback by such defiance, such arrogance, such a calculated challenge to Henry as his new overlord. It was also no less a slap in my face. I opened my mouth to reply, to demand the feudal service due to me, but Henry stilled me with a hand on my arm. His other hand grasped a knife from the board as if he would consider burying it in the costly robes of the Abbot.

"Would you care to repeat that?" Henry invited.

"We are not duty-bound—"

The Abbot got no further. With an upward and downward stroke of his arm, as if he were a blacksmith beating out a horseshoe, Henry hammered the knife to the hilt in the top of the table, snarling an order, the steward leaping to obey.

"You will not insult my wife. You will not neglect your feudal obli-gations. Summon my military commander!"

A brief conversation ensued—or rather a barrage of instructions, to which the commander nodded brusquely. "Do it!" Henry growled, then got to his feet and set his hands to the white cloth that covered the table.

"No!" I managed in horror, gripping hard to anchor the cloth.

It would have been like stopping the encroachment of a military force in full attack. With white-lipped fury, Henry dragged the cloth and its burden toward him. The feast, such as it was, was swept to the floor.

"Out!" he ordered, only to seize a handful of the Abbot's chasuble before he could make it to the door. "Oh, no, you don't. *You'll* come with me. You'll witness this. . . . And you'll be afraid."

And I stood in frozen shock as I watched the first assault on the walls of the city of Limoges that began as soon as Henry could buckle on his mail and snatch up his weapons.

"There, my lord Abbot." Henry smiled thinly at the trembling cleric. "Witness the result of your displeasing me! No abbot, no bur-gher, not even a beggar in the streets can use the city walls as an excuse to withhold from me or the lady what is due to us."

And then as fast as it had descended, the storm was past. Henry left the dismantling to his captains and flung his gauntlets down beside me where I sat in my pavilion, hooking his toe around a stool and sitting in one smooth movement as if nothing were amiss.

"I'm hungry."

"It's your own fault. You threw what there was to eat on the floor. A very respectable salmon, as I recall . . ."

"In a good cause." His smile was rueful, charmingly apologetic, typically Henry. "I don't suppose you could find me something to eat . . . ?"

We all learned to treat Henry Plantagenet with discretion at Limoges. Within two days the walls were razed to the ground, the glory of their new construction completely laid waste, the arches of the fine bridge over the river destroyed. No one dared stand in Henry's path. This blazing, outrageous exhibition of temper was yet another facet to the man who was my husband and whom I loved beyond reason.

As for the rest, my recollections were sweet. Hunting and hawking in crisp autumn days. Nights enclosed in our own private domain in a haze of pleasure. It was a time when I knew I had to hoard the bright memories against the coming drought. For after those four months—nothing. Only endless weeks of vast distance between us, and infrequent news. I clung to the memories like beads on a gossamer thread that could be snapped at any moment if not handled with care. Or like a Book of Hours full of precious jeweled icons to be taken out, lingered over, treasured. Or wept over in private.

I might admit it to no one—but I did all of those.

Oh, I missed him. Through the sixteen long months we were apart when Henry took an army to England. Sixteen months! It was unbearable. The news of battles, sieges, skirmishes. The terrible weight of ignorance. For much of the time I had no idea whether he was alive or dead. The arrival of every courier might bring me news that I was widowed.

Was this to be my marriage?

I feared his features were growing dim in my mind as every night I struggled to piece together the stormy eyes and dominant nose. The lips that could snarl or smile or kiss me into insensibility. Was this to be the rest of my life, loneliness interspersed with occasional bright flashes of joy? Did I love him? If love was missing him, thinking of him, sleeping and waking with his presence beside me, then I was doomed. I would never be dependent on a man, but I missed him so, and when necessity kept me close within my palace, the time hung heavily.

I sighed.

As if he sensed my melancholy, the troubadour, new to my court, sank to one knee, dark eyes fixed on my face as his fingers stirred the lute to life once more.

Lady, I am yours, and yours will stay,
Pledged to your service, come what may.
This oath I take is full and free,
The kind of vow that will hold for sure. . . .

I smiled my pleasure at these verses written personally for me, expressing all the hopeless devotion of a man for a highborn lady. I smiled until Aelith nudged me back to reality.

"If you smile at him like that, you'll find him locked in one of Henry's dungeons faster than he can tune his lute."

"What?"

"Eleanor . . . he has a reputation!"

I looked at the young man who still knelt, eyes shining on me in abject adoration. Bernat de Ventadorn had attached himself to my court when Henry and I had made our progress through the south, and I was not disappointed in his talents.

"He's in love with you," Aelith whispered.

"But I am not in love with him."

"He thinks you are!"

"He does not! It's the role of the troubadour to worship his lady."

"That's not worship. That's lust. Romantic, perhaps, but lust nonetheless."

I looked at him. Handsome, certainly, with fine features and a sweep of dark hair, a tall, lithe figure that carried the clothes of the troubadour with elegance. But I had not considered him as a lover. Was that what people might think? Was that what Henry would think?

Ridiculous! Talented he might be, but Bernat was the illegitimate consequence of an archer's drunken tumble with a willing kitchen maid. Yet others had found him attractive, for he had come to me with the reputation of having seduced the wife of his previous patron.

Of all my joys you are the first,
And of them all you'll be the last,
As long as my life endures.

I sighed again. What woman would not enjoy a handsome man singing her praises in such a manner?

The problem was that Bernat sang the words and sentiments I would have liked Henry to address to me. There was no romance in Henry. Yes, he now wrote to me often, sending me news, keeping me abreast of the troubled politics across the sea, perhaps realizing at last—and not before time—that I would fear for him in the midst of war. Surreptitiously I pulled the latest from within my sleeve and read the rapid script that had become so familiar.

Eleanor,

Events move apace. I faced Stephen at Wallingford and challenged for battle. The English barons decided a parley was more practical. Thank God Stephen is a man of sense. I spoke with him and we are negotiating a truce. I shall be at Winchester. And then on to Westminster, if all goes well.

The brief note looked as if it had been written from a horse's back—as I presumed it had. There were blots and rough edges and the stains of travel.

He's in the middle of a tense situation, the voice of reason chided. *That he bothers to write to you at all is a miracle.*

What was more, he had drawn me rough maps on the parchment with routes and battles, understanding that the names of places would mean nothing to me. Except by now they did. Had not Henry promised that one day I would be Queen of this warlike island? I had made it my business to learn more of this kingdom—and liked little of what I had learned other than the indisputable fact that the King held supreme power, answerable to none but God. The rest made me shudder. The drink of preference was ale, the wine of such poor quality as to be drunk with closed eyes and clenched teeth. I must remember to take my own. And the food—nothing but pottage and onions and red meat. The royal court was itinerant, by God, moving ponderously, constantly from one drafty castle to the next. I would soon change that. I took in Henry's final words, already knowing there was no comfort to be had there.

If I can clip the wings of Stephen's son, Eustace, a permanent peace may be possible. I may be with you soon.

Hope you are well. I know the power is safe in your hands.

Henry

Henry . . . ! Why could you not write to me as a lover? Where was the romance in this letter? Informative, reassuring, but not what my heart cried out for. No yearning, no lingering passion. No hopeless, unrequited love. No word of affection, no endearment, while I suffered more than I cared for. I missed Henry Plantagenet. Moreover, I thought crossly, I could not see Henry being laid low by the temporary absence of his lover. He was more likely to take another—some pretty female who widened her eyes at him—to fill the space! I folded the parchment into sharp creases, frowning at a startled Bernat, and stuffed it back into my sleeve.

Bernat smiled winningly.

I grimaced.

"I suppose it would be sensible to banish him from court," I remarked to Aelith.

"Give him to me instead." Aelith was widowed now from her beloved Raoul, and her eyes shone. I forgot how lonely she must sometimes be.

"I think I'll save him from your clutches, sister," I said, and smiled.

For all I write and sing
Is meant for her delight.

Bernat finished on a flourish and bowed, face flushed with the applause and my reward of a purse of gold coins. Perhaps I should exert some caution. Perhaps I should send him with Aelith when she left. Or perhaps not. Louis, I recalled, had once been insanely jealous of my troubadours, but Louis was a fool. Henry had far more sense.

Henry continued to keep me informed with unsentimental lack of detail.

Eleanor,

Peace with Stephen is made in my favor. The threat from his son, Eustace, who has been venting his anger on the east of the country, has been decided by God. Eustace paid the penalty of greed and choked to death on a dish of eels.

Perhaps I will be back in Normandy before too long.

That was good. Very good. Eustace's death would leave Stephen without an heir, which could only be to Henry's advantage. The crown of England crept closer by the day. With Eustace's death there would be no more battles, no figurehead to lead the English rebels. Henry would be safe. He would come home. My heart leaped and optimism resurfaced. Until my eye traveled down.

*It has come to my ear that your troubadour is causing
comment for his slavish adoration of your own fair person. Send
him here to me. I've need of a man with talent. I'll test his skill
at composing martial tunes to rouse the spirits of my soldiers
who yearn for home.*

*I consider your person to be mine. I'll not tolerate a rival.
Nor will I have you the talk of Europe—more than you already
are. I expect him forthwith.*

Henry

Where was the affection, the undying love? The need to see me
again? Instead, all I got were unfounded accusations. Were all men
capable of such unwarranted spite? Were all men incapable of appreciating the simple beauty of song and music to extol the value of a
woman? Did they have to be quite so crude in their suspicions?

I will not obey, like some meek goodwife! was my first thought. But
my second? If Henry was clawed by green-taloned jealousy, I was not
averse to it. *I consider your person to be mine.*

Did he now? Then come here and prove it!

My loins were hot, but I would not take a lover. Henry filled my
heart and my soul. Bernat de Ventadorn was pretty enough, but no
rival to the Plantagenet.

As a meek and dutiful goodwife, I informed Bernat of his future.

He blanched. No, I could not see him composing military marches
either, but we all had to make sacrifices. I might resent Henry's peremptory demand, but sometimes good sense argued for compliance.

I must leave my love and go away,
Banished I know not where.
For she does not bid me stay,
Though this cruel exile I cannot bear.

That night Bernat's lute sobbed as his voice hung in the rafters,
heavy with emotion.

I sighed and wished my own love would rescue me from this cruel exile.

Bernat de Ventadorn left for England. As it happened, I could not have sent him away with Aelith. She chose to make her home with me at Angers in her widowhood.

"Why would I leave?" she asked when I expressed my pleasure but my surprise. "The Plantagenet spices everyone's life! I'll stay here and watch the fun."

And then Henry was home. The Plantagenet courier bowed low. Henry was at Rouen, his capital in Normandy, to spend Easter there, and I was summoned to join him. Summoned? He would summon me to Rouen rather than come here to Angers? The courier's respectful tones could not quite hide the demand. I did not care. After sixteen months I would have followed Henry to the ends of the earth. I packed up my household, my necessary entourage, and ordered up the palanquin. Then all that was left was to organize my gift for Henry and set off within the day.

Chapter Twenty

I did not know Rouen, nor was I greatly impressed with it, its gray and forbidding walls reminding me too strongly of Paris for comfort, but I was not sorry to arrive. It was a cold, overcast afternoon, the sharp showers of April having made travel unpleasant and the going slow. When I arrived, the castle was teeming with soldiers and officials so that I had to display my consequence to find a space in the courtyard to unpack my household. Henry was back, and the whole household vibrated with his presence.

My heart made a little thud against my ribs at the thought of our reunion.

"My lady. We did not expect you so soon."

"Where is he?" I asked the steward who had come to greet me as I climbed the steps after arranging accommodations for my entourage. Agnes, arms full, and a little body of servants equally burdened with boxes and packages followed me. I had need of them all.

"Ah! . . . That is to say . . ."

His eyes would not quite meet mine. Perhaps he had come to waylay me rather than greet me.

"Tell me." I continued to walk briskly. Although I didn't know my way, it was clear where the main activity was. My ears pricked up.

"My lord is in the Great Hall."

"So I hear." There was some sort of commotion ahead. It was uncommonly loud.

"He's not best pleased, lady."

"Hmm. Bad, is it?"

I knew the steward, a man of integrity. He knew me. He was Henry's man but not without respect for Henry's wife.

"All I can say, lady . . ." His voice dropped to a furtive whisper. "It's like *Limoges*."

I frowned. Limoges. I had no need to ask for further explanation. Limoges had a habit of preying on the mind.

Oh, yes. At Limoges I had learned fast that Henry was a true inheritor of the renowned Angevin temper, and I knew what devastation it could create. It was an amazing thing when in full flowering, and for the briefest of moments there in Rouen, it made me hesitate, glance back to Agnes and then at the steward who awaited my decision. Henry in the grip of anger was a man to be avoided.

"As bad as that?" I asked.

"Worse. My lord doesn't tolerate opposition well. Perhaps you should delay your arrival, lady. . . ."

I considered his wooden expression, his kind advice, then cast it aside. I'd traveled a long way for this meeting. I'd waited until the very limit of my patience. "He summoned me here. He'll speak to me now."

"As you will, lady." *And on your head be it!*

I could hear Henry's furious accents before I even reached the doorway. There I had to wait for the steward to push aside the servants and officials who had withdrawn from the vast hall to take refuge in the outer audience chamber, but eventually I and my little party stood just inside the door, my hand on the steward's arm to prevent him from announcing me, as I watched the cause of the upheaval, fascination warring with wariness. It was not worse than Limoges—the destruction was not likely to be quite as great—but it was a near thing.

"Every time I turn my back . . ." Henry growled, face white, eyes blazing. "If it's not one bloody vassal it's another. And if it's not one of my lords bent on betrayal, it's the King of France raiding along my border. Burned Verneuil, has he? Attacked Vernon? And still calling himself Duke of Aquitaine as if it's a God-given right! The bastard!" The short Angevin accents reverberated from the stonework. "The Vexin's up in arms again. The Vexin's *always* up in arms!"

He flung his arms wide as if to encompass the mess that had awaited him on his return from England.

"My wife's damned vassals are a law unto themselves. While my brother—God rot him!—watches me for every chink of weakness. And I daren't think of what's going on in England now I'm not there. God's Eyes! I thanked the Almighty for Eustace's death, but that was a shade premature. With Louis pinning me down here, I'll warrant those bloody English barons have torn up my pact with Stephen and are sharpening their swords to stir up trouble for me. By God, I'll crush their balls like a nut between two stones . . . !"

His voice harsh and cracked, Henry lunged to sweep his arm along the trestle, sending cups and flagons flying, maps and documents too. Snatching one up before it fluttered to the floor, he tossed it haphazardly into the fire, where it went up in a crackle of flame, the seal melting with a hiss. Henry did not even register the destruction. It could have been the precious agreement with Stephen, signed and sealed between them in Winchester, bought with so much blood and effort. In that surge of blind rage Henry did not even care. Dragging the felt cap from his head, he now proceeded to wrench it into strips, flinging the shredded wool into the air, like a flock of colorful finches, before it dropped to the floor. A precious crystal cup was hurled at the wall, where it shattered into pieces, to lie like tears.

Nor was Henry finished. "I'll have Geoffrey's balls as well for this and roast them over a slow fire!" He might have lowered his voice but it was threatening for all that. He roamed the room, overturning benches, stools, dragging one of the heavy tapestries from the wall, his whole manner without restraint. Hounds fled; servants retreated even farther. Men died when Henry was in a temper. Men who had resisted his depredations had died at Limoges. I remained unmoving in the doorway, my fingers tightening on the steward's wrist.

"And now I hear that . . ."

I shook my head at the steward, who was still intent on announcing me. Could I control Henry, restrain him? Now was the time to see, to prove it or to slink away. Eleanor of Aquitaine did not *slink*. I never had and never would. Henry's ire was not directed at me, so I would advance into the eye of the storm.

Henry would not frighten me.

I walked forward.

Henry's head snapped around.

"Ha! And here's my lovely wife!"

He pounced. He covered the ground between us in a matter of steps. I would not flinch. I lifted my chin. Yes, my heart thundered, my skin chilled to ice, but I was intrigued rather than afraid. Would he actually cause me harm, and so publicly, in this display of terrifying fury? Could I draw the poison from the passion? Only time and experience would tell, and we had had so little time together to discover the limits of our relationship. . . .

"My wife! At last! What took you so long? You should have been here sooner. Did I not command you?" He was within two strides of me now, face flushed as he loosed his attack. So I was to be the object of his ire after all. "Torn yourself away from your milksop singer of stomach-churning sentiment, have you? He slipped out of my grasp fast enough, the miserable whining fool. I suppose he fled back to hide behind your skirts again. Did he tell you I ill treated him? By God, I did no such thing!"

It was true. My less than courageous troubadour had returned to Angers at the first opportunity, and I could not blame him. A military garrison was not Bernat de Ventadorn's métier. But to do so without Henry's permission was more than foolhardy. Henry would not have given his permission, of course.

"Bernat did not accuse you of cruelty, only of lack of sensitivity," I replied coolly. "Is that all you can say to me, Henry, when you've not set eyes on me for over a year? The fact that Bernat returned to me says more about your character than mine. I expect you mocked him unmercifully."

"I did not." For a brief moment reason slid back into his glare.

"Well, not much. By God, Eleanor, he's a poor creature. How can you tolerate him? Did he drip words of honeyed love into your ears?"

"Yes. He is a troubadour and is paid to do exactly that. I am his lady and his patron."

"God's Blood!"

"You weren't there to drip words, honeyed or otherwise." I kept the eye contact, even as I trembled. Henry's gaze raked me with hot fire. "It's been over a year, Henry!"

"Bugger that! I've been at bloody war!"

"I know."

"And I don't like your troubadour!"

"I know that too. I have left him in Angers."

"I'm amazed you can bear to be without him." Henry's eyes narrowed. "Have you heard the gossip? I have."

"Of course. They say Bernat is my lover."

"And is he? Have you let him do more than hide behind your skirts?"

Oh, I was so cool in my replies. I amazed myself, but I would not retreat. "Do *you* think that I have?"

"I think that you are a law unto yourself, madam!"

"Such that I would couple with the bastard of a kitchen wench?"

"You have the reputation for it, madam. *Lascivious* is the word, I think!"

So he was not of a mind to retreat either. Nor would I expect it. I was not unhappy if Henry was jealous. I stepped up my counterattack, it being an excellent form of defense, and even bestowed on him a contemptuous smile.

"Any scandals of my past have at least been with men of birth as good as my own. I do not grovel in the gutter for my pleasure. Unlike you, my lord."

A thunderous silence descended.

"What was the name of your latest slut?" I asked, silky-smooth. "Ykenai? What sort of name is that? A common whore, I understand." I considered my next comment, and decided to risk it. "And I hear that she has carried you a son."

Although Henry had stilled, the emotion did not disperse. He watched me, viper venomous. I shivered. "You have a sharp tongue on you, lady. Have a care."

I tilted my chin. "Oh, I do. I have every care, my lord. I am the epitome of respectability. My *lascivious* reputation is a thing of the past." I showed my teeth again in a smile. "Why would I need a milksop lover when I have *you*?"

"Well, at least that is true! Why would you? I think it's time I reminded you, madam wife!"

He *was* jealous! Delight sang through me as sweet as Bernat's songs as I tracked the easing of the lines around his eyes, the draining of the high color. Henry was mine. The fury was lessening and, with a harsh laugh, he was becoming aware of the avid audience of lords and servants alike, mouths open as they took in every word. I did not care. Let them listen to their betters if they so wished.

"No!" I stated.

"No, what?"

"No, it is not true. I don't have you. Not often. Hardly ever. What are you going to do about it, Henry?"

"You're here now, Eleanor. I'll show you what I'll do about it."

I saw my provocation hit home. Henry raised his hand. I must have flinched. Henry's eyes widened in horror and his hand dropped away.

"You thought I was going to strike you! You did, didn't you? By God, woman!"

"I have no idea. Your mood is black enough!"

"I've never struck a woman in my life," Henry said in a low voice, "and I'm not about to start with you. I've killed a fair few men, but I'll not demean myself by striking a woman, and by God, never you!" The extremity of emotion faded further from the harsh lines of his face as he raised his hand, slowly now, to rub the backs of his fingers over my cheek. "I'll not willfully harm you."

You might through carelessness, I thought. *Not physically, but I think you might hurt me through neglect.* But: "No, I don't think you will strike me, Henry," I agreed. "But how soon before you abandon me this time? An hour, a day? A month? Must I be grateful if you stay in my company for more than a week before your campaigning demands your time? It's a poor return for marriage, Henry!"

"God's Bones, Eleanor! I have a war to fight."

"So you do. I don't dispute it. And when you return from your brave, warlike deeds, you welcome me with open arms. Your words are sweet and seductive. Your touch is soft and tender." I dropped my eyes from his to his hands, which, at this point in our verbal conflict, had gasped my forearms like bands of iron.

"You want sweet words from me, do you . . . ?"

"I might. Among other things."

"What other things?"

"Do you need to ask? It's been sixteen months since I last saw you. Perhaps you would like to kiss me in greeting." The heat of him. It pumped from his skin as if his blood were all flame. His eyes blazed. I braced for another onslaught. "I have never been to Rouen before, I came as fast as I could, I am weary and travel-stained, and all you can do is rant and rail at Louis and Eustace and Geoffrey! No 'Good day, wife'! No 'Welcome to your new home; allow me to see to your comfort'! No 'How I have missed you' . . . !"

"Eleanor . . ."

Henry placed his fingers softly on my lips, then leaned to follow them with his mouth in the most tender of kisses. "Eleanor, you drive a man to the brink of control."

"I think you get to that point without my help!"

He slid his hands slowly from my arms to my shoulders. Once more his lips touched mine, cool and firm and gentle but with a wealth of promise.

"I care nothing for Bernat," I murmured against his mouth.

Henry's laugh was lambent after the storm of emotion. "I know."

"I have come at your command, days of travel when it would have suited me better to remain at Angers and have you come to me. And all you can do is rage and accuse." I drew away a little and placed my palm flat on his chest. "When I have come and brought you a gift."

"A gift . . ."

A bubble of laughter welled within me as I saw comprehension touch his eyes and felt the leap of his heart. "Have you forgotten, Henry? I know you got the news."

"Ah, Eleanor . . ."

It had gone at last, all of it, the final vestiges of his outrageous anger, as fast and unpredictably as it had arrived, slipping from him almost as if it might lie in a puddle at his feet, an unwanted mantle cast aside in a warm room. In a typical wayward gesture Henry released me and fell to one knee, as flamboyant as my despised troubadour.

"Forgive me." His eyes were bright as he looked up. His smile was hard edged with regret, as, picking up the hem of my gown, he kissed it despite the dust and grime of travel. "You are my love. My anger was never against you."

"And my gift?"

"I claim the gift from you. Where is it?"

"It is not an *it*, Henry. It is a *he*."

"A son. My son! Let me see him."

As Henry stood and took my hand to lock his fingers with mine, as if we had never been at odds, I beckoned Agnes from the doorway. She brought the baby and gave him into my arms.

"Here he is."

My son. Our son. I could not disguise my pride in this achievement. I had carried a son, at last. How I had feared that I was truly incapable of a male heir. No matter how confident Henry had been, this anxiety had lived with me throughout my lonely pregnancy with Henry absent and fear of failure strongly present. It had perched at my shoulder like a malicious sprite as I had set my teeth against the agony of giving birth, filling my mind with memories of death. But no longer. Here was my son. My own vindication. Pride and success wove together to fill my heart with love for Henry and for this son. Old enough now at eight months to take notice of his surroundings, he squirmed in my arms and reached out to Henry, who was so clearly his father. The deep russet hair and striking gray Angevin eyes had once again imprinted themselves. Now those eyes latched onto the heavy ring on Henry's right hand.

"This is William."

I had proved my worth to myself and to Henry.

"My son. He's very small."

"He is only eight months old! But he's growing fast."

Henry surveyed the baby with a mixture of astonishment and trepidation as William reached out for the glittering jewel. Then he laughed softly.

"Did I not tell you that we would have a son?" Henry took the child from me with more skill than I ever had in dealing with infants, and allowed him to gnaw on the gold shank that had so taken his attention. "William, is it? For my great-grandfather, the Conqueror?"

"For my grandfather, the Troubadour. All Dukes of Aquitaine are called William."

Henry snorted, causing the baby to look up, eyes wide. "I should have known. A good name nonetheless. Let me look at you, William." Henry held him up with confident hands. William stuffed his fist into his mouth and kicked against Henry's chest. "Already a fighter!" Henry laughed. "As soon as you can walk, William, I'll teach you to ride. You'll ride at my side."

"He has a sweeter temper than you."

"He doesn't have my irritations." Henry allowed the baby to transfer his gnawing to the leather of his cuff.

"His teeth are beginning to show," I said with an irrepressible delight that was quite unlike me.

"He's magnificent. What an achievement, my love. Look at that hair." Cradling the baby's head in his hand, he turned to me. "Are you well, Eleanor?"

So he had remembered to ask at last. "Yes."

"You are as beautiful as ever. I regret I was not with you."

"I was not sorry," I admitted dryly.

"Forgive my temper. I did warn you."

"So you did. Are there rooms made ready for me in this cold place?"

"Come with me."

After depositing William back into Agnes's arms, Henry swept me off. In his bedchamber—not mine—he kissed me, stripped me, and

showed me that the months had been as long for him as they had been
for me.

"Now that we've dealt with the priorities"—his grin was as satisfied
as a cat with a free run of the dairy—"and much to our satisfaction, I
warrant, I'll tell you where I stand with England."

Henry knew me well. Of course I would want to know more than
his brief letters had given me or his scribbled excuses for a map had
suggested. He was already out of bed, a plain tunic belted loosely, soft
shoes on his feet, a cup of ale in one hand, as he stalked around the
bedchamber. On every surface there were signs of his residence, an
untidy clutter that I had not noticed when he had rushed me over the
threshold and into his bed. Rolls and seals and creased documents. A
bag spilling coins across the surface of a chest. A cup and plate bearing crumbs from some long-ago meal. A favorite sword that he had
half cleaned. A heap of abandoned clothing not yet put to rights by
his squire.

I sat up and clasped my arms around my bent knees, touched when
Henry reached to catch up a fur-lined mantle in one hand and cast
it over my naked shoulders against the chill. Sometimes he had the
power to surprise me. Sometimes, when I was not angry, his sensitivity
made my belly liquid with desire.

"I know you've come to terms with Stephen," I said. "A victory, I
suppose."

"I have." He dropped onto a stool before the fire to inspect and
then to gnaw on a piece of previously abandoned fowl. He chewed,
licked his fingers, and dropped the bones in the flames. "Stephen will
fight no more. He's lost the heart for it, certainly with Eustace dead."
He chose another unidentifiable piece of meat. "He'd no wish to face
me at Wallingford. Do you know what his men were saying? That
God himself appeared to fight for me, so many towns and fortresses
had fallen to me." Henry wiped his mouth with the back of his hand.
"I wasn't aware of God prompting my decisions, but it made Stephen
think twice before taking me on. Archbishop Theobald—Stephen's
Archbishop of Canterbury—told him it would be a mistake to join

battle with me. For whether I rode for God or the Devil, I was unbeatable. Theobald is my man for sure. He was already whispering in Stephen's ear that I should be named as his heir."

"Which Eustace resented."

Henry frowned at another chicken leg, but abandoned it to surge to his feet and pace from one end of the chamber to the other and back again. "I can understand Eustace's anger. What man would wish to be disinherited by his own father? But his retaliation was bloody. Do you know what he did?" he demanded, as if I ought to know.

I shook my head.

"He harried a swath of land along the east of the country. Burning and killing and destroying. His own country, his own people. To lure me into a trap, I expect, if I was fool enough to follow him to bring him to justice. It's a godforsaken place, all swamp and river and low-lying land." He sank onto the bed beside me, a flicker of anger in his eyes, but it was distant, like a low roll of thunder, and not to be feared. I said nothing, allowing him to continue. "I know I sometimes do things in the heat of fury, but not in cold blood. Not like that. I can't regret his death."

"Thank God for eels."

"Yes. I prefer red meat, myself." His teeth gleamed white as he shrugged off his displeasure. "Anyway, the outcome—as I wrote—Stephen and I healed our differences at Winchester."

"Where you were recognized as Stephen's heir?"

"Yes! Not only his heir but also his adopted son. Sealed and witnessed by a fistful of worthy bishops and earls. I shall be King of England on his death. I did homage to him and agreed that Stephen should hold the kingdom for the rest of his life, provided that I'm proclaimed king without opposition on his death. I know I've to wait out the term of Stephen's life—but it's a small price to pay."

"All you have worked for."

I watched the play of emotion on his face. Pride, restless ambition, a sense of fulfillment, and underlying it all the impatience that still he must wait. Then he lunged and rolled me and the mantle into his arms.

"This is it, Eleanor. Our empire. And now we have a son to inherit it after I am gone. And there'll be more. See how bright our fortune shines together." He stretched a hand to the side of the bed to scoop up a rolled document from the floor, heavy with seals. The Wallingford treaty. So it hadn't ended up in the flames. It amused me that he should keep it by him. "Here it is. Do you want to read it?"

"Not right now!"

"No. Later. For now I think . . ." He kissed his way along my throat to nibble at my jaw. I purred soft as a kitten. Victory made Henry very desirable, as long as I could distract him from the next step in his planning and bring him back to me.

"One thing, Eleanor."

Clothing mostly restored, Henry gave his attention to a need to make a fast reconnoiter of his possessions. We both knew that Louis would not take news of the birth of the Angevin heir in good heart. Baby William would inherit Aquitaine, thus snatching it from the dower of Marie and Alix. French retaliation was expected. Nor was brother Geoffrey's strained loyalty to be depended on—he still had Maine and Anjou in his sights as soon as Henry looked the other way.

"One thing . . ." Henry repeated.

Yes, he *was* uncertain. "Only one?" I attempted a lightheartedness I suddenly did not feel.

Buckling his sword belt, Henry raised his gaze slowly to mine where I sat on the bed to make some semblance of order in the rat's nest of my hair. All the soft humor of the past hour was suddenly replaced by an unusual hesitancy. His reply jolted me.

"The child."

Ah. The child. A boy. And not mine. When I had heard the rumor I had grieved over it: now I knew it for the truth, from Henry's own lips. Henry's past was his own affair, as was mine, but I resented this child that had been conceived since our own marriage. Anger clenched its fist in my throat—but at least he had not hidden it from me, as I kept the memory of the stillborn child in Jerusalem locked tight within me. I was in no position to be judgmental and swallowed hard against the obstruction.

"Is he yours?" I asked. Of course he was!

"She says so." I raised my brows. "Some will tell you that she's gulled me, fooled me into accepting what's not mine. But I think he is, and Ykenai was never less than honest. I've taken him in exchange for a purse of gold to set her up with a house and a chance to change her profession if she so wishes." His eyes were stern and direct.

"Did you love her?" A woman's question, full of envy, carefully hidden.

"No. I was needy." A man's reply, a careless shrug.

"I don't like the thought of you with her."

"And I don't like Bernat de Ventadorn singing love songs to you!"

"And so?"

"Will you take him?"

For a moment I finished braiding my hair, head tilted to consider the request.

"Why should I take your bastard by an alehouse whore?"

"Because I ask it of you. And because it's you I love."

Easy to say. Abandoning my hair, I picked at the soft pelt of the bedcover, hiding my thoughts.

"He is called Geoffrey," Henry informed me. "If you can't find it in you, then I'll make other arrangements."

"What arrangements?" I knew the words sounded cold and uncompromising, but in that moment, my body still warm from his, it was hard to forgive him.

"I don't know. No—look—I don't want that." I looked up and for the first time saw a shadow of regret chase across his features. "Here's the thing, Eleanor—will you take on his upbringing? He's a fine lad and deserves the best from me. I can't leave him with his mother. Will you do it for me, raise him as my son? He'll not threaten the inheritance of our own children—but I want him. I want recognition of him as mine. Take him, Eleanor!"

I sighed. This would not be a seamless marriage. But why not? Better to have the child of Henry's blood raised under my authority than perhaps used by others with an eye to future power. Bastard children could be a weapon in the right hands. So why not? Geoffrey would be raised with William and the other sons I intended to have.

At the end I could not refuse him.

"I'll do it. But if I catch you with the fecund Ykenai, Henry, I'll crack your skull."

"I'll have to make sure you don't catch me then, won't I?"

With a leer of pure mischief and renewed appetite, he pounced to pin me to the covers. The lacings on his robe were simple to undo.

"You have a generous soul, Eleanor. Have I told you today how your hair reminds me of the sun shining through autumn beeches in England?"

His kisses were sweet and for now he was all mine, all I could ask for. I was content.

I was pregnant before he left.

Disaster stalks us when we least expect it. Perhaps I should not have been so sanguine, so sure of my future contentment. It was some months before Henry returned. That was not the problem—I think I had at last come to terms with our relationship continuing at a distance. Nor was it Geoffrey, Henry's son. He had a charm all his own; he learned to talk early and without cease: no one, not even I, was immune from his childish prattling and his determination to wield the wooden sword—a thoughtless gift from Henry—to the danger of all within reach. No, it was not Geoffrey—I learned to love him as I did my own son. The disaster when it hit was unexpected and beyond my control.

The little cavalcade clattered into the courtyard with Henry at the forefront and I met it with no foreboding. A familiar scene of arrival and chaos followed. I made my way down the steps, William in my arms, Geoffrey at my heels, where he had recently attached himself, whatever I might be doing, and walked unsuspectingly across the courtyard to greet them.

"My lord." I kept the public greeting formal. "Welcome home." And then because I couldn't resist: "I didn't expect to see you so soon. I thought the child would have been born first."

Raising his hand slowly, Henry pushed back the face guard of his closed helm. "Eleanor . . . !" He closed his eyes, opened them.

"Henry . . . ?"

"I had to come. . . . I had to be here."

"Why?" I frowned. "Are we in danger here? I can't think why." Rouen's walls would keep out the strongest besieging force.

With no more ado and in habitual impressive style, Henry slid from his stallion to land in an untidy heap of mail and mud-and-sweat-stained russet cloak at my feet, where he lay inert and did not stir.

"Henry!"

He lay on the stones as if life had fled.

"Henry!" Depositing William on his feet, with no consideration for either my cumbersome skirts or my increasing girth, I knelt beside him, removing the helmet with fingers that trembled, pushing back the coif. "Henry!"

When there was no response, a bolt of fear ran through me to strike at heart and belly. For a terrible moment, until I felt his chest rise and fall under my hand, nausea swam through me and my vision was blurred. I looked up at the knights who surrounded us.

"What's wrong with him?" And then I saw the man who had dismounted to drop to one knee beside me. "Geoffrey. What are you doing here?"

Geoffrey, Henry's sullen, ambitious younger brother, would-be abductor of my person. He was still sullen.

"I've come with *him*," he snarled. "We've made a truce. . . ."

"Or you sued for peace," I snarled back, pulling off Henry's gauntlets, unlacing the mail at his throat. "I suppose you had no choice—since Henry had stripped you of all but one of your castles! Who'd want a landless traitor for an ally?"

"By God! I'm no traitor. . . ."

But I wasn't listening. Every sense was fixed on the man who lay under my hands, as it had been from the beginning. He was unnervingly still. Henry was so rarely still.

"Is he injured?" I demanded. "Wounded?" I did not think so.

"No," Geoffrey replied, unable to hide his disquiet. "The sickness came on him last week. He's been fighting it but he's getting weaker."

Sickness? "Carry him inside . . ." I ordered, struggling to my feet, reclaiming William, who had been rescued from the dangers of inquisitiveness by one of Henry's captains.

So they did, and to his chamber, where they laid him on the bed and I took stock.

Henry's face was gray and sweating along brow and lip, although his skin felt clammy and cold to my touch. He was out of his senses, his body twitching in the throes of some nightmare. What was this? Plague? But there was no obvious rash. The disease of the gut that had carried off both my father and his? But there was no vomiting or voiding. My hands shook even more as I loosed the buckle of his sword belt and drew it from under him. How helpless I felt with no knowledge of sickness and its causes.

I sent for the one source of help I could think of.

"Agnes . . ." I could barely speak for fear. "What is it?"

She touched his forehead, his throat, the place where blood pounded furiously beneath his chin. She frowned heavily.

"An ague of some kind—a sweating sickness. It has him in its grip."

"Will he die?" I hardly dared ask, and dreaded the answer more. They were, I think, the hardest words I had even spoken.

"Not if we can get the fever down. It puts a strain on the heart, lady."

"His heart is strong."

"And so is he—but the fever can draw strength from the strongest."

Here was no reassurance. My belly clenched hard with fear, causing the child within me to kick and squirm. "Do you know what to do?"

"Perhaps. I can try. I've seen it before, when I was with Queen Adelaide at Maurienne. Some say it's bad air, some that it's foul water." She looked at me and gave me the honesty I demanded. "It can be dangerous, whatever the cause."

"Don't let him die, I beg of you." I covered my mouth with my fingers. "I need him."

I knew it for the truth. Not the power, not the security for Aquitaine, not even the hope of a crown, but him. I needed Henry. I supposed this was love, with all its pain and inconvenience.

I let Agnes take charge. She had the skills, but she was of a mind to make me sit and rest. What good putting the child at risk, she snapped, when I at first refused to do as she said. What help would I be to her if I too were sick? True enough. So I obeyed and kept my fear within me.

By the Virgin, it was hard to sit and watch. With Henry stripped of his mail, tunic, and chausses, the predations of the fever were obvious, his skin waxy, his muscles lax. In so short a time, without food but determined to push on home, his body had been pared down to flesh and bone. Without any overt sympathy Agnes set herself with Henry's body servant to make him as comfortable as she could with cloths soaked in cold water to bring down the fever that burned him up.

What a long, frightening process it was, trying to force through his lips an infusion of white willow bark. All I could do was stay out of her way, or sit beside him. And I did, night and day as he thrashed in hot fever or shivered in ice. I held his hand. I talked to him. I talked to him incessantly of things to tie him to this life. I told him of what he would do when he returned to England. Of how his army awaited him to take the throne that was his by right. I described to him the pride he must feel when the crown of England finally rested on his brow. I told him he must recover, that all depended on him. I talked until I had no voice and Henry surely must wake to tell me to shut up.

"You must rest, lady." Finally Agnes turned her attention to me.

I shook my head in defiance. "I rode through Outremer, faced mountains, swollen rivers, flood, and constant attack. I survived Louis's treachery. I survived abduction and imprisonment. A few nights without sleep won't harm me."

"But the child . . ."

"The child will be strong, as is his father. A few more nights will not hurt."

"It might be more than a few nights—he's young and strong, but—"

"No, Agnes." I gripped her hand for comfort, for reassurance. "If I go to rest on my bed, if I sleep, Henry's perverse enough to die as soon as I leave the room. How would I forgive myself for that? I will stay here, Agnes, until we know—one way or another."

I sounded heartless. I knew it. But I was not. My heart was under attack and I had no defense against the pain. By God, he frightened me. Death crouched in the corner of the room like a malign shadow, all claws and teeth, as vicious as one of his Angevin lions. Some days his chest barely rose and fell so that my fears leaped again and again that his weakened body had given up the fight. At other times there was no calming him and I joined Agnes in holding him to the bed, applying damp cloths, restraining him as she forced him to accept drafts of nameless potions. Then there were the hours when he ranted and cried out wordless imprecations and demands. Never my name but Stephen and Eustace, once Geoffrey. Once even Louis. In his delirium, Henry was still campaigning.

He did not ask for me.

It hurt, but the knowledge of my love for him burned with a bright and true flame. I fixed my whole attention on his face, the flushed features carved to a strangely fine elegance by the fever. Could I hold him to this life by willpower alone? I no longer painted pictures of what he would do when he recovered: now I dared him to die, challenged him to leave me. I would not allow it. I would not permit it. I talked and talked until my voice was hoarse, and if he could hear me I thought he must wish me to the Devil. I have no memory of most of it, but I commanded him to step back from the brink. When he stirred and muttered in unintelligible slurrings of words, I gripped his hand in mine and willed him to live. To live for himself and all he envisioned for the future. To live for *me*.

How selfish does love make us?

"I will not let you die, Henry. So make up your mind to returning to life!"

One night, when his ravings terrified me, when we were alone, and because I was sure he could not hear me, I told him I loved him and that to live alone without him would break my heart.

"I love you, Henry Plantagenet."

Had I ever said such simple words to his face? I don't think I had, too wary of opening my emotions to any man. But here was Henry, his life hanging on a thread. Here we were, wed because of some strange, unfathomable force that neither of us questioned or fought against.

Henry, however much I might not have chosen it, was lodged in the very center of my heart.

There was no response. Henry's head thrashed from side to side, sweat glistening on his chest and arms where he struggled to escape the bed linen.

"I love you, damn you! Don't leave me now."

Unable to calm him, afraid of the violence of his movements, I summoned Agnes and we followed the same hopeless routine of cold water and white willow bark in wine. Henry sank into the grip of unconsciousness. Inconsequentially I noticed that his cropped hair was growing long. With a stifled sob I smoothed it back from his forehead.

In the brief interlude, I fell asleep in the chair set at the side of his bed, my swollen ankles propped up on a footstool. When I woke to daylight, my neck was sore, my shoulder painful from sleeping awkwardly. I grimaced and stretched. All was quiet in the room. . . .

With a gasp of fear, I focused on the still figure on the bed.

"Eleanor . . ." The breath of a whisper.

Henry was awake, his eyes calm. His face was thin and gaunt, worryingly so, but his skin was no longer flushed or slick with sweat. For a long moment our eyes touched and held, neither of us finding words to speak, Henry in his weakness, me in a strangely painful and shy diffidence. There was so much I wanted to say to him.

Did I tell him I loved him? I did not.

Did I soothe and caress my husband, newly returned to life? I did not.

"So you're awake and like to live," I said. "And about time too. Do you know how long I've been sitting here? Now I can get some sleep."

"I knew you'd be here," Henry croaked, voice rusty from disuse.

"Where else would I be?" My heart leaped with joy.

"When I was ill"—he spoke carefully, as if choosing every word—"this is where I wanted to be." He stretched out his hand and I took it. "I told them to bring me home. To bring me to you."

I smiled and ran my finger over the strong, steady beat of blood at his wrist.

"You are home. Now you will be well."

There was nothing more to say between us.

Until Henry's next words. "Is Geoffrey here?" he asked.

"Yes."

"Send him to me."

"You need to eat first."

"I need to see Geoffrey."

The familiar flare of jealousy at his single-mindedness sharpened my temper, but I did not voice it. Weak he might be, but his will was as dominant as ever. I stifled a sigh and gave in, acknowledging that the rest of our life together would be like this.

"I hear you've made a truce."

"Yes. Better to have him with me than holding hands with Louis."

"A statesman at last, I see." I smiled wryly against the little ache that his mind was already leaping ahead, away from me.

"I've grown into it." He sighed. "A mug of ale would be welcome, lady."

I walked to the door.

"Eleanor . . ."

I stopped but did not look back.

"Come back when I've finished with my brother."

Now I looked over my shoulder—and returned his smile. "Yes, I will."

So Geoffrey came, with the ale, and I left them to talk tactics. Henry would never change.

It was dark, before dawn. A peremptory knock thumped against the door of our chamber. Now beyond the sixth month of my pregnancy I was unwilling to stir, but Henry, restored to vigor in a disgustingly short space of time after all the dread he had put me through, was awake in an instant, leaping from bed, sword in hand, while I barely struggled out of sleep.

After a brief exchange of information, he was back, snatching randomly at clothes in the light of a candle taken from the messenger.

"God's Blood!" he swore as he stubbed his foot against one of his traveling chests. "Eleanor! Wake up."

"What is it?"

"It's come. Wake up!"

Now I sat up, gripped by his voice, the urgency, the underlying excitement. He was already pulling on his boots, swearing as one of the hounds bounded through the still-open door to rub affectionately against his legs.

"What's happened?"

"Get off!" He pushed the hound away and lunged to kneel beside me, cupping his hands around my face to kiss my lips and cheeks. I could feel his energy all but rebounding from the stone walls. "Stephen's dead. A flux of hemorrhoids. Probably from sitting for so long on a cold throne that didn't rightly belong to him . . ." He laughed in unseemly mirth. "Dead . . . Sooner than I could ever have hoped." Henry was already halfway to the door.

"Where are you going?" As if I didn't know. I tried not to sigh. I would be an abandoned wife again before the week was out, and I did not like the thought.

"To Barfleur. And then to England."

Chapter Twenty-one

*W*hat followed was a day of uproar and turmoil. Weapons, supplies, horses, transport, all the demands of a military campaign marshaled with Henry's habitual concern for detail. He was everywhere, overseeing every decision, as if he had not so recently lain under death's shadow. Had he not spent his whole life in the center of such warlike demands? Had he not planned for this moment when he could come into his own? Henry's vassals were summoned to Barfleur for immediate invasion. With his brothers Geoffrey and William, a clutch of bishops, and a host of Norman and Angevin magnates, Henry was intent on traveling to impress, to put the fear of God into any who might toss a coin on the possibility of rebellion.

"I can't leave England without a king!" Henry glowered, fretted. It was one of the few cogent conversations that passed between us on that day when I barely saw him. He snatched food on the run, writing instructions, issuing orders, wearing down the patience of everyone in his vicinity. "It all takes too long! I should be there now!"

But, by God, he was efficient! Impressively so. Even so, his bottomless energy could be too much of a good thing for mere mortals.

"You're Stephen's heir. No one questions it." I tried to apply cold reason, snatching a handful of manuscripts from him before he could shred them.

"Tell that to the mice who'll start to play while the cat's still in Normandy!"

I did not need him to tell me. I knew the fate of England could still hang in the balance. But that was not the first thought in my mind.

He'll leave me again.

It had been there, as irritating as a tick on a warm dog, since I had broken my fast alone. How long would he remain in England this time before his return? Sixteen long months last time, and I had given birth to my son alone. Would I carry and bear this new child without Henry? More likely than not. And when he wore the crown of England, where would his priorities lie then? Would England take precedence over Normandy and Anjou, over Aquitaine and Poitou? Would the splendor and authority of kingship in England mean more to him than returning to me?

And what of me? I made an excellent regent for him, as I knew. I could hold the reins for him during his absence; I could rule in his name and in my own most effectively, as well as any man. He'd be a fool not to leave me here in Rouen to uphold law and order in his absence. Would I not do the same, in his position?

I sighed over the weight of my belly. I saw no lasting comfort in our relationship together. Henry was a driven man, and I must fit into this vast empire he was creating from these disparate portions of land. I knew it, had always known it, and must bow to the inevitable. Henry had never led me to believe otherwise.

Surprising myself, I retired from the bustle of hall and courtyard, even of solar—how, by the Virgin! could Henry's exigencies even infect the peace of my solar?—and found my way to the chapel, where, despite the cold and my ungainliness, I knelt before the altar. I would rule alone and I would do it well. I would, of course, never beg him to stay. It would be crass of me; nor would Henry agree—so I must not submit to such weakness.

I wept. I might deny it but my cheeks were wet and cold.

The priest bustled in.

"Lady . . ."

I wanted neither his presence nor his empty phrases of consolation and advice, and so, leaving him to the office of the day, I climbed to the wall-walk to pace and watch the ever-changing life in the town below. Well muffled as I was against the autumn chill that touched the leaves with crimson and gold, I knew that this was no time for campaigning—far too late in the year—but that would not stop Henry. I leaned on the wall. With Henry gone, where would I go? Back to Angers? No. Far better Poitiers. I would carry this child in my own Maubergeonne Tower. And when Henry returned, as one day he must, I would come to him again.

My lips twisted with scorn. How had I become this poor creature at his beck and call? Perhaps the distance between us would cause the longing to fade and I could live my life to my own direction. I shivered as the wind picked up, spurring me to turn and beat a retreat.

"Eleanor!"

Henry was below me in the courtyard. I took a breath and arranged a cool smile, as if the turmoil in my heart that matched that around us did not exist.

"Up here!"

"There you are! What are you doing up there?"

Immediately Henry strode toward me, until he stood directly below me, looking up, his face vivid and alive. Never was he so animated as when action beckoned. I stretched my lips to preserve that smile and would have descended the steps if he hadn't bounded up them to meet me, loping along the wall-walk with a pair of hounds at his heels. I sniffed. Perhaps the bitter wind would mask the true reason for any remnants of tears on my cheeks.

"You're hard to find, lady." He took my hand and raised it, quaintly formal since we were buffeted by dogs and a howling gale, to his lips.

"And you're so busy you'd have difficulty locating your own head!"

But I let him kiss my cheek. Looking at me through narrowed eyes, he rubbed the pad of his thumb over my cheek and licked the moisture.

"Tears? Surely not."

"Not! The wind's cold, that's all. This is a day for celebration."

"Then what're you doing up here?"

"Thinking."

"Come and think in your own chamber. I can pack for an army but God knows what a child of one year would need."

A child!

I swallowed. He was taking William. He was taking our son with him but leaving me.

Suddenly the tears were hard to control—until, beneath my cloak, I clenched my hands into fists so that my nails scored my palms. How I kept the smile in place I could not have said. I forced my mind to sift through Henry's intentions. Well, it made good political sense, did it not, to take the baby to show him to his new people and display for the English magnates the infant heir to the throne? Excellent sense. Could I think of one good reason against it? I could not. For a moment I felt raw anguish that I would miss the baby. How unnatural of me, when I had never missed my daughters other than a transitory concern for their well-being. What a strange mother I must be. But Henry had made the right decision, the political decision. William had his own household, his nurse and servants to answer his every need; he was robust and healthy. Why not take him to England? The royal accommodation at Westminster must be quite as acceptable as that at Angers or Rouen, even after years of destruction and civil war. Stephen must have lived in some level of royal state.

What better place for William than the kingdom he would one day rule?

"I'll come to my chamber," I said, "but I don't see why you need me. Agnes would have done the job just as well."

With his hand around mine, first smoothing out my fingers, Henry all but dragged me along. "You're half-frozen. You should have more care of yourself and the child. And since when were you going to pass authority on your appearance to the decisions of your tire-woman?"

I did not understand. "Appearance?" My steps faltered, except that Henry gave me no choice but to trip over his heels.

"Well, I expect you'll have something to say on what you wear for your coronation!" Impatience made him clasp my hand even tighter and bustle me along.

I stopped and dug in my heels. Which brought him to a halt at last.

"What's wrong now, Eleanor?" He expressed a snap of intolerance when his whole world was waiting for his attention. "We haven't time, whatever it is. I want to be on my way by dawn."

"Am I not staying here as regent?" I asked carefully.

"Do you want to?"

"I thought you would need me to stay."

He frowned. "Did I say that?"

"No."

"Then what's . . . ? Ah! You thought I'd leave without you, didn't you?"

"Yes."

He was facing me, hands biting into my arms through the heavy cloth and fur of my cloak. "It will be the most important day of my life when they put that bloody crown on my head. I want you with me. Beside me."

"Oh."

He shook me gently. "Eleanor, sometimes you are nothing more than a foolish woman!"

"How was I to know? You left me before."

"But not this time." And he was pulling me along again. "We'll be crowned together, and this child will be born in England. Does that satisfy you?" Not waiting for an answer, he swung me against him, his arm around my shoulder, my back to the fortress wall. "We won't always be together. You know that. Our life is not made for comfort and our own personal choice of how we live it. Our birth makes us subject to higher things." His kiss was hard and sure. "But for this momentous achievement, the crown of England, my own birthright, we will stand together." He kissed me again. "Do you agree?"

"Yes."

Always partings. Always differences. How clearly he saw things. And so did I. I knew it and accepted it.

"Always remember this moment, Eleanor, standing on the wall

at Rouen with the world at our feet. It's ours to take, our empire to hold and rule, our line of inheritance to create through our children." He smoothed his hand over my rounded belly in a proprietary gesture. "And never forget this. I love you." He lifted my chin. "Look at me. You're very quiet—always a cause for suspicion in a woman!" He growled a laugh. "What do you have to say that I won't like?"

"Nothing!"

"Then tell me what I will like!"

All my anxieties had vanished. I was cold and damp and ungainly, but I had never been more content than I was within the shelter of Henry's arm on the walls of Rouen.

"My heart is yours," I informed him. There! I had said it at last!

"Excellent."

"And I love you too." Why had I found the words so difficult to utter?

"I know you do. So you should. And you'll come to England with me."

"Yes."

"Which reminds me . . ." Before I could react to his deplorably smug assertion that he'd always known I had more than a passing affection for him, we were almost running down the steps, Henry's arm firm and supportive around my waist. "Did you hear what the courier had to say about Louis? He's taken a new bride. The Castile girl, Constance. They were wed at Orleans early this month."

"Oh."

I think I was taken aback. I knew Louis would wed but it was still a strange thought.

"Louis in alliance with Alfonso of Castile," Henry continued. "D'you suppose it's to bolster his strength against my waxing moon of glory?"

I laughed. Louis's marriage meant nothing to me after all. "I'm sure of it. Unfortunate girl! I'll offer up a Mass for her survival through a lifetime of intense boredom. And that she puts Louis out of his misery and manages to bear a son."

Henry's eyes rested, briefly, on my face, but I had no difficulty in meeting his speculative gaze that was entirely too sharp and knowing. He nodded his head.

"Louis was never good enough for you. I'm better. I've always said that."

And pushing me inside the door of the keep, Henry was already marching in the opposite direction toward the stables.

"One more thing." He paused, turned his head. "I won't take that maggot from Ventadorn with me to England."

"Why not?"

"And have him mooning over you? By God, I won't. And he can't sing a rousing tune to save his life. I'll leave it to you to tell him. If I set eyes on him I might just wring his neck for decamping without leave." So he would decide whether my troubadour traveled with me or not, would he? He saw the glint in my eye. "Will you argue the point?"

I thought about it. And thought better of it.

"No, I'll not argue the point."

"Good. He'd have my men crying into their ale for unrequited love. Now go and do it, my love. . . ."

I think he'd already forgotten me, but my heart was light and I went to oversee the packing of my traveling chests, trying to decide how to tell my troubadour that his *dear love* was abandoning him. Henry's word was law.

Upheaval greeted me in my rooms. What to take? How to choose between one gown and the next? Shoes with or without gold embroidery? Mantles with or without ermine trim? In the end I took them all. And as an afterthought, ten warm undershirts. As Henry said— who knew what I might need, and England was a cold country.

Queen of England?

I liked the thought.

Epilogue

THE NINETEENTH DAY OF DECEMBER, 1154

Westminster Abbey, London

It is so cold. I clench my jaw against it and try to forget my first impressions of this city that will be my home for at least some parts of every year. All dirty snow banked beside the roads, compacted ice to trap the unwary, the layered filth and excrement of a city under stress, and the Thames frozen over. However much I might yearn for Aquitaine, this is where I must be when Henry demands it. That much I know.

The vast space above my head presses down on me, the air keen in my nostrils with the slice of a hunting knife, despite the brazier some thoughtful soul has placed beside me. Every time I take a breath my lungs wince, even though two of my undershirts are stretched across my girth. My exhalation puffs out in white mist, as it does from every baron of England who has had the sense to present himself here today. Any lord who has chosen to absent himself on the pretext of ill health or bad weather—well, I don't envy his next interview with his new overlord. It might just be at the point of a sword.

Henry Plantagenet has come to claim his own. And I have come with him.

I can barely feel my feet. My fingers are red and raw with the cold as I fist them inside my mantle. I'm paying a heavy price for being here:

chilblains with their irrepressible itch. But nothing—nothing!—can spoil this day.

To my left in the shadow of a squat pillar stands Aelith, who seems to have made her life with me permanent in her widowhood, even to coming to England with me. I am not sorry. I enjoy her company when Henry—as he invariably is—is distracted. She watches in solemn support as she has done since that day when we waited together for Louis Capet to arrive in Bordeaux to claim his bride. My attention is caught. Beside her my fifteen-month-old son squirms in Agnes's grasp and whimpers. I sense the start of a storm. He's too young for this, but I would have him here. He may not remember, but I will tell him how he saw his mother and father crowned King and Queen of England. And then the storm is averted, for young Geoffrey reaches up his hand and distracts my son with an impish smile over some shared mischief. Geoffrey is a good boy.

Archbishop Theobald of Canterbury approaches with solemn pomp. His broad face is beaming in satisfaction at getting what he wanted for England. I slide a glance to Henry. All I see there is red-hot impatience for this ceremony to be over, but for once the emotion is carefully banked. Henry knows the importance of this moment, the impression he must make.

Behind us stretches a month and more of endless waiting at the port of Barfleur, a month of tempests, gales, and violent seas that kept us penned like sheep for market. Until Henry could wait no longer. He was no sheep but a predator—and as restless as one of the caged lions I had seen in Byzantium. I smile a little as I recall.

"We've been here a month," he all but shouted, stabbing his finger in accusation at no one in particular.

"We are all aware of that," I remarked calmly, although his frustration had driven me to distraction.

"And over there—I could almost spit the distance!"—he jabbed the same finger in the general direction—"over there is England, six weeks without a king. Who knows what mischief's afoot with me shackled here by one bloody tempest after another."

"There's nothing you can do. They know you'll come when you can. . . ."

He flung down the book that had kept his attention for all of five minutes. "I'll risk it. I'll go tomorrow, no matter what." He marched to the door, shouting orders as he went.

I had expected this, but still it lapped around my heart, a rising tide of fear.

"Henry—don't! Remember the *White Ship*," I called after him. That terrible tragedy, the irreplaceable lives lost. When Henry the First had lost his only son, William, casting the country into bloody civil war because the barons would not accept a woman, Henry's mother, Matilda. Was I to lose him to the sea, as that first Henry had lost the light of his life? I could not bear to lose Henry to the waves.

"Bugger the *White Ship*!" he shouted back.

But at the door he spun on his heel and marched back toward me again. With hands cupping my elbows he lifted me to my feet from my huddle beside the fire, so that my needlework fell to the floor, where it found its way under his boots.

"I'm going tomorrow, and you won't change my mind. But you'll not come with me. Not yet. Too dangerous." He eyed my figure dubiously.

Not go? Oh, no! I would not allow this. I had not come so close to be left behind now. I had not tolerated Henry's furious impatience over the past weeks—while I stitched impotently at a panel for an altar cloth, not caring if it was even completed—to be sent home meekly to Rouen or Angers or even Poitiers. Yes, I was afraid of the storms and wallowing seas, but nothing would stop me from sailing with him.

"I won't be left behind, Henry."

"Eleanor . . . !"

"If you're going to England, so am I."

Agnes and Aelith, a critical audience, exchanged knowing glances, probably wagering on the outcome. Henry saw their silent communication and reacted in a predictably male manner.

"Out!" Henry ordered.

And they left. As soon as the door was closed:

"By God, Eleanor! You're in no fit state to travel."

"You invited me to accompany you."

"That was before the delay. Look at you! You're as round and full as an egg!" I barely opened my mouth to deny this unflattering picture. "You're not going to be difficult about this, are you?"

I raised my chin. I was going to be very difficult. "I'm going with you, Henry, even if I give birth on the damned ship."

Henry was not impressed. "Hear me, Eleanor. You're not going!"

"I'll hire my own ship if I have to! I'll sail alone!" Pray God I wouldn't be driven to it.

"I'll lock you up in this miserable fortress if that's the only way I can keep you safe!"

"Show me a prison door that can't be unlocked with a handful of gold!"

"Eleanor! By God!"

"Don't shout at me!"

"I am not shouting!"

"I will not let you leave me here!"

The outcome hung in the balance. I punched Henry not so lightly on the shoulder with my clenched fist.

"God help me!" Now he did shout. I expect Aelith and Agnes could hear from where they were doubtless eavesdropping outside the door.

"I expect He will. But I'll help you more. You need me, Henry!" I would give no quarter.

"Do I need a bad-tempered, opinionated woman who can't follow a plain order even to save her own life?"

"Yes. If you go to England, Henry, then so do I, by one means or another. It's as simple as that."

I felt the moment the balance tipped in my favor.

"Ha! You are a trial to me, Duchess Eleanor."

I tilted my head with a little smile and waited in silence.

"A stubborn, capricious woman! I suppose I shouldn't be surprised." The tension eased into a suspicion of a grin and Henry's fingers relaxed their grip. "If Louis was stupid enough to take you crusading, I suppose I must take you on a short journey to England."

"And you, of course, are not stupid."

"No. By God, I'm not. I know I need you with me. We have a performance to make, my love. And we will play it to the hilt."

No sentimentality here. Off he went to chivy and organize. The embroidery was beyond repair.

So I suffered one of Henry's diabolical campaigns: twenty-four hours of storm-tossed, freezing-cold misery in the *Esnecca,* Henry's Sea Snake, a war galley as wickedly predatory as Henry himself and with no degree of comfort, followed by a makeshift lodging with vermin and lice in the old Saxon palace on the south bank of the Thames at a godforsaken place called Bermondsey. And that dubious accommodation only after a flying visit to the Royal Treasury at Winchester, where the barons did homage. Quaking like a bed of reeds in a high wind they were, all of them gazing with astonished eyes on their new king, who had made a miracle crossing of the Channel, like an avenging angel sent by God to sort out the sins of a weary, war-torn country. But they were all wary. There was not one of them who did not know what had happened at Limoges.

Not one hand or one voice was lifted against us.

"I'll chop off any hands that wield a sword in my presence," Henry had snarled at the first opportunity. Perhaps that had something to do with their acquiescence, on top of the rumor of his reaction when he first set foot in the palace of Westminster, where we had thought to make our residence. Vandalized and stripped by Stephen's supporters, it was beyond words.

Yet Henry found them.

"God's Eyes! Do they live like hogs in a sty?" And this from the man who thought nothing of wrapping himself in a cloak to sleep on the floor alongside his men when on campaign. Who would not always comb his hair from one day to the next unless reminded. "Has no one seen fit to make ready for us? I want food and warmth for my wife. Now! Not in an hour's time! Who's in charge of this misbegotten place? I'll string up his guts for the ravens to eat. . . ."

No, we were not opposed by any dissenting voice.

And here we are now, six days before the feast of the Nativity.

Our filthy travel garments are gone and our robes are of silk and brocade and gauze. Rich embroidery decorates hem and sleeve, over all furred with ermine. Resting on my shoulders beneath my cloak is Melusine's Byzantine collar. I think, whatever her antecedents, she would have enjoyed this moment despite the drear surroundings that enhance none of the fire in the heart of her opals. Today they are dull and gray, gloomily sullen and unresponsive as I touch them with frozen fingers. I shiver. Thank God I brought the undershirts with me. I wrap the mantle discreetly around me, masking the fact that I am well into my eighth month, carrying Henry's child.

Archbishop Theobald anoints Henry's head with holy oil. Then mine. It trickles on my scalp, uncomfortably cold, with a greasy unpleasantness, as Henry's new vassals stand and stare with speculative eyes and hands clenched on sword belts, their expressions masked beneath heavy beards. What a backwater of civilization this is, worse than Paris. These Anglo-Normans are as uncultured and crude as the Franks; they have no wit, no charm, no romance, and are badly turned out. Nor have they any love for the art of the troubadour, although if I have to be fair in my judgment, a score of years of war and devastation are enough to beat the romance out of any man.

God and his angels slept, so they say.

"How fortunate we are," Henry says, turning his mouth to my ear. "I worked and fought for this moment, but it takes the hand of the Almighty to bring it to fulfillment."

"Lives are cheap," I reply.

I had almost lost him. And it was death that had brought us here. Some long in the past, one very recent, altogether a string of them without which Henry would never have made good his claim. Prince William drowning in the *White Ship* all those years ago. Eustace strangling on a pot of eels. And Stephen dead, only a year after the truce at Winchester.

"We will live forever!" Henry chuckles. "Or at least until you've given me a brood of sons to follow in my steps." His hand curves over mine, over my belly.

Theobald holds the crown. A crown commissioned by the Conqueror in imitation of the imperial crown of Charlemagne. Heavy, jewel encrusted, it fits well on Henry's head. Great-grandfather to great-grandson. Henry is still, not a muscle twitching. It is as if he holds his breath, not one hair out of place, not a snagged thread, not an unlatched lace or fastening, not even a grubby hem. The long tunic, all crimson and gold, elegantly lapping over embroidered undertunics, is a statement of power. Jeweled gloves in white kid replace his usual hunting gauntlets. His boots are polished. I doubt I'll ever see him as tidy again.

A crown is placed on my head too, a smaller version, with a jeweled rim and thick gold fleurs-de-lys rising from it. A crown befitting the Queen of England. Not a ducal diadem, not a coronal, but a crown. Heavy, but I will become accustomed. I feel Henry's fingers tighten around mine.

"So it is done. Our son has his empire."

The voices in the abbey are raised in acclamation. I look at the faces. What do they see? Their new king barely come into his manhood? Let him who thinks so beware. Henry may still be young in years, but he has honed his political skills since the cradle. I can see them realize the worth of their new ruler as Henry stands and vows to rule in the precepts of his grandfather, King Henry the First. The days of misery under Stephen are thus swept away with the stroke of a pen, the impression of a seal, the lifting of his rough voice.

We emerge from Westminster Abbey to stand in the gray light of this nineteenth day of December in the year 1154. No sun to greet us, as I might have fancifully imagined. The clouds are low and heavy with the threat of more snow to come.

Before us, our horses stand ready, magnificently caparisoned. And the crowds who line the route we will take shuffle and strain to see. What will they say? Will any man growl and curse and stir rebellion? But no. Voices begin to cheer, increasing in number and volume until the acclamation all but drowns out the dissonant clang of the bells above our head. I raise my hand in acknowledgment—and am immediately aware of Henry's inattention.

I follow the direction of his stare, and see. His eyes rest on a pretty face in the crowd that smiles back at him.

I sigh and transfer my shoe to the top of his boot. Followed by my weight. Henry winces on an intake of breath, and his eye slides back to mine with a quizzical lift to his brow. There is no apology. There never will be, I suspect. For now he is mine; the bond between us holds firm, but I have no illusions.

And yet, surrounded as we are by the crowds and courtiers and clerics, we turn to face each other, there on the steps. A silence. A look, a smile. A recognition of what lies between us and what the future will hold. Even though we make no overt gesture, it is as if Henry touches my cheek with his hand or even with his lips.

Yes, he is mine.

The roar bursts again on my ears as we step forward.

"*Waes hael.*" We are greeted in the old Saxon tongue. "*Vivat Rex,*" thunders in counterpoint from the Anglo-Normans.

Vivat Rex indeed.

Henry lifts my hand to present me to my people with a charmingly courteous bow, redolent of pride. Of victory.

"And *Vivat Regina* also!" he murmurs, his voice hoarse. Henry has done a lot of talking—and a fair bit of shouting—in the past days.

"*Vivat Regina!*" I lift my face and smile at my subjects.

Anne O'Brien taught history in the East Riding of Yorkshire, England, before deciding to fulfill an ambition to write historical fiction. She now lives in an eighteenth-century timbered cottage with her husband in the Welsh Marches in Herefordshire, a wild, remote area that provides much inspiration for people and events in medieval times. Visit her Web site at www.anneobrien.co.uk.

QUEEN DEFIANT

A NOVEL OF ELEANOR OF AQUITAINE

Anne O'Brien

A CONVERSATION WITH ANNE O'BRIEN

Q. What inspired you to write this novel?

A. I have been fascinated by Eleanor since watching for the first time, many years ago, the film *Lion in Winter*, with Peter O'Toole and Katherine Hepburn as Henry and Eleanor, focusing on the later years of her turbulent second marriage. More recently, reading a biography of Eleanor, I realized that her astonishingly eventful life began much earlier. Her marriage to Louis of France, her crusading days, her pursuit of divorce, and an advantageous second marriage had much to recommend them as the dramatic theme for a novel. I could not resist, and so this idea became *Queen Defiant*, Eleanor's story, full of passion and courage and scandal.

Q. What do you think accounts for our continued fascination with Eleanor of Aquitaine?

A. Eleanor lived so long ago—almost nine hundred years—when women, for the most part, had no voice in history. Yet Eleanor's voice rings out loud and clear. What a remarkable role she played, flouting the mores of society in a relentless bid to determine her own destiny. Vibrant, confident, sometimes outrageous, strikingly beautiful, she is the quintessential heroine.

Not content to accept the powerless ignominy of her life with Louis, she seized fate and made it dance to her tune, to fulfill her vision of herself as Duchess of Aquitaine. Eleanor's sense of self-worth, extraordinary in the twelfth century, with the authority of Church and State united against her, appeals very strongly to women today.

And apart from that, her life was never short of excitement and emotion!

Q. Can you tell us a bit more about the period in which Eleanor lived, particularly about the great land of Aquitaine that she ruled?

A. Eleanor was heiress to one of the richest domains in medieval Europe. Comprising Aquitaine, Gascony, and Poitou, it covered much of modern southwestern France. With a warm, temperate climate, it was a land of prosperous towns and farms, with much of the wealth being derived from a lucrative export trade in wine and salt. Aquitaine was far more powerful and wealthy than the Kingdom of the Franks to the north, to whom they nominally owed allegiance.

The people of Aquitaine were of Romano-Basque origin, hence the *langue d'oc*, Eleanor's mother tongue, derived from the language spoken by the Romans. The Aquitainian aristocracy enjoyed a luxurious lifestyle, the men notable for their long hair and clean-shaven faces, the women for their use of cosmetics and their exotically fashionable clothes.

Aquitaine enjoyed strong government under Eleanor's ancestors. They went on crusade and pilgrimage. They consolidated their lands at the expense of their neighbors. The Dukes married strong-minded women. Dominant and defiant of all who challenged their power, the Dukes of Aquitaine were aggressive and confident in their authority. Eleanor, inheriting their blood and their pride, was particularly influenced by her grandfather, Duke William IX. Intelligent, gifted, artistic, a warrior and a poet, he established a sophisticated and civilized court at Poitiers that became renowned as the foremost cultural center in western Europe.

This was Eleanor's inheritance.

Q. It's often difficult for contemporary readers to understand the absolute authority of the Catholic Church during Eleanor's lifetime. Can you give us some insights?

A. Eleanor's own family gives a superb portrayal of the complex relationship between Church and State. The Dukes of Aquitaine acknowledged the preeminence of the Church, but preserved an ambiguous relationship with both the Almighty and the Pope. The Holy Catholic Church and its doctrines might reign supreme, His Holiness the Pope might have the ultimate authority in all spiritual and moral matters, but in reality ruthless pragmatism ran strongly under the surface. The Dukes of Aquitaine would honor God with all due duty and respect, as long as He kept His interference out of their lives and the government of their dominions.

This story illustrates it perfectly: Eleanor's grandfather, Duke William IX, spent his final years in a state of excommunication for his scandalous flouting of the law and morality when he snatched Dangerosa from her husband to set her up as mistress. Taking exception to the interference of the Church, the Duke grabbed his bishop by the throat and threatened to choke the life out of him if he did not absolve him of his sin. The Bishop stood his ground. The Duke decided to compromise, turning the situation with typical sacrilegious wit.

"I do not love you enough to send you to Paradise, my lord Bishop." So the Bishop survived and the Duke died excommunicate, loving Dangerosa to the end. Earthly power and personal gain invariably took precedence. Not all rulers reacted so violently to excommunication as did Louis.

Nevertheless, any ruler with an eye to the stability of his country recognized that it was good policy to have the Church on his side, something Henry of Anjou was to discover when the murder of Archbishop Thomas Becket, at his instigation, inadvertent or not, caused a dangerous rift between the King and his Church. Most rulers wisely found the opportunity to stand patron to religious institutions, to go on pilgrimage, or even crusade, as did both Eleanor's father and grandfather.

Q. *You include songs from some of Eleanor's famous troubadours. Can you expand on her contribution to ideas of "courtly love" and the tradition of having troubadours in the royal court?*

A. Eleanor's grandfather, Duke William IX, established the ideal of courtly love in Aquitaine. He stood patron to a number of famous troubadours, who, influenced by Arab and Greek writers as well as by the cult of the Virgin Mary, developed the codes of courtesy, chivalry, and knightly conduct of a lover toward his mistress.

At a time when marriage alliances were often dry and sterile, the lady having no choice in whom she would wed, the troubadours idealized the mistress as highborn, often married, but a woman who remained unattainable to her suitor. The lover must pay her homage and prove his devotion and loyalty before his love could be acknowledged. The woman was the superior, and it was she who set the pace and tone of the relationship: any suitor who did not comply with her wishes was deemed unworthy of her love. This was at odds with the contemporary notion of courtship and marriage, but was highly popular as an intellectual exercise amongst the Aquitainian aristocracy.

Duke William himself, often known as "The Troubadour," wrote verses and poems, some erotic and blasphemous, some romantic and sensual, celebrating female beauty, carnal delights, and the pleasures of love. Eleanor, brought up in the tradition of courtly love, would have found nothing unusual in a troubadour declaring his undying love for her. To both Louis and Henry, however, raised in quite a different culture, it was completely unacceptable for a minstrel to be seducing Eleanor in music and song.

Eleanor's daughter, Marie de France, became the most famous patron of the troubadours. The treatise *The Art of Courtly Love* was written for her by Andreas Capellanus, her chaplain at her court at Troyes when she became Countess of Champagne, detailing a code of chivalrous behavior for the lover toward his lady.

Q. Paris is depicted as a cold, gray place lacking in any of the cultural refinement with which we associate the "City of Light" today. Was all of Paris as unappealing as Eleanor found it?

A. Eleanor certainly had a biased view of Paris because of the Cité Palace to which Louis brought her. A grim, dark fortress inherited from the previous Merovingian rulers, built with defense rather than comfort in mind, it had hardly been improved since its construction. All the luxury that Eleanor had enjoyed in the palaces of the south was absent. Nor was there any literary tradition or entertainment at the French court to brighten Eleanor's days.

As for Paris itself, it was probably no worse than any other rapidly developing city, such as London, with its overcrowding, its stinking, unpaved, narrow streets, open sewers, and stench of humanity. Paris did, however, suffer from a particularly unpleasant atmosphere in the summer, since the surrounding land was low-lying, badly drained marshland. The population had to withstand damp heat and swarms of flies. The Capets often took refuge at the hunting lodge of Bethizy in the summer.

One of the advantages of life in Paris that Eleanor eventually discovered was the emergence of that city—with London and Bologna—as a center of education and debate with notable scholars such as Peter Abelard. We know that Eleanor listened to the erudition and enjoyed the cut and thrust of well-reasoned argument. Louis often invited the scholars to meet and lecture in the palace gardens.

Q. The devastating loss of life suffered during Eleanor and Louis's Crusade remains shocking to this day. How much loss of life was due to Louis's incompetence as a leader and how much due to actual military aggression from anti-Western forces?

A. The blame for the loss of life must of necessity be shared.

Without doubt the Muslims became a far more effective force at this time. After the success of the first Crusade of 1096–99, four Crusader states had been carved out of the land seized from the Muslims by the Normans to create Outremer, and as long as the Muslim rulers remained divided, Outremer remained secure. The emergence of Zengi, governor of the Islamic states of Mosul and Aleppo, followed by his son Nureddin, both formidable leaders in battle, put the struggle for ownership of the Holy Land on a new footing. It became impossible for the Western states to hold out: by 1291 they were finally driven from the Holy Land.

The failure of the Second Crusade must also be placed firmly on Louis's shoulders. Louis's lack of military skill and leadership, as highlighted in *Queen Defiant*, failed to come to terms with the problems of warfare in this hot, mountainous region where the Muslims employed guerrilla tactics with great skill. It is generally agreed that he led his army into an untenable situation. His unwise choice of tactics and his refusal to follow good advice made defeat inevitable.

As for the number of lives lost in this Crusade, much of this was due to starvation and plague, particularly when the crusading troops were trapped at Attalia and Louis refused to take the obvious route and sail with the remains of his army to Antioch. The army finally disintegrated through desertion and lack of discipline.

Altogether an ignominious outcome for Louis's dream of glory in Jerusalem.

Q. Eleanor seems so unusual in her willingness to flout social constraints of the time—even to the extent of having an affair with her uncle, and marrying the son of her former lover. Yet in your portrayal she is not at all promiscuous or lacking in restraint. What do you think motivated her choices?

A. Eleanor was raised to know what was expected of her: virginity and celibacy before marriage, loyalty to her husband after— although her maternal grandmother, Dangerosa, might not have been the best example of moral behavior for a young girl. Nevertheless, Eleanor would have regarded her marriage to Louis as one that would last for life.

I do not believe that Eleanor was promiscuous. So why did she flout the mores of society by indulging in two affairs, one of them particularly scandalous? I think it was a matter of immediate circumstance, coupled with the fact of Eleanor, a young woman of vibrant spirit, being trapped in such an unsatisfactory relationship with Louis. Both of the affairs were brief, the heart ruling the head, giving and demanding no more than instant pleasure.

The affair with Geoffrey of Anjou—a brief, wild fling of no more than three weeks—was the result of her unhappiness with Louis, who rarely visited her bed and paid her increasingly little attention. Yet here was Geoffrey, a handsome, powerful man, who showed her what it was like to be loved and admired. It would have been very difficult for her not to have succumbed to his obvious attraction to her.

Her affair with Raymond was of a different nature. There was an instant family rapport between them, but they had not been raised in the relationship of uncle-niece, the age difference was not wide, and they had probably met only briefly some years previous to Eleanor landing in Antioch. After the disaster of Mount Cadmos, the physical danger, and Louis's vicious accusations against her, I think she was seduced by the sophisticated world of Antioch and the romance of Raymond's welcome to her. It was not wise, and earned Eleanor condemnation for her behavior from the chroniclers of the age, but I allowed her to give her own justification for what she did.

If Eleanor loved anyone, I think it was Henry. She married him because she saw in him the power to preserve her own dominions, and evidence suggests there was an emotional bond between them. Her marriage to Henry was not undermined by her infidelities, but by Henry's. There is no evidence of Eleanor ever being unfaithful to Henry.

Q. You suggest that under Raymond's rule, Antioch was a beautiful place where enlightened attitudes and religious tolerance promoted prosperity and peace. Was that true for other parts of the Middle East as well, and what led to the bloodbaths between Christians and Muslims that remain part of our common knowledge?

A. The Norman Kingdom of Sicily was another such kingdom where there was much tolerance for different races and religions, allowing Christians, Jews, and Muslims to live and thrive side by side. So Antioch was unusual but not unique in absorbing the different cultures rather than suppressing them. The courts of both Raymond and the Norman rulers of Sicily resembled that of an Ottoman potentate rather than a Western king.

The collapse of such an idyllic situation resulted, as is always the case in history, from the emergence of one particular interest and power over the others. In Sicily, the Catholic Church became dominant. In Antioch it was Muslim reconquest. Tolerance and harmony suffered as a result in both states.

Otherwise in the Holy Land, there was no tolerance, with too much bad blood between the Christians and Muslims. Warfare continued until 1291, when the West had to accept defeat and the Holy Land fell back into Muslim hands.

*Q. What happened to Louis after he and Eleanor parted ways?
What happened to his children?*

A. Since Louis's priority was to produce a son and heir, remarriage was essential. His choice was Constance of Castile, who became his wife in 1154, two years after his divorce from Eleanor. Constance gave birth to two daughters, but died in childbirth with the second. Louis therefore took a third bride, Adela of Blois, who gave him the much-desired son in 1165 as well as another daughter. This son, Philip Augustus, ruled France most effectively after Louis.

Louis appeared to have had no difficulty in enjoying normal marital relations with either of his two later wives. Perhaps neither of them intimidated him as much as Eleanor had. Eleanor's two daughters, Marie and Alix, were wed to two brothers, Henry and Theobald of Champagne, to tie this province into an alliance with Louis against Henry of Anjou. They both raised their own substantial families: Marie's son became King of Jerusalem.

Q. I found your portrait of Henry of Anjou utterly compelling. Was he really as brilliant, mercurial, dynamic, and ambitious as you portray him?

A. Henry was very much the man I have portrayed in *Queen Defiant*. What a pleasure it was developing his character as the man who would prove to be equal to Eleanor in ambition and strength of will.

Henry had enormous energy, spending most of his life traveling from one end of his far-flung empire to the other, covering vast distances in a day. Always restless, always hardworking, he rarely sat at ease, frequently standing to eat meals or conduct business, striding across the room while giving instructions. He even fidgeted through Mass, impatient for it to end.

Henry was intelligent, well-read, but preferred action to ideas. Ferociously articulate, he was able to read and write, still rare skills in the twelfth century even for rulers. Voracious in his search of knowledge, he was endlessly inquisitive, interested in everything that could be picked up and examined. He had a great sense of justice, giving his dominions the first trials by jury to replace trial by combat and ordeal. An able soldier and general, he was also addicted to hunting.

A formidable and forceful character, Henry was complex and unpredictable, exactly the fascinating figure I have made him. The match between Eleanor and Henry would never be an easy one, but there is evidence of an enormously strong bond between them, even in the final years, when their marriage disintegrated.

Henry's ungovernable temper, running swiftly out of his control, was also a historic fact. He could be polite and affable, but when his will was crossed, his wrath was spectacular.

Q. From various sources I know that Eleanor and Henry's marriage did not remain happy, and that he had her imprisoned for long periods. When and why did their relationship turn sour? What kind of life was Eleanor able to create for herself within the restrictions placed upon her?

A. Henry and Eleanor remained compatible during Eleanor's child-producing years, but in 1168, after the birth of their last child, John, in 1166, these years were over, and she chose to return to Aquitaine to rule her own lands, leaving Henry to oversee the rest of the empire. One reason for this decision may have been Henry's infidelities, particularly his setting up of Rosamond de Clifford as his long-term mistress. Certainly relations soured between Henry and Eleanor.

But this was not the main reason—Eleanor, I think, was rarely governed purely by emotion. The final rift was political. Their eldest living son, Henry—William had died young—had been crowned in his father's lifetime and was called the Young King to distinguish him from his father. Allowed no authority of his own despite his title, the Young King rose in rebellion and, with the support of his brothers Richard and John, joined forces with King Louis against Henry. Eleanor took the astonishing step of encouraging her sons in this rebellion, believing that they had justification in their demands. She particularly wanted Richard to inherit Aquitaine and rule it directly in his own right.

Henry put down the rebellion with ease, taking Eleanor prisoner as she fled to Paris to join her sons. Any trust between them was lost, and for his own security Henry kept Eleanor under restraint for the final fifteen years of their marriage, sometimes at Chinon, sometimes in various strongholds such as Old Sarum in England.

Eleanor's years of imprisonment must have been very hard for her. She was treated with courtesy; nor was she kept in total penury, being allowed two chamberlains and a personal maid. Henry made grants of clothing and furs and domestic items such as a bedcover to her, but it was a pittance compared with her earlier wealth. Eleanor must have been lonely, finding time hanging heavily, excluded from court and political life, everything she had enjoyed. Henry never forgave her for destroying their marriage. No doubt she welcomed widowhood when, released, she could return to freedom and to court.

On the accession of Richard the Lionheart, Eleanor continued her mission to keep her lands intact for her sons. Much of the government of the Angevin Empire fell into her hands in these years, since Richard spent almost the whole of his reign crusading.

Eleanor remained vigorous and energetic, a force to be reckoned with, withdrawing from the world only in her eightieth year, when she was consecrated as a nun at her own abbey at Fontevrault. She died there in April 1204 at the age of eighty-two years.

Q. Have you visited the land that would have been Aquitaine in Eleanor's day? What is it like now?

A. I have never been to Aquitaine and Gascony. My visits to France have always been to the north—to Paris and the Loire

Valley—or farther to the east, to the Roman ruins of Arles and Nimes and Avignon. I think it's high time I visited Eleanor's domains. Perhaps next year . . .

Q. What, in the end, do you want readers to remember about Queen Defiant?

A. I hope readers would remember what a remarkable woman Eleanor was. We might not always approve of the choices she made, but we can understand the reasons she made them, appreciating her failings as well as her strengths. She emerges from history as a very real figure, and we are privileged to know so much about her, given the vast distance in time between us and Eleanor's world. She reminds us that our ancestors were flesh and blood, and acted for good or ill. Eleanor pursued her goals, and although happiness was transient for her, it did not deter her: Even as an elderly widow, she still fought for the authority of her sons, and her own power in her beloved Aquitaine.

I hope readers would admire her strength and courage, as I do, in the face of a society dominated by men.

Q. What can your readers look forward to next?

A. I am embarked on a novel about Alice Perrers, a most resourceful woman. Alice, mistress of King Edward III in the final years of his life, was the first royal mistress in England to hold a semiofficial court position. She was supremely unpopular in her day; nor has history given her good press, but there are many gaps and inconsistencies in her story. Her background and rise to power are both obscure. The vicious criticism of her arose from biased sources, particularly from the Church and Parliament, both of which saw her as the perfect scapegoat for the disasters in foreign policy.

My intention is to reinstate Alice Perrers, to create a woman who was far removed from the lowborn, grasping, and greedy woman who challenged class and the social mores of her day and used her position of power with the King purely for her own ends. Alice was a clever, well-educated woman who had her own motives in seizing every opportunity, a pragmatic character who weighed principle against self-advancement. Strong-willed, formidable, precociously well-informed in politics, the law, and finance, she chose to improve her lot in life by fairly unscrupulous means but nevertheless deserves a fair hearing.

I see this reinstatement of Alice as a challenge: to write her story, to win her a sympathetic audience, without making her either innocent or a victim—which I am sure she was not!

QUESTIONS
FOR DISCUSSION

1. What aspect of *Queen Defiant* did you enjoy most?

2. If you've read other novels (or seen plays and movies) about Eleanor of Aquitaine, how does Anne O'Brien's portrait of her compare to the others?

3. Many books have been written about Eleanor. Why do you think writers and readers keep returning to her?

4. Eleanor is only fifteen when she marries Louis, who is only seventeen, yet they act, and are expected to act, as mature adults. Henry is only nineteen when he later marries Eleanor, yet he's already well on his way to becoming King of England. Discuss factors that might contribute to this early maturity, and compare them to contemporary attitudes toward becoming an adult.

5. If you were Duchess of Aquitaine, and found yourself married to Louis, would you have accepted your situation or fought to change it, as Eleanor does?

6. Do you think Eleanor sinned by sleeping with her uncle, Raymond of Antioch? Is her own justification of what she did acceptable? What would you have done in her situation? And should

she have tried harder to return to Antioch, and help Raymond, after Louis brought her by force to Jerusalem?

7. Discuss Eleanor's different methods of dealing with her two husbands, Louis of France and Henry d'Anjou. Was she more successful with one than the other?

8. In general, Eleanor treats the Catholic Church as a power to be manipulated rather than as a source of moral authority. Discuss some of the instances in which the Church's edicts seem capricious, arbitrary, and driven by politics rather than by moral righteousness.

9. Despite her great wealth and position, as a woman Eleanor was often at the mercy of male dominance and authority. Discuss instances in which she had very little control over her own fate, and what she did about it.

10. Eleanor confronted some of the most powerful men of her day. Which male character did you find the most interesting, and why? Whom did you most admire? Whom did you despise?

11. Life in twelfth-century Europe was far different from our own. Do any details stand out for you as particularly colorful, grotesque, or humorous?